DENNIS WHEATLEY

THE MAN WHO MISSED THE WAR

A Novel

THE BOOK CLUB
121, CHARING CROSS ROAD,
LONDON, W.C.2.

THIS EDITION 1946.

THIS BOOK IS PRODUCED IN COM-
PLETE CONFORMITY WITH THE
AUTHORIZED ECONOMY STANDARDS.

MADE IN GREAT BRITAIN
BY HARRISON AND SONS LIMITED
PRINTERS TO HIS MAJESTY THE KING
LONDON, HAYES AND HIGH WYCOMBE

DEDICATION

FOR

IRIS SUTHERLAND

Who was my invaluable secretary through the dark days
of 1941-42, and who has now most generously given
up her rest days from her war job to deciphering my
hand-written manuscript, in order that a fair typed
copy of this present book should reach my publishers
and readers with a minimum of delay.

DENNIS WHEATLEY.

10, Chatsworth Court,
    London, W.8.
       VE Day, 1945.

Contents

CHAPTER   PAGE

    I.   THE CHALLENGE ..   5

   II.   THE GREAT IDEA   14

  III. "IN THE MIDST OF LIFE . . ."   25

  IV.   EAVESDROPPERS NEVER HEAR GOOD OF THEMSELVES   36

   V.   DESPERATE MEASURES ..   47

  VI.   THE UNINVITED GUEST ..   59

 VII.   THE BAD COMPANIONS ..   73

VIII.   THE ENEMY   96

  IX.   THE UNSOUGHT BACCHANALIA ..   108

   X.   THE HORROR THAT LURKED ON THE FORESHORE   123

  XI.   THE SILENT CONTINENT ..   136

 XII.   THE DARK PRINCE   153

XIII.   THE STRANGEST KINGDOM   165

 XIV.   THE SHOWDOWN   176

  XV.   THE COMING OF THE DOG   185

 XVI.   THE WHITE MAN'S BURDEN   198

XVII.   THE TEMPLE OF THE FALSE SUN   218

XVIII.   THE SECRET OF THE MOUNTAIN ..   229

 XIX.   AMONG THOSE OLD IN SIN   245

  XX.   THE VITAL HOUR   272

CHAPTER I

THE CHALLENGE

IF Admiral Jolly had not been nominated to attend the Naval Conference on Victualling and Supply that autumn; if the conference had been convened at any other place other than Portsmouth; if Philip Vaudell's father, Engineer Captain Vaudell, R.N., had not, many years earlier, come to the rescue of the gallant Admiral in a house of dubious reputation not far removed from the waterfront at Wang-hi-way—then Philip's life might have run its normal course.

But the Fates had decreed otherwise. An ugly fracas in a Chinese tea-house, where, on a sultry night long ago, two young British Naval officers had fought back to back against curved knives wielded by an angry yellow crowd, was to have repercussions on the son, as yet unborn, of one of them. By the same spinning of the Three Weird Sisters: a girl-child from an American city was to found a new dynasty in a distant land, a Russian prince was to lose the strangest kingdom ever ruled by mortal man; and Hitler was to be struck a mortal blow at the most critical phase of Germany's second bid to conquer the world.

* * * *

The day was September the 10th, the year 1937, the scene a medium-sized house set in its own trim gardens, looking out across parched grassland to the greeny-blue sea of Alverstoke Bay, near Portsmouth.

Its owner, Engineer Captain Ralph Vaudell, was a careful man; not so much from inclination as from the habit of years, as he had never been blessed with a private income, and his wife had died years before, leaving him to bring up their two children. In consequence, he did not often entertain, but to-night he was giving a small dinner-party, and his women-folk were in an unaccustomed flutter.

Ellen his daughter, whose birth seventeen years earlier had resulted in her mother's death, was for the twentieth time giving a last touch to the flowers in the drawing-room, in between self-conscious preenings before the overmantel mirror to reassure herself that her newly acquired make-up could not be improved upon.

Mrs. Marlow, fat, homely, boundlessly goodnatured, the Captain's governess when a boy and the only mother Ellen had ever known, wheezed and rustled a little as, displaying unwonted activity, she propelled her bulky form in a shuttle service between the kitchen and the drawing-room.

" There! " she exclaimed, coming to rest at last in her favourite arm-

5

chair. "Cook says dinner will be done to a turn by eight, so I only hope they're punctual."

"Don't fuss, Pin!" replied Ellen with assured calm. "Of course they'll be punctual. When the Canon was preparing me for confirmation he used to talk about lots of things that had nothing to do with religion, and I remember him saying once: 'Punctuality is the politeness of princes!'"

"Did he indeed?" Pin Marlow chuckled. "Let's hope he thinks of himself as one then, though a funnier prince than that fat little ball of a man it would be difficult to imagine. Considering how rarely we see him, it's a puzzle to me what led your father to ask him to-night."

Ellen shrugged her slim shoulders: "I think it was just that Father wanted someone outside the Services to meet the Admiral; and the Beal-Brookmans are distant relations of ours, aren't they?"

"Yes, my lamb. The Canon's wife was your dear mother's cousin, though it was only after Mrs. Beal-Brookman's death that he came to live at Gosport three—no, four—winters ago."

At that moment Captain Vaudell came hurrying in. He was tallish, lean, grizzled, in his late forties, and the kindness of his eyes belied the hardness of his mouth. After a swift glance round, he moved over to a small table on which drinks were set, to see that everything on it was in order.

"Where's Philip?" he suddenly demanded of Pin. "Woolgathering as usual, I suppose. Probably forgotten that we have guests to-night."

"What nonsense you talk!" Pin answered placidly. "The boy's not as bad as all that. He'll be down in a moment."

She had hardly finished speaking when Philip joined them. Like his father, he was tall, but he had none of his father's rugged compactness. He seemed all long, ungainly limbs, and his awkwardness was accentuated by large knobbly-knuckled hands which always gave the impression of being out of control. His fine, high forehead and thin cheeks gave him a somewhat ascetic appearance, but his blue eyes were quick and friendly.

His father's glance appraised him from top to toe with a swiftness born of years of professional inspections.

"Well?" Philip inquired, a shade anxiously.

"You'll do." The elder man's mouth relaxed into a faint smile. It was obvious to him that for once the boy had made an attempt to subdue his shock of fair unruly hair, but the sight of the ill-tied bow caused him to add: "It's a pity, though, that up at Cambridge they don't teach you to wear your clothes a bit better."

"That's hardly a tutor's job," Philip shrugged; "and few of the men bother much about clothes. Such tons of more interesting things to think about."

Captain Vaudell could hardly quarrel with that statement, as he knew that his son's whole mind was absorbed in studying to become a Civil Engineer, and, although he said little about it, he was extremely proud of the boy's rapid progress.

Ellen walked quickly over to her brother and re-tied his tie. She had only just finished when Canon Beal-Brookman was announced.

The Canon was a short, fat, red-faced man possessed of boundless energy and a certain artless charm which few could resist. As usual, he was a little breathless, having hurried from one of the dozen meetings which his forceful personality dominated each day in a dogged attempt to enforce social progress on a large, poor and apathetic sub-diocese.

In less than a minute he had wrung his host fiercely by the hand, inquired after Pin Marlow's asthma, complimented Ellen on her adult appearance, given Philip a friendly pat on the arm, and, having accepted a pink gin, sunk it with gusto.

" Good gracious!" he exclaimed a minute later. " I drank that one up pretty quickly, didn't I? Wasn't really thinking what I was doing. Never mind! It's a pleasant change from the innumerable cups of tea that misguided women think it their duty to force upon us clergy. If only they would all provide Earl Grey or Orange Pekoe it wouldn't be so bad. The thick black muck I have to swallow plays the devil with my digestion."

Without any false embarrassment he held out his glass to be refilled just as the door opened and the maid ushered in Vice-Admiral Sir James Jolly.

Although he did not look as fat as the little Canon, the Admiral was the heavier of the two by several stone, and his weight was emphasized by his rather ponderous gait. He was a florid-faced man with a fringe of grey hair round his shiny bald head and blue eyes which he liked to believe were stern, but which had a disconcerting habit of displaying a sudden twinkle at moments when he allowed himself to forget his self-importance. Having shaken hands all round, he gave free reign to his obvious pleasure at spending an evening with his old friend's family. After ten minutes' easy chatter, they went in to dinner.

The meal was orthodox—tomato soup, fried fillets of sole, roast saddle of mutton and Charlotte Russe washed down by a good claret. The Canon ate as though racing against time, but in spite of that he contributed his full share to the conversation. The Admiral talked more readily when any Service matter was touched upon, and Vaudell, having similar interests, naturally encouraged him. Pin and Ellen put in an occasional mild platitude, but Philip remained almost silent, wondering how soon the guests would go so that he could get upstairs again to his beloved books.

At last the nuts and port were put on the table, and the ladies withdrew. The talk then turned upon the old days in China and went on to Singapore with its new vast Naval Dockyard, from a visit to which the Admiral had only recently returned.

" Singapore's the final answer to the Japs all right," he announced with a chuckle. " It's put the lid on any ambitions those little yellow devils may have had in the East Indies and Australasia once and for all." He went on to speak of the great Battle Fleet that the huge base would be able to accommodate when it was completed the following year.

Up to this point it had required a conscious effort on Philip's part to disguise the fact that he was vaguely bored; but now his face lit up with sudden interest and, in a voice made louder than he had intended through a slight nervousness, he exclaimed:

"Surely, sir, battleships aren't going to count for much in any future war!"

"Eh, what's that!" The Admiral turned to him with a startled glance. "What do you know about Naval strategy, young man?"

"Very little, sir. But it's clear to most people that if there is another war the aeroplane will be the dominant factor in it."

"Oh come now! Aircraft will play their part, of course. Very useful for reconnaissance and harassing the enemy by dropping the odd bomb here and there. But they're an unreliable weapon—darned chancy things —and no sane Commander-in-Chief would ever risk depending on his air force to play a key rôle in any major operation."

"I don't agree." Philip's words came hurtling out. "As sure as I'm sitting here, the time will come when great fleets of bombers will render bases like Singapore untenable; and having driven the enemy's Fleet to sea give it no rest until they've sent the last ship to the bottom."

The short pregnant silence which followed Philip's outburst was broken by the sharp crack of a nut. Before the Admiral could speak again, Captain Vaudell laid down his nutcrackers and said:

"You must excuse Philip's wildly exaggerated belief in air power. Armament problems are rather a hobby with him, and because he's going into an aircraft factory when he comes down from Cambridge at Christmas I'm afraid he's come to believe that ' Air ' is the answer to everything."

"But it is, Dad," Philip protested. "Battleships won't stand a chance against the bombers of the future. The Admiralty would do far better to devote any money it's got to building lots of small fast ships."

The Admiral smiled indulgently. "Look here, my boy! I've heard the question debated scores of times—wasted many more hours on it than I care to remember—but there's only one answer. The nation that has the biggest ships will always be in a position to gain and retain the command of the seas."

Taking some pieces of nutshell from his plate and dividing them into two heaps, he proceeded to demonstrate with them on the mahogany table. "It works this way. These bits of shell are ships. Out comes a little fellow from one side. The enemy sends out something slightly larger. The little ship is sunk, or must scuttle back to port. Number one sends out something bigger; the other side in turn has to beat a retreat. Now he sends out a cruiser, say—we'll use a whole nut for that; and number one is sunk again. He sends out a heavy cruiser, that's the nutcrackers here— and the poor old nut is cracked."

With a chuckle at his little joke, the Admiral suddenly stretched out and seized the port decanter. " But here comes the Queen of the Seas—a battleship; and if the enemy hasn't got a bigger one his whole Fleet will have to spend the rest of the war bottled up in port! "

" Quite, sir," said Philip drily; " unless a squadron of bombers comes out and sinks the battleship."

The Canon choked suddenly, as he said later, on a nut; but Philip had a very shrewd suspicion that the violent fit of coughing which ensued had really been caused by the effort of suppressing a burst of laughter. When the Canon had recovered his breath his host suggested that it was time to join the ladies.

While they were drinking their coffee in the drawing-room, it emerged that the Canon and the Admiral had a mutual friend in the Assistant Chaplain-in-Chief to the Fleet. This led to some talk on Welfare Services in the Navy, and thence to the Canon's own labours among the seafaring population of the neighbourhood.

" It's uphill work," he said, with a shake of his dark, bullet-like head. " There's nothing behind us—no good solid funds to draw on. We're entirely dependent on grants from various charities, plus what we can raise locally; and of course, both those sources vary from year to year according to the prosperity of the country."

"And I suppose it's just when there's a slump, and the people start cutting down their subscriptions, that you need the money most," remarked Captain Vaudell.

" Precisely," agreed the Canon. " Having to rely on voluntary charity makes it extremely risky to launch any new undertaking and militates against the steady progress of the old ones. Really, one must confess that these things are far better managed in the Dictator countries. Mussolini has devoted millions of State money to slum clearance in these last few years, and Stalin, I'm told, has erected whole townships of convalescent and holiday homes for the Russian workers in the Crimea."

" That's true enough," the Admiral nodded. " Look how this feller Hitler has tackled the unemployed question. There were eight million of 'em when he came to power, but he's managed to find work for practically everyone on new roads, and canals, and one thing and another."

" And in building a new Air Force to bomb Britain," added Philip.

" He's not building much of an Air Force, dear," Pin Marlow put in. " Mr. Baldwin said in the House not long ago that the R.A.F. is far stronger."

" Then he made a criminally misleading statement."

" That's pretty strong language to use about the ex-Prime Minister, Philip," said his father.

" But doesn't it stand to reason, Dad? Hitler couldn't employ *eight million* men on making roads and canals, and the German export trade is no better than it was when he took over. The only way he's been able to find jobs for these enormous numbers is by going all out on full-scale rearmament. Nine-tenths of those eight million are hard at it turning out guns, tanks, planes and submarines. And whatever the true comparative strengths of the British and German Air Force are to-day, our production is limited by Parliamentary estimates, whereas Germany's is not. That's why they're bound to overhaul us before long and old Baldwin's statement was so wickedly misleading."

" Of course, Hitler is rearming to a certain extent," admitted the Admiral. " There can be no doubt about that. But why should you suppose that his intentions are necessarily hostile towards Britain? "

" Hang it all, sir! " Philip threw out his knobbly hands in a little helpless gesture. " It was the British Empire that defeated Germany last time, wasn't it? The French lost so many men that they were practically out of the game by 1916, and the Americans only arrived in really big numbers towards the end. It's Britain that bars the way to German world domination, so whatever other plans Hitler may have he's bound to have a showdown with us sooner or later. If he doesn't his people will sling him out. The Germans are the last people to go on piling up armaments indefinitely without any intention of using them; and, if Hitler won't play, the Junker Generals will find another leader who will."

" Do stop him, Daddy! " Ellen said in a bored voice. " Otherwise he'll be giving us the whole of the speech he made when the debating society up at Cambridge discussed rearmament last term."

" So that's where you got all this stuff, eh? " smiled Captain Vaudell. Philip flushed slightly. "Not altogether. I've talked these things over with lots of chaps of my age—and we've got pretty good reason to be interested, you know. After all, if there is another war it will be we who'll have to do most of the fighting this time."

" Do you really think there will be? " asked the Canon.

" I can't see what's to prevent it. My generation is absolutely powerless, and, to be frank, yours seems to be hypnotized with the extraordinary idea that, having fought the Germans to a standstill in your youth, there's nothing more you need do about it."

" What would you have us do? "

" Do! " said Philip. " Why, take steps to meet the sort of situation we may be called on to face in five years' time—or less."

" What steps would you have them take? " the Canon persisted.

" Well, look at the Army. When the Scots Greys were due to be mechanized they kicked up a fuss, so the order was cancelled and they were allowed to keep their horses. That simply couldn't happen in any other country, but here the War Office simply said what damn' good sportsmen they were, and purely on sentimental grounds the future efficiency of our crack regiments was sacrificed. The higher ranks of the Army are still packed with fox-hunting squires who haven't the faintest conception of what the next war is going to be like; yet the foreman of any factory you care to go into could give them a pretty good idea. It will be a war of machines and technicians. It will be fought with giant tanks, motorized artillery, cannon mounted in aeroplanes, television sets, and every other man in it will have to be either a motor mechanic or a wireless expert. Yet what are we doing to prepare for such a war? Just nothing! We haven't got a single battery of anti-aircraft guns. Those lunatics at the War Office scrapped the lot after the last war. They scrapped the camouflage units too, and most of the other new ideas that enterprising civilians had succeeded in forcing on them. They won't hear of giving the infantry sub-machine guns, but still put their faith in the bayonet, and if it weren't for public opinion I bet they'd have scrapped the Tank Corps too. Their attitude to it is clear enough from the fact that it's been kept so small."

The Admiral had gone a shade pinker, and his voice was a little gruff as he said: " That's all very well, but there's one thing you seem to forget —money. The Services have to cut their coats according to the cloth they are given. Essentials must come first—barracks, rations, pay, uniforms and so on. Then they have to keep up the equipment they've already got. The income tax payer would have to ante-up quite a bit more in the pound before we could afford to go in for the sort of luxuries you suggest? "

" Yes to some extent, sir, but not altogether. Doesn't it depend on what are considered as essentials? For example, what about the six hundred horses of the Scots Greys that are still eating their heads off? Are they essential? And surely it's better to have one thousand troops equipped with, and trained in the use of, the latest scientific devices for destroying the enemy than two battalions of footsloggers with obsolete weapons? "

The Admiral passed a pink hand over his bald pate. " I'm no soldier, so I can't answer that one. But tell me, you young fire-eater, just as a matter of interest, what do you consider should be regarded as the first essential by the Royal Navy in preparing for any future war? "

Philip smiled. " That's easy. There was only one time when Britain stood in real danger of defeat in the last war. That was after the Germans launched their unrestricted U-boat campaign. You'll know much more about that than I do, sir, but I gather it was absolutely touch and go in 1917. We were losing far more shipping than we could possibly build, and if that had gone on for another few months our war industries would have dried up through lack of raw materials from America, until finally we should have been faced with starvation and compelled to surrender."

" Yes, that was a grim time. But we got the menace under control by the convoy system."

" I know, and maybe the convoy system would do the trick again—or maybe it wouldn't if our enemies happen to have thought up some new device to counter it. Torpedo-carrying aircraft, perhaps, or something like that. Anyhow, sir, if I were their Lordships at the Admiralty I should have only one concern: the absolute paramount and vital necessity of being one hundred per cent. secure in what was found to be our weak spot last time. I would take risks anywhere else and yet face a war with confidence if I could only be certain of keeping our Atlantic life-line open."

The Admiral shrugged. " The protection of our trade routes has always been a first principle of British Naval strategy, and you need have no fears as to the efficiency of the convoy system; particularly as we too shall have aircraft to assist us in convoy protection next time. But their Lordships certainly don't share your views about taking risks in other spheres. It's no secret that under the last Naval treaty we are entitled to build three new battleships for delivery in 1939, and every Ministry of Marine in Europe must know by now that *King George V, Prince of Wales and Duke of York* are on the stocks."

" Good God! " exclaimed Philip. " But that's sheer madness! "

" Philip! " said his father in a sharp warning voice.

" But Dad! " He stood up and once again threw out his large-jointed hands. " Think of the money those great ships will cost! At the very least twenty million pounds! And the Atlantic *won't* be safe for shipping if they're going to rely on the old convoy system of two or three escorts for forty or fifty cargo vessels. The Germans are not like us. They don't neglect the lessons of past wars. D'you think they'll enter the next one with only fifty or sixty U-boats? Not likely! Submarines can be built in parts, and stored in secret. Within two or three months of the outbreak of a new war the Germans may have two, three, perhaps five hundred U-boats at sea. They'll hunt in flotillas, and the convoy escorts will be helpless against such numbers. We'll need hundreds of small, fast submarine chasers and spotting aircraft to co-operate with them. With all these millions we could build them; yet the money's to be squandered on these absurd outmoded monsters that can be blown up in five minutes by half a score of big armour-piercing bombs. I tell you their Lordships are stark staring crazy! "

" Philip! " rapped out his father. " Whatever your opinions may be, to air them with such lack of restraint is positively disgraceful. You will apologize to Admiral Jolly at once! "

For a moment Philip stood there as though he had not heard. His face was flushed, his blue eyes seemed to glitter with the strength of his emotions, and he was trembling slightly. Suddenly he said in a fierce, low whisper:

" I won't! It's the weakness and stupidity of the politicians that your generation has placed in power which is making it possible for the Germans to fight us again. But at least you might see to it that my generation is given decent weapons to fight with when the time comes. No! I'm damned if I'll apologize! " And turning on his heel he marched out of the room

The embarrassing silence which followed his exit was broken at length by a most unexpected remark from the Canon.

" What a splendid young man! You know, I envy you, Vaudell, having such a son. I'm sure our friend here "—he waved a beautifully proportioned hand towards the Admiral—" is far too much a man of the world to resent honest criticism of his Service, even when delivered with a lack of finesse—which, after all, is a common failing in the young. And as a fighting man he will appreciate the courage which is required to make such a stand for one's beliefs."

" Oh—er—quite! " the Admiral muttered, somewhat at a loss now that the Canon had so urbanely excused Philip's extreme rudeness.

" That's all very well, Canon," growled Captain Vaudell. " But the boy was downright insolent, and he'll hear more of this from me before he's much older! "

" No, no! " the Admiral protested. " Please, Ralph. Of course, the boy doesn't know what he's talking about, but, as the Canon says, we must give it to him he has the courage of his convictions. So I'll take it as a personal favour if you'll let the matter be."

" Well, if you really wish it," the outraged parent agreed somewhat reluctantly. " Anyhow, I apologize on his behalf, sir. Er—now, what about a whisky and soda? "

" I accept both with alacrity," declared the Admiral, rubbing his hands.

When his host had mixed the drinks and Ellen had carried them round, the little party settled down again, but not for long. None of them could readily forget the charges of incompetence against the War Office and Admiralty that Philip had made with such bitterness, and half an hour after he had left the room the Admiral and the Canon announced almost simultaneously that they must be getting home.

On going out into the hall they found Philip standing near the stairs, wearing a rather sheepish look. He pulled himself together, and approached the Admiral.

" I'm afraid I was very rude, sir. I—er—feel rather strongly about these things, but I should never have spoken to you as I did while you were a guest in my father's house."

The Admiral's blue eyes twinkled. " Does that mean you would have outside it? "

" Well—yes, sir. To be honest, I think I would."

" Good for you! " the Admiral gave him a friendly pat on the shoulder. " But if you really feel so strongly about the menace to our Atlantic life-line in a future war, why don't *you* do something about it? "

" Hang it all, sir! " Philip smiled. " What can I do? "

" If the menace is as grave as you may think, a new weapon or an entirely revolutionary procedure may be the only answer to it. At the Admiralty we may have little originality in our strategic concepts, but we're always open to new ideas. You are training as an engineer and you are going into an armaments firm. If you think about the problem long enough and hard enough, we may owe to *you* the measures which will keep our life-line open, and so save Britain in her darkest hour. Why not see what you can do? "

CHAPTER II

THE GREAT IDEA

THREE days later, somewhat to Philip's surprise, he received an invitation to dine with Canon Beal-Brookman. As he knew the Canon only as a distant relative and had never even been to his house, he could only imagine that the dynamic little priest was either giving a party for young people or, with their last meeting in mind, wished to talk further about rearmament questions.

Neither proved to be the case. When Philip arrived at the big, rambling rectory, which resembled one vast library, as it had books even in the passages and on the stairs, he found the Canon alone; and during the evening the word "war" was not as much as mentioned; yet, when Philip looked back afterwards, he was amazed at the number of subjects on which they had touched.

Wine was the first, when Philip said on being offered a glass of Amontillado, "D'you mind if I don't: I'm more or less a teetotaller."

"Well," said his host, " if you keep it up you'll save yourself a lot of money; on the other hand, you'll be depriving yourself of a lot of pleasure. Books "—he waved a hand at the packed shelves that lined the walls of his principal living-room—" and wine are the two greatest civilizing influences in the world. If I had my time over again I think I'd be a wine merchant-bookseller, so that I could spread both gospels simultaneously! But perhaps you're one of those who regard alcohol as the 'devil's milk'—eh? "

"Good Lord, no! " laughed Philip. "It's simply that I don't like the taste of gin, whisky or brandy, and, to me, beer is bitter and claret sour. I often drink cider, though."

"I see. It sounds like the case of a sweet palate. Here,"—the Canon pulled the stopper out of a second decanter—" try half a glass of this rich old Madeira. Leave it if you don't like it."

He gave a deep laugh as Philip first sipped the wine, then nodded and drank it down. " Heaven knows what some of my more austere brethren would say if they could see me leading a young teetotaller into the arms of 'the demon Drink'! Still, most of the Blue Ribbon clergy know my views already. True temperance is not the churlish rejection of one of God's greatest gifts to Man, but a reasonable moderation in its use! "

It was hours later when Philip, filled with the well-being which follows an admirable dinner and a mental content begotten of the intimate atmosphere of the great book-lined room, said, feeling confident that he could not give offence: "You know, somehow, when I'm talking to you, I don't feel as if I'm talking to a clergyman at all."

"That's hardly surprising," was the prompt reply. "You see, with people like you, Philip, I put aside my workaday mask and say what I really think, instead of the sort of thing that Christian convention compels me to say when I meet the people I bully from my pulpit each Sunday."

"Do you mean that you don't really subscribe to the Christian convention then?"

The Canon's face broke into a smile. "Only a fool would seek to belittle Christ's greatness or to deny the immense value which the example He set has proved to mankind. On the other hand, only a fool could believe in eternal damnation or many other heathenish conceptions that the Christian Churches inherited from the Jews.

"True enough," Philip nodded, "but if you feel that don't you find it a bit of a strain to carry on as a Christian priest?"

"Not at all. When I was quite a young man I realized that my work was priestcraft—the spreading of the true knowledge of Good and Evil among those ready to receive it, and a life-long fight against lies, meanness, hypocrisy, tyranny, dirt and disease. Ordination in the Church of England was simply the best way in which I could fulfil my priesthood."

The Canon paused, pulled at the lobe of his left ear and went on: "You see, Philip, the thing the majority of people fail to realize is that there are only two basic religions. One is the belief in a beneficent Creator, who imbues each of us with a part of himself which, acting as an inner voice, gives us unfailing counsel at all stages of our journey on the upward path. The other is Satanism, which offers its votaries short cuts to wealth and power if they will ignore the voice and become the servants of destruction, brutality and uncleanness. All the great religions are a mixture of these two. Each holds the hidden core of truth buried under the often meaningless or distorted ceremonies with which many generations of false priests have overlaid it. Or, as in our own religion, entirely Satanic conceptions such as that incredible old brute Jehovah, who revelled in the smell of burnt offerings and blood sacrifices, have become hopelessly mixed up with God the Father, to whom we owe the Creation of all things beautiful. The two original religions existed in all their purity side by side, but as warring entities, in the great Island Kingdom of Atlantis. The confusion arose when that remarkable civilization was almost entirely wiped out by the Flood, nearly eleven thousand years ago."

Philip smiled. "How strange that you, who have just inferred that you consider most of the Old Testament as nonsense, should believe the Flood to have been an actual fact."

"Oh, but it was. There's no doubt about that. Geology, botany, ethnology and lexicology, as well as the traditions and folklore of every race in Western Europe and North and Central America, provide abundant evidence to prove it. But it was not universal, as the author of

Genesis no doubt believed, and Noah's party was by no means the only one to escape. There are practically no Flood legends among the peoples of Asia, and none at all in the folklore of the Pacific. Everything points to the catastrophe having been caused by the subsidence of a great island continent in the North Central Atlantic. Plato has left us a most realistic description of the marvellous civilization which flourished in Atlantis, as it was given to him by an Egyptian priest. Egypt, Chaldea, Mexico and Peru all derived their civilizations from Atlantis and were, perhaps, colonies of the Atlantean Empire before the Deluge. Or it may have been that little parties of cultured survivors landed and settled in these places soon after the disaster. In any case, from Plato's description of the great circular harbour in the Atlantean capital, it is clear that they must have had ships of considerable size, and no doubt many of these were on distant voyages at the time of the crisis. Some must have escaped and, like Noah, landed in distant countries; but many of the ships were probably manned only by rough sailors who would have been absorbed into the local semi-barbaric populations, leaving no permanent civilizing influence behind them—only a legend of the disaster which had overtaken their country and a garbled version of one or other of the two original religions. Hence the ensuing confusion."

"Well, you amaze me!" Philip ran a hand through his unruly fair hair. "I've always thought the story of Atlantis was a complete myth."

The Canon stood up and going over to a corner cabinet that held a small collection of jade and soapstone carvings, brought back from it a curious piece which he handed to Philip with the question: "What d'you make of that?"

Philip turned the bluey-green stone carefully from side to side in his hands. It was about seven inches long, roughly the shape of a conch shell, with a row of holes bored in it increasing in size from the thin to the thick end. The whole was most elaborately carved to represent a man with a conical cap on a head much too big for his body, and a fish's tail. After a moment Philip shook his head. "It's a lovely thing, but I haven't the faintest idea what it is—unless it's some sort of musical instrument that you blow through."

"That's right. It is a very early example of the Pipes of Pan, and the carving, as you see, is as exquisite as anything ever done by the Chinese, although it bears no resemblance to Chinese art of any period."

"No, the face looks like that of a Red Indian, doesn't it? And the design reminds one of the bits of old Mexican stonework that one sees in museums—except that it's much simpler and altogether more delicate."

"Yes. The art of the Incas and Aztecs was, in fact, a debased version of the art of the people who made that—and inherited from them. That is far older than any civilization of which we have a record. It was given to me by an American friend of mine who is a professional geologist. He found it when he was examining some mountain caves in one of the Lesser

Antilles, and he vouches for the fact that it cannot be less than ten thousand years old, owing to the deposits under which he found it. The only possible explanation of the finding of such a gem in such a place is an acceptance of the existence of Atlantis as an historical fact. If there had been any other civilization ten thousand years ago that had advanced to a state of culture in which its art equalled, or perhaps even surpassed, the Chinese, there could hardly fail to be innumerable traces of it."

"How absolutely fantastic!" Philip murmured. "Just to think that this thing was played by a chap who actually saw the Flood—one of the Noahs who didn't get away with it, eh! One who died in the mountain cave where he had sought refuge from the terror of the rising waters!"

It was now close on midnight, and soon afterwards Philip reluctantly left the restful, book-lined room with which he was destined to become so familiar.

Yet he was not to see his new friend again for some months. A week after his first visit to the rectory he went up for his last term at Cambridge, and on coming down, as soon as the Christmas vacation was over, he went into a Southampton aircraft factory. There the excitement of new work, new surroundings and new people kept him entirely absorbed for quite a number of weeks.

It was on a blustery day in March that he ran into the Canon—a short tubby figure with his cassock billowing about him like a tent. He was crossing the road from the church to the rectory, an incongruous form as he battled against the wind which blew his thin, dark hair in wisps about his bullet-shaped head. When they had exchanged greetings, he said:

"I want to talk to you, Philip. Come and dine with me—come to-night." And, as Philip accepted, he added: "We can hear all each other's news then."

That evening, before and during dinner, he encouraged Philip to describe his reactions to the type of people he was meeting in the factory, but immediately afterwards, when they had settled down, he asked:

"Well, what do you think of the news?"

"You mean about Hitler marching into Austria two days ago?"

"Yes."

Philip shrugged. "I suppose it was almost inevitable, since we took no steps to stop him reoccupying the Rhineland. Every time you give way to a people like the Germans it simply encourages them to demand something else."

"Where do you think his eyes'll turn next?"

"I don't know enough about international politics to say, but I wouldn't mind betting that he'll grab quite a lot of territory before those old fossils at Westminster pluck up the courage to set a definite limit on his expansion. Still, sooner or later, they'll have to."

"Have you any ideas when that is likely to be?"

"Yes, I think it will be when Germany makes a formal demand for the return of her colonies. The Admiralty would not stand for that. To allow Hitler to establish air and submarine bases in the Cameroons and Tanganyika, South-West Africa and various other places, would virtually be to surrender the Empire without even a fight—and their Lordships know it. At that point, the Government will be forced to say 'No' to Hitler, even at the risk of war."

" You still think that war is inevitable? "

Philip gave a quick nod. " Every month Germany is growing more powerful. I know for certain now, from people in the works, that her Air Force already far exceeds ours. She may have a dress rehearsal with one of the smaller European Powers, just to gain actual experience in the new technique of co-operation between great air fleets and armoured spearheads on the ground. But it is the war of revenge which will bring about the downfall of Britain that every German is now living and longing for."

" And what progress have you made? "

" Progress? I don't quite get what you mean."

" Surely you've not forgotten Admiral Jolly's challenge to you that night we all dined at your home last September? "

" Oh that! " Philip put up a hand and stroked his lean jaw thoughtfully. " As a matter of fact, I did put in quite a bit of time thinking about it; but when I got back to Cambridge I had to buckle down to my final exams, and since then I've been up to my eyes getting the hang of things at the works."

" How far did you get with your speculations? "

" I had what might be the germ of an idea—that's all. You see, the obvious answer to attacks by great numbers of U-boats on our shipping is more escorts and more anti-submarine vessels. But as the Admiralty has squandered the best part of its money on these absurd battleships— huge things so vulnerable that they each have to have more escorts than a convoy before they dare move out of harbour themselves—there's not the least prospect of our getting the small fast craft we'll need. The only alternative safeguard against a German undersea blockade of the British Isles proving fully effective, that I could see, seemed to be some method of increased shipping space from the United States quickly and at comparatively little cost. I'll go fully into the whole thing again and get something down on paper. Then I'd very much like to have your opinion on it."

" Splendid! " beamed the Canon. " Is a week long enough for you? "

Philip nodded. " Yes, it shouldn't take me more than two or three evenings to draw a diagram of the thing I have in mind."

" Right then! Come and have dinner with me again to-day week."

A week later, after they had dined, Philip collected a long roll of stiff paper from the hall and, clearing a space among the books scattered all over the big table in the Canon's library, spread it out. At the top there stood out in bold letters the words " ATLANTIC RAFT CONVOY."

ATLANTIC RAFT CONVOY

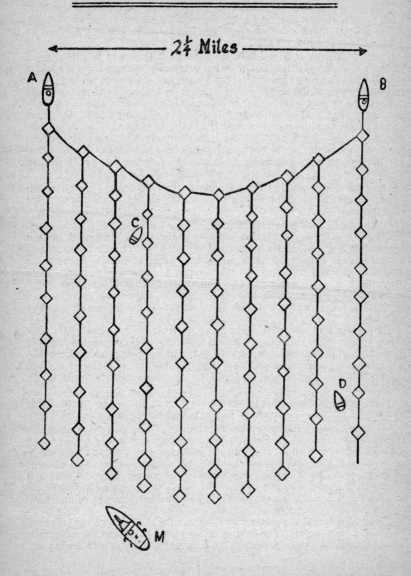

" By jove! " exclaimed the Canon, as he peered over Philip's shoulder.
" Rafts, eh! That's a darn' good idea—if only it's workable. But surely
it will take as much steampower to tow loaded rafts across the ocean as
it would to transport the goods in the hold of ships? "

" Yes, ordinarily it would," Philip agreed. " That was just the snag I
had to get over. My first idea was that every ship coming from the States
should tow a large raft behind it. But I soon saw the objections to that. A
raft of any size would act as such a drag on its towing vessel that it would
increase the time of each voyage to a degree at which we'd almost certainly
lose rather than gain on our imports. In addition, during storms, the strain
on the cables would become so severe that they'd snap; then we'd not only
lose the cargo on the raft, but the rafts themselves, drifting wild, might
prove a serious danger to our other shipping. Nevertheless, it was that
last thought about a raft drifting loose in the Atlantic that really put me
on the right track. Do you realize where it would land up? "

The Canon thought for only a second, then he cried: " Why, somewhere on the coasts of the British Isles most probably—on account of the
Gulf Stream."

Philip nodded, his blue eyes shining. " That's it. The Gulf Stream, and
the prevailing winds, would bring it slowly but surely north-east, until it
beached in England, Ireland, Scotland or Norway. The next step was to
find a way of harnessing those god-given forces of nature, because the
danger to shipping remained if the Americans just launched scores of these
big rafts on to the open ocean, and a percentage of them would be bound
to be lost through being dashed on to rocks or washed up on the coasts
of the Azores, Eire, Ireland and Scandinavia; so this is the scheme I've
worked out."

They both bent over the diagram as he went on to explain it. "My
idea is that a hundred square wooden rafts should be connected together
in ten strings of ten by strong cables, and that the first raft in each string
should be similarly connected to its neighbours. Those lozenges marked
A and B are sea-going tugs attached to the two outermost rafts in the
front line."

" But two ocean-going tugs would never have the power to tow that
number of rafts, if they were of any size," objected the Canon.

" Of course not," Philip replied impatiently. " For power we must rely
entirely on winds and current, but two fair-sized tugs *would* have enough
pull in them to influence direction, and provided they were not required to
steam *against* the current they would be able to some extent to check drift
to south or north of the shortest course between the United States and
Northern Ireland. The pull they would exert should also be just sufficient
to keep the lines of rafts strung out and prevent their fouling one another."

" In calm weather perhaps, but not in a storm."

" No. In a storm any attempt to influence the direction of the raft convoy would be hopeless. The towing cables would snap, and these big rafts
would become a serious danger to the tugs, particularly in a following sea.

In the event of bad weather, the tugs would cast off and cruise at a safe distance from the rafts, then pick them up again as soon as the storm had abated."

"If the storm lasted for two or three days, the tugs might easily lose touch with your Raft Convoy. In the course of one rough, pitch-black night it might be swept scores of miles away from them."

"I've provided against that. Every fourth raft will have a small automatic beacon in the centre. The captains of the tugs ought to be able to keep in view a group of twenty-five lights spread out over an area of four square miles, even in the roughest sea."

"Will your convoy cover as much space as that?" asked the Canon in some surprise.

"Yes. Each raft would be a hundred feet square. That gives a diagonal from corner to corner of a hundred and forty feet. Then I think we should allow a thousand feet interval between each raft and its neighbours, to lessen the chance of their fouling one another in rough weather. Though, actually, I don't see why they should, because, provided the load of each is equal in weight and distribution to the others, the stress of tide and wind should be exactly the same on them all. So, theoretically at least, they should keep station automatically. Anyhow, as I was saying, the frontage of the Raft Convoy when it was fully extended would be just under two miles, and, of course, it would be the same in depth."

"Have you any idea how long it would take to cross the Atlantic?"

"The speed of the Gulf Stream varies from four knots at the mouth of the Amazon to two knots off the coast of Scotland. Allowing for diversions from course, due to cross-winds, it would not be unfair to take the lowest speed of two knots as an average. It is roughly three thousand miles from Long Island to Northern Ireland, so that would take fifteen hundred hours—say, sixty-three days—about three calendar months. But I think there is a way by which we could reduce the crossing to somewhere near half that time."

"How do you plan to do that?"

"By fitting each raft with a long, low sail. It would be only two feet high but a hundred and forty feet in length, erected diagonally from corner to corner of the raft, immediately above its cargo, on eight short masts. And under pressure of a fair wind two hundred and eighty square feet of canvas ought to prove pretty useful."

"Then you propose that each raft should have its own crew?"

"Oh no. That would be impracticable. Apart from the loss of cargo space and the big additional expense of having to fit each raft up with living accommodation and a galley, one could hardly leave two or three hundred poor devils marooned on the rafts during a storm, and on most occasions between the first warning of bad weather and the breaking of the storm there wouldn't be anything like the time to collect two or three men from each of a hundred rafts. Besides, for ninety-five per cent. of their time they'd have nothing whatever to do, so it would be a most appalling waste of manpower."

"True," agreed the Canon. "But sails don't set or furl themselves; and if you left them permanently set they would be blown to ribbons before your rafts were a hundred miles out into the Atlantic."

"I don't think you're right about that. Of course they would if they were ten or twelve feet high, and that's the very reason why I've made them only two feet. I believe that long, low sails stretched on a stout framework will stand a lot of buffeting."

Philip produced another plan, showing a single raft, drawn to a much

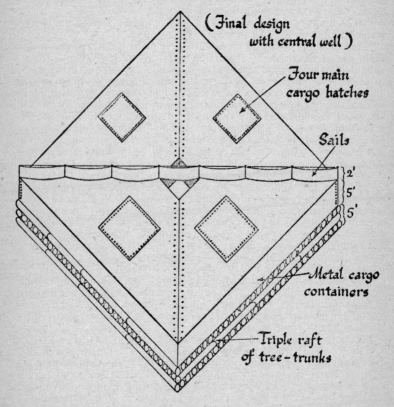

(Final design with central well)

Four main cargo hatches

Sails

2'
5'
5'

Metal cargo containers

Triple raft of tree-trunks

larger scale, and went on: "You see, steel rods connect the thick, short masts together along their tops, and the long sail will be bent to them as well as having the support of a mast every twenty feet laterally. My idea

is that every Raft Convoy should leave the States on a favourable wind
with all sail set, and it would remain so until the wind became definitely
adverse. If possible, the sails would then be reefed, but if the weather
became too bad they would be left to blow themselves out. As soon as the
sea went down and the wind became favourable again, any sails that were
torn would be replaced by new ones."

" Then you *will* need crews? "

" Yes—servicing crews, but not men on each raft. Look, the large
lozenge marked M is the mother-ship of the convoy. Her function is a
dual one; to protect the rafts from sabotage by enemy U-boat crews and
to house the personnel who will service the rafts. She does not have to
be fast or very large. Any old hooker of eight hundred tons or so would
do, provided she is mounted with a good big gun to drive off subs and a
derrick capable of lifting in-board lozenges C and D—which are two
large motor launches—whenever bad weather blows up. The mother-ship
would carry the spare sails, extra beacons, and lengths of cable, and so on.
Every day parties of the men in her would go off in the motor boats and
make the complete round of the convoy, landing on each raft to inspect it.
They would test the beacons, lower as many of the sails as time permitted
if the wind was becoming unfavourable, or fit new ones after a storm, and
keep an eye on cables connecting raft to raft, so that if any of them showed
signs of chafing steps could be taken to prevent the cable wearing through."

" I see," the Canon drew a finger along one of the lanes between two
strings of rafts. " I wondered why you hadn't made the whole thing a
complete network, but, of course, if the rafts were all connected to one
another laterally, as in the front row, the servicing parties would not be
able to get at the inner ones."

" Exactly. I would have preferred to link the whole lot up, because I
believe they would keep station better if each were attached to three or
four of the others instead of only two; but I don't quite see for the
moment how I could prevent the propellers of the servicing launches
becoming fouled by the connecting cables. Still, we may find a way to
get over that."

" The whole idea is most ingenious, Philip. But I'm a little doubtful
whether you'd find the wind of much assistance. The odds against it blowing for any length of time in the exact direction required to drive your
rafts along the shortest course between New York and Northern Ireland
must be pretty high."

" Oh, but that isn't necessary," Philip laughed. " The nearer that course
it is the better naturally; but any wind from the south-west quadrant of
the compass which would carry the convoy towards a two thousand mile
arc—of which Cape Clare in Southern Ireland is the centre—would serve.
You see, there is no way in which these Raft Convoys could be steered
right up to a port. The tugs would serve only to help keep them going in
a generally north-westerly direction. But they would have to be met and
brought in. Each convoy would be able to give its position daily by its

wireless and all British aircraft could be given permanent instructions to keep a look-out for Raft Convoys in the Western Approaches. Then a flotilla of sea-going tugs would be sent out to the place indicated, the convoy would be split into ten, or perhaps twenty, strings, and each of the tugs would tow its own quota of rafts the last few hundred miles to whatever port or ports had at that particular time the best facilities for their reception."

"You certainly seem to have thought of everything. How much cargo would one of these Raft Convoys bring over?"

"A hundred and twenty-five thousand tons."

"That sounds an enormous amount!"

"Well, if each raft is a hundred feet square, that gives it an area of ten thousand square feet. I should make the cargo containers five feet in height; no more as it is the Gulf Stream that we are mainly depending on—the prevailing wind is only a subsidiary factor, and if the height of the containers is kept low the current would more or less neutralize anything but a strong adverse wind once the sails were down or blown out. Five feet in height would give us fifty thousand cubic feet of cargo space, and the measure being forty cubic feet to the ton it comes out at one thousand two hundred and fifty tons per raft, and for the hundred rafts one hundred and twenty-five thousand."

"I do congratulate you," the Canon said enthusiastically. "Of course, there may be all sorts of snags to it that a professional sailor would point out, but for the life of me I can't see why it shouldn't work. Unless the containers are very strong and absolutely watertight they would not be suitable for the transport of the more easily spoiled types of cargo, and the time taken is against anything that would be required on a high priority. But, even if it did take two or three months to get each of your convoys over, it still seems the perfect answer to lifting from our ordinary shipping the burden of the millions of tons of raw materials and tinned goods that we'd need in a war. I take it, too, that these rafts would prove practically unsinkable if attacked by enemy submarines?"

Philip laughed as he rolled up the big sheet of paper. "Yes, in a way that's the cream of the whole idea. A U-boat could sink the tugs and blow the rafts to pieces one by one by gunfire, but to do that she'd have to surface, and she wouldn't dare do that so long as the mother-ship were afloat. The rafts would draw so little water that torpedoes would pass right under their bottoms—even if a U-boat captain considered it worth launching a £2,000 tinfish at one of them. In addition, they are as invulnerable from air attack as anything afloat can be. I worked it out that the total area of the hundred rafts comes to one million square feet, while the area covered by the whole convoy, when fully extended, would be eighty-one million; so the odds against a bomber getting a direct hit on any of the rafts would by eighty-one to one. And the worst that anything short of a direct hit could do would be to capsize one of the rafts or break some of the cables."

" Have you shown this idea to your father yet? '

" No, he's away on one of his duty visits to Devonport at the moment."

" But you will, of course, when he gets back? "

" Yes, I think so," Philip replied a trifle hesitantly.

A little smile twitched the corners of the Canon's mobile mouth. " You're afraid of your father, aren't you, Philip? I mean, in spite of the fact that you have the courage to defy him occasionally when you get yourself really wrought up, you are generally vaguely apprehensive in case he will disapprove of anything a little out of the ordinary that you may do or say."

" Well, yes, I suppose I am. How did you know? "

" Oh, I just sensed it. But you shouldn't be, you know. He's very fond of you, and extremely proud of the way you've buckled down to making a career for yourself. He's said so to me on more than one occasion."

" He certainly doesn't go out of his way to show it when I'm about."

" No, I don't suppose he does. Like so many people, unfortunately, he's tied up in knots and finds it difficult to give expression to his feelings. That's all the more reason why you should give him all the opportunities you can to get closer to you. Age is no barrier between friends, and there is no earthly reason why it should be between parents and their children. I do urge you, Philip, to try to make more of a friend of your father, for his sake as well as your own. And to ask his views on this provides an excellent opening."

" All right," Philip agreed. " He'll almost certainly think I'm crazy, but I'll try the Raft Convoy on him when he gets back from Devonport next week."

CHAPTER III

" IN THE MIDST OF LIFE . . ."

HAVING consulted his father, Philip telephoned the Canon and was again asked to dinner. When he reached the Rectory he found his host in the garden, admiring the crocuses, narcissi and daffodils in his Spring border; but he turned at once on Philip's approach and, taking his arm, exclaimed : " Well, what does he think of it? "

" He was very much nicer about it than I thought he would be," said Philip. " I expected him to say the whole thing was sheer lunacy, but he didn't. He put down his *Times* at once and seemed quite flattered at being consulted. He heard me out to the end too, and then asked all sorts of shrewd questions; but I'm afraid it's no good."

" Why not? "

"He agrees that the fundamental idea of using the Gulf Stream and the prevailing wind is quite sound; but he said that I'm wrong in supposing that because the rafts were all moving in the same direction and under the same stresses they would automatically keep station. He was quite definite that even if we used double cables to connect the rafts they would snap in no time."

"Well, that *is* a blow!" For a moment the Canon was silent, then he went on. "You know, I was really convinced that you had something that might be of inestimable value to the country if we do have to fight the Germans again. However I suppose it's not much good pursuing it further, if your father considers it quite impracticable."

"I'm afraid not," Philip sighed; and to take his mind off his disappointment the Canon changed the subject.

For several months neither of them mentioned the Raft Convoy again; but their three evenings alone together in so short a time had greatly strengthened the bond between them, and it gradually became a regular custom for Philip to dine with the Canon every ten days or so.

Although now twenty-two, Philip was in some ways still young and undeveloped for his age. He had never been a keen dancer and was not very interested in either girls or sport. From the time he had been given his first set of Meccano all his enthusiasm had been devoted to mechanical things and engineering problems. By securing a good opening in a big aircraft firm he had already achieved one of his ambitions, but now, after the excitement of the first months in the works had worn off, he might normally have become more socially inclined. Instead, his friendship with the wise and worldly Canon supplied him with all the new interest he needed to keep his active mind fully occupied. On their evenings together they talked of many things, and Philip, whose education had been mainly devoted to practical subjects, found himself embarking for the first time on the fascinating realm of speculation—of mythology, pre-history, philosophy, ethics, psychology—and he rarely left the Rectory without borrowing two or three books from the great collection that lay scattered all over the house.

From mid-May onwards, whenever it was fine, they spent most of the evening in the old garden. They were out in it one sultry night in September and had not spoken for some time. All the world was worried because Mr. Chamberlain had gone to Munich, and nobody yet knew if he would bring back peace or war. Suddenly, the Canon broke the companionable silence.

"Philip, did you ever do anything more about your Raft Convoy?"

"No. I thought about it for a bit, but Father's objection seemed to create a complete impasse. If the strain would snap the cables how else could one keep the convoy together? There just doesn't seem any answer to that."

"You didn't try to get a second opinion?"

"No."

"Well, I think you should." The Canon leant forward earnestly. "The Powers that sustain Good against Evil made the tides and the winds just as much as they made us. This Nazi thing is evil; few of us can doubt that now. It thrives on the persecution of the innocent and seeks to rule by force through Fear. God knows we're in no state to wage war, but we may have to if we are to save our souls alive! If we have to pass through the fire again, the Great Ones will not forsake us, because, however shy the British people may be of admitting it, they still carry in their hearts the insignia of Saint George. Yet the Great Ones choose strange ways to aid those of their children who stand in dire peril through their own folly, and their maps are far larger than any the puny mind of man could conceive; so it may be that even when the world was young they foresaw this coming hour of trial, and ordained the ocean drift from West to East to be our salvation."

He thoughtfully snapped off the dead head of a late rose before continuing: "I think you ought to put down your whole scheme on paper as clearly but as briefly as you can and send it, or—better still—take it yourself, to the Admiralty."

Philip nodded. "It's queer that you should suggest that, because only this morning I was thinking just the same thing. Unfortunately old Admiral Jolly is out in the Mediterranean now—otherwise, I'd take it to him."

For the next few nights he worked like a beaver, but by the time he had finished his draft Mr. Chamberlain was back from Munich with his piece of paper, and admiring crowds were applauding him for having secured "Peace in our time."

Philip took his draft round to the Canon, who suggested a few minor improvements, and they discussed its prospects.

"I don't stand anything like the chance of securing a good hearing as I did a week ago," said Philip ruefully.

"I don't altogether agree about that," the Canon replied. "The Service Chiefs must have the sense to realize that our having thrown the unfortunate Czechs to the wolves cannot possibly be the final solution of our own problem. Personally, it wouldn't surprise me at all if Chamberlain were for once pulling a fast one on Hitler. The Prime Minister must know how hopelessly unprepared for war we are, and this may be a ruse to lull Germany's suspicions—a measure to buy time—while we set our house in order and re-arm as swiftly as we can."

"Perhaps. If you're right the old Raft Convoy may meet with a good reception. In any case, I'm determined now to do my damnedest to put it over. I believe in it. I'm dead certain that the scheme could be made workable if only the Admiralty technicians got busy on it."

Three days later he obtained a day off from his job to go to London, and by making use of his father's name secured an interview with a pink-faced, youngish Naval Commander in the Plans Division of the Admiralty.

The Commander listened politely to what Philip had to say, scrutinized the drawings, then looked up with a cheerful smile.

"Well, Mr. Vaudell, I must say your idea is most ingenious, but I'm afraid I can't possibly express an opinion as to whether it would work or not. It's a bit Jules Verne-ish if you don't mind my saying so; but, then, so was his book *Twenty Thousand Leagues Under the Sea*—before we had submarines! My difficulty is that you've really come to the wrong shop. It may sound rather silly to you, but in the Plans Division we don't deal with this sort of thing at all. We're only Plans in the operational sense. However, I'll pass your stuff on to the right department for an opinion."

"Thanks," said Philip. "I'd be grateful if you would. But, just as a matter of interest, do you think it looks like a practical proposition?"

The sailor fingered his smooth chin. "The strain on those cables would be terrific, and I'm afraid the whole thing would break up if it ran into an even moderately heavy sea; but, of course, only an expert could say definitely. One small point I would suggest is that each of the cargo containers should have a square hole in its middle: a sort of well, you know, about six feet by six. It wouldn't mean sacrificing very much of your cargo space, and it might prove useful as a refuge for your servicing crew should they be caught in a sudden squall. However, that's a detail. Anyhow, we're very grateful indeed to you for bringing us your idea."

Philip thought the suggestion of a refuge-well a good one, and said that he would incorporate it in his final plan.

Three days later, he received a letter bearing the embossed anchor crest of the Admiralty. He tore it open with trembling fingers, only to find that it contained nothing but a formal acknowledgment of his papers.

The time of waiting that followed seemed interminable. Philip now felt certain that war was impending as the Air Ministry sent a high official to the works to address the senior staff, draughtsmen and shop stewards. The short talk was mainly about Security and the necessity for concealing, even from their families, details of forthcoming increased Government orders; and, after hinting at the gravity of the European situation, the speaker urged the workers to do all in their power to increase output.

Captain Vaudell was also now putting in longer hours at his office in Portsmouth and making more frequent trips to the other Naval Dockyards which he visited from time to time. Occasionally he still had one or two of his brother officers to dinner, and from their conversation one evening Philip learnt to his fury that yet more millions of the all too small Naval Estimates were being devoted to the laying-down of two more huge battleships, which Service rumour had it were to be named *Anson* and *Howe*.

"How soon are they likely to be ready, sir?" he asked one of the guests, a dark hatchet-faced Post Captain.

"They're scheduled for commissioning in 1943," was the prompt reply.

"But surely," protested Philip, "if there is going to be a war it will break out long before that, and with luck might even be all over by then.

Wouldn't it be sounder to concentrate on smaller stuff for quick delivery which would be of some use to us if we have to fight this year or next? "

The Captain shrugged. " Oh, war or no war, we must keep up our long-term building programme, you know."

Quite unreasonably, the episode left a bitter taste in Philip's mouth. Alone in his bedroom later that night, he raged silently against such stupidity.

" Fools! Blockheads! With their Big Ships which in future could be no more than a target for bombs. When would they learn sense? When they found themselves struggling in the oily sea, going down for the third time, after a direct hit had exploded a magazine, perhaps! But, in the meantime, the old diehards at the Admiralty were squandering Britain's last chance to prepare for a modern Naval war. Yet there must be some men with brains and vision at the Admiralty—people who realized that within a few months we might be at war and the fate of the whole free world depends on our ability to keep Britain open and supplied as a base for operating against the tyranny which was gradually engulfing Europe. One of them would see his plan and the raft convoy would be adopted. It simply must be."

The blow was all the heavier when a few days later he received a communication from the Admiralty. The printed slip read: " We thank you for giving us the opportunity of examining your . . . but regret that we cannot at present recommend that an offer should be made with a view to acquiring rights in it." The blank had been filled in with the words " Raft Convoy," and below appeared a meaningless scrawl, which was, apparently, the signature of the Secretary of a " Committee for the Examination of Devices," together with a typed postscript to the effect that his plans were being returned under separate cover.

Philip at once rang up the Canon who, detecting the crushing disappointment in his voice, did his best to console him and asked him to dinner the following night

When Philip arrived at the Rectory he was still seething with indignation that the examiners had not even considered his idea worthy of a personal letter and a few words as to why they had turned it down. The Canon let him rant for a bit, then turned the conversation to other things over dinner, only reverting to the subject of the Raft Convoy much later that evening.

" Do you consider," he asked quite suddenly, " that your great scheme, if adapted solely to commercial ends, would prove a paying proposition? "

" I've no idea," said Philip slowly; then, after a pause, he added more quickly: " But, of course, it would! In peacetime there would be no need for a mother-ship. The spare sails and cables could be carried in the tugs. Twelve men apiece would be ample for their crews, and that's many less than the average freighter carries. The fuel consumption of the tugs would be negligible, and with each convoy one could bring over the best part of a hundred and twenty-five thousand tons of cargo. If a company took it up they would earn terrific dividends."

"That's more or less the conclusion to which I came when I was thinking over your setback last night," smiled the Canon. "Of course, you must remember that you could use your rafts only one way, so you'd have to build new ones for each trip, and new cargo containers, too, unless you shipped the old ones back; but there should still be a very handsome profit. Have you any idea what the building of a hundred-raft convoy would cost?"

"Not the vaguest, but I suppose I could find out by making a series of calculations about the wood and cable and so on that would be needed, and writing to the various firms for quotations."

"Then why not do that? When you've got your figures you could draft a prospectus with a view to floating a company. You see, if you could only get the thing going as a commercial concern our purpose would be served, as the Government would take it over immediately war broke out."

"Gosh, yes!" Philip whistled, then jumped to his feet and began pacing up and down the room. "That's a marvellous idea of yours—absolutely smashing! But the trouble is that it takes money to float companies, and I haven't any."

"Do you know what to-day is?" the Canon asked.

"It's the twenty-first of October, isn't it?" Philip looked slightly surprised.

"Yes—Trafalgar Day. I've always believed that as long as we remember the dead they remember and help us. As you know, I'm not a rich man, but I have a certain amount of private money; and on this day, in memory of our greatest sailor—Nelson—I'm willing to give you a thousand pounds, Philip, to pay the expenses of forming a Company, the ultimate aim of which will be to defeat once more the enemies of Britain at sea."

For a moment Philip was speechless, then he stammered: "It's—it's too good of you . . ."

The Canon held up his hand. "Nonsense! At the worst I stand to lose my money; at the best, I shall come in for some of those handsome dividends on my founder's shares. That's a gamble that any man should be willing to take for the sake of his country. You'll be risking much more, if you accept my proposition, because you realize, of course, that if you succeed in forming this company you'll have to give up your present job to become its managing director."

"Yes, I suppose so—" Philip laughed suddenly. "But what an opening for a young man you're offering me instead. I can hardly wait to get down to making those calculations."

Night after night, for the next two months, he worked like a demon at it, and typed scores of letters to engineering and shipping firms in both Britain and America. He had long ago decided that the cheapest and most practical way of securing the large quantities of wood required to make the rafts would be to purchase a number of the big log rafts that are floated down the Saint Lawrence each summer from the great Canadian lumber camps. They would have to be towed south to the States, as they could not otherwise be launched into the Gulf Stream, but this kind of timber had the advantage that, however waterlogged it might be on reaching Britain, it could still be pulped for paper-making—an additional asset in a war which might well bring about an acute paper shortage. Wood, however, was but one of his problems: he had to get estimates for the making of the cargo containers, cables, sails, launches, and the charter of the sea-going tugs. Then there would be the questions of anchorage for assembling the convoy, of labour, of crews and of offices or agents for the company in both London and New York.

It was Christmas before he had his data completed, and he had reached the conclusion that such a company could not safely begin to operate with a capital of less than £150,000. The hundred rafts would cost over £1,000 each to build and equip; and there were besides the launches, charter of tugs and innumerable other expenses.

By working over the Christmas holiday, he managed to take three days off early in January, and, armed with a draft prospectus and his original drawings, went up to London to visit several financial houses whose names had been given to him by the Managing Director at the aircraft works.

They all proved keenly interested, but at the same time refused to commit themselves. In almost identical words, they pointed out that, while abundant finance would be forthcoming once a single Raft Convoy had made the crossing safely, it might be no easy matter to find investors who were prepared to gamble on so revolutionary a form of sea transport proving successful; and they must consult their partners . . . etc.

Philip was not unduly depressed, as he had realized from the first that he must rely for his capital on born gamblers; but it did not seem to him that it should be very difficult to find such people to put up the relatively small sum of £150,000 in a great money market like London where many millions were hazarded each day.

Yet, as January passed into February, he became more and more anxious and impatient. Time was slipping by and nothing could be done until the company was floated and the capital subscribed. Now and then he received temporizing letters from the firms he had consulted. The investment, they said, seemed to strike people as a particularly risky one, but there were still certain big backers whom they hoped to interest. Finally, as February drew to a close, one by one they intimated politely that they could hold out no further hope and must drop the project. Philip had kept the Canon informed, and when the last of these letters arrived they spent a gloomy evening together. It seemed that there was nothing more that they could do.

A few weeks later Hitler repudiated the Munich agreement, and the German legions marched on Prague. The following day the Canon rang Philip up at the works and asked him to come in to see him that evening.

B

Philip could not get away until after dinner, and when he arrived he found the Canon impatiently awaiting him. He had hardly sat down when the little man burst out:

" You know what's happening? As we sit here those brutish Huns are seizing and murdering every honest independent, free-speaking Czech they can lay their hands on! I could scarcely sleep for thinking of it last night. It's horrible—horrible! Britain can't remain indifferent to this sort of thing indefinitely! "

Philip nodded. " No, the people won't stand for it. You should hear what the chaps at the works say about Chamberlain and appeasement now. Either he'll have to stand up to Hitler or the Government will be thrown out before we're very much older. In either case I wouldn't mind betting that we'll be at war within a year, but, of course, we're still hopelessly unprepared.

" That's just what I wanted to talk to you about. By hook or by crook, we've got to get your Raft Convoy tried out! "

" Oh God! " groaned Philip. " If only we could! Should it prove no good, well, that would be just too bad. But it may be that in it we've got a thing which will save Britain from starvation—save the world perhaps from becoming one vast slave camp ruled by the Prussian jackboot and the Nazi rubber-truncheon. Yet we're powerless even to test it. I'd give everything I possess—or, since that's not much, ten years of my life—if only I could persuade someone to take it up and give it a fair trial."

" I know you would. But listen! Do you consider it essential that the trial should be made with a hundred rafts? Wouldn't twenty-five or even a dozen do? And couldn't the size of the rafts be reduced as well? "

" Certainly," Philip agreed at once. " The size of the rafts and their number don't matter. It's the principle of the thing that we want to prove. But what's the idea? "

" Simply to reduce the initial outlay to the absolute minimum. What do you feel would be the smallest set-up which, if it crossed the Atlantic successfully, would induce the Admiralty to accept your idea as a practical proposition? "

Philip considered for a moment. " One raft wouldn't be any good. It's the strain on the cables connecting a number that has got to be tested. One string of ten would do, then we should only require one tug and one launch. Wait a minute, though! If we reduced the rafts from a hundred to fifty feet square they'd only be a quarter of the size originally planned, so a sea-going launch would be able to give the single string direction as well as service it, and we could cut out the tugs altogether."

" D'you think you'd be able to get a crew that was willing to cross the Atlantic in an open boat? "

" It would be a powerful cabin launch with bunks and a galley, so I don't see why not. Lots of people have crossed under sail for the fun of the thing in far less comfortable conditions. Besides, we've always agreed that the first trip ought to be made in the summer, so the odds would be all in favour of good weather."

"That's true. Well, how much money do you think you'd want to build a convoy of ten fifty feet square rafts and to finance such a trip?"

Producing a pencil and an old envelope from his pocket, Philip made a few rapid calculations before replying: "Ten to fifteen thousand pounds; fifteen ought to cover it easily."

"And you'd be prepared to supervise all arrangements and bring the convoy across?"

"I'd jump at the chance; but the devil of it is that I doubt if it would be any easier to find fifteen thousand than one hundred and fifty thousand."

The Canon smiled. "Much easier, Philip. The greater sum is far beyond my means, but my mother left me the best part of £25,000, so by selling out capital I can easily provide you with the sum you require, and a good bit more if necessary."

"But," expostulated Philip, "say the whole thing is a failure—your income would be reduced by more than half!"

"That's a risk I must take," answered the Canon imperturbably. "I've often felt like breaking into this money in order to further various interests I have at heart; but I've always resisted the temptation from the feeling that in the long run I should be able to do more good if I kept the capital intact and applied the income each year to charity. But this thing is bigger than any charity, and it may be that I was meant to save the money until now for this purpose."

"If you really feel like that about it I'll work out exactly how much I shall need to begin putting matters in hand right away."

"That's it! There's not a moment to be lost if you're to make your attempt as soon as the weather is suitable. The sooner you succeed the sooner the Admiralty will be convinced and give orders for the big rafts to be made in large numbers."

Philip laughed. "You're taking it for granted that I shall succeed!"

"Of course you will! I've felt from the beginning that we were receiving Divine guidance in this just as Noah was inspired to build his Ark. Because a number of parties of Atlanteans escaped the Deluge that is no reason to discount the story of Noah, you know. All accounts agree that the Atlanteans were warned of the impending catastrophe, and Noah set himself to preserve not only his family but as much of the culture of his nation as he could. He would naturally have taken on board a selection of domestic animals for breeding purposes, but the 'Zoo' was no doubt symbolical of the many other things he saved for future generations. He could not save his people, because they would not hearken to him; but you and I may perhaps save ours if we follow with unflinching resolution the counsel which the gods have put into our hearts for their own high purposes."

B 2

Elated as he was on his way home that night, Philip could not but feel some slight misgivings when he thought of certain practical steps which he must take before he could actually launch his enterprise. He would have to give notice at the works, and also inform his father of his intentions.

In the course of the next week he wrote a number of letters, making further inquiries about the cost of rafts of a reduced size, smaller quantities of tackle and the prices of sea-going motor launches which might be for sale in the largest American ports. He then got down to lists of the stores that would be required for himself and a crew of five on a three months' voyage. When the replies came in he made a final cast and decided that the job could be done for £13,000. Putting all particulars into a large envelope, he delivered it at the Rectory the next morning on his way to work. That night he found a note from the Canon waiting for him at home. It read:

DEAR PHILIP,

Many thanks for your budget. I've had no time to do more than glance at it yet, but you seem to have thought of everything. This is only a line to let you know that I instructed my brokers last week to sell £10,000 worth of my securities, and the additional £3,000 can be made available at any time. So go right ahead. Don't waste a minute. I see from the paper that Sir John Anderson is to issue us all with Air Raid Shelters and gas masks, so at last the Government must be taking matters really seriously. I intend forming an Air Raid Defence Squad, as those of us who are wise will consider ourselves as already at war.

It is a terrible prospect; but I count our venture as starting from this moment, and from to-day I shall fly the flag of Saint George from the spire of the church, with the prayer that he may give you his special protection.

Blessings upon you—

JOHN BEAL-BROOKMAN.

Philip knew there was now no turning back, and that day he gave in his notice. The Works Manager was surprised and distressed but they finally parted with mutual expressions of good will, and Philip was told he might go at the end of the week.

The last few days at the works passed very swiftly. Philip called twice on the Canon, but on each occasion he was out at meetings of the new committee he was forming to undertake first aid and other war activities.

On the Sunday night Philip decided that he must face his father. All his boyhood fears of his reserved and practical-minded parent had returned with redoubled force, and he knew there would be a most unholy row about his having chucked up his job to go off on what his father would call a wild-goose chase. By the time dinner was over he had worked himself up into such a state of inward panic that he felt convinced that his father would turn him out of the house.

He went through a positively ghastly hour after dinner in the sitting-room, waiting for his sister Ellen and Pin Marlow to go to bed. Between surreptitious glances at the clock which seemed to crawl, he pretended to read a book, but Ellen was more than usually irritating with her affected chatter, and even old Pin unconsciously added to his torture by declaring she meant to finish the jersey which she was knitting before going upstairs. The clock eventually struck ten, their usual hour for saying good-night, but to-night they sat on, and it was his father who at last brought the boy's agony to an end by remarking, a few minutes later:

"Well, I think I'll begin to lock up."

Without even knowing that he was about to speak, Philip heard himself say in what seemed to him a strained and remote voice: "If you don't mind, I'd like to have a word with you before you go to bed."

There was another interval while the women collected their belongings and said good-night. But Philip did not mind now; the die was cast. The moment the door had closed behind them he stood up and blurted out the gist of what he had to say.

His father did not interrupt him, but simply stared at him, his mouth hardening into a thin straight line; then as Philip's spate of words petered out, Captain Vaudell began to speak; quietly at first, but with gradually rising anger.

He declared that his son was an impracticable visionary, and the Canon a fool for encouraging him. Neither of them knew the first thing about the sea and its titanic power which would fling these crazy rafts about as though they were matchsticks. He demanded that this absurd project should be given up immediately and that Philip should make his apologies at the works and ask to be reinstated.

Philip stuck to his guns, and there followed an hour of bitter wrangling, until both of them found themselves repeating the same arguments over and over again. At last, Captain Vaudell saw that it was useless to persist further, and said:

"All right, Philip It's clear to me that you have allowed Beal-Brookman to hypnotize you into visualizing yourself as a kind of Crusader. But let me tell you that if you had any real sense of patriotism you'd stick to your job in the aircraft works, which is now one of the highest national importance. However, if he is determined to throw away his money I can't stop him, and, as you are now of age, I can't stop your doing what you like. But I will not conceal that I am bitterly disappointed in you, and you must not expect any support or sympathy from me in this connection."

They left it at that, and all next day Philip could settle to nothing from distress over this quarrel with his father. In recent months they had been getting on so much better, and he hated the thought of leaving home in a few weeks' time with this ugly breach between them. Yet he felt there was nothing he could do which would be likely to bridge it before his departure, and he was now more than ever determined to see his enterprise through.

In the afternoon he went for a long walk with the idea of trying to quiet his turbulent thoughts. Coming back he passed the church and saw the flag of Saint George flying from its steeple. He squared his shoulders and threw up his head. His course was set, and nothing should stop him. Nothing.

As he entered the house he found his father standing in the hall. There was no hardness in Captain Vaudell's face to-day. His eyes were full of kindness, if a little sad, as he stepped forward and said:

" Philip, I've been waiting for you."

For a second Philip was filled with a new apprehension. He feared that his father was going to plead with him, and he knew that whatever it cost him he could not go back on his decision; but Captain Vaudell went on:

" I'm afraid I've got some bad news for you. I know how bitterly disappointed you'll be, but the fates seem to be against your making your attempt to cross the Atlantic. The money to finance your project won't be forthcoming after all."

" Why! What on earth d'you mean? " Philip's voice hardened suddenly. " You haven't seen the Canon and persuaded him to call it off, have you? "

" No, Philip," his father answered gently. " I wouldn't do a thing like that. The Canon had a heart attack this afternoon. He's dead."

CHAPTER IV

EAVESDROPPERS NEVER HEAR GOOD OF THEMSELVES

For the moment Philip was quite stunned by this totally unexpected and tragic news. Somehow he could not think of the dynamic little Canon as dead, or realize that he would never talk and laugh with him again. Among the chaotic jumble of his thoughts he was conscious of his father's statement that the money for the raft convoy would not be forthcoming after all, and that he had thrown up his job to no purpose; but now, in the first shock of his personal loss, these seemed but minor matters.

" I know what close friends you had become," Captain Vaudell went on, " so quite apart from your raft idea this must be a great blow to you. I'm most terribly sorry, and I only wish there was something I could do."

" Thanks," murmured Philip, " thanks; but I'm afraid there's nothing you *can* do." He turned towards the stairs, adding: " I think I'll go upstairs to my room for a bit, if you don't mind."

" That's right, old chap. Have a lie-down. In fact, I'd slip into bed if I were you, and Pin will send you up something on a tray for dinner. By the bye, I wouldn't worry yourself about having given notice at the works. The way things are moving these days I'm sure they'll be only too glad to have you back. Still, I think you could do with a bit of leave, so I should take things quietly these next few days."

On the Tuesday Philip tried to reorient himself. He had not realized before how dependent he had become on the Canon, but it now seemed as if his whole world had fallen to pieces. There were a few young people whom he had known all his life living in the neighbourhood, but he had seen little of them since he had gone up to Cambridge, three years before, and he had made no new friends since coming down. There was no one now to whom he could turn who really talked his language, and no one at all who knew about the rafts and could give him a glimmer of hope that it might yet be possible in some way or other to arrange a trial. As he thought how near he had been to proving the theories in which he had such confidence, he almost choked with rage and frustration.

On the Wednesday afternoon he went for a long walk, during which he strove to think of new avenues he might explore in the hope of finding backing for his venture. The very fact that the Canon had died seemed to make it more imperative that he should not be let down, and that a way should be found; but Philip cudgelled his brain in vain.

When he reached home Pin roused him from his futile mind-searching by telling him that a Mr. Pickering had rung up to say that he hoped that Philip intended to attend the Canon's funeral the following day, as he would like to have a talk with him afterwards. Pin had no idea who Mr. Pickering was, and had assumed that he was a friend of Philip's; but Philip had never heard of him, and was much puzzled as to what the stranger could want.

Philip and his father attended the funeral together. There were no coaches as the coffin had only to be carried across the road from the Rectory to the church; but the verger told them that seats had been reserved for them in one of the front pews, and this did not strike them as odd in view of the fact that they were relatives of the deceased. However, their connection with him was sufficiently distant for them to be surprised when a dapper, youngish man stepped up to them after the burial and, introducing himself as Mr. Pickering, the Canon's lawyer, asked them to accompany him back to the Rectory.

A few other people had already congregated in the big book-lined room Philip knew so well: two old spinster cousins of the Canon, his doctor and another elderly man, both of whom proved to be executors of the will, his housekeeper and the other servants. Mr. Pickering announced that, up to a short time ago, certain well selected charities would have materially benefited by his deceased client's demise; but just before Christmas he had instructed his solicitors to draw him a new will under which, while the original legacies to individuals remained unaltered, the bulk of his estate now went to his second cousin, Mr. Philip Vaudell.

After the list of legacies had been read out, Philip and his father had a short talk with Mr. Pickering from which it transpired that, by wise investment, the Canon had materially increased the patrimony left him by his mother; so that, even when all the legacies and duties had been paid, Philip would come into not less than £20,000 and, in addition, all the Canon's furniture, silver, objets d'art and books, which, if sold, would realize several thousands more.

As they drove back from Gosport along the Alverstoke road, Captain Vaudell said: " Now that you have come into this money I suppose you mean to go on with your enterprise? "

" Yes," replied Philip quietly. " He didn't leave it to me for that purpose, as at Christmas-time we still had hopes of raising a much bigger sum in the City. But I think he'd expect me to carry on now; and, to tell the truth, I've done little for the past three days except cudgel my wits as to how I could possibly get hold of the money."

" In that case I won't make any further attempt to dissuade you. It seems a pity to—er—unload this nice little fortune when you've just come into it. Twenty thousand pounds doesn't often come one's way; and I don't mind telling you that these days it's devilish hard to build up a nest-egg of even one-tenth of that sum. Still, it's your money, and if you're determined to use it on your rafts at least one can give you credit for your patriotic motives."

" Thanks, Dad. Thanks too for being so decent about the Canon, and everything, these last few days."

They left it at that, and six weeks later Philip, having with the help of Mr. Pickering formed a company called Raft Convoys Ltd., landed in New York.

He arrived there with only one personal introduction. It was to a friend of his father's, a Commander Foorde-Bilson of the United States Navy, whose home was in Belleville, a pleasant city suburb to the north of Newark, on the other side of the Hudson River, about twelve miles from Central New York. It so happened that the Commander was absent on the Pacific Station that summer, but his mother and two young sisters, Jean and Lexie, made Philip welcome and extended to him that boundless hospitality which is such an outstanding feature of the American character.

They immediately proposed that he should be their house-guest for as long as he liked; but, knowing that he would have to be in New York for at least two months, he felt that he could not possibly accept, and excused himself on the grounds that his business necessitated his living nearer the shipping quarter of Manhattan. They laughed and said that he would regret it during the great heats of the summer but that he could always change his mind; and, in the meantime, they moved him to another hotel which was not only more comfortable but considerably cheaper. Mrs.

Foorde-Bilson insisted that until he found other things to do he must always spend his week-ends with them, and the Foorde-Bilson sisters took him out evenings on a round of parties.

The new and colourful life into which he now entered, where the hustling, crowded streets of daytime gave place each evening to dashes in fast cars to country clubs, and midnight bathing parties in private gardens, was a great change from the placid existence he had led at Gosport. A little shy at first, he soon got used to the spontaneous friendship shown him on every side as a protégé of the Foorde-Bilson family, and began to enjoy himself thoroughly; but he did not allow his new social life to interfere with his purpose in coming to America. Soon after his arrival there the "Pact of Steel" had been entered into by the Berlin-Rome Axis, and for those who had eyes to see there were plenty of indications that Hitler now had the bit between his teeth.

Philip soon discovered that, for the smaller size and number of rafts that his revised scheme required, it would be more economical to place the whole contract in the hands of a New York builder than to float great rafts of lumber all the way down the coast from the mouth of the Saint Lawrence. Having put the contract out to tender with a number of firms, he closed with one that undertook to deliver the whole string, complete with cargo containers, sails, beacons and cables ready for sea, by July the 20th. It irked him that the earlier part of the year had slipped away without his being able to make any of these physical preparations, as he would have preferred to attempt his first crossing in June; but he consoled himself with the thought that, even if he could not get off till the beginning of August, he should still have at least eight weeks of good weather ahead, and with the aid of the sails he hoped to accomplish the voyage in something less than that.

His next concern was the purchase of a suitable sea-going motor launch and, having examined a number, he settled on a broad-beamed forty-footer with sleeping berths for six and diesel engines. On delivery it was brought across the Hudson to the New Jersey bank so that he could give Jean and Lexie and their friends evening picnics up-river or downstream past Ellis Island in it; and he spent many hours taking the engines down and going over every part of them with meticulous care so that there should be no likelihood of one of them breaking down once he was out in the open ocean.

On one of the rafts he intended to ship the most miscellaneous selection of cargo he could find, in order to test the effects of a voyage of six weeks to two months by raft on as great a variety of goods as possible. But he was also anxious to obtain cargo for the other nine rafts, if only he could persuade some firm to trust him with it, as he felt that for all ten to make the voyage fully loaded would provide a much more telling trial than if nine out of the ten had to go over in ballast. Accordingly, he inserted an advertisement in a New York shipping paper offering cut rates for cargoes to any port in Great Britain, to be shipped by escorted raft, period of voyage six weeks to three months.

The immediate result was a visit from a reporter, one Jeff O'Dowd, who worked on the shipping paper to which the advertisement had been sent.

"What's the big idea?" Jeff wanted to know. "What's all this about escorting rafts to Europe?"

Philip had not bargained for his idea being given to the world through the Press, but he was quick to realize that, as he could not prevent them from printing anything they chose, the wisest course would be to give the rakish-looking Mr. O'Dowd a correct account of his intentions.

Having adjourned to a nearby drug-store, where Philip partook of a pineapple sundae and Mr. O'Dowd indulged in a somewhat more sustaining refreshment, they discussed the matter for half an hour before parting with mutual satisfaction. Jeff had his story, and Philip had succeeded in steering clear of any inference that this new commercial venture of his was actually being undertaken with the hope of being able in time of war to save his country from starvation.

The next issue of Jeff's paper carried a three-column headline on its main page, running: " ENGLISHMAN TO HARNESS GULF STREAM "; and Philip read the article below with considerable satisfaction, since he felt that, while his small " ad " might have passed unnoticed by many readers, few people could remain ignorant of the new cheap cargo service he was offering after the appearance of the main page splash.

The same afternoon he received a telephone call from a Mr. Eric Eiderman, which resulted in his making an appointment to call at Mr. Eiderman's down-town office the following morning.

When he arrived he was shown in straight away, and a tall, thin, fair-haired man, who was seated behind a handsome desk, stood up to greet him

" Glad to know you, Mr. Vaudell. Sit right down and tell me all about this new idea of yours."

Philip gave him a friendly smile. " When we spoke on the telephone I gathered that you'd read O'Dowd's article, so there doesn't seem much more to tell. My first convoy will consist of ten rafts, each of which will carry approximately three hundred tons of cargo, and I propose to sail early in August. For my second trip I hope to have rafts four times that size and many more of them; and I should be happy to give anyone who takes space in the first convoy refusal of similar space in the second at the same rates, although to other people they will be considerably higher."

" If there ever is a second convoy," Mr. Eiderman remarked with a flash of even teeth. " If you don't mind my saying so, Mr. Vaudell, you're a much younger man than I expected. Well, I've got nothing against youth, but you won't mind my asking about the folks who sent you over here. Would any of your principals be directors of other shipping companies? "

It was a nasty one but Philip faced it squarely. " No, this is an entirely independent venture. My only partner died a few months ago, and I formed a small company, which I've called Raft Convoys Limited, out of the bulk of the money he left me."

"Indeed. Then you are quite alone. How interesting! But, as no one has ever done what you propose to do before, how about insurance? No firm would be prepared to take such a risk unless the goods were fully covered."

"I quite appreciate that and I got a quotation from Lloyd's before I left London. Naturally, it is prohibitive, but once a Raft Convoy has crossed the Atlantic successfully it will come down to quite a reasonable price. In the meantime, for this first trip I do not intend to accept any but the least valuable types of cargo, as I should then be able to pay the premium on them myself and thus cover the owners against loss."

"I get you, Mr. Vaudell. You're prepared to make a loss on your first trip and count that as part of your initial expenses. I'll say that's a sound decision, although insurance money doesn't compensate for annoyance to customers through loss of goods, you know. However, maybe we could do business on the lines you mention. As you may have gathered, we're General Merchants. Most of our trade is with Norway, and the firm owns three lines that run under the Norwegian flag. Still, that's neither here nor there. My job is to ship goods to Europe the cheapest way, and your scheme certainly opens up mighty big possibilities. If I help you to get going, what would you say to giving me an option on a percentage of your cargo space in all your future convoys at a rate to be fixed now?"

"I'd have to consider that," Philip hedged. He felt that Mr. Eiderman's inquiry was only the first of many which might result from Jeff O'Dowd's article, and he did not want to sell too much space in advance at a cut rate.

"Well, what about lunching with me to-morrow? You could think it over in the meantime and let me know then."

"That's very kind of you but I'm booked up to-morrow," Philip lied, wishing to gain more time for other inquiries that might come in.

Eiderman consulted a little book. "How about next Thursday?"

"That would be fine," Philip agreed.

"O.K. then. Call for me here round one o'clock and we'll feed at the Norwegian Club. Meantime, I'll go into the question of what bulk cargoes we'll be having for delivery in Europe this fall. I'm certainly glad to have met you Mr. Vaudell. Yours is a very interesting proposition." The tall, lean, Nordic-looking American stood up, flashed his white teeth again, shook hands with Philip and pressed a buzzer for him to be shown out.

Philip's expectations regarding numerous other inquiries were not fulfilled. To his surprise and disappointment not even the suggestion of another inquiry reached him between his visit to Mr. Eiderman and the morning of their luncheon appointment; but by then Philip had persuaded himself that, to begin with at least, there might be considerable advantages in dealing with one firm only.

At the office Eiderman introduced him to a fat man with thick spectacles and hair cut *en brosse,* named Thorssen, and the three of them repaired to the Norwegian Club, where they ate an excellent lunch.

Unlike Eiderman, who had hardly a trace of foreign accent, Thorssen spoke in a thick, guttural voice, and it soon transpired that he was still a Norwegian citizen, whereas Eiderman had lived nearly all his life in the States and had become a naturalized American many years ago. The pair proved good hosts, and by the time the party had finished with the innumerable tempting *hors d'œuvres* offered on the huge *smörgasbord,* Philip was already on excellent terms with them both.

After lunch, over coffee in the smoking-room, Eiderman produced a list of possible cargoes which would not carry a high insurance rate, and a draft contract between his firm and Raft Convoys Ltd. They haggled a little about terms but Philip did so only as a matter of form, since he felt that if the venture was successful the proposed concessions were not a very serious matter. His one anxiety now was to clinch the deal and prove to the British Admiralty that cargoes could be brought safely by raft from the United States to Great Britain.

Philip did not know a lawyer in New York, so he secured an introduction from Mrs. Foorde-Bilson to her attorney, a kindly, bespectacled old fellow named Irving Ducross. He said at once that he knew little about shipping law but would get the contract vetted by a firm that specialized in such matters, which he did. It was returned to Philip by the week-end as a perfectly fair and straightforward document, and was signed by both parties in Eiderman's office on June the 18th.

The only thing which now remained was to secure a suitable crew of five to man the launch. As she would be able to do no more than correct the general direction of the string of rafts in mild weather, an expert navigator was not required, and Philip had learnt sufficient navigation from his father to take an observation of the sun and work out his position from it. He already knew the engine backwards and enough about radio to send, receive and do minor repairs to the set if necessary; so he did not need any very highly skilled help. An assistant engineer, a radio operator and three able seamen to service the rafts, one of whom must be able to cook, were the crew he had in mind, but if he met with difficulty over securing the first two he was willing to take five seamen of average intelligence, as he knew that he might have trouble in finding men willing to sign on for such an unusual trip.

It was this which caused him to consult Eiderman, who was now taking a great interest in the whole venture, and the blond, lean-cheeked shipping agent responded at once.

" The answer to that one lies in what you're prepared to pay. Maybe it'll need double, or treble, the normal wage to tempt five shell-backs into standing for six to ten weeks in what's hardly more than an open boat. But as you need only five of them what are such wages but a bagatelle compared with your outlay on building and insurance? "

" That's true," Philip concurred, " and I'd naturally anticipated having to offer high wages. The thing is how's the best way to set about finding takers? "

" I'll have a word with Thorssen. He'll find you five squareheads from one of our lines. They'll be tough guys but I think you should not mind that. It's better so for such an undertaking."

" So long as they are decent fellows I don't mind how rough they are."

" Leave it to me then. But it's early yet, and there's no point in your paying retainers for longer than you have to. Towards the end of July will be time enough to get your crew together."

The next few weeks slipped by very quickly. During the daytime Philip was busy buying the miscellaneous cargo which he intended to ship on his Number One raft, and arranging for such supplies as oil for the launch and beacons, additional sails, medical stores and food for the voyage; all of which were to be shipped in the Number One raft owing to the launch's limited accommodation. In the evenings and over week-ends he continued to enjoy a hectic time with Jean and Lexie and their friends. New York was now stiflingly hot, so he often slept out at the Foorde-Bilson house, and at the beginning of July they at last persuaded him to move out there permanently. Jean was the prettier of the two girls, but Lexie was more fun. She also took much more interest in Philip and was making him into quite a passable dancer. Not unnaturally, this propinquity with an attractive young woman was having its effect, and Philip found himself devoting much more time than ever before to thinking about red lips, dark curling eyelashes and the graceful curve of long silk-stockinged legs; yet he did not allow his mind to be distracted from any essential preparation for his voyage.

There was one bad hitch over the construction of the cargo containers which prevented the completion of the rafts by the promised date; but they were delivered a week later, on July the 27th, and, after Philip, Eiderman and Thorssen had given them a very thorough inspection, declared to be satisfactory.

Thorssen had in the meantime secured a crew, which he presented to Philip down at the dock. Their leader, Hans Auffen, who was to act as bo'sun, was a huge man with a cast in one eye. A small, scrawny-necked man called Dirk had been taken on as wireless operator and cook; a third, Jan Schmaling, admitted to being an engineer who had lost his ticket, and there were two others, both big, bovine-looking men with cropped heads and china-blue eyes.

They all spoke some English and appeared willing enough, but they were as tough a looking bunch as could have been found on any dockside. As he surveyed them, Philip wished that he had taken the trouble to go down to the British Seamen's Mission and try his luck there, before appealing to Eiderman. It was only now brought fully home to him that he would have to share extremely cramped quarters with five such habitués of the

fo'c'sle for many weeks and, since that had to be, he would have much
preferred them to be men of his own nation. However, he felt that it
was too late to alter the arrangement that had been made for him, so, having satisfied himself that all the men fully understood for what they were
signing on, he took them over one of the rafts, explained the sails and
the beacons and gave instructions as to how the cargo was to be stowed.

It was August the 8th before the loading was finally completed, and now
it only remained to await a suitable wind. Thorssen had arranged that
one of the ships in which he had an interest, the *S.S. Regenskuld,* then in
New York harbour, should tow the launch and convoy down the Hudson
and out to sea, releasing it only when there was no longer any danger of
its fouling other shipping, or being driven back on to the shore through
a sudden veering of the wind. Philip and Eiderman's company were the
only people interested in the venture, and Eiderman said that he was
greatly in favour of keeping the whole thing quiet in case other people
should muscle in on it; so, as there was to be no special send-off, Philip
agreed that there was nothing to prevent his sailing the moment conditions
were considered favourable.

For three days he waited with an impatience that even Lexie could not
banish; then, on the afternoon of the 11th Eiderman 'phoned to say that
he had just had a report in from the " Met " people, who predicted fair
to strong winds from the south-east for the next four to six days, and
Philip agreed to sail that night.

There was little packing left to be done, but Lexie insisted on going
upstairs to help him with his bag and, when it was done, collapsed on the
bed in floods of tears. Sitting down beside her, Philip somewhat awkwardly put an arm round her shoulders and drew her dark, curly head
towards his. This was the first occasion on which he had ever held a
weeping girl in his arms, and he felt considerably embarrassed, but he
told her that he liked her much better than anyone else he had ever met,
that he was not really going into danger, that he would send her a cable
the very moment he arrived in England, and that, as soon as his business
there was settled, he would be coming back to New York to arrange
another convoy.

She cheered up a little then, and after she had dried her eyes they
kissed and hugged each other, and both agreed that they had been the
most frightful fools to waste such countless opportunities during the past
three months when they might have done the same thing. He said how
wonderful her hair smelt, so she gave him the ribbon from it which he
put away carefully in his pocket-book. Then Lexie bathed her eyes and
they went downstairs, slightly pink of face.

Jean was away from home dining in the country that evening; but Mrs.
Foorde-Bilson produced, as by a miracle, three of Philip's favourite
dishes for dinner. Then she and Lexie accompanied him in their car,
through the late dusk of the summer evening, across Jersey City and the
river-ferry to the dock where the *S.S. Regenskuld* was moored.

Eiderman was waiting for him with an apology for Thorssen's absence. It appeared that the Norwegian had been prevented at the last moment from coming to see Philip off. Eiderman had announced his intention of going on the *Regenskuld* to see the Raft Convoy actually cast off in the ocean, and after Philip had made his farewells to Lexie and her mother the two men went on board.

The ship's master, Captain Sorensen, received them on the quarter-deck and took them to his own day cabin, which he placed at their disposal; then he showed them two sleeping cabins in which bunks had been prepared for them, as it was proposed that the *Regenskuld* should not cast off her tow rope until six o'clock the following morning, when she would be well out in the open sea.

It was just after ten o'clock when she left the dockside, drawing the launch after her, while five tugs followed in procession, each towing two of the rafts, the port authorities having stipulated that this arrangement should be followed as a reasonable precaution against the rafts fouling other shipping in the crowded harbour.

While still in the dock, Philip and Eiderman had been standing in their shirt-sleeves on account of the torrid heat, but after passing the Statue of Liberty they struck a light breeze which forced them to put on their coats. Captain Sorensen remarked as they did so that to him it smelt like rain. Philip assumed that he was thinking of a thunderstorm, as the night was extraordinarily sultry, but otherwise clear, and looking back he could discern the molten silver of the foam churned up by the tugs glistening in the reflected glow of the million lighted windows of Manhattan's skyscrapers.

Eiderman had attended to all the clearance papers on Philip's behalf, and for the best part of an hour they were busy in the cabin while these were being checked and handed over. When they came out on deck again the *Regenskuld* had passed the Narrows and was slowing down so that the tugs could come up with her and begin the complicated procedure of stringing the rafts into a single line. Though there seemed to be endless fussing to and fro and almost continuous hooting for a long time, they actually made a good job of it and had the whole convoy lined up ready to put to sea in just over an hour. Soon after midnight the tugs gave hoots of farewell, the *Regenskuld* replied and, taking the full strain on the towing cables, headed in a north-west by westerly direction, with Coney Island on her port quarter and the light of Sandy Hook flashing almost dead astern.

They were going slowly now, not much over four knots, owing to the great weight they were towing. For another half-hour Philip and Eiderman strolled up and down the deck, then the latter suggested that, as they had to be up very early next morning, they might as well turn in, so they said good-night and went to their respective cabins

Philip undressed and got between the sheets, thinking as he did so that these might be the last few hours of carefree rest he would enjoy for a long time to come; but for some time he could not get off to sleep. It was over-excitement, perhaps. The little scene with Lexie that afternoon had awakened in him long dormant emotions, and now there was the stupendous thought that, after all these many months of waiting, planning and disappointments, he was at last really setting out to prove his great idea, which might mean so much to Britain in her hour of need.

At length he fell asleep, but only to become the subject of a most vivid dream. He was back in the Rectory library talking to the Canon. His fat little host was not seated, as was his wont, in his favourite armchair but walking agitatedly up and down.

"You're behaving like a blind fool, Philip," he said angrily. "Unless you rectify your mistake in time you'll be dead in twenty-four hours. For goodness sake get up on deck immediately."

Philip woke with a start. Insistent, commanding, the Canon's voice was still ringing in his ears. "Get up on deck immediately."

For a moment he lay still, trying to argue with himself that to leave his warm bunk on account of a dream was really the height of absurdity, yet he could not get rid of the feeling that something must be wrong with the string of rafts and that he ought to go up to have another look at them. Perhaps he had overlooked some vital factor which might yet be rectified at this eleventh hour before he entrusted himself and his crew to the launch and the ocean next morning. Getting out of bed he slipped on his dressing gown and slippers and went up on deck.

He found that the night was darker than before. There was no moon, and swiftly moving clouds now obscured most of the starry sky. When he reached the stern rail he could no longer see all the rafts and could only count five ever smaller streaks of foam where they ploughed up the sea; but, thousands of yards away, he could clearly sight the last beacon, although the raft that bore it was hidden from him.

All seemed well so after a moment he turned and began to make his way back to his cabin. It was then that he caught the sound of voices coming through an open skylight. He paused because there seemed something unfamiliar about them. Suddenly he realized what it was: someone down below was talking German!

Kneeling down, he peered beneath the raised, glass-filled mahogany frame and found that he could see one wall of a cabin. Against it leant his bullet-headed bo'sun, Hans Auffen, next to him stood the scraggy-necked Dirk, and then came one of the big, doltish-looking squareheads. But none of them was talking. They were listening with evident respect to someone else whom Philip could not see, yet whose voice he now recognized as Eiderman's.

Philip had been on the Modern side at his public school, so knew enough German to understand the gist of what was being said; but as he first con-

centrated on catching the words he got only the end of a sentence which
had something to do with being able to reach Boston by Friday.

"*Jawohl, Herr Kapitan,*" Hans Auffen replied in a guttural voice, and
every muscle in Philip's body seemed to go rigid as he heard Eiderman go
on:

"It is important that you should all tell the same story on your return.
While inspecting a raft, he slipped, struck his head, fell in the sea and went
under, disappearing before you could get close enough to help him. Without a Captain you were not prepared to face the trip to Europe, and you
could not tow the rafts back against the current; so you decided to abandon them and make for the nearest port. This is a very simple task so I
shall accept no excuse for bungling. You have only to hit the young fool
on the head and throw him overboard. I care nothing what happens to
the rafts so long as he is prevented from carrying out this dangerous
experiment."

"*Heil Hitler!*"

CHAPTER V

DESPERATE MEASURES

THE night was still warm but suddenly Philip was gripped by cold. In
these last few minutes a chill seemed to have run right through him,
turning his blood to water. He rose from his knees a trifle unsteadily and
made an effort to grasp the full implications of what he had overheard.
At first he could hardly believe his senses. It seemed impossible, unbelievable, that Eric Eiderman, whom he had come to know and like, could
really have just given orders for his cold-blooded murder.

Yet, even as he was beginning to doubt the evidence of his own ears,
fresh sounds reached him from below. A sudden shuffling, a click of
heels; then, like a rumble of doom, came the voices of the five who had
been chosen to murder him raised in a baleful, unquestioning acknowledgment of their orders: "*Heil Hitler!*"

Those menacing, fanatical syllables were, Philip realized, the key to the
appalling situation in which he found himself. Eiderman was not a
Norwegian born, but a German; and whether he was a naturalized American or not he was a secret agent of the Nazis. Having seen the article
about the proposed Raft Convoy, he had been shrewd enough to realize
at once that this was no mere attempt to undercut current shipping rates
by the introduction of a new method of sea transport, but a device which,
if successful, might in war-time defeat the blockade of Britain by submarines. Obviously, no price could be too high for Hitler's secret repre-

sentative to pay, if it would strangle such a scheme at birth, before the slow-moving British Admiralty became interested in it.

Suddenly, Philip's mouth twitched, and he was filled with silent laughter. It was caused by the thought that, although his own people would not listen to him, the Germans thought him dangerous enough for them to go to considerable trouble to kill him. It was the greatest compliment he could possibly have been paid, and seeing the funny side of it released the tension he was under, causing his blood to flow warmly through his veins again. Yet the second his mind turned to the future he became extremely perturbed.

He saw now why Eiderman had expressed such interest and satisfaction when he had learnt that Raft Convoys Ltd. was a one-man venture unbacked by any of the big British shipping concerns; and why he had urged so strongly that the date of the sailing of the convoy should be kept secret. Naturally, he did not want any publicity given to the project which he could possibly stop, because the wider the knowledge of it became the more likely it was that someone else would attempt to interest the British Government in it after Philip had been eliminated. But that was of no importance now, the thing that mattered was—how far was Captain Sorensen a party to Eiderman's designs?

Philip felt that much hung on this: his life perhaps. One thing was certain: after what he had heard there could be no question of his sailing with that cut-throat crew. By thinking up some plausible excuse he must get the *Regenskuld* to tow the convoy back to New York, where, once safely ashore, he could have a showdown with Eiderman, and later secure another crew from the British Seamen's Mission. Walking on tiptoe he made his way back to his cabin.

While he dressed as swiftly and quietly as he could, he again speculated about the possible position of the Captain. If Sorensen were in the business, immediately he was asked to take his principal passenger and the rafts—which were the whole object of the trip—back to New York he would guess that Philip had smelt a rat, and send for Eiderman. Then the fat would be in the fire, and Philip felt that he might find himself in about as desperate a situation as he could possibly imagine. On the other hand, the more he thought about it the more unlikely it seemed to him that Sorensen was involved. From the little Philip had seen of him the old sea Captain did not seem at all the type who would agree to become accessory before the fact of murder. The odds were that he and his ship's company were acting in perfectly good faith; but, even if that were so, he would be extremely surprised to receive an order to put back to port, and Philip began to rack his brains for a plausible excuse.

After some minutes of hard thinking he decided to feign illness. He could say that before he had left London he had been warned by his doctor that he ought to have his appendix out, that he had ignored the warning at the time, but a sudden attack of acute pain in the last hour had brought it home to him that it would be absolute madness to chance a two months' voyage on which no doctor would be available.

A glance at his watch showed him that it was just after half past two. It occurred to him that the Captain might have turned in, but he thought that unlikely, owing to their proximity to the coast and the unusual shortness of the trip. Very quietly he closed the door of his cabin behind him and went up the companionway to the bridge.

To his relief he saw Captain Sorensen standing near the binnacle, and the Captain, catching sight of him at the same moment, turned and came towards him.

" Hello, jong man! What do you make opp herr? " the short, thickset old sailor greeted him in a friendly voice. " Et iss aarly yet, an' der iss anoder two-tree hour before we to your launch let you down."

" I know," replied Philip; and adopting a voice that he strove to keep clear enough to be comprehensible, yet low and panting to suggest that he was in serious pain, he went on to tell him the story about his appendix and ask him that with as little delay as possible the *Regenskuld* should tow the whole convoy back to New York.

" Dis iss bad," muttered the Captain sympathetically. " Kom into my cabin an' I gif you der goot Schnapps. But for me to about ship der order from Mister Eiderman muss kom."

Phillip followed him down to his cabin, now fairly certain in his mind that the Captain was not in the plot to murder him. He hated the taste of the Schnapps but drank the fiery spirit off with a little shudder, then proceeded to reiterate his request.

" I haf tell you," repeated the old sailor, " to about ship der order from Mister Eiderman muss kom."

" He's certain to be asleep, so why bother to waken him? " argued Philip. " And, after all, this is my show, I'm paying for the rafts to be towed out to sea just as I paid for the tugs and all the rest of it."

" *Ja, ja,* I do not argue wid you over dat. You pay Eiderman maybe, but Eiderman charter der *Regenskuld* for der job, see? So he der boss roun' herr ess, an' eff you want me to about ship der order from Eiderman muss kom."

Realizing that it was futile to argue further, Philip thanked the old fellow for the Schnapps and, still making a pretence of being in pain, by holding his tummy, retired to his cabin.

It seemed that his choice now lay in waiting until six o'clock when everyone would come on deck and expect him to go over the side into the launch with the five Nazi assassins; or going along to tackle Eiderman then and there.

On thinking it over, it seemed to him that if he waited until dawn he would be at a greater disadvantage, as Eiderman would then have at his disposal his five thugs, and perhaps even further aid if, as was quite possible, there were a number of other Germans among the ship's company. If Eiderman found himself thwarted, he would be capable of doing all sorts of mischief with such a bunch at his orders, the least of which might be the scuttling of the launch and the sabotaging of the contents of the Number One raft. Moreover, to wait would give it away to Captain Sorensen that he had only been shamming illness, and by that he might lose the Captain's goodwill. No; it would be better to tackle Eiderman now, while he was alone.

As he walked along the passage he noticed an iron turnscrew with a square hole in its brightly polished rounded brass top, hanging on a hook. It looked a pretty useful weapon, so he took it down as a precaution against Eiderman cutting up rough, then advanced boldly towards his enemy's cabin. He could feel his heart pounding in his chest but he knew that his only hope lay in showing a bold face and trying to bluff his enemy.

Streaks of light coming through the ventilator above the door indicated that the German was still awake. Philip did not knock but with one turn of the brass knob threw open the door. Eiderman, clad in a silk dressing-gown, was lying on his bunk reading.

" Hello! What the hell . . .? " he exclaimed, sitting up with a jerk but he broke off suddenly as he saw the grim look on his visitor's face.

Philip wasted no time in beating about the bush. " If you want a row, we'll have it : but I don't think losing our tempers would do either of us any good at the moment. I'm on to your little game and I'm not playing; so I must trouble you to come up on the bridge and tell Captain Sorensen that he's to about ship and tow the convoy back to New York."

" So! " the German sneered contemptuously, and putting down his book thrust his hands deep into his dressing-gown pockets.

" Come on! " said Philip a trifle nervously. " Sorensen is expecting you. I've already told him that my appendix has flared up and that I've decided not to risk the voyage. That's a good enough excuse for you to tell him to turn back."

" And what do you propose to do if I refuse? " Eiderman said calmly. " Beat me over the head with that big spanner? "

The disdain in his tone made Philip flush. He was seeing Eiderman now with new eyes. The narrow skull was that of a fanatic who would stick at nothing to gain his ends; the smile was as false as the gleaming white teeth behind it, and the steely-blue eyes were as hard and soulless as agate. How he could ever have trusted this man Philip could not think, but in spite of his loathing for him he managed to keep control over his temper, as he replied :

" *Herr Kapitan,* you will either do as I say or face the music. I'll tell Sorensen that you've been planning to have me murdered and insist that he radios the nearest patrol boat to come out and investigate. Then, in front of the U.S. officers I'll accuse you of being an American citizen in the pay of a foreign country—Nazi Germany. I know I've got no proof of that, but the police might persuade one of your thugs to talk, and in any case as far as the authorities are concerned you'll be a marked man from now on."

"Say, you're smarter than I thought," Eiderman acknowledged, swinging his feet off the bunk and standing up. "That would certainly be most inconvenient. My old friend Heinrich Himmler would not be at all pleased to learn that his best officer in the United States had become the target for every little Federal agent's suspicions." Suddenly his voice hardened, as he added: "Such revelation I will not permit."

"All right then! Come up to the bridge and tell Sorensen that he's to turn round."

The cabin was quite a roomy one. Philip was standing with his back to the door, which he had closed behind him. Eiderman was about six feet away beside the bunk from which he had just risen. Without a word to Philip he turned his back, walked a few more paces to the porthole end of the cabin and pulled open a drawer in the dressing-table which stood beneath it. Glancing over his shoulder he remarked jeeringly:

"You British are a wonderful people, are you not? So sporting! You never hit an enemy from behind." Suddenly he whipped round with a big automatic clutched firmly in his hand.

Pointing it at Philip he went on: "You young fool! What impertinence even to think of crossing swords with me. You are scheduled to die in a few days' time, at the first sign of even moderately rough weather. All you have succeeded in doing is to advance the hour of your extermination. I propose to kill you here and now!"

Philip paled under the threat. He had half feared that when Eiderman had moved over to the dressing-table it had been to get a weapon, yet somehow he had not been able to bring himself to strike the German down while his back was turned. Now it looked as if he were about to pay for his quixotry with his life.

"You—you'd better be careful," he stammered. "If you let that thing off one of the sailors will hear it and—and come rushing along to find out what's happened."

At that moment a roll of thunder sounded and the rain came sheeting down on the deck above. Eiderman bared his white teeth in a mirthless grin. "Listen to that," he snarled, jerking his head slightly towards the cabin ceiling. "Even God is now fed up with protecting so stupid a people as the British and when we need it sends us Germans the weather that suits us best. The crew will keep to their quarters while it rains like this, and no one upon the bridge could hear a shot fired down here."

"Even if they don't Sorensen will want to know what's happened to me," Philip burst out. "If you kill me you'll swing for it—I mean, go to the electric chair."

"You are wrong! I am no novice at removing unwanted meddlers from my path. Many times I have had to do so in the interests of my beloved Fuehrer, and you, I think, have already provided me with a good explanation for your own death."

" What the hell d'you mean?"

" You have told Captain Sorensen about your appendix, have you not? You have pretended suddenly to be very ill to-night as an excuse to get back to New York. Very well. How can we be certain that the appendix is the cause of the trouble? It might be peritonitis or a hæmorrhage—something which would flare up suddenly, causing you to collapse here in my cabin in about one minute's time. Actually the cause will be a bullet through the stomach. But no one except Auffen and myself will know that. I shall partially undress you, plug the wound to stop it bleeding, cover up the bullet hole in your clothes, lay your body on my bunk and respectfully cover it with a sheet."

Philip stared at the tall thin man. The palms of his hands were damp, but he felt an entirely detached fascination in listening to this callous account of what was to be done with his dead body. Almost automatically he began to argue.

" You seem to have forgotten that in cases of sudden death like that there's always a post-mortem."

Eiderman laughed. " You young fool! There is no doctor in this ship and we are now outside United States territorial waters. After Sorensen has had a look at your face, and felt your pulse and heart if he wishes, I shall bring Hans Auffen here to sew you up in a piece of canvas. Then to-morrow morning, instead of your going off with your rafts, you will be buried at sea."

" Sorensen may not agree to that," cried Philip, desperate now that he saw the trap he had helped to fashion closing so surely about him.

" He *will* agree!" The German's thin mouth became a sneering line.

" He would not turn back to New York without an order from me, would he? That old Norwegian fool at least has the sense to know who is the master here. He will do what I tell him!"

Stepping forward a pace and thrusting out both his chin and his pistol, Eiderman became even more threatening as he went on: " Before you die, little Englishman, it is good that you should understand that soon there will be only two kinds of people in this world—Masters and Slaves. We Germans, who are the natural Master Race, will at last come into our own. Every other race will either submit—or be liquidated. France, Holland, Belgium will give us little trouble. The Balkan countries are too ill equipped to offer any resistance, and it is so long since the Scandinavian peoples went to war that they have forgotten how to fight. In Europe that leaves only Britain; and you British are so stupid you will not even have the sense to realize the hopelessness of fighting—so we shall have to wipe you out. Don't think either that your Raft Convoy would have saved your country. It was a good idea, a very good idea, but as your proverb says, ' One swallow does not make a summer!' Also, even quite a number of clever young men are not enough to save a country which allows itself to be led by a lot of old men who think only of party politics. That is where we Germans have been so wise in abolishing political parties for the National Socialist State. Above all, we have our mighty Fuehrer to lead us——"

Almost as though some invisible presence were standing beside him and had whispered a warning in his ear, Philip suddenly felt convinced that, worked up as Eiderman now was, when he reached the end of his peroration he would exclaim: " Heil Hitler!" and simultaneously press the trigger of his gun. Philip knew that the sands of his life were running out.

The German's words, fast increasing in tempo as his voice became louder and more guttural, were now lost on him. He still remained near the door, tense and rigid, his eyes riveted on Eiderman's, no longer with fear but with a strained vigilance, as he waited for something—he hardly knew what—to happen.

Suddenly the sign he watched for came. Eiderman's eyes flickered, his voice rose almost to a scream and he threw up his head. At that second Philip cast himself forward, lunging out with every ounce of strength he could muster behind the heavy turnscrew. The distance between them was too great for the blow to fall on Eiderman's head or body, but the attack was so unexpected that he had time neither to pull back his gun nor squeeze the trigger. The rounded brass head of the turnscrew caught him on the thumb, and he dropped the pistol with a screech of pain.

If Philip had had more experience of such desperate fighting, he would have followed up his advantage by beating down the German's guard and stunning him. Instead, he rashly dropped his weapon and made a dive for the automatic. At the same moment Eiderman plunged forward in an attempt to retrieve it. Neither succeeded in his object; instead, they crashed into each other and rolled over together on the floor.

For the next few moments they fought with silent ferocity, each struggling to get a stranglehold on the other's throat. Physically, they were fairly evenly matched. In height and weight there was little to choose between them. Philip had the advantage of age as he was nearly thirty years younger than his antagonist, but he had never gone in much for games and was soft in comparison to Eiderman, who had spent the best part of those thirty years as an officer in the German Navy.

Backwards and forwards they rolled, only to be brought up with a bump, owing to the confined floor space in the cabin. First one was on top, then the other. At last, Eiderman managed to straddle Philip and, his white teeth exposed in a snarling grin, began to bash sideways at his face. Philip took two smashing welts on the left ear, which momentarily stunned him; then, exerting all his strength, he threw the German off. Eiderman promptly kicked him in the face, but, fortunately for Philip, he was wearing soft bedroom slippers.

They were panting now as they strove to get a new grip on each other. The sweat ran down their faces and both were marked from blows. With a great effort Eiderman pushed Philip off and staggered to his feet. As he stepped back he kicked the iron turnkey, which gave a metallic clang as it slithered against a stanchion. Stooping he grabbed it up and raised it high above his head. Philip was still half-crouching on the floor, now absolutely at his enemy's mercy.

In the split second that he huddled there staring up, he knew that one blow from the great key would be enough to bash out his brains. In a desperate effort to save himself he flung his body back, sprawling head-long across the floor. The blow fell but, overshooting its mark and with its force largely spent, caught him on the thigh. In his violent twist to avoid the blow his head struck the leg of a chair and his right arm shot under it. As he thrust out his hand to raise himself his fingers came in contact with the butt of Eiderman's automatic. Snatching at it he rolled right over. The German was towering above him and had lifted the heavy iron to strike again. Philip thrust up the pistol and pulled the trigger.

For a moment Eiderman remained quite still, his arms above his head, a demoniacal look of hate and fury on his lean features. The shattering report of the pistol seemed to echo round and round the cabin, a wisp of blue smoke trickled from its barrel. Then, as the reverberation died away, the light went out of the German's eyes, his knees buckled beneath him and he slumped sideways across Philip's legs. As Philip strove to free himself, there was a loud rattling from Eiderman's throat, one of his hands clawed spasmodically at the air, then dropped, and the sound ceased.

Still gasping for breath, Philip stumbled to his knees and stared down at his would-be murderer. The Nazi was not a pretty sight. His mouth lolled open, the flashing upper denture had fallen forward and from below it oozed a trickle of dark blood. There could be no doubt that he was dead.

Philip's first reaction on seeing Eiderman fall had been one of triumph. Never before had he had to fight for his life, and all the exhilaration of primitive man at his first victory surged through him as he savoured his own escape and witnessed the death throes of his adversary. But he was hardly on his feet when the full implications of what had happened struck him.

Eiderman could have killed him and, no doubt, got away with it; but his having killed the German was a very different matter. He could not go to Captain Sorensen and say that Eiderman had died of a sudden hæmorrhage with the least hope of such a statement being credited. Neither could he call on the wall-eyed Hans Auffen to sew up the corpse in canvas for burial at sea.

For one wild moment he thought of attempting to arrange matters so that Eiderman's death looked like suicide. But that was impossible. Even if a motive could be suggested, the position of the wound showed at a glance that it could not have been self-inflicted. The bullet had gone in under the ribs, travelled up through the body and come out at the neck. And when it came to a motive for murder Philip saw at once that Sorensen would think they had quarrelled. The Captain knew that one of them had wanted to turn back at the last moment. He might quite reasonably assume that the other had large financial interests in the venture and so had refused to do so. High words could easily have followed, and although the pistol was Eiderman's only the person with him could have fired the shot.

All these thoughts rushed through Philip's brain in a few seconds. Hardly a minute had elapsed since the shot had been fired. The rain was still pelting down overhead, but Philip cast an anxious glance at the door. When the pistol had exploded it had sounded like the bursting of a bomb. It seemed impossible that no one should have heard it.

Some strange instinct caused Philip to tiptoe as he stole to the door, opened it, and peered out. There was no one in the passage. Shutting it again he bolted it and stood for a moment gazing down at Eiderman's body in bitter despair. It seemed to him now that this unscrupulous servant of a maniac master had trapped him as surely by his death as if he had carried through undiscovered his original assassination plans. It now looked as if, instead of being knocked on the head and thrown overboard, his victim was headed for a murder trial.

Such a trial, Philip knew, would take many weeks. Even if he could succeed in proving that Eiderman was a German agent and that he had killed him in self-defence, by the time he was once more a free man the summer would be gone, and there would be no hope of testing his Raft Convoy till next spring. By that time Europe might be in flames, and once war actually broke out it would probably be impossible even to get permission to try out the idea. But would he be able to prove anything against the dead man? And if he failed to do so what would the outcome be? He would be dead long before the spring. They would send him to the electric chair.

The more he thought about it the more convinced Philip became that he would find it extremely difficult, if not impossible, to prove anything about the conspiracy against his life. Eiderman's determination not to allow any accusation to be made against him argued his conviction that he believed himself entirely unsuspected up to date. If the American Political Police did not even suspect that he was working for the Nazis, what weight would Philip's bare word carry? As for the five thugs, he could prove nothing against them either, and it was not they who would be grilled now, but himself.

With sudden determination Philip opened the door of the cabin's tall, narrow hanging-cupboard. Bending down, he stripped off Eiderman's silk dressing-gown and threw it, as though casually abandoned, on the bunk. Exerting all his strength, he lifted the dead man and propped him upright in the cupboard, hung up his jacket in front of his face and spread a spare blanket he found there over his feet to sop up any blood that might drop from his wound. Having locked the door and pocketed the key, he carefully mopped up the little pool of blood on the cabin floor with a rubber sponge from the washstand. Slipping the catch of the pistol to safety he put it also in his pocket, picked up the turnscrew, switched out the light and stepped into the passage, closing the door softly behind him. There was every chance now that anyone looking into the cabin would think that Eiderman had got up and left it. Sooner or later the body would be discovered, but not until Eiderman had been missed and a serious search made for him—and that might not be for several hours to come.

As Philip replaced the brass turnscrew in the corridor his face was flushed but his jaw was set in a grim line. He was damned if he would stand trial for the murder of one of Hitler's filthy Nazis and most probably be executed for it! What an ignominious end to all his plans! No, he wouldn't submit to that without a struggle. Anyhow, he would give them a run for their money and, with a little luck, he would yet contribute something of real value to the defeat of Hitler and all his greedy, treacherous Germans.

Walking quickly but quietly to his own cabin, he crammed all his belongings into his handbag. As he thrust in his travelling-clock he saw to his amazement that it was only just after three. It seemed hours since he had gone up on to the bridge to speak to Captain Sorensen, yet that had not been much over twenty minutes ago. He looked round in vain for a strap, some cord or a piece of string, and, finding none, snatched up the face towel from the basin. Pushing one end of the thin towel through the handle of his bag, he turned round and passed the other end under the back of his braces before knotting the two firmly together. It was an awkward way to carry the bag, dangling and bumping against his behind, but it left both his hands free, which was what really mattered. After a last glance round, he left the cabin.

It was still raining, and the thunder, more distant now, rumbled from time to time. Eiderman had been right about the crew remaining under cover while the deluge lasted. When Philip reached the deck there was no one to be seen, and keeping to the deepest patches of shadow he quickly made his way aft.

Gazing astern he could see the launch, but only one of the following rafts was now visible. For a moment he feared that some of the cables must have already snapped, but a second later he caught a glimmer of light through the teeming rain and knew that it must be the beacon halfway along the string, on Raft Number Five.

It looked a long way from the stern of the *Regenskuld* to the bow of the launch—very much further than he had thought. When he had first had the idea in Eiderman's cabin of escaping from the ship by sliding down the cable hand over hand it had seemed quite an easy thing to do; but now, as he gazed at the awful gulf beneath him and the dark, turgid waters being churned up by the screw, he feared that he was going to lose his nerve. Yet behind him lay certain arrest and trial: not just a hold-up of a week while he got together another crew, but months of anxiety and uncertainty, the total waste of his idea if war did come to Britain and, quite probably, at the end of it all, the electric chair for himself.

Steeling himself for the effort, he climbed over the taffrail and, his feet still on the ship, grasped the cable firmly, thanking all his gods that he had chanced to have with him a pair of gloves. He was stooping now, his bag dangling out behind him and proving a much greater weight than he had expected. He had half a mind to take it off and abandon it, but that would have meant climbing back across the rail; and he had an uneasy suspicion that, if he once got his feet on the firm deck again, he would not be able to screw up the courage to leave it a second time. He drew a deep breath, gripped the cable with all his might and swung himself off.

The next six minutes seemed like six hours. With his legs wrapped round the cable while it slithered between his thighs and hands, he went down monkey-fashion, slipping and checking alternately, and gasping with pain each time the cable, which felt red-hot, cut through the gloves and seared his palms. The last ten yards were the most difficult. He had reached the bottom of the curve and could slide downwards no further, but had to haul himself along hand over hand, while his bag swinging under him flopped and splashed about in the sea. Three times waves washed right over him, and he almost lost his grip, but, at last, with a sudden spurt of energy he reached the prow of the launch, grabbed it and drew himself aboard.

For some minutes he lay flat on his back up in the bows, panting from his exertions. Then, when his breathing became a little easier he relieved himself of the bag which had proved such an awkward burden, and set about disconnecting the cable by which the *Regenskuld* was towing the launch. This was not a difficult matter, as he had thought it a wise precaution to have all the cables used in the Raft Convoy fitted with patent release gear at both ends. He had reason now to be glad of his forethought, as he had only to pull out a split pin. There was a faint splash as the end of the cable hit the water, and the first Raft Convoy was now adrift on the open ocean

Philip wondered how long it would be before Captain Sorensen realized that he had lost his tow. The *Regenskuld* had been proceeding at only three or four knots, owing to the great weight she was pulling, but now she would naturally go much faster. The lookouts would not miss the convoy as their attention was concentrated forward, and owing to the rain, it might be some time before the loss was realized, provided the increase in the speed of the ship did not immediately become apparent to those in her.

As soon as the launch had dropped half a mile behind the ship, Philip took his bag along to the cabin and left it at the bottom of the broad, shallow steps, but he did not dare to switch on a light for fear of attracting attention It would have been useless to get the engines going, as the launch had nowhere near the power required to tow the rafts in any direction other than that in which the current was already carrying them; so there was no way in which he could increase his distance from the *Regenskuld*—he could only hope that she would proceed on her course and be over the horizon by the time dawn came.   At last her lights disappeared in the rain, but Philip still felt it wiser not to show a light himself.

The night was warm and the rain soon decreased to a steady drizzle, so, although Philip was wet through, he did not feel cold and remained on deck. He had plenty to think about with his recent escape and the uncertainty of what now lay ahead.   After all, he thought, people had crossed the Atlantic in canoes, so there was no earthly reason why he should not make it in a forty-foot launch. He knew the boat's engines like the palm of his hand, and enough about radio to signal if he wished to. He had food enough for months and a great variety of other supplies. Having no crew he thought it unlikely that he would be able to service the rafts so far as their sails were concerned, but he could make an occasional inspection to see that the cables were not fraying.

At the first sign of the sky lighting, Philip began to haul on the cable by which the Number One Raft was attached to the launch. After a steady quarter of an hour's hard work the two came together with a slight bump. He next proceeded to push and pull with a boathook until he got the launch flat alongside the raft, and then tied her up there.

As dawn began to break he anxiously scanned the eastern horizon, and soon his worst fears were realized. He could make out a ship, which he felt sure was the *Regenskuld*, and she was coming towards him. Evidently some time during the past two hours she had discovered her loss and turned round. He knew that since he had failed to lose her in the night he had only one hope. It was the chance that the people in her would not see the launch but imagine that he had abandoned his rafts in order to escape in it to the coast. It was with this in mind that he had hauled the launch close alongside the raft and tied her there on the side where she would be furthest from the ship if she had turned back on her track.

For the next half-hour he waited and watched from his concealed position as the *Regenskuld* gradually grew nearer. His throat was dry and his lips parched from his anxiety. If they spotted the launch it was all up, and his attempt to escape would make things look blacker than ever against him at his trial.

The ship came to within half a mile, then she altered her course slightly. With his heart in his mouth he watched her for another few minutes, then he gave a sigh of relief. His ruse had succeeded and she was coming no nearer.

A quarter of an hour later he had to perform the tricky operation of easing the launch round to the east side of the raft, otherwise anyone looking astern from the *Regenskuld* might have seen him. But the ship continued on her course, and by half past six she was hull down over the horizon.

Looking back at her, he felt a tremendous elation. Not only had he outwitted his enemies but he was at long last setting out on the great venture of which he had dreamed for so many months. What matter now if it was him alone against the ocean? All the more glory! He laughed suddenly out aloud at the thought: "Himself alone against the ocean!"

As his laugh echoed across the water he heard an angry voice say behind him: "What are you laughing at? An' where the hell are we?"

Swinging round he saw that a girl was standing scowling at him from the cabin steps.

CHAPTER VI

THE UNINVITED GUEST

JUST as some four and half hours before—although it seemed as many days ago to Philip—he had hardly been able to believe his ears when he overheard Eiderman give orders for his murder, so now he could scarcely trust his eyes. Yet there could be no doubt about it: a girl was glaring balefully at him from the steps that led down to the cabin.

"Where are we?" she repeated angrily. "What would we be doin' at sea here in a little boat like this?"

Philip did not reply immediately; he was still busy taking her in. She was, he guessed, about twenty, of medium height with well developed bust and hips, yet smallish in appearance; this, as he realized later, being accounted for by the fact that her absurdly high-heeled shoes gave her a tallness out of proportion to her figure. Her hair was of the violent red that small boys rudely call "carrots" and in its present state of disorder looked as though it had not been brushed for a week. Her face was round and freckled, its only striking feature being a pair of not very large but very bright eyes. Although it was high summer she was dressed in a pleated cloth skirt of strawberry tartan with a jacket to match, and a cheap nondescript fur tie round her neck. A large brooch, earrings, three bangles and two rings—the exaggerated size of the stones showing clearly that they were all imitation—completed the picture. By and large, Philip summed her up as an unattractive, tawdry-looking little thing.

Meanwhile, she had been using her sharp blue eyes on him. She put

him down as twenty-one—two years younger than he actually was—six
feet in height, with an attractive, loosely-knit figure. He was wearing
a pair of old grey bags and a pale blue, short-sleeved sun-shirt; but
nearby lay his Glenurquhart tweed jacket, which he had spread out to
dry, and she knew that had cost good money. The early morning sun
glinted on his fair hair untidily tumbling across his forehead; it also lit up
the stubble on his chin and the patches of greasy dirt with which he was
still blotched from his monkey-like journey along the cable. Yet, beneath the dirt she read in his well-proportioned, ascetic face the signs of
culture; so she decided that he was a college boy who had taken the
motor-boat out to sea for some crazy notion, and bet herself a new mas-
cara outfit that he would prove both a highbrow and a sourpuss.

"Say, are you as dumb as you look?" she cracked suddenly. "Or is
it jus' that your mother never taught you to talk?"

Philip smiled. "I may be dumb the way you think but I'm certainly
not dumb physically."

"Then give, will you! What'll we be doin' here, right in the middle of
the ocean?"

"We're not. We can't be much more than fifteen miles from the
American coast yet. If we were higher out of the water on the deck of
a ship you could still see it, I expect."

"Holy Mary and all the Saints be praised!" exclaimed the girl. "We'll
have no difficulty in gettin' back then. And I scaring myself into thinkin'
I'd been asleep for a week and woken up heaven knows where!"

Letting any question of "gettin' back" pass for the moment, Philip
enquired: "How do you come to be on this launch?"

"'Tis quite simple. By the time I'd gotten through the dock gates the
evenin' had caught up wit' me. The night is no time to choose a ship to
go to Europe in, an' there was this motor-boat bobbing alongside the
steps. It sure seemed a good place to sleep in; and sleep sound I did till
ten minutes ago."

"D'you mean to say you never heard the hooting of the tugs, or the
thunderstorm, or anything?"

"Would I be tellin' you the contrary if I did; an' do I look the kind
of dumbcluck who would be wastin' her time joy-ridin' in this boat instead
of gettin' her a liner?"

"So you are going to Europe, eh? But when one does that one
doesn't just walk down to the dock and choose a liner—one books a berth
through a travel agency," Philip explained in humouring tones, not altogether free from superiority.

Looking up again she smiled for the first time. "Have a heart now!
What's a poor girl to do? 'Tisn't all of us can afford the passage money,
even to go steerage. When I get to Paris I'll be needin' my savin's if I'm
to live respectable; an' what harm will it do one of those big shipping
companies to take me over an' me weighin' next to nothin' at all?"

Philip was completely puzzled. With her gaudy clothes and trashy jewellery the girl looked like an East End tart, yet she spoke of going to Paris and living respectably on her own savings in the same breath as she confessed that she had deliberately intended to cheat some shipping company out of her passage money.

"What's your name?" he asked, with a smile.

"Me name's Gloria," she replied, and seeing his smile deepen added with asperity: "An' what may there be to laugh at in that?"

"Nothing," he said, sobering hastily. "But you're Irish, aren't you? And I somehow expected you to be called something simple, like Mary."

She flushed to the roots of her red hair, and looking down began to fiddle with her ring. "Ah, just fancy you thinking that! Well, Mary's me christened name if you must know, but I chose Gloria for meself. Don't you like it?"

"Yes I think it's very pretty. What's your other name?"

"Smith, but I spell it with two 't's'" came the rather astonishing reply. "'Tisn't so easy to change a surname, an' how would an artist ever succeed with a name like Mary Smith?"

"So you're an artist," said Philip, wondering if she were a juggler or contortionist or merely did the usual small-time song and dance act.

She nodded. "That's why it's crazy I am to get to Paris. The masters in the Latin Quarter are the tops. Oh, jus' to think of the pictures I'll be painting this time next year!"

"Have you been studying art for long?" Philip enquired, once more endeavouring to adjust his ideas about this strange companion Fate had seen fit to thrust upon him.

"Why, sure I have, ever since I was a wee bit of a thing. But 'tis only since I began to work in a factory that I could afford the classes. My mother—she's Irish as you guessed I was—was against it. But me poor Dad—he had education and sent me to a good convent school—was the great one to encourage me. He died of the drink, bless his ould heart, but before he had the final fit that carried him off he made me swear by the bones of the Saints that I'd never give up me paintin'."

Philip cast a quick glance round him, scanning the sea to north, east and south, then clambering on top of the launch's cabin he peered over the raft to westward. There were a liner, two tramps and a fishing trawler in sight, but none of them was less than two miles distant, and, while he could see them clearly it was doubtful if they were even aware of the presence of the Raft Convoy—unless the lookouts in their crow's nests had reported it—owing to its lowness in the water. Jumping down again he said to Miss Smith:

"Going from the sublime to the practical, d'you happen to know anything about the art of cooking?"

"Why sure!" The small freckled face lit up. "I'm hungry too. Jus' show me the way to your stove!"

He took her down into the cabin, the far end of which had been arranged as a small galley, showed her the cupboards that contained crockery and stores, and opened the refrigerator, which he had filled to capacity with fresh food only the previous day.

Leaving his uninvited guest to cook breakfast, he went back on deck, untied the launch from its position close up against the Number One raft, and, as it floated clear, started up the engine. In less than two minutes he had taken up the slack of cable, and although it could not be said that the launch was actually towing the convoy, it was exercising a definite pull upon it in a north-easterly direction. Having lashed the wheel into position so that the launch would keep its course, he returned to the afterdeck where the self-styled Gloria was now setting out breakfast.

She tucked into her grapefruit, scrambled eggs and coffee with such heartiness that Philip got the impression that she must have been half-starved and, curiosity overcoming his good manners, he asked her when she had last had a meal.

There was a moment's silence before she cried: " Now, come to think of it, not a crust have I had since I threw the cereal dish at me mother's head yesterday morning!"

" Your decision to go to Europe was quite a sudden one, then?"

" Indade it was, though I've long dreamed of makin' the trip. Me sister's to blame in the first place for the softie she is, but me mother the more so, for it's the black-hearted wickedness of her that drove me from me home." Upon which pronouncement Gloria suddenly burst into a flood of tears.

Philip did his best to comfort her and, with none of the shyness he had experienced only the day before in a similar situation, put his arm round her shoulders; but his sensations then had been very different. He felt that he was definitely in love with Lexie, whereas he had only a vague curiosity and pity for this strange little waif to whom he was now making soothing noises. Moreover, the subtle French perfume that had gone to his head from Miss Foorde-Bilson's beautifully coiffured curls was of an entirely separate world to that of the cheap sickly scent which flowed over him in waves from Gloria's dishevelled and, he suspected, unwashed tresses.

After a little he persuaded her to stop crying and during the next hour succeeded in extracting enough further information about her to form a coherent version of her history.

Her father, Alphonse Smith, was the son of an English father and a French-Canadian mother. He had been a journalist by profession and, being a good linguist, had been sent by the paper for which he worked to Russia as a War Correspondent in 1914. Soon after his arrival in St. Petersburg he had met and married Gloria's mother, Sheila O'Neill. Sheila was the illegitimate but acknowledged daughter of a rich Irish merchant, with a business of many years' standing in St. Petersburg, and his Russian mistress. But at an early age she had been sent back to Ireland to be brought up by her father's relatives, and she had only rejoined him in the Russian capital a few months before the outbreak of war.

For some two years Alphonse and Sheila appeared to have lived quite happily, but on the outbreak of the first Russian Revolution he decided that it would be safest to send her and their first child, Gloria's elder sister Maureen, to his mother's people in Canada. Gloria herself was already on the way and was born some months after their arrival in Quebec.

It was at this point that the trouble had begun. Sheila had not only taken an intense dislike to her French-Canadian in-laws but scandalized them by her behaviour with numerous young men in the Forces, who were either going to or returning from the European War, while the unlucky Alphonse was passing through the dangers of the Russian Revolution and later detained by his duties as a journalist in South-Eastern Europe.

As Gloria said sadly of her erring mother: " 'Twas the Russian in her, and, shamed as I am to say it, she has not the morals of a backyard cat."

Whatever the cause of Mrs. Smith's indiscretions, these culminated in 1918 when she put her babies in a home and ran away to New York with an American officer who had been in Quebec on liaison duties. He soon threw her over, and she lived with half a dozen other men before at last being traced by her still loving Alphonse. She had refused to leave New York, so he took out naturalization papers and they started married life afresh; but it had not been a success.

"The Russian in her" had continued to make Mrs. Smith wayward and temperamental, so from then on it was the sad and sordid story of two quite decently educated middle-class people slipping gradually lower in the social scale through immorality and drink. The children were spared much of it in their early years through being placed by their father in a convent, where the Irish sisters mothered them; but it could not be hidden from them that their own mother spent much of her time in dubious night-clubs or away from home, and that their father had taken to drink on that account. His work had suffered, and his earnings dropped in consequence, and, finally, after a long spell of only intermittent employment, he had drunk himself to death soon after Gloria's fourteenth birthday.

By this time Maureen was a pretty girl of nearly seventeen and, seeing in her daughters a source of income, their mother had taken them both away from the convent to have them taught dancing. As soon as Maureen was old enough, a place had been found for her in a cabaret, but Gloria had jibbed at following in her sister's footsteps. Although she did not admit it, there could be little doubt that she was the plainer of the two, and she had had constant rows with her mother about devoting the time when she should have been practising her dancing to sketching and painting. Whether she could in due course have got a job in a cabaret had she so wished was not revealed, but the fact was that, her mother having refused to support her further unless she worked, she had gone into a Christmas Card factory, where she earned enough to keep herself and pay her fees at art classes in the evenings.

Maureen meanwhile had gone the same way as her mother, and was always being pointed out to Gloria as an example of how a " sensible " girl could get herself furs, joy-rides and a good time all round without working for it. This had had little effect on Gloria, as, knowing that Maureen allowed her mother to bully her into handing over two-thirds of her earnings, she had only contempt for her weak-minded sister. The final crisis had arisen when Maureen had fallen ill. Money had begun to get short in the Smith household, so the depraved old mother had first pressed Gloria to go out with one of her sister's elderly men friends, who had seen and taken a fancy to the younger girl, and on her refusing had stolen the girl's last week's pay packet from her handbag.

This had proved the finishing touch. On discovering the theft Gloria flung her sister's cornflakes at her mother's head, retrieved her savings from their hiding-place, packed her best things in a bag and left home for good, with the bold idea of going to Europe to study art.

When the somewhat garbled recital eventually came to an end Philip could not help wondering how much of it was true. He had never moved in circles where it was even remotely likely that a mother would deliberately urge her daughter to take to prostitution as a means of livelihood; but the young woman beside him spoke of the whole matter with such complete naturalness that it was difficult not to believe her.

After a little pause she said: " Come now, it's I who've done all the talkin' so far. Will you be tellin' me something about yourself for a change?"

As he started off by giving his name and saying that he was an Englishman, she exclaimed: " So that's why you talk so queer ! Yet I remember me poor old dad had something of the same high-hat way with him when speakin' to strangers; only not so pronounced."

Philip laughed. " Surely the boot's on the other foot? You talk the queer lingo of an Irish girl brought up in America, whereas you should speak like me, seeing that you're the daughter of an Englishman, and therefore English."

"'I am nothing of the kind !" she declared hotly. " Was I not tellin' you but a moment back that me father took out his naturalization papers in nineteen-twenty, an' but for a few months as a wee babe I've lived in the Bronx all me life. 'Tis American I am, an' one hundred per cent. American at that."

Having soothed her down, Philip went on to describe his home at Alverstoke, his family and his education, with the sudden realization that so far there was little in his life to interest a stranger.

Apparently his companion felt that too, as when he paused for a minute she took the opportunity to ask him what time he thought they would get back to New York.

Actually, he had just been considering the best way of leading up to the subject of the Raft Convoy, and, instead of replying direct, he asked her a question.

"If you had managed to stow away in a ship going to Europe to-day, as you planned, do you think you would have succeeded in avoiding discovery for the whole voyage?"

"Well, I would have to come out to eat, wouldn't I? An' I hadn't figured on trying to stay hid all that time."

"You evidently don't realize, then, what the accepted treatment for stowaways is when they're caught."

"What would it be?"

"They're put to work on some menial task, like washing the dishes, to earn their keep."

She shrugged. "A gal like meself wouldn't be minding that."

"But wait a minute! That's not all. When they reach the port on the other side they're locked up in a cabin. Then they are let out on the return journey to work their way back; and when they arrive at the port where they originally stowed away they are handed over to the police as vagrants."

"D'you mean the shipping people wouldn't let me land in Europe?" Her blue eyes blazed.

"That's right. I'm not fooling," he assured her.

"Well, what d'you know—of all the lousy bums!".

"Still," he said, nerving himself for the plunge. "You don't have to worry about that now. It may take you a bit longer to get there this way, but when we do reach Europe I wouldn't dream of preventing you from landing."

"Say that again," she murmured, coming slowly to her feet.

"I was just trying to break it to you as gently as I could that we're not going back to New York."

She looked wildly round her. "D'you mean you're figuring to cross the ocean in a cockleshell of a boat like this?"

"That's the idea."

"The guy's crazy!" she announced.

"No," he countered. "I'm perfectly sane and I've been planning this trip for a very long time. Actually, it hasn't turned out by any means as I originally intended and your presence provides yet one more unexpected complication; but I have no intention of turning back just because you smuggled yourself on board, so you'd better make up your mind to grin and bear it."

At this she became really angry, and stooping down waved a small clenched fist in his face "Say now, you can't do this to me! I'll not be drowned because some sap of a boy gets it into his head that he's a

new Christopher Columbus. 'Tis back to New York we'll be goin' an'
that quickly now, or 'tis meself ye'll have to reckon with."

" Sit down !" snapped Philip, his eyes hardening.

" I'll not sit down," she screamed. " 'Tis you who'll be gettin' to
those great feet of yours an' turnin' the boat around. Me poor ould
dad was born in England an' 'twas himself used to say that all the
English are crazy. But I'll not be murdered by one of the crazy
English. Put a sock in it now an' take me back where I belong this
instant !"

" It's no good," said Philip. " As a matter of fact, I couldn't, even if I
wanted to. You saw that big raft we were tied up to when you first came
up from the cabin—it's bobbing along there behind us now? Well, we're
towing that and nine others like it. At least, not exactly towing, but
guiding to some extent; and if we turned round we'd be heading against
both the current and the wind, so we couldn't possibly make it. In fact,
the best we could hope for would be to slow them down a bit, because
their pull would be much greater than ours, and they would slowly carry
us further out to sea."

Gloria cast her eyes up to heaven. " Holy Mother of God preserve me
from such imbecility ! Poor sap that you are ! Has it not entered that
thick skull of yours that if we untie the big wire to the raft the boat
will be free?"

" What, abandon the rafts ! " cried Philip. " No damn' fear ! "

" Is it then that you mean to stay hitched to the rafts till we get some
place? But no ! That cannot be. 'Twould be craziness piled on
craziness, for nowhere at all would we get but spend our whole lives
driftin' roun' and roun' in the ocean."

" No, we shan't. The Gulf Stream will carry us to Europe in two
months—or three at the most."

" Three months, is it? Now Saints hear him ! An' if there's a wee bit
of a storm it's dead we'll both be in three hours." Suddenly Gloria
dashed across the short afterdeck and, flinging herself on the release gear
that held the towing cable, strove to undo it.

Jumping to his feet Philip was at her side in a flash, but she did not
understand the mechanism, and was bruising her fingers in vain.

" Stop that !" he shouted, grabbing her by the wrists and pulling her
away. " If you won't behave sensibly I'll have to lock you up."

For answer she kicked him with all her force on the shin and, as he
released her with a cry of pain, followed it up by striking him on the side
of the face with her clenched fist. Dodging a second blow, he seized her
arms again and lugged her, scratching and wriggling, towards the cabin.
While he was half-pushing and half-carrying her down the broad flight
of steps, she suddenly swivelled her head and sank her teeth savagely in
his arm. As he jerked himself away, one of her high heels twisted under
her, and she sat down with a wallop on the cabin floor. Snatching the

opportunity, he grabbed the key from the door, backed up two steps and, pulling the door to, locked it from the outside.

Having looked to his hurts, Philip angrily plumped himself down in the stern to consider how best to deal with his uninvited and now hostile guest when next they came face to face as, sooner or later, they were bound to do. As his temper cooled he had to admit to himself that the girl had done no more than seek shelter for a night in the cabin of the launch, and it was certainly pretty tough on her that, as a result, she should be compelled to go on a long voyage, during which acute discomfort must be faced in times of bad weather, and possibly great danger. Yet there could be no question of taking her back. No inducements, no threats, no pity for anyone else concerned, would now have influenced Philip to abandon his rafts. In bitter mockery she had called him a new Christopher Columbus, but he felt much more like a Crusader. He had a self-imposed mission that might be the saving of his country, and he meant to see it through.

There was, of course, still the possibility of sending an S.O.S. to the nearest westbound ship. When it approached he could request that his passenger be taken aboard for transit to New York, and Philip considered this seriously for some time; but he decided that he simply dared not risk it. If Eiderman's body had not already been discovered, it almost certainly would be before the day was out. As soon as that happened the New York police would be informed, and Mr. Philip Vaudell's description circulated with the information that he was wanted for questioning in connection with murder.

Philip could not be certain that his ruse of hiding the launch behind Raft Number One early that morning had succeeded, but he had every reason to suppose so; and, if his hopes were justified, the police would devote all their energies to hunting for the launch among the hundreds of miles of creeks and bays in which he might have attempted to conceal her anywhere between Cape Cod and Delaware Bay. On the other hand, if he stopped a passing ship to put Gloria on board, it would be known in New York that night that he had not fled back to the coast and landed at all, but was still at sea with his rafts; and the following day an aircraft would be sent out to spot them so that a patrol boat could pick him up and bring him in to stand his trial.

There was, he knew only too well, the very considerable risk still to be faced that, on sighting the rafts, a passing ship might alter course to investigate and, coming too close for the concealment of the launch, compel him to reveal himself and supply the answers to questions prompted by idle curiosity. But the further the rafts drifted from the vicinity of New York the less danger of that there would be, owing to the divergence of the many traffic routes from the great port; and Philip, as a sailor's son, had a very good idea how seemingly illimitable, desolate and empty the vast open spaces of the ocean could be.

After some thought he decided that when a suitable opportunity offered he would tell Gloria all about the origin of the Raft Convoy and see if he could reconcile her to the long voyage through interest in its purpose and the prospect of the reflected glory if the venture proved successful.

However, as he could now see no less than seven ships on various points of the horizon, he decided that he had better keep Gloria locked up for the rest of the day in case she should be overcome by the temptation to signal any craft that came near enough to see her. In consequence, when, half an hour afterwards, there came a violent banging on the cabin door and angry shouts, he ignored them.

Glancing at his wrist-watch, he was amazed to find it was only a quarter past nine, since to him—as yet not accustomed to noticing the position of the sun—it had seemed that it must be approaching midday. He was now beginning to feel reaction from the great and unusual strain that he had been through during the previous night, and it suddenly struck him that it was well over twenty-four hours since he had had any sleep. That accounted for the feeling of limpness he was experiencing, and the fact that he could hardly keep his eyes open, now that he had relaxed. He did not want to go to sleep during the daytime, while he was still in this busy shipping area, but he could not escape if pursued or avoid any visit that the curious might choose to inflict on him, so there was no vital purpose to be served by his keeping awake; and the subconscious knowledge of that caused him to drop off before he realized what was happening.

When he awoke it was late afternoon, and his first thought was that he was hungry. His next was of Gloria. The radio had been switched on, and dance-music was coming from the cabin. Since he had locked her in there she was now in control not only of the galley but also of all his edible stores. He wondered if she had cooked herself any lunch—it was not his fault if she hadn't.

As he got up he saw with some alarm that an old-fashioned sailing barque, flying the Finnish flag, was no more than half a mile distant and standing towards him. Fearful of attracting attention by moving about, he sat down again, and spent an anxious half-hour watching her tack back and forth on his starboard beam. At last she had definitely passed without hailing him, so he breathed freely again. But not for long. In the distance, from what appeared to be dead ahead, an oil tanker was now coming up. She gave him another half-hour of acute trepidation, although she eventually slid by a good mile away to port.

Two such close calls in so short a time made him wonder how many others he had had while he was asleep, and convinced him of the wisdom of having left Gloria locked up all day. Moreover, it made him feel that it would be most unwise to release her until darkness had fallen. In consequence, all through the long summer evening, for some four seemingly interminable hours, he endeavoured to busy himself with little jobs about the deck and in the engine-room, in an effort to stave off his hunger.

When twilight had come and visibility dropped to about half a mile, Philip felt he might safely switch on his beacons and navigational lights and go below. Unlocking the cabin door, he nerved himself for another encounter with the temperamental Miss Smith.

He did not, as he had half-expected, receive a crack on the head from a saucepan. She had switched off the radio some time before, and was sitting there quietly in the semi-darkness.

" Hello! " he said, as he turned on the light.

" Hello! " she replied. " Was it nice bein' up there on deck all day? "

" Oh, all right. As a matter of fact I slept a good part of the time. Sorry I had to lock you up, but I hope that to-morrow it won't be necessary. Have you had anything to eat? "

" Thanks, yes. All I was wantin'. But how's yourself managed all these long hours?'"

He gave a rueful laugh. " To tell the truth I haven't, and I'm darn' hungry."

She stood up at once. " 'Twas your own silly fault, but now you've apologized I'm not one to bear malice. Just lay up that table, an' I'll have supper ready in no time at all."

Evidently she had taken the opportunity of exploring the cabin thoroughly during her enforced confinement, as she now seemed to know where everything was kept, and with a deft, efficient touch which compelled his admiration she very soon had an appetizing meal cooked and on the table.

The eating of it provided him with the best opportunity he had so far had for studying her closely. No one, he decided, could possibly call the round freckled face opposite beautiful, but it certainly had character. There was something about the jaw-line and the set of the eyebrows above the bright blue eyes which could flash so angrily. Then he thought again of the account of her life she had given him that morning. If it was true—and he now saw no reason to doubt it—she had had a pretty raw deal, poor little wretch, and had put up a darn' good show in an extraordinarily tricky situation.

He was inclined to discount her victorious preservation of her virtue to some extent, on the grounds of temptations and rewards connected with immorality being in direct ratio to the good looks of the young women concerned, until he remembered that an embryo-doctor friend of Cambridge days had told him that it had been proved through scientific observation in clinics and police courts that professional prostitutes were plainer as a class than either shop girls or factory workers, and that looks had no relations at all to morality. It seemed, therefore, that Gloria must be given full marks for her refusal to be bullied into following her mother's and sister's example, and when she asked him what he was thinking about he frankly said so.

She laughed and, after a moment, replied: " 'Tis an old saying that vice does not pay. An' believe me 'tis a true one, as you'd know if you'd seen all that I have. 'Tis a fool's game for a girl that's ambitious, an' how would I ever get one of me paintin's in the *Salon* if I wasted the best years of me life anglin' for men?"

"How long is it since you got this great urge for painting?" Philip asked.

"I guess I've had it all me life. When I was only a wee thing playin' around with chalks an' the like me poor ould dad said that one day I'd make a name for meself. But it's hard to become real good when you have your living to earn. Evenin's an' week-ends is all the time there is, an' 'tis steady work that gets results in art, same as in everythin' else."

Going over to the bunk she had chosen for herself, she pulled from beneath it an old suitcase in which she began to rummage, as she went on: " 'Twas terribly difficult to know what to bring. Not that I'd be tryin' to fool you that me wardrobe rivalled the Queen of Sheba's. I have me warmest suit on me back already, and me only dacent dance frock is right here. I mean, in the way of me drawin' an' paintin'. I've left albums and albums back home but maybe you'll think these few not too bad."

Philip knew nothing about the technicalities of art, but it was obvious to him that the girl had talent. She had brought only two small canvases, one a painting of a negro's head and the other a street scene; but there was a folio with the best part of a hundred drawings in it. The street scene was done in a very modern style, and he thought it rather messy, but the head had a tremendous vitality about it, and the drawings, most of which were anatomic studies, were, he felt sure, of a very high standard.

As he looked slowly through them he made a number of admiring comments, before he finally remarked: "I think they're terribly good. I only wish I could discuss them with you properly, but the trouble is that I know practically nothing about art. These last few years I've spent practically all my time studying engineering."

"Why, that's interestin' too," she smiled kindly. "Gettin' somethin' yourself has conceived in your mind done jus' the way you wan' it is creation sure enough, whether 'tis a bridge built in steel or a still-life on paper."

"That's right," he said eagerly. "And that's exactly how I feel about crossing the Atlantic with these rafts. You see, I first thought of the idea nearly two years ago. I've spent thousands of hours planning the job, and I've dreamed about it for months. It's never been done before, you know; and now that it looks as if another world war is inevitable it's terribly important that it should be done."

She shrugged. " 'Tis nonsense you're talkin' now. There'll be no world war. A little bit of a scrap in Europe maybe, but we Americans are wise to things now and we'll not be drawn into your muddles a second time. But will you be tellin' me how driftin' across the ocean at the pace of a tortoise is goin' to help any sort of a war? "

Philip asked nothing better. He told her the whole history of his struggle and did his utmost to impress upon her the fact that if their voyage were successful it might enable him to save his country from starvation, should the war, that so many people in Europe now considered as certain, actually break out.

She listened to him patiently and asked several shrewd questions, and it was clear that she was considerably impressed; but, as she appeared to have little more interest in Britain than in any other European country, it was scarcely to be expected that she would become really enthusiastic about the object of the voyage. After a little, she sighed and said:

" 'Tis a great patriot you are, Mr. Vaudell; but 'twas a black day for me when I picked on your boat back in the harbour there. This day the blessed Saints have been kind an' the sea like a mill-pond, but what of to-morrow an' all the days after? One puff of the wind an' I'll be as sick as I was the time I got plastered on hooch at the Art Students' dinner-dance. Sure I'll be dead of sea-sickness before we're half of the way over."

" No, you won't," he tried to reassure her. " However good the weather a small boat like this always tosses about quite a bit; so the fact that you haven't been sick yet proves that you'll be a good sailor. If you do have a bout you'll soon be all right again."

" 'Twas all of a week before I recovered from the hooch, an' two-three months is a real terrible time. I doubt if there'll be two-three days together in all of it that we'll be free of the wind, so it's murderin' me you'll be by forcin' me to come with you."

" I'm sorry," said Philip. " Really I am, but I'm afraid there's no alternative."

" Ah, but that's just where you're wrong." She bent forward quickly. " It come to me all of a sudden this afternoon. I was lookin' out of a porthole an' I saw a ship. Then I sez to meself, sez I: 'We'll be passin' lots more ships an' if we signal one that's headin' for New York it'll stop to ask what we be wantin'. Then himself can be asking them to take me on board an' be rid of me; an' I'll be blessin' him all the days of me life.' "

Philip shook his head. " No, I hate to disappoint you, but it can't be done. As a matter of fact, the main reason why I kept you down here all day is because I was afraid that if a ship came within hailing distance you might try to attract the attention of someone in her."

" But, merciful Saints, why shouldn't I? "

" Because I don't want anything to do with any ships on the way over, particularly vessels going into New York. I want to keep my, er—I mean, the whereabouts of the convoy secret as far as possible. That may not sound an awfully satisfactory reason to you, but I'm afraid you'll have to be content with it."

c*

For a moment she sat silent then she looked up with a faint smile. "So you're scared of that Hitler an' his Nazis already, eh? For shame, man! He's only a great bag of wind, and so near as this to America not one of them would dare to touch a hair of your head."

Philip resisted the temptation to enlighten her and give his real reason for being so anxious to avoid the attention of all New York-bound shipping. Instead, he took her taunt with a smile, and said: "Perhaps. Anyhow, this show means a lot to me and I'm not taking any unnecessary chances."

"Well, if that's the way you feel—" She left the sentence unfinished, and went on: "I'll be doin' the washin'-up. There's a cloth there for you to be dryin' the things on."

Together they cleared away the débris of their meal, and shortly afterwards Philip said: "I expect you'd like to be turning in soon. I'm going to have a look at the engine."

"O.K.," she replied laconically and, humming a little tune to herself, she walked over to a small mirror that she had hung above her bunk and began to pull the pins out of her flaming red hair.

The engine-room was situated forward and reached by a separate hatch, which necessitated going out on deck. The night was fine and starlit. One glance at the pointers of the Dipper carried his eye to the Pole Star, and he saw that they were still heading in the right direction, although the speed of the launch was so slow as to be almost imperceptible. As he listened to the note of the engine, he smiled. His long days of work upon it had been well worth while. It was purring like a Rolls. Having checked the gauges and made a very slight adjustment to the fuel supply, he whiled away half an hour looking over his stock of spare parts, then returned to the main cabin.

Only one light was now on, and Gloria was tucked up in her bunk with her face turned to the wall. It took him only two minutes to undress, switch out the light and slip into the bunk opposite. He began to think about his strange and exciting day, which had started with the appearance of Gloria. It seemed extraordinary to think that this time last night he had still believed Eiderman to be his good and helpful friend, and that he had not even known of Gloria's existence. And now Eiderman was dead and Gloria sound asleep only a few feet away from him on the other side of the cabin. He wondered how long it had been before they had discovered Eiderman's body. He wondered too what would happen when he reached England. Would there be a warrant out for his arrest? Probably, and, as Eiderman had been killed in United States territorial waters, it was quite on the cards that the United States Police would apply for his extradition. That was a most unpleasant thought to sleep on, and it would be quite time enough to worry about it when he was nearing England.

His thoughts turned again to Gloria. What a strange little person she

was; in some way so young, in others so sophisticated. He began to
wonder whether, if given the choice, he would rather have her or not
with him on the voyage. It would have been terribly lonely cooped up
in the launch for six, eight, perhaps twelve, weeks without a soul to whom
he could talk; and, provided Gloria did not become permanently either
sullen or ill, she promised to be much better company than the crew of
five roughnecks he had left behind, even if it had not been their intention
to murder him. Gloria, too, seemed quite a passable cook, which was
an unlooked-for blessing. True, the violence of her temper was apt to
make her dangerous at times, but he felt that things had now more or
less sorted themselves out. The fact that she had refrained from making
a fuss when he had refused her request after dinner to put her on a ship,
and had gone quietly to bed without locking him out of the cabin, or
some nonsense of that kind, showed clearly that she had accepted the
situation, and he did not think he would have any more trouble with her.

Having reached this happy conclusion, he drifted off to sleep. Later
he dreamed that he was on a toboggan, then that he was in a speed-boat.
The waters were rushing past, and he was going faster—faster—faster.
The dream ended in a terrific crash. The launch stopped with a shudder-
ing jerk. Next second he was flung violently from his bunk to come
smashing down on the floor of the cabin.

CHAPTER VII

THE BAD COMPANIONS

For a moment he lay in pitch darkness, wondering if he were awake or
still dreaming. Then the navigational lights flickered and went on again.
Their faint glow coming through the portholes showed him that he was
lying full length on the cabin floor, which was now tilted at a sharp angle.
In the brief but violent process of being hurled from his bunk his head
had come into collision with the beam above it, and now ached
intolerably.

Putting a hand to it he tried to concentrate and realized that the launch
must have piled up on something. His next thought was of Gloria, and
he shouted her name. There was no reply. He staggered to his feet and
slithered down the sloping floor to her bunk. It was empty; and her
clothes had gone from the next bunk on which she had laid them.

With a sudden fear that the launch might be holed and in danger of
sinking, he grabbed his dressing-gown and pulled it on as he stumbled up
the short companionway. He saw at once what had happened. The
starlight was quite sufficient to show that the launch had piled up on one
of the rafts. But how, in God's name, had it managed to do that, Philip

asked himself? A moment later, he knew. The engine was still running. Clambering forward to switch it off, he swung himself over the edge of the engine-room hatch and came face to face with Gloria.

The light was still on there. By it he saw that there was a slight cut on her forehead, from which the blood was trickling. Her eyes were dilated, and her face was very white. Otherwise, she appeared to be unhurt and in full possession of her senses.

"What the hell have you been up to?" he snapped.

"What the hell would you think?" she snapped back. "Since it's the lousy heel you are an' won't take me back to New York, 'tis meself an' the blessed Saints I must rely on to get me there."

He grabbed her by the arm and shook her. "Tell me what you've done this instant!"

"I undid the cable an' turned the boat around. How was I to know that in less time than it takes to powder me nose 'twould go crashin' into a rock?"

"You little fool, it's not a rock we've hit but one of the rafts. Get out of my way!"

Thrusting her aside, he took over the controls of the engine, which was still throbbing rhythmically, and put the gear lever into reverse. There was an ominous grating for a moment, then the action of the screws took effect; the stem of the launch drew away from the raft and suddenly fell back into the water with a loud splash.

Stopping the engine, Philip waited for a few moments tense with anxiety. As a precaution against rough weather, he had had watertight compartments built into both the bow and the stern of the launch, so he did not think there was any great danger of her sinking under them; but he was afraid that she might have been holed forward which would cause the compartment there to fill and make the future handling of her most damnably difficult. If she were badly holed, the weight of the water would soon cause her to go down at the head and give the deck a new slant; but, as it remained level, he knew that the damage could not have been very serious.

"You'd better get back to the cabin and bathe that cut on your head," he suggested to Gloria, and following her up on deck, he proceeded, with the aid of an electric torch, to make as thorough an examination as possible of the launch's bows and the smashed side of the raft. The launch still seemed all right above the waterline, but one of the big metal cargo containers on the raft had been stove right in. He decided that it was better not to attempt to pick up the cable that Gloria had cast off till daylight, so, hauling the launch alongside the raft, he made her fast. On returning to the cabin he found Gloria back in her bunk and apparently asleep. It was still only a little after one o'clock, so he scrambled back into his own bunk, and, after ruminating a little on how best to deal with his problem child, fell asleep again.

When he wakened it was full day and the first thing he noticed was that his feet were now several inches lower than his head. Evidently the impact of charging the raft during the night had caused the launch to spring a leak, as she was now down by the bows. The sole consolation was that it could only be a comparatively small leak, otherwise the forward compartment would have filled much more quickly. It was annoying, but it could be dealt with, and he decided that in the process of dealing with it the unruly Gloria should be taught a lesson.

Jumping over his bunk he wrapped his dressing-gown round him and went over to her. She was lying on her back with one bare arm thrown up round her head. Her breathing came very softly through moist, slightly parted red lips, and he noticed that her dark lashes were long and curly as they lay fanlike on her cheeks. She looked very young, and it seemed a shame to waken her, but he hardened his heart and, shaking her by the shoulder, called out:

"Gloria! Wake up! The launch is sinking!"

Her eyelids fluttered up and the bright blue eyes stared at him, then with a gasp of "What! What's that?" she sat up.

Turning away he ran to the hatchway, only pausing with one foot on the first step to fling over his shoulder: "Come on! Quick as you can! I shall need all the help you can give me."

Her dawning realization that the cabin floor was sloping forward did the rest. In two minutes she had pulled on a skirt, a jumper and a pair of shoes, and came clattering along the deck towards him.

When she arrived he was plumbing the forward compartment with a long wire, which showed that there was water in it up to a depth of nearly four feet. He knew that the water had now reached its level and would not increase, but he turned a scared face to Gloria and exclaimed:

"Good God! We've shipped four feet of water, and if it gets up to five we'll sink! I must take up the floor boards in the cabin so as to crawl along the bilge and stop the leak, but before I can do that we must get the level of the water down." Pointing at a small hand pump he went on quickly: "If you don't want to spend the next two months on the raft you'd better put everything you've got into that while I get the floor boards up and work the other pump in the engine-room."

Obediently she grasped the pump handle and began to turn the wheel for all she was worth, while he hurried back to the cabin. But when he reached it, instead of taking up the floor boards, he unhurriedly washed, shaved and dressed, and then began to prepare breakfast for himself. He was careful not to cook anything in case the smell gave him away, but he opened a tin of ham and another of pineapple chunks, and made himself a pot of tea.

An hour afterwards he thought he would go up and see how she was getting on, but first of all he ruffled his hair and smeared his face and hands with some black from the stove to give himself the appearance of having been slaving in the bilge.

With aching back and straining muscles Gloria was still turning away at the wheel of the pump, but she let go of it with a little gasp, and drew herself painfully upright as he approached.

"Well, how're you makin' out?" she panted.

"Not too badly," he replied, drawing the back of his hand wearily across his eyes as though he were almost dead-beat. "I think we'll save her—that is, if you can manage to keep it up." He took the depth of the water with his dipper again, and added: "You're doing well. It's down to two feet six, but I won't be able to fix things till the deck is level. How often have you been resting?"

"Just a few minutes now and then."

"That's right. I couldn't do this and the job I'm doing at the same time, so you mustn't crack yourself up."

"'Tis terribly hungry I am," she grumbled. "Couldn't we be gettin' ourselves some breakfast now an' finish when we've eaten?"

He shook his head. "No, that would be fatal. If you stopped pumping for half an hour the water would be back to four feet and we'd have to start the whole job over again. Rest when you feel you must, but remember that every minute of rest means two minutes' more pumping later on."

Having planted this disturbing thought in her mind, he added: "Neither of us must let up until the deck is level and I can get at the leak." Then he hurried back to the cabin as though his presence were required there as a matter of the utmost urgency.

He had meant to go round all the rafts that morning to see if any of the cables were showing signs of strain, but that was impossible so long as the launch was out of action. There was nothing else he particularly wanted to do, so he picked up the latest James Thurber, which was among the books he had bought before leaving New York, and lay down on his bunk to enjoy a good laugh over that author's brilliant nonsense.

After reading for a little, owing perhaps to his having been roused in the middle of the previous night, he became drowsy, and putting down his book closed his eyes. Over an hour slipped by before he opened them again, and then it was with a start, to find a flushed and enraged Gloria staring down at him.

"So this is the way himself acts the great sailor, is it?" she flared, planting her feet apart and her hands on her hips. "All his talk of savin' us from sinkin' by crawlin' around down in the bilge while I'm sweatin' blood at that pump. Ah, if only I had the strength of a man I'd be givin' you the bum's rush right over the side of the boat!"

Shooting his long legs out of the bunk, he stood up and faced her. "Now, listen to me! The sort of thing you did last night might easily have killed us both. We're alone here and at the mercy of the ocean."

"You're telling me!" she interrupted, stridently.

He ignored that. " There's no reason at all why we should come to any harm provided we both play the game. By that I mean take all reasonable precautions and good care of our equipment. But, if the launch or its engine becomes seriously damaged, it may well cost us our lives. A few hours' hard pumping is not a very severe punishment for having risked both our necks, and there's at least a chance that the memory of it may help to drive home what I've just said. Anyhow, one of us had to pump the water out of the forward compartment, and as it was your fault that it got in there I saw no reason why you shouldn't be made to get it out. Now that you've got the water down I really am going along to try to stop that leak."

She turned away suddenly without a word, and he could not tell if it were to hide tears of repentance or sullen anger. Picking up a hammer, blow-lamp and other tools that he had put ready, he went up on deck.

It was, of course, actually quite impossible to reach the forward compartment by way of the bilge, and the real way into it was through a manhole in the small triangular foredeck. Having unscrewed the trap, he lowered himself into the dark, narrow space below, and, with the aid of his torch, began to look for the leak. It was some time before he found it, and, when he did, it was indicated only by a slow trickle of water seeping between the timbers. He was no expert at repairing boats, but knew just enough to check the flow temporarily at least, while thanking his gods that it was no worse.

The job had to be done by artificial light, and to complete it he had to kneel down in the smelly water that still remained slopping about the keel. In consequence, he had not once glanced up at the manhole by which he had entered during the half-hour it took to do the work. Now, on getting up from his knees, he saw with horror that while he had been busy the manhole had been replaced.

Filled with apprehension he first pushed then banged upon it, but it did not budge a millimetre. With rage and dismay he accepted the awful truth which had already flashed upon him. While he had been too occupied to notice, the incorrigible Gloria had stolen up, replaced the mantrap cover and screwed it down.

For ten minutes he pummelled and called and cursed and banged, but all to no purpose; so eventually he gave up and endeavoured to make himself as comfortable as he could until it should please his tormentor to release him. But he soon found that his choice of positions varied only in the degree of discomfort that they offered, since the space under the foredeck could hardly have been bettered if it had been designed specially for purposes of torture by a Gestapo expert. It was not high enough for him to stand upright in it, and the floor, curving sharply away from each side of the keel to form two of the three walls, sloped to such an extent that he could not even find a flat surface for his feet; and, in the meantime, the water washed and eddied round them.

Eventually, he found that the least acutely painful position was sitting down in the shallow water on the keel itself with his back against the stem post of the launch, but the keel was not very wide, so its two edges cut into his behind, forcing him to kneel or stand half-bent for relief at frequent intervals. After a time, there being no ventilation, the place became abominably hot and stuffy.

For hours on end he thought of all the jolly things that he would do to Gloria when he did get out; but when she actually released him at eight o'clock that night he did nothing. After the best part of ten hours in this ' black hole of Calcutta ' he was so exhausted that he only managed to climb out with her assistance, and she was clearly a little frightened by the state to which she had reduced him.

It seemed too that she was not only frightened but distressed; as, when he collapsed upon the deck croaking hoarsely for water, the moment she had fetched it she cradled his head on her breast and began to murmur little phrases of comfort to him as if he were a baby.

When he had recovered to some extent she served the supper which she had already prepared for them both, and during the meal neither said a word about the tricks played on each other, which had caused one of them to spend a most exhausting morning and the other an extremely painful afternoon. Honours were now even, and by mutual if unspoken agreement they entered upon a truce. But they spoke very little over the meal or after it.

As the launch was still tied up alongside the raft there was no point in Philip going to look at the engine; but, after his suggestion that they should make an early night of it, to which Gloria agreed, he went up for a breath of air on deck. The weather was still fine, the sea calm, and what little wind there was still came from within a few points of South-East. To-morrow, he thought, I must take an observation and find out where we've got to. That is, if that little devil doesn't play some other dirty trick on me. But he really felt too tired to worry very much at the moment, and going below turned in, to fall asleep almost at once.

The next morning, again by unspoken agreement, the truce was continued. Immediately after breakfast, Philip took a sounding of the forward compartment and found that the water had risen only three inches since he had patched the leak some twenty hours earlier. Provided it got no worse, ten minutes' pumping a day would be sufficient to keep it down, and if the flow did increase he could always reduce it by re-patching, so he felt that he no longer had any cause to worry about the results of Gloria's desperate attempt to get back to America.

The launch was still tied up to the raft, and he clambered on to it to examine the damage that had been done to the cargo container. In mounting the raft the launch's bows had ripped a great hole in the container and smashed some of the wooden boxes inside it. The trouble now was going to be that the moment anything approaching a swell got up each wave that hit the raft would pour in and out of the hole and ruin the cargo. Philip had intended to do his best to fix a canvas screen over the hole, but on getting close to the wooden boxes he saw for the first time from the smashed ones that they contained only loose earth.

Evidently, having planned for the rafts to be abandoned to drift until they either became waterlogged and sank, or were battered to pieces on some probably desolate coast, Eiderman had felt that it would be absurd to waste good German Secret Service money on providing a genuine cargo.

At first, Philip was furious at this new trick which had been played upon him. Now only his own goods on Number One Raft could be used to provide evidence that various commodities might be thrown violently about during a crossing of the Atlantic by raft without harm coming to them, whereas he had been counting upon producing scores of additional exhibits from the mixed cargo on the other nine rafts. But he soon realized that the harm done to his experiment would be comparatively small. To have brought nine of the rafts over in water ballast would have been most regrettable, but being filled with wooden cases was a very different thing. If the cases arrived without becoming waterlogged or otherwise damaged, it stood to reason that whatever had been put in them would have done so too; so for his purpose the fact that the boxes were full of earth really did not matter.

Then he suddenly saw something else. The very fact that the boxes were filled with earth might prove his salvation if he ever had to face his trial for Eiderman's murder. Provided the rafts reached Britain safely, it would now no longer be his bare word against Thorssen's when the defence sought to establish that the Norwegian's late co-director had been a Nazi agent. Down in the cabin, Philip had the Raft Convoy's manifest with the long, long list of goods that the Norwegian Company were supposed to have shipped with him. When it could be proved that all these bales and boxes contained only earth they would have to do some pretty remarkable thinking to provide any sort of explanation.

Although his thoughts had been occupied by Gloria for a large part of the two days and nights since he had made his escape from the *Regenskuld* he had, mainly subconsciously, been very worried indeed about the probability that when he did reach Britain he would find himself arrested and extradited for trial to the United States. Now, if that happened, the boxes filled with earth would put a very different complexion on the matter, and this did a great deal to relieve his mind.

All the same, he felt that it would be wise to stick to a decision he had taken on his first morning at sea; not to send out any message on his radio until he was within one hundred miles of the coast of Europe and actually needed tugs to come out and tow him in. It was annoying, as before sailing he had promised to let his father know every few days how he was getting on by sending a short message which, it had been arranged, would be relayed by any of H.M. ships that picked it up. Fortunately, as it now turned out, Eiderman had persuaded him to avoid any publicity, so, although there was a definite news value about his voyage, he had no hook-up with American Press or broadcasting services, which might have sent an aircraft out to look for him if he had failed to radio to them; and Thorssen's firm, with whom he had arranged to communicate, doubtless assumed that he was lying low in some American coastal town or village. In consequence, although his silence might cause his father considerable anxiety, his best hope of reducing any chance of his being hunted by the American authorities and taken back to New York lay in maintaining it.

The raft with which the launch had collided as a result of Gloria's desperate attempt to regain her freedom was Number Three in the string. Casting off from it, Philip started the launch's engine and did a tour of his whole convoy, stopping for a little at each raft in turn. He did not board any of them, but came near enough for him to have a good look at the sails on each and the coupling of the cables. The ten rafts were no longer in a line, but formed an irregular zigzag spread out over a mile of water, but none of the sails had so far blown out, and all the cables were in order. Ending up at Raft Number One, Philip next set about hauling in the cable that Gloria had disconnected. This was no light task but eventually he got it hitched to a small winch and, once he had recovered the sunken end, it was easy to re-shackle it to the gear in the stern of the launch. An hour later, having set an approximate course by the sun, he had the satisfaction of seeing that each of the cables in turn had gradually taken up the strain, so that now the string of rafts was once more in a straight line.

Just before midday, he got out his sextant and at twelve noon took an observation of the sun. For the thirty odd hours during which the launch had remained tied up to Raft Number Three he had no exact record of their course, or the speed they were making. However, he knew that, owing to the favourable wind, their speed had been considerably greater than he had anticipated, and, having taken approximate figures, after half an hour with his book of logarithms he had completed his ' day's work,' which gave the surprisingly satisfactory result that the Raft Convoy had, by midday, covered some hundred and sixty miles of its journey.

Over lunch he told Gloria, hoping that she would be persuaded of the folly of making any further attempts to get back to America, and become resigned to the voyage, but her only comment was to remark darkly: " Ah, just you wait till we strike one of those hurricanes that whisk away whole houses and tear up great trees by their roots! 'Tis then you'll be askin' me pardon on your bended knees for bringin' me to me death in a watery grave."

However, that afternoon she suggested that he should sit for her, and he willingly agreed, as he was both intrigued by the idea of having his portrait done and interested to see how good she really was. He was somewhat peeved when after a two-hour sitting she refused to let him see what she had done, but she protested that to complete it several more sittings would be necessary, and she did not wish him to see it before it was finished.

When they woke next day they found that the wind had freshened and the sea was quite choppy, but Gloria did not appear to be affected by it, and cooked and ate breakfast without any suggestion that if it got worse she might be ill. Actually by ten o'clock the wind had dropped again, so Philip took the precaution of refuelling the launch from the main supply of oil, which was stored in one of the cargo containers on Number One Raft. Then, in the afternoon, he sat once more for his portrait.

During the following two days they were again blessed with sunshine and light winds from the south-west, so that their progress filled Philip with a quite justifiable elation. Having worked out his position as at noon on August 17th he found that in five days they had travelled three hundred and ninety miles from their starting-point, and, so far, every mile of it had been in the right direction.

It was just after supper on the 17th, after a fifth long sitting, that Gloria declared the portrait finished. She had rigged up a makeshift easel to which it was pinned, and getting up Philip walked over to look at it.

" By Jove, that *is* good! " he exclaimed, as he studied the excellent drawing. He had never before realized that he was such a good-looking fellow, but she had brought out his fine forehead, kind eyes, and the line of his determined chin, so that, while it remained an unmistakable likeness, these gave the impression that he might well be a great leader of men in whom brains were coupled with physical attraction.

" I think it's absolutely grand," he continued enthusiastically. " And if you can do this sort of thing you ought later on to make a packet of money as a portrait painter."

" Sure an' I will! " she agreed with a laugh that had a slight edge to it. " 'Tis a thousand bucks a time I'll be charging for a portrait in oils the like of that when I get back from me studies in Paris. And d'you know why? But of course you don't, so I'll be tellin' you. It's like enough to that long face of yours for yourself to be thinkin' you look like that. But you don't. Not a bit of it! That's how you'd like to look—and maybe flatter yourself you do. An' that's why you'd pay me the big money if you were a rich guy and meself rented one of those Ritzy studios in Greenwich Village. Now, just take a look at yourself as you are."

As she finished speaking she unpinned the drawing and disclosed another beneath it, on which, unknown to Philip, she had also been working during those long sittings.

It was again an undeniable likeness, but no one could call it a pleasant portrait. This time she had stressed the thinness of his face to the point of emaciation, made his strong jaw look sullen and given his big forehead a narrowness that suggested the bigot. It was the face of a stubborn man with a one-track mind, and it entirely lacked any quality which might be expected to appeal to a young woman.

The sight of it was admittedly a shock to Philip, although he knew that it was as much a libel as the other one had been an outrageous piece of flattery. He swallowed hard, stared at it for a minute, and then said quietly: " If I had needed anything to convince me that you have real talent this would have done so. It's damn' unpleasant. It isn't true. But it is the work of a very clever artist."

Gloria was so taken aback that she remained there tongue-tied until, after a moment, he turned and strolled away towards the engine-room.

He knew very well that Gloria had made the second drawing because, for some reason best known to herself, she desired to humiliate him; most probably in revenge for his keeping her with him against her will. That must be so, as had she done it only as a practice study she need never have let him see it. In consequence, he decided that it would do her a great deal of good to know how it feels to be humiliated, and he planned a sharp lesson for her, which he took the opportunity to deliver after supper that night.

" You know, Gloria," he began, " I've been thinking about that second drawing you showed me this afternoon. Quite possibly I do look like that, and you obviously feel that it does us good to see ourselves as others see us. Unfortunately, I lack the talent to do a pair of portraits of you, but perhaps I can achieve the same effect by a word-picture. We won't bother about the first, as I have no doubt that you think of yourself as a Venus, although, actually, apart from the colour of your eyes and hair, you're rather a plain little girl. What I should like to get at is the you behind the face, as all really great artists succeed in doing with their sitters, and as you did in a way with those two travesties of me on which you've been working so hard these past few days. But then again, I don't profess to be a psychologist, and I don't really know you well enough yet to name the things that are really good or bad in your character."

He paused for a moment, then went on: "As a result, I'll have to confine myself to mentioning a couple of points about you that you'll do well to correct if you really want to get on in the world. The first is your way of speaking. There's nothing objectionable about it and, in fact, a touch of the Irish brogue is not without its fascination. But, if you succeed as an artist and wish to gather the full rewards of your labours by not only painting the great and wealthy but also mixing with them on terms of equality, you will have to learn to speak English like an educated American—and not like an Irish peasant who has been dragged up in a New York gutter."

Gloria's blue eyes were flashing, and her mouth was half-open to speak, but he held up his hand and fired his second shot. " The other point is cleanliness. To-morrow morning it will be exactly a week since you left home. During that time, although the weather has been perfect, you have not once washed your head, and as far as I know you haven't even had a bath. It's true that owing to lack of space here we can only run to a salt-water shower, but that's perfectly adequate, and if you'd turned it on I'd have heard the water running, because there's only a thin partition between the shower and the engine-room. Now, most of the people who can help you on the road to success while you are still little known will do so much more readily if you talk their language; although that won't matter if you succeed in painting really big stuff. Then, even the greatest leaders of thought and fashion and patrons of art will stand for your talking Cockney or Bowery at their dinner tables. But there is one thing that none of these people will stand—no, not if you were Michael Angelo himself. They will not ask to their houses a girl who smells! I don't happen to be your best friend, Gloria, so I can tell you quite bluntly that it's time that you learnt to wash all over at least once a day."

Her face had gone so scarlet during this brutal recital that her freckles had temporarily disappeared. Her mouth opened to speak, then closed; it opened and closed a second time. Philip sat there quite fascinated.

Suddenly she grabbed up the breadknife and lunged at him with it. If he had not jerked his head back he might have lost an eye. Next second she was on her feet and coming round the table at him. He sprang up and sidestepped swiftly, placing the table between them. Her blue eyes blazing murder, she glared across it, made a feint in one direction and with the agility of a cat leapt at him from the other. Dodging the blow, he jumped away to the far side of the table once more. He now had his back to the companionway. By turning and making a dash for it he felt sure that he could get on to the ladder and have the door slammed in her face before she could catch up with him.

He was terribly tempted to do it, but he knew that if he allowed her to chase him from the cabin he would lose face to such a degree that he would never be able to stand up to her on equal terms again. Even at the risk of receiving a nasty wound, it was up to him to get that knife away from her somehow, and prove that at least he was not a coward who could be intimidated by displays of temper in a girl.

Twice more she came at him and he dodged round the table; then an idea for getting the best of her suddenly came to him. Stooping forward he seized the water jug and flung its contents in her face. Temporarily she was half-blinded, and even as she let out a scream of rage he grabbed her wrist. One sharp twist and the knife clattered upon the deck. As it did so she kicked him on the shin. Letting go of her wrist he drew back his hand and delivered one sharp slap on the side of her face. Suddenly, she seemed to go quite limp. Her arms fell to her sides, and she burst into tears.

This time he did not attempt to comfort her. He just said: "If you put on any more of these homicide acts I shall shut you up in the forward compartment, where you trapped me the other day, and keep you there. Now you'd better get undressed and go to bed."

He spent the next hour up on deck, and when he returned to the cabin he found her apparently asleep. Having got into his bunk, he did not waste any time speculating on his future relations with his difficult passenger, but read until he felt sleepy, then put out the light.

Hours later he woke with a start. The portholes showed the grey blur of early morning. There was a sudden tightness in his throat as he saw the vague outline of a figure bending over him. It flashed into his mind that Gloria had got hold of the knife again and meant to stab him to death in his sleep. Thrusting out his hands with a half-strangled cry, he sat up.

She stepped back with a grim laugh. " So—'tis frightened you are ! An' I don't wonder ! But there's no need to be. 'Tis just that I've spent most of the night thinkin', and I've somethin' to tell you."

" Eh! Well, er—what is it? " he muttered, not very cordially.

" I've been thinkin'," she went on, " that as rude as you are there may be something in what you say. But I can alter me speech and me ways, whereas you'll never be able to alter the bones of your face!"

Having fired this devastating shot, she turned on her heel and got back into her bunk. From it, a quarter of an hour later, faint snores announced that she was fast asleep, whereas Philip found it impossible to drop off again; not from any hurt to his vanity, which troubled him little, but from wondering how he was going to put up with his tormentor for another seven to ten weeks without wringing her neck and throwing her over the side.

His disposition was naturally a kindly one, but he caught himself feeling almost a smug delight when the following afternoon dark clouds began to pile up in the east, a rising wind broke the surface of the sea into a million white-capped wavelets, and spray began to blow on to the deck of the launch. After as perfect a week as he could have hoped for, it now looked as though they were in for a really dirty spell, and that, he felt, would at least give Gloria something other than rubbing him up the wrong way to think about.

By nightfall the seas had increased to a strength which caused him to consider the advisability of casting off from the rafts, but he knew that if he once did that, virtually single-handed as he was, it would be impossible for him to pick up the cables again until the rough weather abated; and, as the storm might last for several days, during which he could not go altogether without sleep, he feared that he might lose the convoy. Having decided to remain hitched to Number One Raft, he became so concerned as to whether the cables would hold during this, their first really severe test, that he forgot all about Gloria and, wrapped in his oilskins, spent the night either on deck or in the cockpit of the engine-room.

Morning dawned with the sea still running high, but on looking back as the launch drove over the highest wave crests Philip could count six of the rafts in a rough line behind him, so he had little doubt that the other four, though out of sight in the troughs beyond more distant waves, were still linked securely in the chain. With sober satisfaction he went down to the cabin to see about some breakfast.

It was immediately apparent that during the night Gloria had been extremely ill, but at the moment she was sleeping. He cleared things up and got himself some coffee, toast, and marmalade, refraining from cooking anything in case the smell might make her worse. She wakened just as he had finished, and he tried to persuade her to have something to eat, but all she could manage was the juice of a grapefruit.

Having bathed her face and provided her with a clean basin, he went on deck again. The sky was still dark and the storm by no means over. He spent the morning as he had spent most of the night—at the controls of the launch, checking her for a few moments to let the cable slacken, letting in the gear to give her enough speed to secure steering way, heading her towards the next big wave, then, immedately it was past, cutting out and reversing his engine again before she could be brought up with a jerk by the cable attaching her to the raft.

Playing the launch thus was not unlike being a great fish on the end of an angler's line. It was a terribly tiring business, and he had been at it for many hours. By midday he was desperately weary, and decided that he must get some sleep. Within a few minutes of his having shut off the engine the launch had swung round sideways on to the waves and begun to wallow badly. He could not help that. The worst that could happen was that she would drift into one of the rafts, and he felt confident that if she did the waves were not now strong enough for serious damage to be caused by the collision.

Below he found that the greatly increased rolling of the launch had brought on another bout of Gloria's sea-sickness. As soon as it had eased a little he gave her a drink of water and sponged her face; then, still fully dressed, he flung himself exhausted on his bunk.

When he awoke it was evening. The launch was still rolling horribly, but Gloria was asleep. He got himself some cold food and put a plate of biscuits and fruit near her against her waking; then he went back to the engine-room for another long spell of fighting to keep the launch on a more or less even keel. At four o'clock in the morning he threw in his hand again, shut off the engine and fell asleep where he sat.

On the third day the storm gradually abated, but it was not until the evening that Philip felt he could really take things easy. By that time, Gloria, now a rather wan and pathetic little figure, was sufficiently restored to get up and cook a dish of scrambled eggs for their supper. Both of them were so done up that they went to bed immediately they had fed, and slept the clock round.

It was now the 21st of August. Having made a tour of rafts in the morning and found all well, except that eight of the sails had blown out, Philip shot the sun at midday. Once again, owing to lack of definite checks on speed and direction, many of his calculations had to be based on guesswork, but, using such data as he had and being reasonably conservative when in doubt, he came to the conclusion that, although the storm had driven them somewhat to the southward of their course, it had been in the main well behind them and helped them considerably; so much so that they were now fully 700 miles from the American coast. That afternoon and the following morning he spent in re-fitting the sails that had been blown out by the storm and servicing the beacons, so he had little time either to improve his relations or quarrel further with Gloria.

Good weather now seemed set fair to bless them again, and to while away the time Philip suggested two forms of recreation: bathing and fishing.

At first, Gloria was a little nervous of going over the side of the launch, but after he had done so she said that she would like to if only she had something suitable to wear. He offered her a pair of his white shorts, and told her that there were numerous flags in the locker, and that out of some of them she could make herself a top. Two hours later she came up from the cabin, and his eyes almost popped out of his head with fury when he saw that she had selected his one and only Union Jack to cut up and make into a kind of ill-fitting waistcoat.

That the gesture had been deliberate he had no doubt at all, as he knew that in the United States the Stars and Stripes, or 'Old Glory', as the Americans called it, is treated with a reverence which far surpasses the respect which any other people give to their national flag. He was so angry that he could have hit her, but he controlled his wrath with the mental reservation that he would not let the insult go unavenged.

When she had swum about for a quarter of an hour she called up to him to help her back on board. Looking down at her he shook his head.

"No, since you have chosen to cut up my country's flag and make it look ridiculous, I am now going to make you look ridiculous—or at all events ashamed. I'm not going to help you up till you take it off, and you can walk back to the cabin with your top half naked."

With a completely expressionless face she heard him out, then trod water while undoing the offending waistcoat, wriggled out of it and threw it up to him, before grasping the hand he held out and scrambling up on deck.

She made no attempt to turn her back as he held out a towel that he had fetched ready to cover her directly he had won his point. Instead, to his utter amazement, she stripped off the white shorts, flung them squelching at his feet, and drawing herself up stood there stark naked in front of him.

" You poor sap—fool, I mean! " she corrected herself quickly. " I guessed cutting up the old Jack would make you pretty sore, but if you think 'tis ashamed I am of my own body you've got me all wrong. I earned me fees to go to an art school by sitting as a model an' half the art students in New York have seen me in the nude. 'Twas only to save your blushes, prig that you are, that I made meself the wee coat."

With a laugh at his obvious discomfiture she turned away and walked slowly down the steps of the cabin.

Her sudden correction of the word " sap " to " fool " had not gone unnoticed by him. Since she had recovered from her sea-sickness she had been less talkative, and except when she was excited she now clearly made an effort to choose her phrases with some care. He knew too that she had started to use the shower twice a day, so it looked as if she really meant to carry out her boast that she could change her speech and her ways.

His resentment at being called a prig was sufficient to cause him to decide that he would bathe naked himself the following morning; but the moment he came on deck he regretted his decision. Gloria was sitting up in the forward part of the launch, and she deliberately stood up to get a better look at him. It was the first time in his life that he had ever disported himself in front of a girl wearing nothing, and as he felt, rather than saw, her eyes run over every part of him appraisingly, his face went absolutely crimson. In his haste to escape what he felt to be her positively indecent interest he stubbed his toe, mucked his dive and did a belly-flop in the water.

Two minutes later she climbed gingerly over the side, also naked, and having lowered herself into the water began to swim towards him. For a moment, for no conceivable reason, he panicked wildly, then he saw her smile as she said :

" 'Tis a nice body you have. One that any man might be real proud of, an' I'd like to draw it. Will you let me? "

Somehow the request restored his self-confidence, but at the thought of her last effort he replied : " What, and let you portray me as ' the living skeleton '? No thanks."

" I wouldn't do that," she laughed. " Your hips are almost too thin, but your shoulders an' legs are the tops. I guess I was pretty naughty yesterday—cuttin' up that Union Jack. I'm sorry. It's just that I get awful angry when I think about bein' cooped up here for so long. D'you realize that but for you 'tis in Paris I'd be this very day? For the delay to me—my career—you sure owe me a little practice. Will you be obligin' me now? "

Mollified by her apology, and entirely forgetful that, had she not come aboard the launch, it was much more likely that she would have been

under arrest as a stowaway than enquiring about art schools in Paris,
Philip consented almost before he realized what he had done—and that
afternoon found him posing as her model, instead of trying his hand at
fishing as he had intended.

They bathed together again the following afternoon, then he gave her
a second sitting, and afterwards they fished for two hours; catching one
large round spikey fish which they threw back into the sea and three
smaller ones which made very good eating for their supper. When he
turned in that night Philip felt for the first time that his relations with
Gloria were beginning to show a definite improvement, but, unfortunately,
there was soon to be a new cause for contention.

On August the 24th the Chancelleries of Europe were rocked by the
news that Ribbentrop and Stalin had signed a Russo-German non-
aggression pact in Moscow. Philip learnt of it from the B.B.C.'s ten
o'clock news bulletin on the morning of August the 25th, and the more
he thought about the matter the more worried he became. He had always
felt that so long as Germany and Russia continued in a state of latent
antagonism there was some hope that the peace of Europe would be
preserved. Hitler had promised his people so definitely that never again
would they be called on to wage war on two fronts simultaneously, yet he
never let pass an opportunity of denouncing the Bolsheviks as the arch-
enemies of the New Order in Germany and the cornerstone of his dip-
lomacy was the Anti-Comintern Pact. While he kept up his policy of
insulting and vilifying Russia it seemed that he would be taking a very
considerable risk if he picked a quarrel with the western democracies;
since, once he was fully committed to a war with them, what would there
be to prevent Russia deciding that her last chance of self-preservation
lay in forcing a two-front war on him before he had, perhaps, defeated
France and Britain, and she had to face him on her own?

But now the whole picture had been altered overnight. By this non-
aggression pact Hitler had secured his rear, so he was now free to make
the most outrageous new demands on the smaller Powers, and no doubt
ready if his bluff were called to support it by force of arms.

From this fateful morning onward Philip listened in to every major
news bulletin, not only in English but also in French and German; and
it was this that drove Gloria nearly into a frenzy. She liked the radio
for its dance music, and she did not mind hearing the news once a day,
but to have to listen to bulletins every hour that Philip was not busy in
either servicing the rafts or in the engine-room was more than she could
bear. Yet every time he came down to the cabin he could not resist the
temptation to ignore her protests and switch on the radio.

During their first twelve days at sea he had been too occupied with
other matters to pay much attention to what was happening in Europe, but
once he had picked up the threads again he soon realized that a major
crisis was now brewing. The Danzig Nazis were following exactly the

same tactics as their Sudeten brethren had done the year before. There were the same old stories of a gentle, music-loving German minority being beaten up by foreign police and Customs officials—only this time the villains of the piece were the Poles. The Czech villains of last year were now being starved, flogged and tortured to death in concentration camps by the gentle music-lovers. There were the same old inflammatory speeches by the Nazi leaders; the same old efforts by the spineless politicians of the great democracies to bully the unfortunate accused into going nine-tenths of the way to meet Hitler's "positively last demands," and thus putting the chain round their own necks, by which in one jerk he could later drag them to the slaughter at any moment he chose.

Philip listened to the drama fascinated and appalled, becoming every day more preoccupied and gloomy. For months past he had believed that war would come within a year, yet now that it seemed so near he endeavoured to persuade himself that it would be averted at the last moment. Somehow, he had always thought that he would be given time to prove his Raft Convoy and see it in production by the Admiralty before hostilities actually broke out.

It was now the end of August, so he had been nearly three weeks at sea, had passed through one serious storm and covered over 1,300 miles of the Atlantic crossing, yet the string of rafts was still intact, and he had not been carried any material distance from the course he would have chosen; so he therefore considered that the feasibility of the project had already been established. But it would be another month at least before he could complete his crossing and provide physical evidence of his triumph. That meant that if war broke out now over the Polish crisis six weeks at the absolute minimum must elapse before the Admiralty experts had definitely satisfied themselves about the Raft Convoy's performance, and placed orders for others to be made in the United States; and winter would then be coming on. It looked like spring now before the British Mercantile Marine could be given any substantial relief by Philip's new weapon. And if there was war how would Britain fare during these long dark winter months ahead?

He tried to interest Gloria in the news bulletins by telling her that the fate of every country in the world for the next two or three generations probably hung on what was happening in Danzig during these fateful days, but she simply was not interested.

"That man Hitler's just a buffoon!" she kept on repeating. "And what you're so scared about I can't think. I knew a German boy back home in New York, an' he often told me that there's nothin' to be gotten out of wars either by winner or loser. That's why the Germans don't want another war; an' 'tis only the likes of you with your scaremongerin' nonsense makes all this talk of war possible."

Next day Germany and Poland were at war.

"Well," said Philip grimly, as he switched off the wireless. "How about it now?"

She shrugged. "Poland is only a little place, so 'twill all be over in five minutes."

"It won't if Britain and France come in. And Poland is not a little place. It has thirty-five million inhabitants—people like you and me. Haven't you got any sort of feeling for them? Can't you conceive how frightful it will be for them to have their country overrun by those hordes of blood beasts and to be turned into slaves?"

"Of course, I'm sorry for them," she replied hastily; "but I think they're great fools all the same. They'd not have got in this mess if they'd been sensible people. But that's just the trouble, an' it's always been the same in Europe. Quarrel an' fight, quarrel an' fight; an' most times 'tis sheer greed at the bottom of it. These Kings and such don't give a fig how many of their people they kill so long as there's another piece of land for the grabbin'. If I had me way I'd bang all their heads together!"

On the 3rd of September Britain declared war on Germany, but Gloria was not in the least perturbed and only vaguely interested.

In vain Philip tried to make her understand that the great forces now aroused in Europe could not leave America untouched. He tried to explain how Britain would be fighting America's battle and giving her a chance to arm, and how, if she did not take that chance and Britain were defeated, Hitler would within a few years have the most powerful fleet that had ever dominated the oceans, and escorted by it and a colossal air force the German Army would invade and conquer America. But she refused to take him seriously.

Europe and its war were as far removed from her as the war in Manchukuo had been from him. The fact that her father had been an Englishman gave her a natural bias in favour of Britain, but her feeling was a purely academic one, and she made it plain that she would regard anyone who might so much as lift a finger to draw the United States into the conflict on the side of Britain as an enemy of her country.

With such a lack of sympathy between two people cooped up together at a time of crisis, it was hardly surprising that they found the next few weeks drag so appallingly. When it was fine—and they only met one other period of bad weather, which lasted for four days—they swam or fished together, but rather because to have done otherwise would have been to display open hostility, than from choice. Philip sat as a model for a number of sketches, most of which he thought very good, and an understanding was reached about the radio, by which it was agreed that news bulletins should be reduced to three a day. But neither of them seemed able to settle anything for very long because, except when sketching, Gloria was intensely bored, and Philip was worrying himself silly about what was going on in England and how quickly he would be able to get into the war once he got there.

After their third day out from New York no ship had passed within a mile of them, and, the first storm having driven them some way to the south of the main sea line between America and Britain, they had not even sighted many ships after that; but now they were approaching Europe they began to see ships more frequently again.

It was on the last evening of September that Philip said just after supper; " Well, Gloria, I'm sure you'll be glad to hear that your ordeal is nearly over. When I worked out our position as at midday to-day, I found that we were less than a hundred miles west by south of Land's End."

" Well, what do you know; that is good news! " she exclaimed. " We've been mighty quicker than you expected, haven't we? "

" Yes, we've been lucky. If we'd been swept up to the north we might have taken several weeks longer and eventually landed up in the Faroes or Norway. As it is, the southern arm of the Gulf Stream, which is still powerful enough all these thousands of miles from the Amazon to give Southampton a double tide, has carried us right in. To-morrow morning I mean to open up the wireless-sending apparatus and arrange for tugs to come out to tow us in. So if all goes well this will be your last night at sea."

For a moment she was silent, then she said: " 'Tis a great thing that you've done, and you've a right to be pleased with yourself. I've no doubt 'tis your father will be killing the fatted calf for you by this time to-morrow."

" Yes, I expect so, if he's still stationed at Portsmouth, but he might have been sent to sea. Anyhow, my sister and dear old Pin, who's been a mother to us both, will be at home; and I'm sure they'll do their best to make you comfortable."

" Holy Saint Bridget! " cried Gloria, surprised into her worst Irish. " An' will you be after tellin' me why they should be doin' anythin' of the sort? "

" Oh well," he shrugged, " you don't know a soul in England do you? And now there's a war on things may be difficult. In any case, I'm afraid you'll have a certain amount of trouble with the immigration authorities as you haven't a passport. We needn't tell them you came aboard as a stowaway and we could say that your passport was in your handbag which got swept overboard in a storm. Anyhow, we ought to be able to fix that trouble somehow, but it may not be at all easy for you to get a permit to go to France, and you must have somebody to help you find your way around. So I think the best thing would be for you to come and stay with us for a bit, anyhow to begin with."

" 'Tis very kind you are. Much kinder than I deserve, and I'll try hard not to be a bother to your sister and Mrs. Pin. But I'll be mighty bashful. Your father's a captain in the British Navy, isn't he, and I've never been inside a great house in me life, let alone stayed in one."

Philip laughed and tried to reassure her. " It's nothing like a great

house—just three recep, six bed and the usual offices, as the house-agents
say! You'll find old Pin an absolute dear—her proper name is Mrs.
Marlow, by the bye. Anyhow, we're not rich or terribly social, so there's
really nothing to be the least bit frightened of. Still," he paused for a
second and went on more seriously, "there's one thing I must warn you
about. I shall give you the address and all particulars of how to get
there, but I may not be able to go with you, and it may even be some
little time before I'm able to join you."

"And why would that be? If it's to London about your rafts you're
going right away, I'd rather go with you."

"No. It's not that. There was no point in my telling you before, but
I'm wanted by the American police, so when we land I may be arrested
and taken off to prison."

Gloria's eyebrows shot up. "Holy Saints defend us now! What sort
of crime have you been committing?"

"I killed a man. I know you still think that Hitler is just a buffoon
and that the Germans are nice, kind people, so I'll tell you what happened to me. Then, perhaps, you'll understand a bit better what slimy,
unscrupulous swine we're up against."

He told her the story of his negotiations about cargo with Eiderman,
of how he had only learned at the eleventh hour on the *Regenskuld* of
the plot against his own life, and described the final scene in which the
German had been shot. He wound up: "You see now why I couldn't
possibly let you signal a ship that might have taken you back to New
York. If the American police had learned that I was with the rafts during
our first few days at sea, they would almost certainly have come out and
picked me up. I don't much mind what happens to me now, but, so
long as my Raft Convoy idea remained to be tested, I couldn't possibly
afford to risk it."

She stood up, came round the table and laid a hand on his shoulder.
Then, using the nickname of "Boy" which she had taken to calling him
on account of his youthful appearance, and in a soft voice that he had
never heard her use before, she said: "Oh, Boy, why didn't you tell me?
Why didn't you tell me about that dirty German and that the cops were
after you because you'd bumped him off?"

"What difference would it have made if I had?"

"Why, all the difference in the world, you poor babe! Do you
remember tellin' me that first day how stowaways were made to work for
their passage? Well, what would any girl have thought? ' 'Tis lucky he
thinks himself to have gotten someone to cook and clean for him and
niver a cent to pay for it. That's why he won't signal a ship, and if it's
drowned I am on account of his crazy venture not a fig will he care.' "

"I see," he grinned. "That's was why you played me up, was it?"

"Sure. I felt that by cookin' an' such I was earnin' my keep, but I
saw no reason at all to make meself pleasant beyond that. And all the

time you were worried out of your wits that they'd come after us and get you. Poor Boy! I certainly could kick meself now for the way I've been treatin' you all these weeks."

"I'm afraid I haven't been all that marvellous myself," Philip apologized : "but I thought you were just a cross-grained little devil whose one idea of fun was to make other people lose their tempers. Still, it's nice to have found out that we might have been quite good friends, even if we have taken seven weeks to do it, and this is the last night of the trip."

They talked on for another half-hour or so a little awkwardly, before they both went to bed, feeling slightly ashamed of themselves, yet filled in some odd way with a happiness and excitement which was not altogether due to the fact that they expected to land safely in England the next day.

First thing in the morning Philip began to tune in on his wireless-sending apparatus. He was not a radio expert and at first the mass of traffic, mainly owing to the war, with which the air seemed to be crammed, confused him. But he kept on sending out the call-signs that his father had arranged should be allotted to him before he left New York, and eventually received a satisfactory answer; then he sent the message that he had prepared and, having received an acknowledgment, sat back to await a reply to his request for tugs.

It came three hours later. "Heartiest congratulations on success of your original and courageous undertaking. Regret no tugs immediately available but Pompey will pick you up further up Channel to-morrow. F.O.W.A."

As a sailor's son, Philip knew well that Pompey was naval slang for Portsmouth, and he guessed that F.O.W.A. stood for "Flag Officer Western Approaches." Evidently his father had given the Admiralty full particulars of his enterprise, and they had passed the whole story on to the Admiral responsible for Atlantic waters who, unable himself to help, had passed on his request to bring Philip in to C.-in-C. Portsmouth. The delay was disappointing, but there was a certain exciting consolation in the thought that, instead of being taken into the Bristol Channel, Falmouth or Plymouth, he would be towed into the Solent and so complete his unique and perhaps epoch-making fifty-one day voyage by arriving virtually on his own doorstep.

However, on going on deck round about eleven o'clock he had an uneasy feeling that the delay might prove extremely annoying as well as disappointing. The sky had been overcast all the morning, and now it was beginning to blow. By midday the familiar white horses that Gloria had learned to dread were topping the wavelets.

By a rough calculation based on his observation taken the day before, and his now practised judgment of speeds, Philip reckoned that they were some sixty miles or less south-west of the Lizard and that, if they continued on their present course, they should pass some thirty miles to the south of it during the night. But the trouble was that the wind had changed. It was now blowing from the north, and they were still out in the open ocean, not yet having come under the shelter of the coast of Cornwall.

Within an hour it was clear that the Raft Convoy was no longer making its way into the entrance of the Channel. In spite of the fact that Philip kept the launch heading north-east by east, they were drifting south. With the wind in its present direction there was no risk of his being driven on to the rocky Cornish coast, so he turned the launch north, head on to the rising seas. He could do no more now than prevent its rolling to some extent and hope that the storm would die down by the following day.

They were cheered considerably about half past five by an aircraft bearing the red, white and blue circles of the R.A.F., which came down quite low overhead and circled round twice before flying off again in the direction of the English coast. It might have been a coincidence but Philip felt certain that it was the long arm of the British Navy which had sent out an aircraft to locate them and, now that they had to face another storm, it was comforting to think that they were no longer quite alone, but had friends ashore who were concerned for their safety.

As night closed down dark and menacing, squalls of rain began to add to their discomfort. The wind had veered again, but not in their favour. It seemed that an ill fate had decreed that they should be caught in the first of the autumn gales, and that they were in for a real nor-'easter.

Philip remained in the cock-pit of the engine-room fighting desperately to keep the launch head on to the waves, which seemed to be increasing in size every moment. The storm was far worse than either of the two bouts of bad weather that they had struck while crossing the Atlantic and at two o'clock in the morning, loath as he was to do so, he decided that he must disconnect the launch from the chain of rafts, otherwise when the cables slackened the Number One Raft might be hurled right on top of them.

Gloria was sick but refused now to remain in her bunk for more than a few hours at a time, and insisted on crawling along the deck from the cabin to the engine-room to bring him biscuits and a thermos full of hot coffee.

When morning dawned, the sea was running mountains high, and for minutes at a time they could see no further than the great green valley across which they were sliding, while from the crests they caught only a swift glimpse of other crests breaking into great curving rolls of foam; but Philip managed to keep the Number One Raft in sight, and never let it become more distant than two crests away from him.

At nine o'clock Philip decided that he really must take a rest, but the launch began to roll so dangerously within five minutes of his leaving the steering-wheel that he had to hurry back to it. It was not, however, till two hours later that he became really alarmed.

He suddenly noticed that after each wave had broken over the bow of the launch the water was taking much longer to slide off. He guessed the cause in a second. The pounding of these great waves was so heavy that the forward compartment had sprung a leak again, where he had only been able to patch it, and had gradually filled with water. This, he knew, was serious, and he was now so tired that he could not keep the launch nose on to the storm for much longer. If he let up for more than a few minutes a cross sea might hit them, half-swamping the cabin and the engine-room; and, with the forward compartment useless as an airlock to help keep them buoyed up, the launch would go under.

His brain was so numbed with weariness that it almost refused to function, but he knew that he had got to do something about the situation before very long, because otherwise he would not have the strength left to do anything at all. The launch could not live through another night of this and probably not even another few hours. Waves were constantly breaking over the forward compartment, so there was no possible hope of pumping out the water, even if he could have reached it without being swept overboard. Yet, terribly aware as he was of the deadly peril which now menaced them, he was so exhausted that he could think of no measure which might avert the final catastrophe.

Suddenly, above the screaming of the tempest and the thunder of the waves, he heard a voice. As clearly as though the words had been spoken in a quiet room, the vigorous tones of the dynamic little Canon smacked home in his ears.

" Philip, what's the matter with you? Use your wits, man! Abandon the launch and get on the raft at once. It's your only chance."

He needed no second urging. The dream in which his dead friend had driven him up on to the deck of the *Regenskuld* so that he might learn of the plot against his life was still vivid in his memory. He knew nothing whatever about spiritualism, and this was no time to consider the implications of these occult manifestations; he accepted them instantly as Divine intervention, and as though an electric current had been turned on inside him he suddenly felt a surge of new energy and determination.

Lashing the wheel, he made a dash for the cabin and, shouting to make Gloria hear above the storm, told her to pack at once as the launch would not last long and they would be safer on the raft.

She took it well and shouted back: " How long can you give me? "

" Half an hour—an hour if you like," he yelled: " but we mustn't leave it too long, and the sooner you're ready the better."

She nodded, and grabbing the handrail to save himself from falling he stumbled up the stairs again, then lurched along to the wheel. Now, he began to ease the launch bit by bit nearer to the raft, as opportunity offered, and after half an hour he was within thirty feet of it on its lee-side.

To his relief he found that, although it was not very high out of the water, the great solid bulk of it provided much more shelter than he had expected. Edging the launch still nearer, he managed to get a grip on the raft's narrow platform with a boat-hook, and pulled himself alongside.

D

The next ten minutes were risky work. As the raft and launch soared up great mountains of water, or slid down into seemingly bottomless valleys, he took his life in his hands tying the two vessels together. At last the job was done, and Gloria, who was already standing by, was able to pass him up some of the things that she had packed. She seemed to have collected everything that was movable at the bottom of the cabin stairs, and Philip spent nearly half an hour throwing the bundles and cases she passed him on to the wide flat surface of the raft. Then he helped her up and, choosing a propitious moment when the launch and the raft were on the same level, half-lifted and half-pushed her from one to the other Two minutes later, as they came level again, he sprang after her.

They had not been any too soon in abandoning the launch, and were still lying flat on their faces breathlessly wriggling their way forward towards the centre of the raft, when one of the ropes that held the launch to it snapped. It immediately swung outward, and as the second rope parted it was whisked away like a cockleshell in the storm.

"That's the end of the old launch," cried Philip in Gloria's ear. "Thank God we managed to get on to the raft! It can't sink, anyhow."

"No," she shrieked back. "But 'tis hundreds of miles we must have been driven by the storm, an' with the launch you've lost your radio-sending set. Will anyone ever be able to find us now?"

CHAPTER VIII

THE ENEMY

EVEN as Gloria spoke they saw the launch again. Head down, stern up, it seemed to balance precariously for a moment on the crest of a monster wave, then it disappeared from view. With it, as she had so grimly pointed out, they had lost their only means of giving their position when the storm subsided, so that they could readily be found and picked up. But they had little time to worry about that now. Their situation was still near-desperate, and every ounce of energy that still remained to them was required if they were to save themselves and their scanty possessions from the fury of the tempest.

Having landed on the lee side of the fifty foot square raft, they were on that part of it least exposed to the buffeting of the waves, which, every time they struck, sent huge cataracts of water high into the air. Every few moments these great columns of spray would come hurtling down on the flat surface of the metal cargo containers with a smack and a swish, leaving not one inch of dry space on the whole two hundred and fifty square feet; and occasionally a wave larger than the rest would sweep right over the whole area.

Only one thing prevented Philip and Gloria being swept from their insecure holds into the sea. This was the six foot square well that had been left in the middle of the cargo containers. The centre of each wave that washed over the raft broke on this, pouring into it and out through the scuppers which ran under the cargo containers for that purpose. As Philip realized that it was to this they owed their temporary safety, he blessed the name of the Naval Commander in the Plans Division at the Admiralty, who, so many months ago, had suggested these wells as refuges for servicing crews should they be caught by a squall on one of the rafts. The two castaways now wormed their way towards the well, pulling and pushing their most precious packages with them as they went. Philip had to make four journeys to get the other things, but twenty minutes after landing on the raft, they and all the things they had brought were in the six foot square hole.

It was only five feet deep, the height of the cargo containers that surrounded it, so when standing upright they could see out over the flat tops of the containers and were exposed to the full force of the gale; moreover, it was impossible to sit down as every eight or ten minutes one of the larger waves poured into it, temporarily submerging them up to their waists. They were safe there, but, as Philip looked at Gloria's dead-white face, he wondered how long they would be able to stand this frightful buffeting before they collapsed of exhaustion and exposure.

His eyes were still on the girl's face, when she suddenly lurched forward and was terribly sick. A wave swamped over them knocking her off her balance, and she fell to her knees. He pulled her to her feet and held her to him as the water gurgled away down the chutes. As the raft had no keel, method of propulsion or steering gear, there was no means of keeping it even moderately steady. It rose and fell, sometimes with a sickening swiftness, and often one corner of it cocked right up in the air at a terrifying angle, while water cascaded from its flat surface. Philip was a good sailor, but the motion was too much for him, and in another few minutes he was forced to give way to an agonizing retching which made him feel he was going to choke up his heart.

When he had recovered a little he saw that Gloria had slipped to her knees again and was leaning half-unconsciously against one of the four round manholes in the sides of the wall, by which cargo could be stowed in the containers as well as by other manholes in their tops. Pulling himself together with an effort, Philip set to work on the bolts that held the manhole nearest to him in place, with the idea that if they could get inside one of the containers they would at least be out of the wind and escape being drenched every few minutes.

The bolts were stiff, but he found a makeshift lever among the gear brought from the launch and, after a quarter of an hour's hard work, desperation lending strength to his efforts, he managed to get the manhole open. Climbing through, he pulled Gloria after him and, one by one, rescued the sopping packages from the well; then he slammed to the circular iron door and, stumbling over Gloria's legs in the darkness, fell upon the heaving floor, where he was abominably sick again.

How long they lay there neither of them was afterwards quite certain, but Philip thought that it was two nights and a day. He remembered getting up on several occasions to peer out through the manhole door, but whether it was dark or light no change was evident; great gobbets of water still smacked down on the cargo containers, and every now and then, after tossing of more than average violence, the well was half-flooded by a spate of foaming water.

Inside the compartment all the elements of a nightmare caused them hardly to know when they were awake or asleep. To keep out the water the manhole door had to be kept shut, with the result that they were lying in pitch-black darkness. As they had nothing on which to fix their eyes, it seemed to them as if they were being whirled round and round and jerked up and down like cherries in a cocktail shaker. There was no ventilation and no heating, so it was both stuffy and cold. The only thing with which to ease the discomfort of the hard floor on which they lay or crouched was the bedding from the launch, but this was still soaking wet. For many hours neither of them was more than semi-conscious, and, at such short intervals as either was sufficiently *compos mentis* to think of the other, it was only because their companion's presence was recalled by the sound of chattering teeth or fitful groans.

At last Philip was brought out of one of his long bouts of miserable timeless inertia by the suddenly crystallized knowledge that the floor was no longer pitching up and down beneath him with the violence of a bucking horse; it was merely soaring and sinking alternately with comparative gentleness that was not altogether unrestful. On standing up, forgetful of the low ceiling, he bumped his head; but after fumbling for a moment he found the manhole and opened it, to discover that it was day and that the square well no longer had water slopping about in its bottom. It came to him then that his clothes had dried on him, and he took some comfort from the thought that sea water is said never to give people either rheumatism or a chill.

Having climbed through the hole, he drew himself to his full height and looked slowly round the horizon. A stiff sea was still running, and on every side lay the same grey, desolate prospect of racing, foam-flecked waters. The sky overhead was still black and lowering, but the wind had dropped, and it looked as if the worst of the storm had blown itself out. There was no ship in sight, no aircraft, and no sort of indication as to in which direction the nearest coast might lie.

Only one thing gave Philip a rather grim satisfaction. Rafts Number Two, Three and Four were still attached to Number One, and that, he felt, went a long way to prove his contention that, provided the load of each raft were equal in weight and distribution to the others, the stress of tide and winds should be exactly the same on them all. As four rafts had remained connected through such a tempest, he had little doubt that the other six were not far distant, and that most, if not all, of the cables connecting them had also held; so that, had they and many more been in the care of a trawler carrying two launches to act as mother-ship, as he had originally planned, she would soon have rounded them all up.

It was nice to think that there would at least still be part of his convoy to show when the destroyer, which he had no doubt would be sent out for them, arrived on the scene to pick them up; but all the same it was damnable luck that the good weather had not lasted for another forty-eight hours so that the launch and her whole string might have been towed in triumph to a safe anchorage in Southampton Water.

He heard a movement behind him and turned to see Gloria emerging from the hole. Her hair was matted, and there were dark rings under her eyes. As he took her hand to help her, he recalled how she had refrained from making a single complaint during their night and day of ordeal in the launch, and the courage she had displayed during the perilous business of transferring to the raft. He began to say what a good show he thought she had put up, but she cut him short.

"Oh, there's no nix to it, Boy. I was so mighty scared that it just stopped me being sick until we were safe on the raft here. But where will the storm have taken us? Have you any idea at all?"

Philip shook his head. "Until the sun comes out I can't even get an observation that will give us a fix; but I'm afraid we've been swept a long way south. We're probably somewhere in the Bay of Biscay."

"Where would that be?" she startled him somewhat by asking.

"It lies between the western coast of France and the northern coast of Spain."

"And how far are they from Portsmouth?"

"Anything from two to seven hundred miles."

"Holy Saints! An' I thought Europe was a small place! Will your friends in the Navy ever be able to find us now?"

"Oh, I think so," he spoke more confidently than he felt. "I'm sure they'll send an aircraft out spotting for us, and once we've been located they'll probably arrange for something to come out from the French coast to pick us up."

"Then I'd be able to go straight to Paris, wouldn't I? That would be fine!"

"Yes, provided you can satisfy the French Immigration officials."

For a moment they stood in silence, then he added: "I don't know about you, but I'm jolly hungry. Shall we see what we can find to eat?"

She sighed. "What wouldn't I give for hot coffee an' hamburgers, right now. Still, there's half a cold tongue—the salt water won't have harmed that—an', if the sea hasn't gotten into the tins, there's plenty of biscuits to be eating with it."

They began to rummage among the bundles and packages that they had salvaged from the launch. Everything was still damp and unpleasantly sticky from briny sea water, but the lump of tongue, when extracted from the table napkin in which it had been wrapped, proved perfectly edible, and enough biscuits for their immediate requirements had escaped a wetting.

Gloria had no watch, and Philip's had stopped, so they had no idea what time it was and could only guess that when they had finished their meal it was about three o'clock in the afternoon. It was now the first week in October, and the darkness of the sky threatened an early nightfall, so they felt that they would not have any too much time to make themselves more comfortable while daylight lasted and set about it right away.

Of the four cargo containers, each occupying a quarter of the raft's area, one had been devoted exclusively to oil, for refuelling the launch while the convoy was at sea, and was still well over half-full. The other three contained the selection of mixed goods that Philip had purchased in New York with a view to testing how the various items would stand up to a two months' voyage and probably a much rougher passage than they would have had in the hold of a ship.

Before leaving the cabin, Gloria had had the sense to pack up his instruments and the books that he used for his nautical calculations, but she had not thought to bring the papers that he kept in the drawer of the table; in consequence, the manifest giving details of the cargo on the raft, and the contents of each numbered case, was lost. All they could do was to open a package at random here and there.

It was not easy work as the bales and cases were stacked close together to prevent their shifting, and the only light they had was that which percolated in through the open door of the manhole; moreover, they both soon began to suffer from a most painful crick in the neck, owing to lack of headroom. Gloria had managed to save all the cooking utensils from the launch, and Philip knew that, if only he could locate them, there were cases which contained both oil heating stoves and primuses among the cargo, either of which would have served for cooking. There was also a great quantity and variety of food. But, during the afternoon and evening, all they succeeded in gaining access to were potatoes, sugar, garden implements, raw cotton, molasses, ball-bearings and rubber sponges.

The bale of raw cotton opened up and spread out proved a most welcome substitute for their damp bedding, and with more of the biscuits off which they had made their evening meal they ate some spoonfuls of sugar, knowing that it would help to keep up their strength.

Next morning they found that the sea was calmer and that the sun had come out, so they carried up all their damp bedding and belongings and spread them out to dry on the deck made by the flat roofs of the containers. For breakfast they had the rest of the tongue, but they now found themselves exceedingly thirsty, and, having nothing at all to drink, set to on a determined and more systematic examination of their cargo.

Philip succeeded in removing the main hatch in the top of one of the containers and this gave them much easier access to a good part of its contents. Moreover, while they worked in it the head of one or other of them was always partly in the open above the hatch level, so it was easy to keep a lookout for the aircraft which they felt sure must be seeking them.

Many of the things they could reach most readily were of little use to them, as it was in this container that all the extra sails for the rafts had been stored, together with the great lengths of rope and twine, spare cables and beacons, etc.; but Philip felt certain that the case containing the oil stoves was also there somewhere. During the course of the morning they came across carpets, a case of ladies' shoes, a crate containing six bicycles, a quantity of fireproof asbestos sheeting, twelve electric fires and several bundles of cheap curtains and tablecloths. Philip had bought all these things and innumerable others through a wholesale trading company in New York, with the idea that when they had served their turn as test cargo he would, by having brought them freight-free from the U.S.A. to the United Kingdom, be able to re-sell them at quite a decent profit; but none of them seemed of much value to him now.

A little before midday they saw a British aircraft to the west of them, which appeared to be cruising quite slowly. Both of them sprang out of the hatch and began to wave lengths of the blown-out tattered sails from the stunted mass of the raft. But the crew of the aircraft did not see them, and it flew serenely on.

Philip took an observation of the sun and worked it out that their latitude was now 46° 42″ North, so his surmise that they were about on a level with the centre of the Bay of Biscay proved correct, although he found that they were well outside it in the Atlantic, approximately on the Tenth Meridian West. However, he knew that these calculations were subject to a very wide degree of error now that he could only guess at the time by the height of the sun in the heavens, and was not even quite certain what day it was.

Not having discovered any further food supplies, they had to make an unappetizing lunch off some more sodden biscuits, and their thirst was now really beginning to worry them seriously; but early in the afternoon Gloria found a crate of grapefruit juice, and afterwards they came upon several sacks of coffee beans, a case of corned beef and another of tinned corn; so, although they could not yet make coffee, their evening meal had more substance and variety.

Just as dusk was falling they saw another aeroplane, this time flying in towards the French coast, but it gave no sign that they had been seen, and they turned in, hoping for better luck next day.

It came to them in one form at least, for one of the first things that

Philip found when they resumed their examination of the cargo after breakfasting off sweet corn and grapefruit juice was the crate containing the oil stoves. They proved to be of two patterns. There were a dozen of the simple round variety used for heating, and six double stoves measuring about two foot six by one foot six and standing about three feet high, designed for the use as cookers in holiday camps. Their joy was almost as great as if a rescue party had suddenly appeared alongside, since, having plenty of oil, there was now nothing to prevent their boiling kettles of sea water to get supplies of fresh water, so that they could make coffee, as well as heat up some of the bully beef and sweet corn for a hot meal.

While Philip was taking his midday observation, they again saw the British aircraft of the day before, or one exactly like it, but once more it failed to see them, and, as Gloria pointed out, they had no proof that it was actually looking, since it might quite well be employed on any of a dozen forms of war activity.

Philip's reckoning showed that, although the storm had now entirely abated, they were still drifting south, and this increased the anxiety that he had been feeling for the past twenty-four hours as to where they would now fetch up. The Gulf Stream, having warmed the shores of Northern Europe and dissipated its force against them, merges with other currents, the principal one of which flows south along the coast of Portugal towards North-West Africa. The storm having prevented the Gulf Stream from depositing Philip and Gloria on some part of the Channel coast, it now looked as if, caught up in this other current, they were liable, unless they were rescued fairly soon, to be carried down to the Tropics. On the other hand, since the winds in these parts were extremely variable it was quite useless to set fresh sails and, unless they got into the North-East Trades, they might drift about for weeks.

Since the going down of the storm they had sighted quite a number of ships, mostly in the distance; but two that had been coming towards them appeared almost deliberately to have turned out of their course. A third did the same on the day following the discovery of the oil stove, and a reason for this strange behaviour was given to them in a most unpleasant manner. The cargo ship concerned, after approaching to within a mile of them, suddenly veered sharply away and two minutes later brought a gun into action against them.

"Holy St. Bridget, is it mad they are!" exclaimed Gloria, as a shell whistled overhead and burst behind them, sending up a great spout of white foam.

"No," replied Philip, pulling her down into the dubious safety of the cargo container. "This raft is so low in the water that it can't be seen properly from that distance, and those jittery fools have taken it for a U-Boat."

Only two more shells were fired at them, both of which landed several hundred yards away: no doubt the gunners at that stage of the war were still somewhat amateurish; but Philip knew now that only a warship would risk approaching them, and if one did there was a most perturbing chance that they would be shelled much more accurately long before the ship's crew realized that their target was only a raft.

On the fifth night after the sinking of the storm they saw a distant light emitting regular flashes which swept like arcs across the darkened sky, and Philip identified it from his manual as the Lighthouse of Cape Finisterre on the north-west corner of Spain. When morning came they could see the Spanish coast as a vague bluish blur on the horizon. For an hour or so their hopes ran high that the raft would be washed up there, but the coastline gradually receded until, by early afternoon, they had lost sight of it altogether.

Some days later their hopes were again raised when a large British seaplane, after flying right over them, turned round and flew back to have another look before resuming her original course. Philip said it was a Short Sunderland on the Lisbon-Southampton run and would definitely report the rafts on its arrival at base, so their rescue within a few days was now certain. They would most probably be picked up by a lifeboat or tug which the British authorities would arrange to have sent out from Lisbon. But the days passed, and no rescue craft appeared.

It was possible that the aircraft had been shot down before getting back to its base in England, or that its crew had seen the raft but not the people on it. If the latter were the case, the fact that no launch was reported as in company with the rafts would lead to the assumption that it had been sunk and Philip drowned in the storm that had come up so quickly after the receipt of his message by the Admiralty. The British Navy had more important things to do during a major war than send valuable personnel to inspect a derelict string of rafts, and Philip, realizing this, now began to feel despondent of their chances. If he were believed dead, all further search for him would cease, and he had to accept the possibility that by this time his family had been told that the launch was missing, presumably lost, and that there was therefore small hope of his own survival.

The thing which infuriated him much more than being a castaway was the loss to Britain of his idea just as it had been proved practical. If only the authorities could have seen the excellent shape in which the Raft Convoy had arrived off Land's End, he felt sure they would have taken it up; but now that it had failed to complete its voyage and been scattered by the first autumn gale, it was highly probable that the whole scheme would be pigeon-holed and forgotten. He was fretting badly too about both his inability to get home and join up and the fact that he no longer even had any idea how the war was going. As part of his cargo he had shipped three of a new make of American radio, but so far he had failed to find the cases in which they were packed, so, since abandoning the launch, they had had no news of the outer world at all.

D*

Meanwhile, as they slowly drifted south a hundred miles or so off the coast of Portugal, they were gradually adapting their curious accommodation to their needs and making it more comfortable. They had converted the limited surplus space in the cargo-container in which they had first taken refuge into a kitchen; that of another into a sitting-place lined with rugs and home-made cushions consisting of raw cotton tied up in tablecloths; and that of a third into a bedroom which, having slept in company for so long in the cabin of the launch, they shared without giving the matter a second thought. The fourth container smelt too disagreeably of oil for them to enter it except when they needed a fresh supply of fuel for their cooking-stove, but on its top Philip had rigged up a canvas bath out of some of the spare sails, and he was intrigued to see that Gloria used it as often as he did.

It seemed that, nothing daunted by her now somewhat uncertain prospects of a safe and speedy arrival in Paris, she was determined to pursue her social education. A score of times a day she said to Philip: " How would you say so-and-so? " until there were moments when he almost regretted having aroused her interest in her mode of speaking. She questioned him, too, upon innumerable points of behaviour in the life of the upper classes, many of which he found it by no means easy to answer; but there was little work to do on the raft and, apart from swimming every morning, talking was their sole recreation during the long hours that they sat in the October sunshine watching for a ship or aircraft to come near enough for them to signal.

He found her mind an amazing jumble of mainly unrelated facts and absurd misconceptions, scarred like a gruyère cheese with pockets of abysmal ignorance. Her strong suit was the lives of famous painters, which she admitted was the only serious reading she had ever done, and upon this subject she was infinitely better informed than Philip. It had, as a by-product, given her a patchy background of certain periods of European history since the Renaissance. Her father, the French-Canadian-British journalist, also seemed to have passed on to her a considerable store of miscellaneous knowledge; but, after leaving Europe, Alphonse Smith appeared to have lost interest in world events, so Gloria knew little of what had happened outside the United States since the 1914-18 war; and it was clear that from the time of his death, in her fourteenth year, all trace of British sympathies had been removed. No doubt owing to the influence of her Irish mother, she had come to regard the British as a greedy and unscrupulous race whose Machiavellian statesmen had been the niggers in most of the international woodpiles.

By the time they had been drifting south for a fortnight they had opened up enough of the cargo to provide themselves with a good range of tinned meats, fruits and soups, as well as a supply of flour, oatmeal and soap, but the further they penetrated among the closely packed stacks of goods the more difficult it became to get at the ones still further from the hatches, and, now having most things they required readily available, they would not have persisted further had it not been for their mutual desire to unearth one of the radios. .

After almost three weeks of unbroken sunshine the weather began to deteriorate again as they reached the latitude of Gibraltar. It was not rough but misty, and with the mist came a damp chill that drove them off their sun-deck to seek shelter and occupation in another examination of their cargo. At about four o'clock in the afternoon Philip gave a cry of triumph; a case that he was opening had revealed one of the radio sets for which they had sought so long in vain. Lifting it carefully from its packing, he carried it out to the well of the raft, where the light was better, fetched the dry batteries of which he had already unearthed a store, and began to adjust it.

He was just about to switch it on when Gloria, who was kneeling beside him, suddenly exclaimed: "Listen!"

A second before she spoke he, too, had caught the sound of voices.

She sprang to her feet, but he seized her arm and pulled her down again. The speakers were talking in German.

Placing a finger to his lips to enjoin silence, he let her rise cautiously until they could just peep over the edge of the cargo container. Not more than fifty yards away, and only slightly obscured by the mist, was the conning-tower of a U-boat.

The submarine had surfaced and was lying still upon the water. On her deck near the base of the conning-tower stood a little group of sailors. It was they who were talking as they peered through the mist towards the raft.

At that moment Philip would have given ten years of his life for a depth-charge and the means of firing it. The fact that he was a civilian did not even occur to him. These were his country's enemies: the blond beasts who had forced a most bloody war upon his father's generation and were now setting about the methodical destruction of his own contemporaries. In the very first month of the war, while he was still able to listen to the radio on the launch, they had made it plain that they were not going to hamper themselves with any half-measures this time. From the beginning they had exulted with a sadistic joy in the massacre of helpless women and children, as their air force brought fire and horror to the Polish towns, and, just as Philip had himself predicted times without number, they had initiated a reign of terror at sea by their ruthless policy of sinking at sight, and afterwards machine-gunning the poor wretches who took to the boats.

Although he realized his complete inability to do any material harm to the great undersea warship, wild plans for attempts to sabotage her were already beginning to bubble in his brain, when, to his horror, he heard Gloria give a low cry of delight.

"We're saved, Boy!" she exclaimed. "Saved at last! Come on, let's. . ."

She got no further. Clapping a hand over her mouth, he dragged her down and positively hissed into her ear:

"You little fool! D'you think I'm prepared to be taken prisoner and carted off to Germany for the duration? I'd rather die first."

"Let me go!" she spluttered, wrenching her head sideways. "You've got no choice. 'Tis coming here they are, in a boat!"

Her words confirmed what Philip had suspected and feared from his last glimpse of the submarine. Even through the murk the large object that some of the Germans were handling had looked vaguely like a dinghy that they were about to put over the side.

"They're not going to get me if I can help it!" Philip snarled. "Or you either!" He gave her a push towards one of the manholes. "Go on—in you go!"

As he pushed her head first through the opening she began to cry out in protest but her voice was muffled because her body almost filled the aperture. The moment she was through he scrambled after her.

"I'll not be kept here!" she was declaring angrily. "Anything's better than being stuck for ever on this lousy raft. They'll land me some place, and I don't give a dime if it is in Germany."

"They'll more probably rape you first and chuck you to the fishes afterwards," snapped Philip.

"You're nuts! I'm a citizen of the United States of America. They wouldn't dare lay a hand on me. They wouldn't dare!"

Philip caught the faint splash of oars breaking the eerie silence created by the mist outside. The approaching menace was now too near to waste further precarious time in argument. He and Gloria were standing face to face, their shoulders stooped and heads bent, owing to the low roof of the cargo-container. Clenching his right fist, he jerked it up, jabbing her hard on the side of the jaw. Her head hit the roof with a bang. She made a little choking noise, and pitched forward against his knees; then she rolled over and lay still.

Having pulled the manhole shut, he fumbled for Gloria's wrists in the darkness and, finding them, began to drag her away from the opening, in among the cargo. As they had now lived in these confined quarters for close on a month, he knew the warren of narrow passages they had so far made among the bales and boxes as well as he did the situation of each piece of furniture in his own bedroom at home. Within two minutes he had pulled her to the furthest extremity of the deepest alleyway. Another minute was sufficient for him to drag a big bale across it, so that they were completely hidden from anyone standing at its entrance. Yet even as he worked, bruising his hands and tearing his nails in the blackness, he could hear the hated guttural voices again, now coming to him deadened by the shell of the cargo-container. Then there came the clatter of boots on metal above.

"*Jemand zu hauser?*" shouted a voice, and Philip's heart almost missed a beat. The suddenness of the emergency and Gloria's obstreperous conduct had given him little time to think. He had taken it for granted that, if the Germans did not actually see the raft's occupants they would naturally assume it had been abandoned. He had forgotten that the apparatus which he had fixed up above one of the heating stoves to give a small but constant supply of fresh water was always kept going, and that his unwelcome visitors had only to glance through the manhole of the next compartment, the entrance to which formed Gloria's "kitchen", to see her cooker alight and the tinned stew of steak and carrots which they had selected for that day's lunch already heating upon it. No wonder they were shouting: " Anyone at home? Come out let's have a look at you! Come along! It'll be the worse for you if we have to fetch you! "

The voice that was bawling in German became more angry and imperative, then it suddenly ceased. There was a long silence, broken only by an occasional muffled cry or the sound of a bump. Gradually the noises drew nearer until Philip realized that his enemies were searching among the cargo in the next compartment; then they stopped altogether.

Crouching there in the stuffy darkness, Philip waited for what he felt to be at least an hour, although, actually, it was less than a quarter of that time. He began to hope that the Germans had given up the search and gone, but he feared that they might be busy still in hunting among the cargo in the container on the opposite side of the raft, so he did not yet dare to move.

Suddenly Gloria groaned. Philip started as though he had been stung. His mind had been so concentrated on listening for sounds of the enemy that he had momentarily forgotten all about her.

" Hush! " he whispered urgently. " Hush! "

She groaned again and muttered: " Holy—holy Saints, where am I? "

" You're all right. But for God's sake keep quiet, or the Germans may hear you! " As Philip spoke he heard them again himself. They had not left the raft, and some of them were now talking together in its central well.

" The Germans! " exclaimed Gloria, struggling up into a sitting position.

At that moment the manhole was flung open with a clang, and there followed the sounds of someone struggling through it.

In the darkness Philip reached out with both his hands. They touched Gloria's shoulders, and a moment later closed round her throat. " If you make one sound," he breathed, " I'll choke you. D'you hear? I'll wring your neck—if it's the last thing I ever do! "

The darkness had become a faint greyness. There were the sounds of tramping feet, then chinks of light from an electric torch shone between the boxes.

" *Kommen zie aus!* " suddenly barked a voice, and it went on in German: " Come on! Come out of that! We know you're there! "

CHAPTER IX

THE UNSOUGHT BACCHANALIA

PHILIP strove to control his breathing. His hands were light but firm on Gloria's throat. He knew that, if she did decide to risk a scream, he could not possibly check it before the damage was done and the first half of it had given away their position. He knew, too, that Gloria was no fool and would be quick to realize that no man, however powerful, could strangle a physically fit young woman without the sound of the struggle and the kicking of her heels against the nearby boxes being heard by the searchers, who at the very most could be only thirty feet away.

" Come now! We have searched the others, so we know that you must be in this one," the German voice went on. " If you come out and answer our questions, we will treat you fairly. But if we have to fetch you we will give you a beating that you will not forget."

There was a pause; and Philip felt the muscles of Gloria's throat swelling under his hands.

The voice came again. " I will give you while I count ten—*Eins! Zwei! Drei! Vier!* "

Philip knew that Gloria's mouth was opening. He could feel the pressure of her chin upon his thumbs, but did not dare to squeeze her throat lest he should check her breathing and precipitate the dénouement which he dreaded.

" *Funf! Sechs! Sieben! Acht!* " went on the voice.

Suddenly, on the inspiration of the moment, although he knew that Gloria's throat was already tensed for the cry which might bring about his death, he released his grip on it and, leaning forward so that his face was within a few inches of hers, breathed: " Please—oh, Gloria, please! "

" *Neun! . . . . . Zehn!* " cried the German, but Gloria made no sound.

After a second's pause the officer in charge of the party shouted at his sailors: " Get busy, you men! They must be here somewhere. Ferret them out, and be quick about it! "

There followed the same bumping and scraping of boxes as Philip had heard half an hour before, but it was much nearer now. He wondered miserably if he had been justified in first forcing and then entreating Gloria to keep silent. Had he allowed her to disclose herself in the first place, they might have treated her with more leniency than they would when they found her after their long and tiring search. Yet he felt certain that his judgment had been right when he had sought to conceal her, even against her will. He had not thought then that any search would be made for them, much less one so thorough, and every instinct he possessed cried out against allowing a girl to place any reliance on the chivalry of a crowd of young Nazified German sailors.

Time stood still for Philip. The search seemed to go on interminably, and the strain of waiting was so great that he was now almost tempted to cry out himself in order to end it. He felt he should have known that, if the Germans once set about making a search, they would do it with their usual thoroughness. The chances of his remaining undiscovered were practically negligible, and when they found him he thought that the odds were a hundred to one that they would kill him. They never bothered to take any prisoners from the ships they sank, so why should they bother to take him all the way back to Germany? By the end of September the wireless had already been giving accounts of the Gestapo's deporting of Polish women by the thousand and murdering of Polish men in a deliberate policy of race annihilation. If they were doing that to the Poles they certainly would have no scruples about doing it to the people they hated above all others—their arch-enemies, the British—and a bullet in Philip's stomach would mean one Englishman the less.

He began to speculate then as to whether it would be a bullet, or if they would knock him on the head and throw him overboard. But perhaps they would throw him overboard without knocking him on the head, for the fun of seeing him swim round and round until he could support himself no longer and went under.

That was the sort of sport that those U-boat crews, all picked men from the *Hitler jugend,* enjoyed. They had been trained since they were children to betray their parents and take a delight in sadistic cruelty; and, as treachery and brutality had been two outstanding characteristics of the German race for close on a thousand years, Hitler's youth instructors had had the best possible raw material on which to work. Yes—they would most probably kick him around a bit first so that he could not swim too far, or long enough for them to get bored waiting for him to drown, then push him over the side. And poor little Gloria? What would these perverts, whose Aryan appearance cloaked a morality on a lower plane than a gorilla's, do to her?

They had finished one side of the compartment, shifting every box and package in it. Now they were starting on the other. Philip was cursing himself for not having got out Eiderman's gun. If he had had that he might at least have put up a fight with it; but he had not even thought of the weapon since noticing it among the things of his Gloria had saved from the launch. On the appearance of the U-boat he had not even recalled the fact that he possessed a pistol, and he had been much too occupied with Gloria to think of it until he had got her under cover, and the search was already under way.

Somewhere, sounding a long way off, a whistle blew. The faint blast was instantly followed by a loud shout of warning.

"*Achtung! Achtung!*"

A crate was dropped with a crash. There was a swift scampering of feet towards the manhole, then a fainter cry.

"*Frisch! Frisch! Ein Englischer flieger!*"

"Good God!" gasped Philip. "What fantastic luck! An R.A.F. aircraft."

Turning to Gloria he fumbled for her hands and pressed them. "Bless you for keeping quiet, Gloria—bless you! We'd both be dead or dying now if you hadn't—or I would anyway—shot out of hand before they bolted."

Gloria pulled away her hands and tenderly felt her jaw as she muttered : "You—you just wait! You'd wish you *were* dead if you knew what was coming to you!"

But Philip did not hear her. Throwing caution to the winds in his excitement, he pushed aside the cases behind which they were lying and, while the boots of the Germans were still clattering overhead, made for the manhole. As the search-party had rushed out still clutching their torches the place was in almost total darkness again, and during the past twenty minutes they had shifted two-thirds of the cargo. In consequence, whichever way Philip turned he stumbled into obstacles. Soon he had lost his sense of direction altogether, and a good two minutes elapsed before he finally found the door.

The first thing he noticed when he got outside was that the mist had lifted. He could see the U-boat clearly now, and the little boatload of men from the raft were at that moment scrambling on to her deck. The British aircraft was roaring up from the direction of Gibraltar. Evidently the U-boat had been lurking there in the hope of catching some of the shipping passing through the Straits; but the R.A.F. patrol had spotted her.

With lightning speed the Germans, conforming to a perfect drill, pulled in their dinghy and made a dash for the conning-tower. As the last man disappeared and the conning-tower hatch snapped shut, the submarine was already submerging. By that time the aircraft had circled into the U-boat's fore and aft line and was almost dead overhead. Her first depth charge sent up a great ragged pillar of water while the U-boat's periscope was still feathering the surface, and not more than thirty feet beyond it.

"Well done!" yelled Philip, as two more spouts of water rocketed upwards. "Go on! Go . . ."

His sentence was never completed as at that second the concussion from the first explosion hit the raft. Philip bit his tongue, and Gloria would have been thrown off her feet if she had not clutched at him to save herself. Twice more the raft shuddered and rocked. By the time it settled down again the water spouts had disappeared and the aircraft, having circled once, was heading back towards Gibraltar.

The realization that, instead of watching the action, they should have being doing everything possible to attract the attention of the crew of the aircraft to themselves dawned on Philip and Gloria too late for them to do much about it. In the hope of rectifying their stupid omission they both climbed hastily on to the open surface of the raft and waved the lengths of torn sail which they always kept there ready; but the aircraft did not turn round, and it soon disappeared from view.

So far as they could see there was no wreckage on the gently heaving water, and they felt that if the U-boat had been badly hit or forced to come up to the surface the aircraft would have remained on the scene to make certain of her kill. Her flying off so quickly suggested that she had either used all her depth charges or that her fuel was running low, so she was returning to base to pick up further supplies and would come out again as soon as possible in an endeavour to locate the U-boat and have another shot at her. The occupants of the raft could only hope for that or that their presence had already been seen and reported.

As Philip was about to jump down into the well again he heard a sudden patter of feet behind him. He half-turned, wondering what could possibly have caused Gloria to break into a run. Too late he realized that she was running at him. Her right foot shot out with all the force of her muscular body behind it and caught him square on the bottom, precipitating him in a wild flurry of arms and legs over the five foot drop into the well.

He fell with one arm doubled under him and both his knees and head came into violent contact with hard substances. For a moment he lay there dazed, then he painfully began to pick himself up, while she stood there on the edge of the drop, her hands on her hips, her blue eyes flashing.

"Maybe that'll learn you to be using your fists on a girl!" she declared angrily. "And there's lots more of the same coming to you yet."

His head was now aching as though it were about to split, and feeling it gingerly he found that a bump had risen on it the size of a small egg. His knees were also aching but they did not worry him so much as his arm, in which he feared he had broken something. Knowing that he was in no state to enter into an argument, he forbore to answer, but turning his back on her got through the manhole into their sleeping place and lay down to wait until the worst of the pain from his numerous injuries had subsided.

He was allowed little time to do so. Barely a minute had elapsed when he heard her shouting for him. "Boy, come here! Come and see what those devils have done to our kitchen."

He ignored her summons, so she came and popped her head through the manhole and cried: "Would you believe it now? Those vandals have smashed our cooking-stove to smithereens, and the water distiller that you made so cleverly. They've stolen lots of our stores too. I've had no time yet . . . "

She stopped in the middle of her sentence. Most of her drawings had been sadly stained with sea water during the great storm; but they still had a decorative value, and she had fixed up a number of the best on the walls that formed the inner corners of the two cargo-containers in which they used the limited free space to lounge in dull weather or sleep at night. In the dim light of the sleeping place certain additions to her drawings had not caught her eye before, but having noticed one her glance flashed round, and she saw that one of the German sailors had defiled them all with crude obscenities. Being mainly nudes they lent themselves particularly readily to the grotesque and misplaced sexual symbols with which they had been garnished.

Climbing through the manhole she stared, with head bent, at each of the drawings in turn, the flush on her face gradually deepening from pink to crimson. Suddenly she gave a sob and sinking to her knees burst into tears.

"What's the matter? " muttered Philip unsympathetically. "You don't have to worry about the cooker because we've got others. As soon as I'm feeling fit enough I'll unpack one for you."

"It's not that," she wailed. "Oh Boy, have you seen what they've done to my drawings? How can men be such beasts? "

Dropping down beside him she let her head fall on his shoulder, expecting him to comfort her as he had done a number of times before on occasions of crisis during the past three months. Instead, he jerked violently away, crying:

"Oh God! My arm! "

Her tears ceased as suddenly as they had begun, and she knelt up to peer down at him in the semi-darkness. "What is it, Boy? Is it really hurt you are? "

"Of course I am. What the hell do you expect? By kicking me over the edge like that you might have broken my neck."

"Well, you should not have hit me."

"I wouldn't have if you'd had the sense to listen to reason."

"An' then to threaten to choke the life out of me body——"

"I had to try to stop you from giving us away somehow. I'm still wondering why you didn't at the end, when you had the chance? "

" 'Twas because you said please, and seemed so scared. You were like a little child rather and appealed to the mother's heart in me. I'm glad though that I didn't call out now. From the way they've smashed our things for no reason at all and their filthy scrawls all over me drawings they couldn't have been very nice people."

Philip groaned. "The Germans are *not* ' nice people ' and never have been ' nice people.' If only you, and lots of other young men and women like you, had been taught *that* in your night schools instead of that we

British are a decadent grasping race, which rushes into war at every opportunity goaded on by a lot of nigger-beating, port-swilling old Colonels, the world really would have been a safer place for democracy."

"Now, now! 'Tis exciting yourself you are," she tried to soothe him, but having started to get himself worked up he would not stop.

"'Nice people' indeed! The Germans are a race of born fighters. They don't consider that there is any point in living unless they can get themselves into a war. That's why all through the Middle Ages and right up to a hundred years ago any nation that wanted more troops for its campaigns used to hire Germans. They were always ready to fight for anyone who would pay them. Britain, France, Holland, Sweden, Austria —anyone would do, and they didn't in the least mind fighting one another. Then with Prussia to lead them they became a nation and waged their own wars against anyone they thought weak enough to prove an easy prey. And did you ever hear of the Germans being generous or merciful when they finished a war victoriously? Of course not! No race can make a profession of fighting for generation after generation without becoming brutalized. The Germans are brutes, beasts, swine born to the trade of murder, and the sooner everyone in the world realizes that the sooner we'll get them under once and for all and have peace again."

"Maybe you're right," murmured Gloria; "but it's no good going on at me in this way. I'm not the President. I can't bring the United States into the war alongside Britain and France."

"No one said you could. I'm only asking you to take a realistic view of things and not behave like an irresponsible little fool if these Nazi swine come back and pay us another visit."

She sat back quickly on her heels. "Say now! D'you think they might?"

"Well, it doesn't look as if the U-boat was sunk, does it? So, if they surface near us, there's quite a chance that they might think it worthwhile to come and collect some more of our stores."

"We haven't checked up on what they've taken yet. How d'you feel now? Are you all in one piece enough to come help me have a look around?"

"I'm feeling like hell!" Philip declared frankly. "My head will get better in an hour or two, but I'm worried about my arm. I'm afraid I've broken something in it."

Gloria immediately expressed genuine contrition for having really hurt him, then helped him off with his coat. They gently prodded the arm all over but could find nothing definitely wrong with it, and Philip decided that he must have wrenched his shoulder. She made him a sling for his arm and put a cold compress on his head, then they made a tour of inspection to see what loss and damage they had sustained owing to the coming of the Germans.

After making a full examination they came to the conclusion that, while two or three Germans—about a third of the party—had spent the whole hour or more of which the visit had consisted in searching for them, the others had employed themselves transporting a selection of stores to the U-boat. The licentious additions to Gloria's drawings had no doubt been made by one of the men while waiting for the dinghy to return and load up again for a second or third trip, and the cooker had probably been slashed with a heavy hatchet, then kicked over in a moment of vindictive rage just before the Germans had abandoned the raft. The newly discovered radio had been stolen and, consciously or unconsciously complying with the tradition of professional burglars, one of the visitors had left his card in the form of an unpleasant mess on the kitchen floor.

All things considered, the results of the visitation might have been far more serious. There were five more oil cookers and two more radio sets among the cargo which could easily be got out. The fresh water still could be mended in a day, and there was such a large quantity of food among the cargo that the Germans had not had time to make off with even a twentieth part of it. The only permanent injury sustained was the mutilation of six of Gloria's best drawings, with which she had hoped to impress some leading Art Master in Paris sufficiently to induce him to take her at a very modest fee. When Philip suggested that she could cut off the heads and other untouched parts and throw the spoilt bits away she would not hear of it, but said that later on she would try to get the marks out; where that was impossible she could cover them with extravagant draperies under which the form of the original figures would still be discernible to the artist's eye. Meanwhile, the drawings were left as they were.

During the afternoon Gloria got on with the cleaning up while Philip sat on the open deck nursing his injured arm and keeping a sharp lookout for the R.A.F. aircraft; but to his disappointment it did not return. They went to bed that night still shaken by their ordeal of the morning but hopeful that other aircraft reconnoitring for U-boats from Gibraltar might find them in the course of the next few days.

When a week had passed and they had seen only one aircraft in the far distance they had to adjust their ideas once more. They might still be lucky and have a plane fly right over them or meet a ship which would come close enough to see their signals, but they needed no telling now how staggeringly vast are the open spaces of the ocean and how few and far between, once one is off the great Trade Routes, are the ships that plough it.

After almost touching the north-western tip of Spain they zigzagged in a south-westerly direction until they were too far out to be within sight of shipping passing along the Portuguese coast. Their best chance of being picked up had been as they crossed the great shipping way between America and the Mediterranean ports, but now they were passing out of this into a much less frequented zone off the north-west coast of Africa.

There was a chance that they might run into a ship on the South African service or that the raft might be washed up on Maderia or the Canaries but Philip thought it more likely that, unless another storm interfered, the North-East Trades would carry them on to the African coast. When that would happen was almost unpredictable. Ever since they had been torn away from the Gulf Stream they had no longer been travelling under a steady impulse but much more slowly and erratically. On average they were now drifting at the rate of about ten miles a day in a generally southern direction, so it seemed that they should strike the bulge of Africa in anything between forty and eighty days.

The one thing that now kept them reasonably cheerful was the weather. During the latter part of August and the first half of September, while they were crossing the west and central Atlantic, it had, in the main, been pleasantly warm; but as the days began to shorten bathing from the launch had lost most of its attraction, and during the first weeks on the raft an occasional nip in the October wind had given warning that Europe's winter was about to set in. But now, although it was early November, day by day it was gradually becoming warmer again. Whenever the wind blew from Africa, having crossed hundreds of miles of scorching sands, it was soft and balmy, and the sea began to take on a new colour: a real, deep, brilliant blue.

For long hours they could now forget their extraordinary predicament and the uncertainties of the future while lounging like a couple of holiday-makers on the broad flat deck of the raft. Day after day the sky remained a cloudless, cobalt blue, and they swam or lay basking in the sunshine, idly watching for the appearance of the schools of porpoises, dolphins and flying-fish that inhabited these pleasant waters.

For some days after the brush with the U-boat Philip had remained almost *hors de combat,* but his sprained shoulder gradually got better. He was then able to sort out the muddle in which the Germans had left a good part of the cargo and open up several fresh cases to make good those they had taken away. Having provided Gloria with a new cooker, he next unpacked another wireless. To his great relief it worked, so they were once more able to listen in.

He was amazed to find that, during the five weeks they had been without news, nothing seemed to have happened at all. Polish resistance had almost ceased before he had been cut off from the world; and apparently the Germans and the Russians had now divided Poland amicably between them. That was hardly surprising, but the lack of activity on the Western Front struck him as quite extraordinary. Like most uninitiated people he had expected the Allies to launch an autumn campaign while the Germans were still to some extent occupied in the East. They had done nothing of the kind, yet it was transparently clear that no nation could hope to win a war simply sitting down behind a great fortified wall and making rude faces at the enemy.

This lack of activity consoled him to some extent for not being able to get into the fight. Somehow it seemed to make the whole war much less urgent because it more than ever confirmed his own view that the conflict would be a long one. Britain had dropped so far behind in the armaments race that it was going to take a long time for her to equip her new forces. The crux of the whole thing was, as he had always felt so intensely, could she keep her supply routes open against the U-boats long enough to equip her new armies and create a really powerful air force? He had striven so hard to help in that and prove to his country that there was a way out so he felt that fate had played him a scurvy trick in cutting him off from home before he had even had a chance to turn in the highly satisfactory results of his experiment. But there was nothing he could do about it now, so he settled down to wait as patiently as he could for landfall.

One thing, however, had begun to trouble him strangely and, because of it, he could no longer enjoy complete peace of mind for any length of time. As he tried to analyse this new feeling of his he came to the conclusion that he had first been conscious of it soon after the Nazi submarine men had been on board the raft; in some subtle, rather frightening way it had originated from the befouling of Gloria's drawings.

Ever since that day of their first bathe from the launch, when he had made her take off her Union Jack waistcoat and she, in a gesture of defiance, had pulled off her shorts as well, they had always bathed naked together, and gradually they had drifted into the habit of dressing and undressing in front of each other without giving it a thought.

At first, Philip had been a little shy of looking at her when she was nude, but he had posed for her many times as a model, and she so obviously regarded his form as just a matter of masses, curves and lines that he soon began to look on hers in the same way. But now, for the first time, he became conscious of her body. He would catch himself looking at it, and he began to hurry over some small task in order to get up on deck when she was about to swim so that he could watch her undressing.

He knew that he had never been in love with Lexie Foorde-Bilson. Even if he had stayed longer in the States he doubted now whether their liking for each other would have ripened into more than a rather pleasant flirtation. He had hardly given her a thought for weeks past. On the other hand, he did not think that he was in love with Gloria. The strange and frightening legacy the German had left behind on those drawings which Gloria refused to destroy was not love; and he certainly did not wish to marry her.

He had been brought up to believe that one should have principles and stick to them. Captain Vaudell had never said very much to his son about women, but he had indicated pretty clearly that one respected decent girls, making up one's mind either to marry them or leave them alone. There were plenty of the other sort for all tastes and pockets, and they should be treated well too; though they knew what they were up to and invited men's attention for their own amusement or gain. Gloria, in spite of her very dubious antecedents, must, Philip felt, be definitely classified as a " decent " girl.

They had on more than one occasion discussed sex relationships, and Gloria had made her own views perfectly clear. She said that she thought it a great mistake for a girl to make a habit of going to bed with odd men because she felt temporarily attracted to them or because they could give her a good time. That sort of thing nearly always ended badly for the girl, and, having seen quite enough of the seamy side of life, she was convinced that the game was not worth the candle. On the other hand, she was no prude and had declared that, if she fell in love with a man who was unable to marry her, she would be quite willing to live with him. But, to her, marriage was the thing. If a girl married reasonably well, she argued, it gave her security from want, the respect of decent people, and enough leisure after the housekeeping was done to pursue any hobby or art in which she might be interested.

" What about babies? " Philip had asked on one occasion.

" Yes," was the reply. She definitely wanted babies. She hoped that she would find a husband who was well enough off to give her a house-girl, so that she would not become a household drudge but could go on with her painting. If she could she felt sure that she would be able to earn sufficient to pay for a nurse. If not, that would be too bad. She was very fond of children, and she meant, if she could afford to bring them up in comfort, to have two girls and two boys. She added with somewhat startling frankness that virginity was a definite asset so far as marriage was concerned, since the steady, marrying type of man was much more likely to make a girl his wife if he knew her to be chaste; that was why she was still a virgin.

Remembering all this, Philip knew that any temptation to seduce Gloria that he might experience must be rigorously suppressed, although, had he felt otherwise, he was so inexperienced that he would hardly have known how to set about it. Yet, the fact remained that he could no longer keep his eyes off her in the daytime or sleep at night because of her presence.

Towards the end of November he realized that she had become aware of the change in the way he regarded her. As it was so much warmer they had taken to sleeping up on deck instead of in the stuffy cargo-container; and she began to slip over the side for an early swim before, as she thought, he was awake, excusing herself later in the morning from bathing with him. Later in the day she would try to choose a time when he was busy or asleep to swim again. She no longer walked about without anything round her middle, but even while sunbathing wore a coloured towel in the form of a loin-cloth.

Unfortunately, this scanty raiment, the colour of which she varied almost every day from the wholesale stock that formed part of the cargo, made her body even more alluring and, with an apparent perversity in view of these new reticences, she began to take much more trouble with her hair, trying out different styles, each of which seemed to make her more attractive.

Much sun-bathing had tanned her body a lovely golden-brown, and her skin was satiny-soft. A dozen times a day Philip found himself aching to stretch out a hand to stroke her, and whenever she brushed against him, as she occasionally did when getting down into the well or through one of the manholes, his heart seemed to stop, and it was all he could do to keep himself from trembling.

During the first week in December they were suddenly seized with a new excitement. The sun now played a much greater part in governing their lives than the time signals sent out by the wireless; and waking as usual at dawn one morning they saw land to the south-east of them.

Philip knew that they were in the latitude of the Canary Islands, and later that day he was able to confirm that the land, now due east of them, was Fuerteventura. In the meantime, two other pieces of land had become visible in the west. They were more distant than the first, but their great peaks towering to the clouds made them quite unmistakable as Grand Canary and Tenerife. The channel between the islands was fifty miles wide at its narrowest—and they were too distant from either to make out even the houses upon the nearest, let alone any human beings who might have been on the shore.

By nightfall they were entering the channel and a few scattered lights appeared along the coast of Fuerteventura. On the offchance that some of these might be the lights of fishing boats which would approach nearer, they stayed up into the small hours, but most of the lights had disappeared long before midnight, and the remainder seemed to be fixed and possibly were the breakwater beacons to tiny village harbours.

Next morning Fuerteventura was still in sight and, as they were only drifting slowly southwards, remained so for the whole of the day. In the afternoon a small fishing fleet of native craft with dhow-like sails passed within two miles of them but failed to see their signals. When evening came Fuerteventura was dropping below their limited horizon, although the more distant Tenerife was still visible, owing to the much greater elevation given to it by its 12,000 feet volcano; but the morning after that both had disappeared and the castaways were once more surrounded by an unbroken prospect of shimmering blue sea.

It was about three weeks later that Gloria discovered the rum. On the face of it, the discovery could not have been better timed as it was made on Christmas Eve. In fact, Gloria was hunting through some of the still unexplored cargo to see if she could not find some exotic additions to their Christmas dinner.

Her first impulse was to call Philip to come down and help her open the case, but she suppressed it on the sudden thought that it would be much more fun to save her find as a surprise for him next day; so she opened the case herself, got out a bottle and mixed the whole of it with an equal quantity of orange juice which she had been saving for the following day's celebration.

Next morning they exchanged the presents they had been surreptitiously making for each other. Hers to him was a portait of herself, and as she gave it to him she said rather shyly:

" It seems a fool of a present when I'm within a few yards of you day after day. But we must be rescued some time, and I thought maybe 'twould be a sort of souvenir for afterwards, if you ever wanted to think of me at all."

" But Gloria, it's lovely and a most charming thought," he assured her quickly. " I shall think of you often, too. After all, we've been alone together now for over four and a half months, so we know each other better than lots of couples who've been married for a year. I mean, that is . . . " he broke off a little awkwardly, then added with a rush: " I could never forget you."

His present for her was a piece of barbaric jewellery which he had made himself. It was a collar, in the Egyptian fashion, of many necklaces, a pendant to hang between the breasts and bracelets to match. He had made them from several hundred coffee beans, patiently stringing them together before colouring them in a bold effective pattern with some of Gloria's own paints. She was delighted with it, especially as he had gone to so much trouble on her behalf: a fact which pleased her more than the prettiness of her new ornaments which were just the type to appeal to her. She stripped off her own jewellery, to which she had clung tenaciously through all the hazards, and insisted on his putting on his presents to her. With nervous fingers he fixed the clasp of the collar at the back of the neck.

Philip had favoured having their Christmas dinner in the middle of the day, but Gloria had pointed out that, as they always had their main meal at midday, it would make more of a change to feed at night. Besides, if they had only a light snack between breakfast and dinner, they would have much better appetites. In consequence, they spent most of the day lazing and sleeping, and it was not until the sun was going down that Gloria produced her rum and orange concoction. She had cooled it as they did their water by keeping the vessel containing it out in the sun all day but wrapped in a succession of wet cloths.

As she produced the drink and poured out two generous rations, he exclaimed: "By Jove! So you kept a bottle of the orange squash up your sleeve for the big occasion! How clever of you! "

She smiled and handed him a tumbler. " I kept back quite a number of our fruit drinks. But this is something special."

He took a pull and smacked his lips. " You're right there! Whatever have you put in it?"

" Have a heart, now! Don't be tellin' me that, as well as hidin' away that case of rum for all these months, you don't even know the stuff when you taste it."

" I suppose I ought to," he laughed. " I've had it in puddings and I rather like it; but I don't think I've ever been offered it as a drink before. Scotch, gin and brandy are the three spirits one finds in most English homes and as I happen to like none of them I'm practically a teetotaller, except for an occasional glass of Madeira or Port."

" No wonder you never thought to search for this case of rum, then. But there have been times when I'd have given the eyes out of me head for a nip to quiet me tummy against the bad weather."

The bad weather of which she spoke seemed a long way behind them now. The sea, quiet as a mill pond, lapped gently at the edges of the raft, whose great bulk floated with such solidarity that it might almost have been a square flat-topped rock. As the sun went down, a ball of golden glory, into the waters to the west and the violet twilight of the tropics closed in about them, they began their meal.

Gloria's artistic imagination enabled her to make the best of their strangely assorted resources by boldly serving together various foods, the mixture of which would normally have been regarded as queer, and she had been at great pains to overcome the definite limitations with which they were faced by the complete lack of certain items. This evening she had surpassed herself, but, even so, the real high spot of the feast proved to be the liquor that went with it.

The rum and orange mixture appealed to Philip's sweet palate, and the disguised alcohol had none of the sharp breath-taking quality which he so disliked. Gloria made no secret of the fact that, after all these weeks on the wagon, it was a great treat to be drinking just for the enjoyment and fun of the thing once more. As the meal progressed they drank drink for drink, toasting each other and each other's countries, and clinking glasses and knocking back " no heel-taps " to the damnation of the Germans. After an hour they were both merrily tipsy; by the time they had finished dinner they were laughing uproariously at entirely pointless jokes and feeling absolutely on top of the world.

They tuned in to some hot jazz on the wireless and began to dance, but had to give up because they were too unsteady on their feet, so they sat down side by side and began to make the night hideous by a raucous rendering of sentimental choruses.

Presently the moon came up. Between them they had finished the first bottle of rum that Gloria had mixed with the orange squash, and Philip went to get another.

" Y'know—y'know," he declared thickly, as he pulled the cork, " if thish's being tight . . . I like it."

Gloria shouted with laughter, then she suddenly stopped and said quite seriously: "Si' down! Si' down, you're rockin' t'boat."

He sat down heavily, poured her a noggin of neat rum and slopped three fingers into his own tumbler.

As they drank he spluttered a little, laughed immediately he recovered and tipped the rest of the potion down his throat. He now felt very flushed and hot. Suddenly, an idea came to him. "I got it!" he cried. "Shwim! Let'sh go for a swim!"

Putting a hand on his shoulder she hoisted herself unsteadily to her feet. "O.K.! Race you to it!"

Undressing, though they had few things to take off, they broke no records, but staggered about bubbling with laughter at their own and each other's difficulties in getting out of their clothes.

By the time they had stripped they had forgotten all about their race and stood for a moment face to face swaying slightly, while the bright moonlight silvered their naked bodies.

Gloria raised her hand to her throat. "Me necklace," she muttered. "Can't go in wi' me necklace. Help me—take it off."

As Philip approached her she suddenly lifted her arms. "Mush' kiss you!" she declared. "Never kissed you for me necklace. Dear Boy! Happy Christmas!"

They swayed together. Philip's arms went round her body as hers locked round his neck. When his lips met hers he found that they were moist and parted. He had never kissed a girl that way before. That kiss and the feel of her golden satin skin pressed close against him did something inexplicable to him. In a single instant it had sobered him of the alcohol but filled him with a new, different drunkenness aroused by her. His clasp tightened about her till she gasped, then suddenly they lurched, lost their balance and fell.

Neither of them was hurt or even cried out, and his grip upon her hardly relaxed as they rolled over until, somehow, they were lying among the mattresses and cushions on which they had sat during dinner.

For a few minutes they hardly spoke except for his murmurs of her name between their even more violent kisses. Once she cried out and suddenly began to fight him off from her, but a moment later she was making half-sobbing, half-laughing noises and kissing him again.

Gradually they became quieter until they were lying there motionless, still clasped in each other's arms. But they were now beginning to feel the delayed effects of the rum. For a time Philip tried to fight down his rising nausea, then, with a muttered "Sorry," he simply had to break away and lurch to the side of the raft in order to be sick.

When he returned he found that she had left their couch on a similar errand, as he could see her crouching in the distant corner of the deck, and there was no doubt that she was being very ill.

On her return he wanted to speak to her but could think of nothing to say. Both mentally and physically he was feeling frightful. He would have given anything now for what had happened not to have happened. It had all been totally different from what he had expected and, except for the first kiss and the feel of her in his arms at the beginning, bitterly disappointing. He wondered how she felt about it and, much as he dreaded entering on a discussion of the subject, by an effort of will he forced himself to invite one by looking up at her and saying: "Well, how are you feeling?"

"Like hell!" she muttered, avoiding his eye; and turning away she began to rearrange her own mattress. Next moment she flopped down on it with her back towards him, and burst into tears.

He went over, knelt down beside her and laid his hand on her shoulder. He wanted to explain that he had not meant to make a mess of things and that he was terribly sorry if he had hurt her. But the words simply would not come, and with her head still buried in the pillow she threw up an arm to thrust him away.

Feeling more miserable than he had ever done in his life, he lay down himself, but the alcohol was still working on him, and, although the sea remained calm, as soon as he closed his eyes he felt as though the raft was not only heaving under him, but going round in circles as well.

Somehow he got off to sleep but only to wake in the dawn with the immediate knowledge that something had gone very wrong and that his head was aching as though someone had hit it with an outsize in sledge-hammers. Between pulsing throbs of pain the memory of all that had occurred the night before flooded back to him.

He went over the side for a swim, but evidently his moving had aroused Gloria, as shortly afterwards she, too, came in; but directly she saw him she looked quickly away and swam off out of sight round the corner of the raft.

After his dip he felt slightly better and, in spite of a nasty headache and evil-tasting mouth, decided to tackle Gloria at the earliest opportunity. Immediately she climbed out on to the deck he said:

"Look here! It's no good our being stupid about what happened last night. I'm terribly sorry . . ."

"So it's sorry you are!" she cut in sarcastically. "'Tis easy enough for the man to be sorry, but that doesn't give the girl back what she's lost, does it?"

"Really, I *am* most terribly sorry, and it wasn't altogether my fault. You kissed me first, you know."

"And what if I did?" she flared. "If all men were like you not a girl in the world would be safe at Christmas-time the second she'd a mind to thank a guy for giving her a present."

"But hang it all!" he protested. "I swear to you I didn't mean to. I wouldn't have dreamed of it if it hadn't been for all that damned rum I drank."

"What's that?" Before, she had been sullenly angry, but now she glared at him with blazing eyes. "Have you the nerve to sit there an' tell me I'm so unattractive that 'tis drunk you have to be before you'd make a pass at me! By the Holy Saints, it's true though! 'Tis the first time you've been drunk in all these months, and 'tis the first time you've ever . . . Oh, for the shame of it—I could drown myself."

"Oh hell!" exclaimed Philip, standing up. "I've said the wrong thing again. I didn't mean that at all."

The blood had drained from her face. Very quietly she hissed: "I hate you. I . . . hate . . . you!" Then she turned, lowered herself into the well and went into their old sleeping-place, where she remained for the rest of the day.

Philip, with a bad hangover adding to his other worries, spent a wretched morning. He cooked himself lunch and offered Gloria some, but she refused it. In the afternoon he slept and awoke feeling only a little better. In the early evening she came on deck munching some biscuits and sat there for a while, but she would not speak to him.

He mooned restlessly about, wondering how long this distressing state of affairs would last. For the time being at least he was cured of all desire to sleep with Gloria, and, so far as he could judge, he would never wish to do so again; but he did wish she would take a reasonable view of things and be civil.

They both went early to bed, and just as Philip was falling asleep the thought entered his mind that it needed only two or three days like that which had just passed for the two of them, compulsorily confined together as they were, to reach such a degree of hatred that one of them would murder the other. And Gloria, lying only a few feet away from him, was thinking exactly the same thing.

It was perhaps the naturally extreme antithesis for the equally unreasoning passion which they had shown for each other the previous night. But neither of them could be expected to recognize that; all they could do was to hope that something would occur to break the ghastly tension which it was beyond their powers to break for themselves.

Something did happen. They awakened the following morning to find that, after a journey of nearly five months, the raft had beached itself during the night on the shores of Africa.

CHAPTER X

THE HORROR THAT LURKED ON THE FORESHORE

GLORIA woke first, and her excited cry roused Philip. From the observations which he took every few days he knew that for some time they had been drifting almost parallel with the north-western coast of Africa and between forty and fifty miles from it; but he had not checked their position since Christmas Eve, and it was December the 27th. In the past three days a current must have carried them shorewards, and the fact that they had not seen any coastline on the horizon the previous evening was accounted for by its lowness.

For as far as they could see on either side the foreshore sloped gently upwards to a ridge of low sand-dunes which were unbroken by any signs of human habitation or even a group of palm trees. It was very far from being the kind of landfall of which they had dreamed so often, but after all these weeks afloat the fact of the raft having beached itself was a tremendous event.

It had grounded on a spit of sand and, now that the tide was rapidly running out, had begun to tilt a little. There were still a hundred yards of gently lapping wavelets between the raft and the beach, but the water was both clear and shallow. On a common impulse Gloria and Philip slipped over the side and splashed ashore.

Shouting and laughing they ran side by side along the beach, then up the nearest sand-dune to its crest. The prospect was not by any means alluring. It was just sand-dunes and yet more sand-dunes until the yellow distance melted into the pale blue of the early morning sky.

" What a mightly lonely spot," said Gloria in a hushed voice, when she had regained her breath. " What part of Africa would we be in, Boy? "

"This is Rio de Oro," replied Philip, " and it belongs to Spain. The Sahara Desert runs right up to the sea here. In fact, thousands of years ago, when the Atlantic was quite a bit higher than it is now, the whole of the Sahara was a great inland sea joined to the ocean, and this strip of coast was part of the sea bottom. That's why it's one of the most desolate spots in the world."

"How far does this empty bit go?" asked Gloria.

" Rio de Oro stretches for about eight hundred to a thousand miles, and to the south of it there's another six hundred miles of the French West African coast which is much the same. The nearest fertile country is Morocco to the north and Senegal to the south."

" But doesn't anyone live in these parts at all?"

" Oh yes. There are a few small towns and villages dotted along the coast. It may mean a day or two's walking but we're bound to strike human habitations sooner or later."

"The Saints be praised for that! " sighed Gloria with relief. " But, d'you know, I'm feeling slightly seasick?"

" Yes. The ground seems to be going up and down, doesn't it? " Philip laughed. " It's only because we've been afloat so long. We'll soon get used to it again."

They returned to the raft for breakfast and afterwards studied Philip's atlas. Gloria was appalled to see that in the irregular triangle of yellow marked Rio de Oro only two places were shown: Kedda, about a third of the way down it and about thirty miles inland, and Villa Cisneros, a port considerably nearer to its southern border. Philip said he thought that they had landed somewhere to the south of Cape Bojador.

The observation that he took proved him to be correct and he worked out that they were about a hundred and twenty miles from Kedda. The sun was now scorching down on them and, as Philip pointed out, they would be mad to undertake a march of that distance in such terrific heat without very careful preparation.

They were too excited to sleep, but rested in the shade during the afternoon and carried a picnic supper ashore in the evening. During their weeks at sea they had seen many fine sunsets but few to equal the glory of the one they watched from the African shore that evening. Soon after the sun had gone down, however, they were startled by an uncanny rustling and clicking in a patch of large bleached conch shells near which they were sitting.

Philip flashed his torch on the patch, and they were alarmed to see among the white shell a score of black, spidery-looking bodies. It was a company of land-crabs which had evidently been attracted by the picnic meal.

At the sight of them Gloria screamed, but the crabs did not scuttle away either at the sound or at the flashing of the light. They remained there motionless, staring with a quiet menace. Then, after a moment, some of the nearest ones began to advance, making swift little rushes forward.

" Quick! " gasped Gloria. " Back to the raft, Boy! Back to the raft! " And she fled down the shelving beach into the water.

Philip remained only long enough to grab up the picnic things before following her; and, as he ran, it filled him with considerable perturbation to think that the difficulties of their journey along the coast would be enormously increased if each night they had to protect their stores—and perhaps themselves—from similar companies of big crabs.

On the following day the preparations for the trek to Kedda, or any village in that direction, were begun, and the work entailed was considerable.

From some of the sails they fashioned a simple low tent, to shelter them from the blistering sun during the midday heat, and two large knapsacks in which to carry their supplies. Then they had to make a careful selection of foods combining nutritious value with lightness of weight, and to distil an extra quantity of fresh water. At last everything was ready, and early on the morning of January the 1st, 1940, they took a last look round the raft, every corner of which they had come to know so well, and went ashore.

The going was not easy as the additional weight of the heavy packs seemed to make their feet sink into the soft sand, and every now and again they had to cross a patch of broken conch shells, which meant that they had to pick their way in order to avoid stumbling or bruising their feet.

From ten o'clock until three in the afternoon they rested, blessing the forethought which had led them to provide themselves with a tent, then went on again till eight o'clock, when they called a halt for supper and the night.

With occasional intervals for rest they had been on the move the best part of eight hours, and, in spite of the modest pace forced upon them by the sand, Philip felt that they must have covered twenty miles at least. Yet all day they had come across no sign of human habitation. Mile after mile of the same flat, sandy coastline had opened up before them as they rounded the headland of each long shallow bay, and only on three occasions had the prospect been enlivened by groups of stunted palms clinging precariously to life among the sand-dunes.

Unaccustomed as they were to any exercise other than swimming, they found that the long trudge had played havoc with the muscles of their legs; but once they were able to unload their packs the very thought that they were not going any further that night temporarily dissipated their tiredness, and as the sun was going down they cheerfully set about the preparations for their evening meal. Yet they were only halfway through their supper when the thing that Philip had been fearing happened; he caught the sinister click and rustle that told him as plainly as if he could see them that some land-crabs were coming out of their holes.

Gloria caught the sound too and turned a white face towards him. "What's that?" she asked sharply, although she already knew.

"It's some more of those beastly crabs," he said, striving to keep out of his voice the uneasiness he was feeling. "They won't do us any harm. It's the food they're after. I think we'd better move camp further inland."

Collecting their things as quickly as they could they trudged up the slope to the top of the nearest sand-dune and, before bothering to re-erect the tent, sat down to finish their meal.

To their annoyance and alarm the respite proved to be a brief one. Within ten minutes of their settling down the clicking sound, which Philip thought must be made by the knocking together of the crabs' long shell-encased legs, came again from the seaward slope of the dune.

As Gloria stood up Philip signed her to stay where she was, and grabbing a thick piece of wood that they used for the main strut of the tent he advanced to the brow of the hill. For the past half-hour night had been coming down, and the rapidity with which it descends in the tropics had left just enough light for him to make out twenty or thirty of the creatures coming up the slope towards him.

The instant they saw him they halted with the precision of well-trained troops at a given word of command, but after a moment first one then another began to come forward again in little furtive rushes. Hoping to scare them off, Philip ran forward and slashed at the nearest of them with the thick stick he was carrying, but the brute dodged the blow with cat-like agility. Meantime the others had all halted once more, but as soon as he ceased his futile blows they came on again, passing out of range of his blows to either side of him.

" Boy! Oh quickly! Help! " came a cry from Gloria, and hurrying back to her he found that she was standing between the haversacks and that eight or ten of the crabs had formed a half-circle within four or five feet of her.

They were repulsive beasts, very much like great spiders, nearly a foot in height and considerably more across. Their bodies were small but their legs were long and very hairy, with sharp, dagger-pointed claws. As they crouched there, they remained quite still, except for their mouths which moved continually with a kind of slobbering twitching.

Rushing at them with his stick, Philip drove them from in front of Gloria, but only for them to form up in a series of furtive sidlings behind her, while another dozen or more came scrambling over the brow of the slope to fill the gap he had made. A few more minutes and they were completely encircled by a ring of thirty crabs at least, and others were still appearing out of the surrounding gloom.

" We must go further inland," muttered Philip. " They won't follow us there. They're filthy-looking brutes but there's nothing to be frightened of."

Picking up his things he began to strike out at the crabs again, and they gave back as he moved forward; while Gloria, carrying the other haversack, followed close upon his heels. As they advanced the number of crabs in front of them decreased, but only to swell the ranks of those behind and on either side of them until there was no longer anything left to strike at, and they were walking across the sand-dunes accompanied by a sickle-moon-shaped phalanx of the crabs that stopped when they stopped and advanced when they advanced, keeping in perfect time with them.

" What—what'll we do?" whispered Gloria in a scared voice, after they had covered the best part of a mile. " I'm scared, Boy, and I'm tired. I'm so tired I could drop."

" I know. I'm tired too," Philip agreed. " But I feel certain the brutes won't go more than a certain distance from shore. D'you think you can make another mile?"

" Yeah, I'll make it somehow," she muttered.

They trudged on for another twenty minutes, then Gloria suddenly pulled up short. " It doesn't seem to be working out," she said, casting a frightened glance over her shoulder. " There's just as many of them following us as ever."

Philip halted beside her. " If we could go on walking away from the coast long enough I know we'd shake them off, but the trouble is that I daren't go too far inland in case when we wake up to-morrow we find that we're lost in the desert."

" A lot I'd care if only I could sit down some place where these things couldn't get at me."

E

"They won't attack us—it's the food they're after."

"Well, they'll get it when we're so tired that we just have to quit walkin': an' maybe they'll go for us too, then."

That was just what Philip had been thinking. He knew nothing of the habits of the African land-crab, but he remembered hearing stories of ship-wrecked sailors having been attacked in their sleep and eaten by land-crabs in some of the Pacific islands.

"Perhaps we'd better give them the food then," he said for a moment, "but we haven't got anything like enough loose food to satisfy this lot—nearly everything we've got is in tins."

"You'll have to keep them off with your stick while I'll be diggin' a hole in each of the tins with the opener. If they can smell the food they'll worry the tins with those long spiky claws until they've got out every morsel."

"That's the idea, and the longer it takes them to get the food out the better. You realize though that if we give these devils all our food we'll never be able to reach Kedda without assistance? Neither of us is up to marching a hundred miles on nothing but water."

"Sure; but we could go on for another day and maybe we'd come upon a village."

The crabs had now formed a thick, rustling, clicking circle round them, and it seemed to undulate with a peculiar life of its own as Philip lunged forward with his stick.

Without more ado they set down the packs and, while Gloria crouched at Philip's feet, fear lending speed and strength to her fingers as she jabbed the opener into tin after tin, he moved round and round her, swiping at the more daring of the brutes as they pressed forward, and throwing out each of the tins as she handed them to him at the spot where the crush of crabs seemed densest.

As they worked he talked all the time, partly with the idea of trying to keep Gloria's mind occupied and partly to sort out his own thoughts as to what was the best thing to do. His conclusion was that as soon as most of the crabs were occupied they should break out of the ring with any food they had left. But the problem was which way to run? He decided, since they had no idea how far the crabs might follow them in-land, that it would be best to get back to the beach. Land-crabs, he believed, did not go into the sea; so, if necessary, they could throw them off by wading out into the shallow water.

The starlight was now sufficiently bright for them to see the results of their appeasement measure. Each thing they had thrown out was instantly pounced upon by a number of the crabs, but apparently the brutes were endowed with sufficient intelligence to realize that there was more stuff in the knapsacks, and the bulk of them seemed content to wait until something was thrown near enough for them to be fairly sure of getting at it before it was submerged under the hard, hairy bodies of some of their companions. In consequence, Gloria had nearly used up her supplies before even half the crabs had been given something to occupy them.

As soon as Philip realized the situation he said: " Save what's left and we'll make a break for the beach. If they come after us we can throw the rest of the things out as we go, to delay them."

" Give me a minute now, to stab holes in the rest of the tins," said Gloria quickly. "Then, when I say the word, we'll go."

They managed the break-out as the crabs drew back immediately Philip began to thrash about with his big stick; but, as he had feared, all of them that were not busy eating came clicking and rustling on their heels.

For the first half-mile they ran, but within two minutes of dropping into a walk the crabs caught up with them, so they began to throw out the rest of their supplies. These were soon exhausted but provided them with a spell which enabled them to run on again. When next the crabs caught up with them Gloria started to throw all the other things out of her knapsack, regardless of their future value.

" Steady on!" cried Philip, as he saw one of their precious water containers crash on the scaly form of one of the great spider-like creatures. " If you do that there'll be no going on to-morrow."

" Who cares!" she sobbed. " They'll eat us if we can't get clear. I know they will!"

Philip had an uneasy feeling that she was not just giving way to panic, but was right. The crabs might not be bold enough to attack them so long as they were able to remain on their feet and put up a fight, but would do so the moment they sat down or showed any signs of exhaustion. Throwing out the food had greatly reduced their numbers, and a few more remained behind to tear at each of the things that Gloria was now sacrificing, so he began to follow her example.

By the time they had reached the beach all their water bottles, utensils, torches and other impedimenta, including the two haversacks and the tent, had gone; but at least they were now free of their encumbrances and not more than a dozen crabs were still grimly sticking to the chase. For the past ten minutes they had been alternating between a fast walk and a jog-trot. Now, by making a final effort, they left the remaining crabs well behind and, after running a last quarter of a mile southward along the shore, turned west to splash out through the shallow water until it was up to their knees.

For the best part of an hour they stood there supporting themselves first on one foot and then on the other; miserable, dejected and so tired that they could have cried. Yet they did not dare to wade ashore.

A million stars twinkled brightly in the velvet sky overhead, but their light was not enough to show the beach clearly at that distance, and many patches of shadow might be hiding groups of their repulsive and terrifying enemies. The only sound was the murmur of the great combers on a reef further out, on which the ceaseless Atlantic swell broke its force before lapping the foreshore. Every muscle of their bodies ached and their legs seemed about to fail under them. Their anger and despondency were further increased by the knowledge that they had had their journey for nothing. Having abandoned their water bottles they could not now go on the next day; instead, they were faced with a long and tiring trek back to the raft.

At last the moon came up, and its strong silvery light showed that many of the frightening patches of shadow on the beach were due only to inequalities in its surface. Cautiously, and still keeping a sharp lookout for the least movement, they splashed their way ashore; but nothing stirred, and, sighing with relief, they flung themselves down on the soft sand just above the tidemark.

Philip still feared that the crabs might reappear and attack them if they were both asleep, so he determined to remain on watch for as long as possible, but he made Gloria put her head in his lap. Almost at once she fell into the heavy slumber of exhaustion. He managed to keep his eyes open for another hour or so, but he was afraid to move in case he disturbed her, and having to remain still proved too much of a handicap for him as a sentry. His chin slumped on to his chest, and he gradually slipped forward until, without knowing anything about it, he was faintly snoring.

In spite of his fatigue, owing to his uncomfortable position he woke early, and, immediately he recalled that the day held for them a twenty mile journey without food, water, or even shelter from the sun, he roused Gloria, so that they could make the most of the early morning hours. There was no breakfast for them to cook and no equipment to be packed, so, after washing their hands and faces in the sea to freshen themselves up, they set out to retrace their footsteps of the day before.

As they were now free of burdens they travelled much more comfortably and swiftly for the first part of the journey, but their troubles began soon after ten o'clock. With a power which now seemed to increase every minute, the sun shone full in their faces, and in all that desolate landscape there was nowhere that offered shelter from its rays. When they felt they could no longer face it they took refuge for an hour in a dip behind the highest sand-dune they could find, lying flat in its bottom, but in less than an hour the sun had uncovered the whole hollow, and the sand round them became almost scorching to their touch. By midday the sea seemed to be the only place where they could get relief for their parched bodies, so they undressed and went in.

By contrast the water seemed, at first, ice-cold and made them gasp, but it refreshed them enormously as well as alleviating, to some extent, their thirst, which had been troubling them considerably for the past hour or more. After a little they fetched their hats and put them on, before sitting down in the shallows, submerged up to their necks; but even so they remained acutely uncomfortable until they judged that the worst of the day was over and came out to dress and resume their journey at about four o'clock.

The last half dozen miles were grim going, as, although both of them had had ample opportunity to get hardened to the sun during the past few weeks, they had never before had to remain exposed to it for a whole day; and its heat on the raft had always been greatly tempered by the surrounding water, whereas on land it not only scorched down from overhead but was also reflected upwards from the shimmering sand. Both of them knew that they had been badly sunburnt from the way their skins were hotting up, and the painful scorching set in long before they reached the raft.

At last, as they dragged their weary feet over a small promontory, the raft came into view. Philip silently thanked all his gods as it was now no longer an uncomfortable makeshift quarter which had been the means of saving their lives in a desperate situation. It was drink and food in abundance, shelter, cleanliness, comfort and all the amenities for which two castaways could reasonably ask. It was home, and something more even than that, because they both knew now that without it they would have been condemned to die of thirst and exposure to a merciless sun, becoming food for the crabs, perhaps even before death overtook them, on that grim and inhospitable shore.

With unutterable relief they waded out to the spit of sand on which the raft lay, and clambered aboard to relieve their thirst with the first bottle they could lay hands on in Gloria's old " kitchen." But that night they were in such pain from their sunburn that they could get no sleep and could lie flat only on their backs, which were the least affected.

The following day they had nasty yellow blisters on their arms, necks, foreheads, hands and insteps; and, at times, were almost delirious. They had set out for Kedda on the 1st of January, and it was the 8th before they were really free of the pain of their burns and could bear to wear any clothes on their bodies without acute discomfort.

In the meantime, they had fully discussed their misadventures, and Gloria declared that nothing in the world would induce her to set out on any second attempt to reach Kedda.

Philip agreed but pointed out that, while they had not had the good fortune to strike a fishing village during a whole day's march to the north, there might quite well be one only a few miles away round the next headland to the south; so it was decided that when they were fully recovered from their burns they should make a day's expedition along the coast which they had so far not explored.

With vivid memories of the midday sun still fresh in their minds, they not only made another tent from some more of the sailcloth, but also two hats with huge floppy brims which would protect their shoulders as well as their heads. Then, well before dawn on January the 12th, they set out.

The coast that they traversed differed in no way from that they had seen to the north ten days earlier; but they made better going as they were travelling lighter, having only the tent, one bottle of water and their lunch to carry. Philip reckoned that they covered about fourteen miles before the heat became so intense that they had to set up their tent and take shelter; but during the whole trek they had not come across a single sign of any inhabitants of this barren land.

At four o'clock they started back and when sunset came they were still a good two miles from home. Soon after sundown they heard again that horrid all too familiar clicking. Before long a number of the land-crabs were following a few yards behind them and furtively keeping pace with them on either side. They were both very tired after their many hours of walking, but, in spite of that, Gloria insisted on breaking into a run in order to get away from their horrible companions.

Alternately walking and running as the crabs came up with them, they covered the last mile and, with renewed relief, waded out to the square squat bulk on the sandspit, which they had now come to regard as their only sanctuary from the creeping horror that lurked on the beach by night.

When they talked over the situation on the following day Gloria said that she never would have believed that any part of the world could be quite so deserted. So Philip produced his atlas and showed her that the population in Rio de Oro was given as less than one to the square mile, which meant that, allowing for the two towns there was probably only one village in every four or five hundred square miles of territory; perhaps even less as most of the inhabitants outside the towns would be roving tribes of Bedouin Arabs, maintaining a precarious existence by moving from oasis to oasis with their flocks.

Philip was anxious to think up some method by which oil or fire could be used to keep off the crabs and thus make possible a longer expedition to the north, but Gloria declared that nothing could ever persuade her to spend another night on shore; so it seemed that the only thing for them to do was to wait until they were either sighted by some coasting vessel or a caravan trekking along the sand-dunes.

For three weeks they took turns at keeping a look-out in between spells of collecting shell fish from the rock-pools to vary their diet, but the only vessels they saw were steamers far out to sea, and the monotony of their vigil was broken only once by the sight of human beings on the land. These were two Arabs mounted on camels. Philip saw them through his binoculars as they rode up to a distant promontory, to remain there for a few minutes looking out to sea before turning inland and riding off again.

His knowledge of desert Arabs was derived almost entirely from exciting fiction which he had read in his schooldays, and he had not the least idea if Bedouin tribes were, as portrayed in these stories, still cruel, treacherous and hostile to Europeans, or whether the civilizing influence of motorcars and aeroplanes during recent years had changed them into mild-mannered,

friendly characters. One thing which somewhat perturbed him was that
the two men he had seen had been draped from head to foot in a blue-
black material, instead of the usual white *burnous*. He remembered that,
according to his fiction, this particular raiment was worn only by the
Toureg Arabs, the fiercest of all the tribes, who were so dreaded throughout North Africa that they were known as " The Forgotten of God."

It was this new uneasiness as to the kind of treatment they might receive if they were discovered by a troop of wild tribesmen that first made
Philip consider the possibility of endeavouring to re-float the raft and
manœuvre it down the coast until they reached Villa Cisneros.

Gloria agreed that, since it looked as if they might remain where they
were for months without a ship coming within hailing distance of them,
it was a good idea; so at the next low tide they both went over the side to
make a full examination of the sandpit and see what chance there was of
getting the heavy raft off it.

The raft had been so well made in the New York shipyard that its
triple float of huge criss-crossed logs showed little sign of wear. Only
about a third of its bottom was actually above water at low tide, but this
one corner of it was now firmly embedded in the sand, its weight having
worked against the spit with every incoming tide for the past five weeks.
However, Philip thought that, if they dug the surrounding sand away
at every low tide, they would gradually create a depression in the spit
where the raft's corner rested on it; so they set to work with the gardening
tools that had formed part of the cargo from the U.S.A.

It was slow and tiring work as every spadeful of sand dug out had to
be carted far enough away in a bucket to ensure that it did not seep back;
but gradually the depression took shape, and as it deepened the tilt of the
raft slowly lessened, until on the afternoon of February the 20th, under
the lift of an unusually high tide, it floated free.

Against this exciting eventuality, they had prepared two long implements made from several lengths of stout wood securely tied together,
which could be used either as poles or sweeps, and an anchor consisting of
all the heavy metal objects they could find, collected into three sacks, one
inside the other, and firmly attached to a length of cable. The idea was to
pole their unwieldy craft through the shallows from day to day, and to
anchor it in as sheltered a spot as could be found each night.

At the moment they were virtually anchored by the cables which still
attached them to Number Two raft and the other two of the original
string, which had been washed up with them on the African coast. Philip
had left the connection for fear that a tide should carry the Number One
raft off in the night when he and Gloria were both asleep; but now he
knocked out the shackles, and picking up one of the long sweeps began
his first attempt to guide their floating home towards the southern pro-
monotory of the bay.

As long as they were able to remain in the calm waters close inshore it
proved easier than he had expected, but a ridge of rocks ran out from the

cape, and to get round it they were forced to find a gap in the reef and go out through it into the open sea. Here, the great Atlantic rollers were pounding with their dull thunder, and, although in the calm weather they broke quite harmlessly against the raft, it became extraordinarily difficult to control it. By a desperate prodding they managed to stave the raft off the reef and pole it in through the next opening round the corner; after which they felt that they had done quite enough for a first effort, and anchored for the night in the far bay.

Next day they successfully negotiated two more capes, and the whole of the day after was spent in poling down a long straight stretch of coast towards a group of sand-dunes that formed another headland. It was that which proved their undoing. When in the cool of the early morning, they began to manœuvre the raft out through a channel in the reef they found it to be too deep for them to reach the bottom with their poles, and the backwash of a big wave suddenly drew them out of reach of the reef itself.

For some minutes they did nothing, expecting to be swept in again, but it seemed that the raft had become caught in a local current as it began to drift along quite quickly almost parallel with the reef but gradually edging a little further from it. The second they realized what was happening they began to thrash the water with their long sweeps, using every ounce of energy they had, but their efforts were unavailing. Out there among the breaking surf it needed far more than the strength of any man and girl to influence the course of that huge, square floating bulk, and after half an hour of frantic paddling they gave up, realizing its futility, and collapsed panting on the deck.

Apart from the time of the great storm, the three days that followed were as anxious as any they had spent since the Raft Convoy had started on its way across the Atlantic. Every hour carried a hope that a change of the wind, the next incoming tide or a sudden break in the weather would cause the raft to be driven ashore again; but, on the contrary, it gradually drifted further out until, on the evening of February the 26th, the low coast of Africa was only a smudge on the skyline, and on the morning of the 27th it had finally disappeared.

Philip moodily made a fresh study of his atlas and charts and reported his findings to an equally gloomy Gloria.

" The prevailing winds here are the North-East Trades, and the currents appear to run more or less with them. So it looks as if we'll be carried right back across the Atlantic again and make our next landfall in Brazil."

" Brazil is it? " she tossed her red head. " To be sure, it was a great idea of yours, this raft; if it's travel one would be wantin', an' to see the world. Still, seein' we've been cooped up together for over six months now another six or eight weeks of each other's company won't prove the death of us."

Philip hastened to agree and tactfully refrained from challenging her estimate for their second crossing of the Atlantic. The current towards Brazil was nothing like so powerful as the Gulf Stream, and, if the winds proved contrary or erratic, it might have little influence on their direction. On leaving America he had had an absolute faith in his Raft Convoy being brought to within easy towing distance of a European port, and, as they had drifted south from Gibraltar, he had been pretty confident that they would sooner or later be washed up on the North-West coast of Africa, but now he had no firm conviction at all about what land they were most likely to see next, let alone when they would see it.

He knew from sailors' tales of casting bottles over the sides of ships with messages in them addressed to their sweethearts that such flotsam often took five—ten—or even fifteen years before it was washed up, and, after all, the raft was scarcely bigger by a calculable fraction when compared with the immensity of the seas. They might just bob about like an empty bottle, driven first one way then another by the caprice of the winds and tides for months or even years without getting anywhere at all.

With these gloomy thoughts he became almost obsessed during the next few days, so that Gloria began to worry about his depression and did her best to cheer him up; until the coming of another storm gave them something else to think about.

This time it was all that they had experienced before, only worse. They had never believed that the raft could tilt to such an angle without capsizing completely. For two nights they were at the mercy of a tropical hurricane, and at the end of the second day they doubted their ability to live it out. On the first signs of the storm they had made everything as ship-shape as possible in preparation for it, then retired to their old sleeping quarters with sufficient iron rations to last them several meals, and closed the manhole firmly behind them. But by the second evening Philip could bear the confinement no longer. The lack of ventilation, the smell and the nausea were such that he felt that, if he did not get a few mouthfuls of fresh air, he would choke and die in one final bout of sickness. Pulling on his oilskins he opened the trap and wriggled through it.

A foot and a half of water was slopping about in the well, and he had hardly closed the manhole when a big wave came right over the raft, temporarily submerging him up to the chest. For a second he gasped, then, as the water receded, got a firm grip on the short central mast of the raft and began to take in the terrifying spectacle around him.

The great storm had brought an early dusk, and the light was already fading; yet it was enough for him to see the white crest that topped a huge wave across a hundred yard long slope of water which rapidly became a towering wall, before which he instinctively gave back. It was at that moment, just as the wave was about to break, that he caught sight of a vague, dark blur only a few feet away from him and wondered what it could possibly be that cast such a deep, almost solid, shadow in that corner of the well.

E*

The spate of water from the wave flooded all about him, temporarily blinding him with its spray, but when he could see once more his breath caught in his throat with something between fear and intense excitement. His eyes almost starting from his head in amazement, he stared open-mouthed at the corner of the well. Where before there had been only a vague black shadow there was now a seemingly solid figure. Within a few feet of him was standing a man, or at least a presence in human form.

CHAPTER XI

THE SILENT CONTINENT

It was not until the presence turned its face towards him that Philip suddenly realized its likeness to the Canon. He had never seen a ghost before, yet somehow he had no doubt at all that he was face to face with the spirit of Beal-Brookman.

"You are naturally surprised to see me," the figure remarked in a conversational voice. "But I asked permission to visit you for a special purpose. How are you getting on, Philip?"

Philip was so astonished that he could only falter: "Oh—er—all right."

"I'm glad of that because I feared you might be worried. You have no cause to be, you know."

"Er—thanks." Philip swallowed hard, then suddenly found his tongue and went on quickly: "When I said I was all right, though, I didn't mean that I was at all happy about being adrift like this. The old Raft Convoy turned out a hundred per cent success, but before they could tow us in we got caught up in a storm, and now we're God knows where."

"I know. I was so pleased that the Raft Convoy proved successful. But you must not worry about being unable to give the full results of your success to the Admiralty. That is quite immaterial now, as you may have already realized if you remember what I once said to you about the Great Planners."

Philip shook his head. "I'm afraid I don't quite follow."

"It was when we were talking of Atlantis, I think. Anyhow, I told you that the Great Ones often achieve their ends by methods which seem absurdly devious or even quite inexplicable to those who are still on earth. They have an end for you, or perhaps it would be better to call it a mission."

"I see," said Philip cautiously. "What do they want me to do?"

"I'm sorry, but I'm not allowed to tell you, because any foreknowledge of it would prejudice your own testing. What I *can* tell you is that your Raft Convoy idea was all part of the great design, because if you had not thought of that you would not be here or able to reach the place to which you are being sent."

" Oh, I say! If you know when the raft is going to be washed ashore you might at least tell me that! "

" No, that is forbidden. All I can say is that you have a long voyage and an even longer ordeal in front of you. That is why I sought permission to come to you to-night. I wanted to urge you to meet whatever difficulties and dangers you may encounter with a stout heart. They will all be opportunities to practise fortitude and courage, and if you survive the earlier tests you will need those qualities in a very high degree when you reach your journey's end. You are a chosen vessel, Philip, and if you prove equal to the burden that has been laid upon you no man of your generation will have done more to help bring about the defeat of Germany."

As it finished speaking the apparition began rapidly to disintegrate.

" One moment! " shouted Philip. " Don't go! Please don't go! " But the likeness of Beal-Brookman had already disappeared, and he thought that he was alone again until Gloria's voice came from behind him with the question:

" What is it, Boy? What are you shouting for? "

He turned to find her leaning half out of the manhole, and replied a little awkwardly: " Oh, nothing. I was just talking to myself."

" You were not," she said firmly. " You were talking to someone else. I heard you."

He motioned to her to go in, followed her, and sitting down asked her seriously: " Do you believe in ghosts? "

" Indeed I do! " She crossed herself quickly, and even by the light of the swinging oil lamp her drawn face seemed to go a shade paler as she added: " But don't tell me we've to add a haunting to all our other troubles."

" No, there's nothing to be frightened of. Of course, I may have been dreaming—walking and talking in my sleep—but I don't think so. Anyhow, it seemed to me that I was talking to Canon Beal-Brookman, a great friend of mine who died just on a year ago."

" What did he want with you? "

" To tell me that we need not fear being drowned, but that we have a very long journey in front of us. It seems that the ' Powers that Be ' decreed that we should spend a long time on this raft until it eventually carries us to a place from which we may have great difficulty in getting home, but when we do I . . ." He broke off suddenly and gave a not very convincing laugh. " Well, I shall be offered the opportunity of assassinating Hitler, or something."

" 'Tis nothing to joke about," she said soberly. " Such visitations are permitted by the good God and His Blessed Saints only as a warning to us. Indeed, this one makes plain much that was hidden."

" How d'you mean? "

" Why look at the way we've missed chance after chance of bein' rescued all these weeks. If a ship ever does come towards us sure an' the night will be upon us before she's near enough to see our signals. And when we did get ashore in Africa what happened then? 'Twas chased off it we were by those lousy crabs, and in no time at all we found ourselves back on the raft adrift on the sea again."

" That's quite true," he admitted. " It does look rather as if our extra-ordinary voyage had been ordained. It was the Canon, too, who appeared to me in a dream that saved me from Eiderman, and his voice that told me to take to the raft when the launch was sinking under us."

" You never told me that."

" Didn't I. Well, it's the sort of thing one never cares to swear to after-wards, because it seems too fantastic to be true, however real it may have seemed at the time.   I didn't see the Canon then—I only heard his voice—but it was clear to me as the sight of him was to-night."

Gloria nodded.   " Let's hope he'll prove our Guardian Angel, then. Anyhow, the weather seems to be the better for his visit."

There was no doubt that during the past quarter of an hour the storm had eased; so now that the raft was gyrating less frantically they settled down again to get some sleep.

On the following day a high sea was still running, but the weather had improved enough for them to be able to straighten up the disorder that always resulted from a storm.   A part of the cargo had shifted, causing some breakages, the most serious of which was the radio set; but Philip unpacked the third and last one to replace it, and they could only hope that no further misadventure would rob them of it before they reached their unknown destination.

By the time that all traces of the hurricane had disappeared it was getting on for mid-March, and Philip's observations showed that they were very slowly drifting south-westwards towards the coast of Brazil. An uneventful month followed, and they were still over a thousand miles from the South American coast when the radio gave the stupendous news that on the 9th of April Hitler had invaded Denmark and Norway.

At last, after all these months of inactivity since the conclusion of the Polish campaign, one of the great antagonists had made a move, although it was far from being the orthodox offensive that most people had expected.

The Allied military commentators were full of optimism and appeared to think that Hitler had stuck out his neck.   They had ample excuse for their attitude in the pronouncements of a no less distinguished person than the Prime Minister, who was presumably the best-informed man in Britain. Mr. Neville Chamberlain told the House that Hitler had " missed the 'bus." The only conclusion to which Philip could come a few weeks later was that either the Government and its military advisers dwelt in a cloud-cuckoo land of their own and refused to accept the information that they were given, or that the much vaunted British Secret Service had fallen into decay between the two wars and was now no more good than an old rattle.

To Philip's surprise and secret amusement the Nazi invasion of Norway brought Gloria into the war on the side of Britain, and her attitude changed from one of mildly benevolent neutrality towards the Allies to one of violent and voluble denunciation of the Germans.

For some reason that remained obscure she regarded the Czechs and Poles as troublesome, bellicose people who liked wars and therefore had no right to complain if they got hurt in them; while, to her mind, Britain and France were senile, top-heavy states with possessions far greater than they were capable of managing efficiently. If they wanted to keep their ill-gotten gains it was only fair that they should have to fight for them every quarter of a century against some younger, more virile nation such as Germany. But Norway! And poor little Denmark. They were neutrals—*real neutrals*—people who did not want to fight and had nothing to gain by fighting. As she said in one of her early outbursts on the subject:

" Why, it's just terrible Hitler attacking people like that, and without warning too! It's pretty near as bad as if he'd planned a secret landing in the United States."

" He would plan one," said Philip drily, " if it wasn't for Britain in between. What's more, if we weren't fighting him and he did land an army in America you'd be in a pretty mess, because there's damn' little you'd be able to do about it."

" Hell! We'd do plenty! " Gloria's blue eyes sparkled.

" I don't doubt you'd want to, but you couldn't; anyhow not until those million men of your first emergency call-up are trained and you have built up a really sizeable Air Force. If Hitler landed an army in the United States before that, you'd have a pretty thin time."

" Don't you worry. 'Twouldn't even get there! Maybe our Air Force isn't all that hot yet—I wouldn't know—but I do know we've got a mighty fine Navy."

Philip nodded. " Yes. That might save your bacon—provided that the Nazis hadn't landed in Canada or Mexico and established air bases in one or the other first. When you say you've got a fine Navy what you really mean is that you've got a lot of big ships. Well, so have we; but it still has to be proved that they are going to be worth the thousands of men and invaluable seafaring talent that is locked up in them. Just look here a minute."

Opening the atlas, he pointed to the Skagerrak. " See that nice piece of open water there between Norway and Denmark. It is nowhere much less than a hundred miles wide. The Germans have to send all their reinforcements and supplies across that to maintain their armies in Norway. Now, the British and French Navies together are at least four times as strong in capital ships as the Germany Navy. Yet they dare not go in and cut the German supply route. The simple fact is that, for the first time in this war, apart from its basic function of blockade, the Navy has been given the opportunity to play a major strategic rôle, but finds itself incapable of taking it.

"In Nelson's time it was different. He swept those waters and sailed his fleet right round through the narrower Kattegat to bombard Copenhagen. In his day a British battle squadron would have cruised there for weeks, or months, if need be, until the German Armies in Norway, entirely cut off from their bases and denied all warlike supplies, were compelled to throw in their hand. But it can't be done in Nineteen Forty. The poor old Admirals still go on building their big ships, but at least they have the sense to know that one little aircraft sneaking out of a cloud with one armour-piercing bomb may prove a match for the biggest of them at any time. And as for sending the British Fleet to cruise in the Skagerrak in the face of the Luftwaffe—well, by the end of the week there wouldn't be any British Fleet."

By early May they were within a few degrees of the Equator and there, to their dismay, they became becalmed. It seemed that they had entered a tract of ocean uninfluenced by any current, and hardly a breath of wind came to ruffle the blue waters that shimmered faintly under the blazing sun.

Then on May the 10th came the news that the Germans had at last launched their attack against Holland and Belgium. To Philip it seemed that this great battle might prove the crux of the whole war, and it irked him bitterly to be away from home and so utterly helpless to aid his country's cause at such a time. Gloria heard him the night the big news came through angrily stamping up and down the deck quoting Shakespeare's "King Henry V."

> "And gentlemen in England now abed
> Shall think themselves accursed they were not here;
> And hold their manhood cheap while any speaks
> That fought with us upon Saint Crispin's Day."

Looking up from the well where she was sitting, Gloria asked: "Would is be Saint Crispin's Day to-morrow, then?"

Philip suddenly stopped his dramatic pacing and laughed. "Good Lord no! At least, I don't think so. As a matter of fact, I haven't the faintest idea when it is."

Gloria was now taking a real interest in the war, and during the desperate days that followed they pored over the atlas together every time a fresh news bulletin came in. But Holland was forced out of the war in four days, and the Belgian Army, after displaying great gallantry, was compelled to surrender after seventeen. Through incompetence in the French High Command and a widespread lack of will to fight among their troops, a long sector of the Allied front collapsed at Sedan, the German armour was forced through the gap at breathtaking speed to the

Channel coast, and the British, with another French Army, were cut off in the north.

"Surely they'll break through?" said Gloria one night towards the end of May. "From the map there, it looks quite simple. Why don't they, Boy?"

Philip grimaced unhappily. "Perhaps they will. There must be half a million men in that pocket, and you'd think that if they all went hell-for-leather at the German corridor they'd cut clean through it like butter. But the trouble is that in modern war so much depends on weapons. The British have practically no armour, and the tanks we have got don't even mount as big a gun as our tanks had in the last war, so they're chicken-feed for the Germans. Even the arms of the infantry are a quarter of a century behind the times. They have no automatic rifles and there's not a single sub-machine gun owned by the British Army. As for parachute troops or flame-throwers—our Generals consider things like that to be comic opera! 'Our Archers did darn' well at Crècy, you know, but a jolly good new weapon called the Bayonet was brought in during the Seventeenth Century!'—and that's just about as far as our Staff College at Camberley has got."

"Oh, come now! They can't all be fools," Gloria protested. "And you say there's no graft in England, so what's the real reason for this?"

"It's the system. Nobody is ever held responsible now when they have occupied a high appointment and either made a mess of things or just drawn their pay and done as little as possible. There is never any inquiry held as to why even the most elementary things are overlooked or shelved. There are at least a score of men who have held very high positions, and by either their stupidity or neglect have largely contributed to bringing Britain into her present danger. But they will never be tried and publicly disgraced. The Service Ministers will say that it was the fault of the Service Chiefs and will be given opportunities to make further muddles elsewhere; and the Generals and Admirals, who either had not the sense to understand the requirements of their Services for a modern war or else lacked the guts to fight the politicians for them, will drift happily into retirement with good pensions and K.C.Bs."

Soon afterwards came Dunkirk with the Navy and the Air Force going to the rescue of the stranded Army. Once again, as Philip pointed out, the bulk of the officers and men of the Royal Navy could play no part in a major operation which was pre-eminently a Naval responsibility. They had to remain biting their thumbs in Scapa Flow and other safe harbours, tied to their big ships which were much too vulnerable to risk anywhere within striking distance of enemy aircraft. But the destroyer flotillas, aided by volunteer sailors in their little ships, did the job with the calmness, efficiency and courage for which the Royal Navy has ever been famous, and added yet another chapter of glory to the proud annals of Britain's seafaring men.

On June the 10th the raft actually crossed the Equator, although it was still moving so slowly as to be almost becalmed. The days were sweltering and the greater part of them had to be spent under cover of a large awning that Philip had rigged up on deck some days after the virtual disappearance of the wind. By this time both of them were baked almost mahogany colour and, owing to the long periods they spent in the water, could have taken prizes for their diving and swimming in any regatta.

Bathing and fishing were, in fact, practically their only recreations. Gloria still did a little sketching, occasionally, but she seemed to have lost much of her enthusiasm for her art. The routine of their days had formed itself even before they had landed on the African coast, and it was rarely altered except through adverse weather.

On waking they swam, then had their early meal. The morning passed in preparing food, shifting cargo, cleaning, cooking, washing, and the scores of odd jobs necessary to their daily lives. During the hottest hours of the afternoon they adopted the Spanish siesta, then they bathed again and, on most days, fished a little before dinner. Some evenings they listened to the radio, but others they just talked, and, whenever they stopped to think about it, they found it quite amazing how quickly the time went.

Italy's entry into the war surprised Philip. The disaster which had overtaken the Allied Armies in France had not shaken his faith in Germany's ultimate defeat. He knew that it would now be a long stiff business, but he felt convinced that sooner or later the United States would come to Britain's assistance, so the only thing that filled him with real concern was his old worry as to whether the Navy would be able to keep Britain's Atlantic Life-Line open. Yet, even if they failed, he felt instinctively that Britain would never surrender, and that with the Empire behind them the King and his Government would continue to fight the war from Canada. Therefore, it seemed to him that, although he had never thought Mussolini a fool, the Italian Dictator was certainly behaving like one now, as he was sacrificing a safe and extremely profitable neutrality for almost inevitable defeat and personal liquidation in a few years' time.

The news of the collapse of France was grim, but the blow was to some extent deadened by coming at the end of nearly ten weeks of unrelieved disaster. In view of the military situation, one could hardly blame the French for seeking terms for their armies in Metropolitan France, but Philip spent hours cursing the treachery of the French politicians and the cowardice of Marshal Pétain which immobilized the great resources of the French Empire and prevented the war against the Axis being carried on from North Africa.

Towards the end of June a light breeze arose, which carried the raft slowly but surely on a new course, slightly west of south, down the coast of South America, although still several hundred miles from it.

After the fall of France there came an ominous pause in the war. It had now assumed its own individuality and was not, after all, to be merely a repetition of 1914-1918. Yet the present situation had more than a superficial similarity to 1802 when Napoleon's Armies were massing at Boulogne for the invasion of England. Then, as now, in her great extremity Britain had been given a great Englishman to lead her. William Pitt, aided by a brilliant band of Admirals, had humbled the pride of France and brought the schemes of the ambitious Corsican to naught; and now Winston Churchill, equally well served by his Air Marshals, was to use Britain's new Navy—the Fleet of the Air—to render the might of Germany impotent and turn all Hitler's past victories to ashes in his mouth.

For those outside the picture the Battle of Britain began almost imperceptibly in ever-increasing attacks by the Luftwaffe on British shipping and the southern ports. But by mid-August it was obvious even to Philip—thousands of miles away in the middle of the South Atlantic—that one of the most titanic battles in the history of the world was now in full swing.

Hour after hour, he waited impatiently for each fresh bulletin and listened to those staggering figures of German aircraft—three, four, even five to one—shot down compared with the Royal Air Force losses. Gloria, too, was enthralled and once asked him, with awe in her voice:

" But how do they do it, Boy? The Germans are swell fighters—you must give them that. They're brave and they've got good machines. Yet the R.A.F. puts it over them every time."

" I suppose we owe it more than anything to Lord Trenchard," Philip replied. " He is a Marshal of the Royal Air Force, and for years during the peace he fought a most desperate battle. He battled to keep our Air Force as a separate Service and to prevent it being brought under the Army, as the Generals and many of our statesmen wished it to be. How he managed to win his fight with such a tremendous weight and influence and interest against him God only knows; but he did, and the policy, arming and training of the R.A.F. continued to be governed by airmen instead of by soldiers. I think the fact that the R.A.F. is a young Service has saved it from a lot of the deadening taboos which often stifle initiative in the others, and as flying is much more exciting than footslogging I don't doubt that a pretty high percentage of our more adventurous young men have gone into the Air Force; but I'm quite certain that wouldn't cut any ice if the basis of the thing had been wrong.

" The pride of place which in all German minds is given to the Army caused them to slip up in laying down the policy of the Luftwaffe. They went in very strongly for dive-bombers and that sort of thing, owing to their conception that the main role of an Air Force is to assist the Army. Our people did not make that mistake. The British doctrine is that the first function of the Air Force is to drive the enemy Air Force from the skies, and its second function is to destroy the enemy's capacity to make war. If it can do the first, the Army obviously won't be bothered by the enemy's dive-bombers, and, if it can do the second—smash up all the enemy's munition factories—all the Army will have left to do will be to hunt the stragglers out of the rubble. Anyhow, the Royal Air Force was organized and trained to fight an air war, and they have been given the finest machines that British mechanical genius could conceive. That's why they're shooting the Germans to hell."

It was some ten days later—on September the 4th, to be exact—that a major tragedy occurred in the small world of the raft. Philip switched on the radio as usual that morning for the eight o'clock news, but nothing happened. Examination disclosed that the batteries had run out and they had no more. To their consternation they found themselves still thousands of miles from any land and now completely cut off from all the news of the outside world.

Throughout September and early October they continued to drift a little erratically, but mainly on the same course. Once they heard distant gunfire, which told them that the war at sea had even reached these southern latitudes, and once another raft, a poor makeshift affair with three dead bodies on it, remained floating for two days in their vicinity. They now rarely saw a vessel, even hull-down on the horizon.

These autumn days were spring in the Southern Hemisphere, and, as they moved even further southward, they were extremely grateful for this fact. Although they had now left the airless and torrid heats of the equatorial region, fine, calm weather and the pleasantly hot days of a normal summer were travelling south with them, and they were able to continue their swimming and lazing in the sun.

By mid-October they had reached the latitude of Cape Town, and it was soon after this that Philip noticed on the chart he kept that their main direction had now altered to south-east, and it looked as if they were about to pass South Africa and enter the great watery wastes that lie below the Indian Ocean.

It was early in November that they saw the first trails of weed. It grew in long bright green streamers, rather like smilax, and at first they noticed only comparatively small patches of it several miles apart. After another three or four days, however, the patches had become great banks, and the sea, now as calm as a mill-pond, was split up into a number of channels intersecting the innumerable verdantly deceptive islands of this strange archipelago.

At first, the change of scene, after the wearisome monotony of the empty ocean, was pleasant, but on the fifth day after they had first seen the weed they realized that they had now entered an area devoid of currents and that their drift had become so slow as to be almost indiscernible. Their latitude was a little south of the 50th parallel, and the temperature very similar to that in the English Channel in June, but it irked them badly to be hung up. The weed provided them with two changes in their diet— small, soft-shelled crabs and baby octopuses, both of which lived among it in great numbers—but it also very nearly proved the death of Gloria.

Before setting out on his original voyage, Philip had realized that he and the crew of five that he had intended to take with him would have to live entirely on tinned foods for from eight to fourteen weeks, so, as a precaution against scurvy, he had shipped a large consignment of tinned spinach. It was partly to the fact that he and Gloria made a meal from one of the tins about every ten days that Philip attributed their excellent health. They still had a large part of the consignment left, but the sea-weed's delicate green looked so fresh and its shoots were so tender that they thought it possible that it was one of the edible kinds and decided to try it as a vegetable.

The result was surprising. Philip felt no ill effects whatever, but within an hour poor Gloria was rolling on the floor in agony and choking for breath, while great beads of sweat bedewed her freckled forehead. There could be no doubt at all that she had been seriously poisoned, so Philip gave her an emetic and forced her to keep awake, even when her pains temporarily lessened; which, with his very limited knowledge of medicine, was the only method he knew of dealing with such a situation.

There were times during the night when from the violence of her vomiting and subsequent spells of complete exhaustion he felt certain she was going to die; and it was during those anxious hours, while he was doing all he could to alleviate her suffering, that he realized how much her loss would mean to him.

After their one most unfortunate experience he had been too frightened to attempt to make love to her again, although he had frequently been tempted to do so, particularly during the more sultry nights when they had often bathed by moonlight together. Yet their perpetual closeness and dependence on each other had formed a strong bond between them. Occasionally the little habits of each would get on the other's nerves, but they were both too well balanced to allow such small irritations to affect them seriously. During their long companionship they had come to respect each other and to admire many of the qualities each possessed. They were rarely silent for very long, never dull and always in good spirits; and, as Philip tightly held Gloria's hands during her terrifying convulsive spasms, he was very conscious of all he owed to her.

It was three days before he felt reasonably sure that she would recover, but in the meantime, she had broken out in an ugly rash and was so emaciated by fever that she could hardly sit upright without assistance. Philip formed a theory that she was what doctors call an " iodine hound " and thus allergic to the drug, which is found in considerable strength in certain seaweeds. However, they never knew for certain if it was this or possibly some bad crab-meat in her portion of the weed that had caused the trouble. The rash gradually subsided, but for a long time she took things very quietly, and it was mid-December before she was her old self again.

The long, pleasant, sunny days ran on until the 18th of the month, when the sky became overcast, and that night they took all precautions to meet another gale. It was by no means so severe as the last they had experienced, and it blew itself out in thirty-six hours. To their surprise and delight, when they next ventured out they found that the storm had carried them out of the area of the weed. The raft was once more floating in open water, and a pleasant breeze was pushing it along.

They soon found they were travelling south and east again, and as they moved through the Fifties to the Sixties they enjoyed the long twilights and short nights that would have been their portion had they been in Scotland during the latter part of the summer. But, from the end of January, the nights began to shorten, as the autumn of the Southern Hemisphere was now setting in.

The two months that followed were by far the most unpleasant they had so far experienced. There was no severe storm, but the sea was almost continuously choppy. There was rain, mist and, at times, hail, while the temperature fell steadily, until even during sunny spells they could never sit out on deck unless well wrapped up. Swimming and sunbathing were only happy memories, and, apart from fishing to maintain their food supply, their only diversion was watching—with a certain trepidation for their own safety, the gambolling of the huge whales that frequented these far southern waters.

Their only consolation for the increasing cold and hardship—and a very dubious consolation at that—was the thought that soon they would again strike land. Philip's workings showed beyond dispute that they were heading for the Antarctic Continent, and, unless the raft were caught up in a contrary current, it could hardly fail to beach itself before the end of March.

Anxious as they were for any turn in their fortunes which offered a prospect of their eventual return to civilization, there was little cause for rejoicing over the likelihood of being able to land in the Antarctic. The atlas showed that the great sub-continent had been neatly divided into segments, the largest of which were dependencies of Australia, Britain and Norway. Most of the coastline was marked, while many bays and promontories had been given names, but there were no towns and, so far as Philip knew, no permanent settlements of any kind—nothing but a few scattered whaling stations which were occupied only during the southern summer—and the Antarctic winter was rapidly approaching.

At the beginning of March the raft entered the area of ice-floes which forever fringes the mysterious Southern Continent. Sometimes they were wide, flat stretches and at other large ice islands that towered from the water, their cliffs shimmering in the pale sunshine and often pierced with deep blue caves. The castaways soon came to know when they were approaching one of these great ice masses well before they actually sighted it, as the snow on them threw a whitish reflection into the sky, and the temperature always fell by several degrees.

Whenever they were in the vicinity of the floes and bergs they kept themselves shut up to preserve as far as possible the warmth of their quarters; but at such times they found plenty to do, as they were now preparing clothes and equipment to enable them to face the rigours of the Antarctic. Fortunately they had a considerable variety of materials, and Philip had always heard that the best protection against extreme cold lay not in very thick garments but in many layers of thin ones, so they planned their outfits accordingly; and, in addition, made themselves warm hoods and big padded fingerless gloves such as boxers wear.

On the 25th of March they made landfall, after having covered an erratic course of not less than 10,000 miles since leaving North-West Africa, at an average drift of about twenty-five miles a day. The coast that rose before them was grim in the extreme. It consisted mainly of the permanent ice foot formed by great glaciers pushing outward, from which huge chunks broke off each year to float away and melt in the warmer waters to the north; but here and there it was intersected by bays of stark, black basalt rocks. At intervals along the coast there rose extinct volcanoes, the sides of which glistened with snow and ice, except where sheer cliffs exposed the dark rock of which they were composed. On the 27th, in a flurry of light snow, the raft grated on the pebbly beach of one of the small bays.

Philip at once threw out their home-made anchor, and, as it was still before midday, they went ashore to climb a five hundred foot hill that lay only about a mile from the beach, to see what was to be seen from it.

The walk and climb took longer than they had expected, so when they got to the top of the hill they had little leisure to remain there if they were to get home before dark, yet time enough to take in the uninspiring scene. To the south there was a range of mountains, rearing snowy heights to the leaden sky; while to the east and west stretched the rugged inhospitable coast, behind which lay a rolling tundra, whose hollows were already filled with snow. Despondently and, for them, in an unusually long silence, they made their way back to the raft.

From fear of depressing Gloria, Philip had said little about the Antarctic while they were drifting towards it, so she had painted it as very similar to Alaska, of which she had read accounts at home; cold and desolate perhaps, but at least sparsely peopled with fur trappers and Eskimoes who had sledges and dogs. She had also expected great pine forests inhabited by reindeer, wolves, foxes, bears and many other animals. Instead, the stark emptiness came as a shock, and she found something appalling in its dreadful silence.

That night Philip explained why it was that such a great difference existed between the territories in the neighbourhood of the two Poles. Although the central Arctic is a great empty ocean, the bulk of the ice cap never melts and each winter stretches down unbroken to the northern lands of America and Russia, so men and animals from both continents have always had easy access to its outer fringe, and on the lands within the

Arctic Circle there has never been any bar to such hardy types of vegetation spreading as will withstand the rigours of the climate. On the other hand, the Antarctic, although a vast land mass far bigger than Europe and also coated in ice and snow for the greater part of the year, is entirely cut off by sea from all the other continents and has no aboriginal tribes such as the Eskimoes living in it. Owing to the sea barrier, no land animals have ever migrated there, and even the indigenous vegetable life is of the lowest forms.

Yet, in some way that Philip could not explain it seemed even worse than he had anticipated, and, although he tried to talk cheerfully about the whaling stations that must lie somewhere along the coast, they both recognized without discussing the matter that it would be absolute madness to attempt to reach one of them until the coming of spring.

They went ashore again several times during the next few days, explored the bays adjacent to the one in which the raft was anchored, and struggled up to the summits of four more hills, but nowhere could they discern any trace of men ever having set foot in that part of the world. By the end of a week a fringe of ice had begun to form along the coast, and by late April the raft was firmly frozen in, with several miles of ice stretching out into the open sea beyond it.

Philip took the elementary precautions, which were all that one with so little knowledge of Antarctic conditions could do, such as keeping two holes in the ice open for fishing, and they settled down to face the hardships of the winter. The days were already becoming absurdly short, and soon the sun, if it appeared at all, was only a pale ball low on the horizon for an hour or two a day.

Two problems which had already caused them some concern now began to assume really troublesome proportions; the one was snow-glare and the other condensation. To protect their eyes they made canvas masks with narrow cross slits and never came out of their living quarters without wearing them. The iron cargo containers in which they lived proved a more difficult proposition as, owing to the intense cold, the iron had now become not only redhot to the naked touch but sweated from the heat of the stoves, so that the floors gradually became covered with pools of water. To get over this Philip knocked a number of cases to pieces and remade them into low wide benches upon which bedding and other items could be kept permanently out of the wet. The water was then allowed to accumulate and mopped up into buckets each morning.

The cold outside was bitter if there was the least wind blowing, but otherwise the lowness of the temperature did not unduly worry them, although they had to be careful about frostbite. This was quite harmless if taken in time but caused very severe pain if even temporarily neglected. It always took effect without the slightest warning, the blood draining away from the afflicted part and leaving a white patch on the skin. If the circulation were at once restored all was well; otherwise when the bite thawed out the place swelled up alarmingly and later became a most painful blister. After learning this from bitter experience they made it a routine to examine each other's faces for these dangerous white patches every ten minutes or so when they ventured out from the shelter of their quarters.

The raft had long since been snowed up, and to get in and out of it they now had to traverse a long, sloping tunnel which they had made through twenty feet of snow. Down at the bottom of this they were as warm as Eskimoes in an igloo, and they soon discovered the wisdom of the Eskimo practice of passing the greater part of the long night of the Arctic winter by eating infrequently but very heavily, then sleeping until they feel really hungry again.

Whenever they did venture outside they found a fantastically bizarre world of unrelieved whiteness. The swelling of the ice as it froze ever thicker caused it to crack and erupt like a volcano hurling huge chunks of lava into the air, and often altering the landscape to seaward in a single night to such an extent that it was barely recognizable. Had the raft been frozen in while still out in the open sea it would inevitably have been slowly crushed to matchwood or rent to pieces by one of these terrible ice-quakes which seemed to shake the whole bay; but, fortunately, it had beached itself on a flat strand of pebbles, so there was hardly any ice under it. It had been forced up a little and tilted sharply to one side, but sustained no damage, and every blizzard buried it deeper under the great layer of snow that protected its inmates from the almost unbelievable degree of cold above.

Yet this grim world was not entirely uninhabited. Large colonies of seals were frequently to be seen lying placidly on the ice of the bay, and flocks of big Emperor Penguins stood about, chattering importantly. Both were absurdly tame, and soon after their arrival, with some reluctance, Philip slew his first seal with a hatchet. The fresh meat proved a most welcome change from their tinned fare, and they found its liver to be a real delicacy; so henceforth seal became a staple item of their menu.

The icy wilderness also proved a constant source of new beauties. Sometimes the sun, a low red disc, and the moon, a yellow globe, were both up together; at others double haloes appeared, or the lights of the Aurora Australis flashed in weird and bewildering patterns to the south. For nearly two months at the height of the Antarctic winter, the sun did not come above the horizon at all, and only a faint greyness dimmed the bright starlight for an hour or two at midday. Then the long twilights came again; a dawn that merged imperceptibly into sunset, while the mountains of the frozen world were tinged with the most resplendent and glowing colours.

At last the days began to lengthen, and they slowly set about preparations for their journey. They made another small tent, similar to that they had abandoned to the land-crabs in Africa, two more knapsacks and a three-layer double sleeping-bag; and went into the most minute particulars as to how much weight they could carry and the selection down to the smallest item of things they meant to take with them.

Snow falls became less frequent, the sun mounted higher in the heavens each day, and its warmth began to melt the accumulated snow of winter, while the tunnel down to the raft grew shorter and shorter until finally it disappeared. Early in October noises like the reports of big guns far away to the north told them that the thaw had really set in; the great ice barrier was cracking up, and huge chunks of it were flaking off as icebergs to float away and melt in the warmer water.

By mid-October they were impatient to be off. The sooner they could reach a whaling station the sooner they would stand a chance of getting to Australia and so home. They had had no news of the outer world for many months, and both were anxious to know how the war was going. Philip never forgot the strange vision that had come to him in the storm, and he felt that, if he were to be of any use to his country, as the Canon had so clearly stated he would be, his first job was to get back to it. In consequence, when a good spell of weather set in, although the nights were still cold and snow still occasionally fell, they decided to set out, and on October the 17th, for the second time, they abandoned the security and comfort of the old raft.

Philip had determined the latitude and longitude of the bay in which they had wintered as 67° 30′ South and 77° 10′ East, so they were in Princess Elizabeth Land and about 150 miles east of a great bay marked on the map as MacKenzie Sea. He felt that this was much the most likely spot anywhere within a thousand miles of them in which to find a whaling station; so they set off westward along the coast towards it.

For the first four days the weather remained good and their journey was uneventful. The going was easier than it had been along the sandy African shore, and no scorching sun had compelled them to waste several hours each day, so in the four days they reckoned that they had accomplished nearly two-thirds of their journey. At the point they had now reached, the map, which they had torn from Philip's atlas, showed a great cape running out into the sea, and beyond it the big bay that was their goal. To follow the coastline would have meant at least two days' hard marching, whereas by heading inland across the base of the cape it appeared that the bay could be reached in one; so on the fifth morning they decided to take the short cut.

Up to midday the ground was very similar to the surface they had already traversed, but its character then began to change. Almost unnoticeably at first it sloped upward, until they found themselves plodding up quite steep slopes, on which patches of snow were still lying; the land became broken with ugly fissures which they had either to jump or make considerable detours to by-pass. In consequence, evening was upon them before they realized how late it was, and before they could even get a glimpse of the sea beyond the ridge they were compelled to camp for the night on these black, barren uplands.

During the night the weather broke, and it snowed again. Philip was not unduly alarmed because he knew it was too late for blizzards and that at this season of the year it was unlikely to go on snowing for long. But it was worrying all the same, since the ground was now snow-covered, and it would be difficult to pick a way among the rocks over its treacherous whiteness.

Within half an hour of their setting out his worst fears were realized. Gloria gave a cry, grabbed at his arm, missed it and fell. As she tried to stand again, she moaned, and to their utmost consternation it was soon apparent that she had sprained her ankle.

She found it quite impossible to walk, and Philip could not carry her as well as the store of food upon which their lives depended. The only course was to make camp again so that she could rest her foot and hope that it would be well enough for her to proceed the next day.

Judging by the swelling and puffiness that soon appeared, the sprain was a bad one, and the only treatment of which they could think—snow compresses—seemed to have no effect. Gloria still could not stand the following morning, so they spent a second miserable day huddling under the bivouac tent on the windswept ridge that had been their undoing.

Philip was really worried now. They had set out with sixteen days' rations. Six days had been allowed for the journey, four days to explore the bay and another six days for the homeward journey if they found no whaling station on the MacKenzie Sea. Actually, they had spent five days on the journey and two on the ridge, so they had only nine days' rations left. That meant quite definitely that they would have to abandon any idea of pushing on to the bay, since with Gloria badly lamed it might take them all of the nine days to get back to the raft.

The third day she still could not walk more than a few steps without suffering acute pain, so they had to spend yet another day and night shivering on the ridge. By this time they were both grimly aware that it was courting death to remain there very much longer, and on the fourth morning they decided to make a great effort at least to cover the few miles which would get them down to the lower levels, clear of the snow, where they would be able to find shelter from the biting wind.

Gloria made a sling for her foot to keep it off the ground, then using the bivouac pole as a crutch on one side, and supported by Philip on the other, she began the exhausting business of hopping along, while he walked slowly beside her. In this fashion they covered about half a mile, but she found it a terrible strain to carry the whole weight of her body on her good leg, and the more tired it grew, in spite of frequent rests, the more she became inclined to stumble. A snow-covered snag of rock on which she trod caused her to lurch against Philip who was also at that moment on uneven ground, and in attempting to recover his balance he caught his foot in a hole and they fell heavily together.

Muttering imprecations Philip picked himself up, but Gloria had wrenched her injured foot again and, refusing his aid, lay there sobbing in the snow. In vain he besought her to make another effort. She only urged him to leave her there and make his way back to the raft alone, which he flatly refused to do; so the only thing for it was to pitch their minute camp once again.

That night, as Philip lay sleeplessly turning over and over in his mind their desperate plight, he came to the conclusion that she was probably right and that their best hope lay in his making his way back to the raft. They had seven days' food left. Unhampered by luggage, he might be able to get back in four days and return with a fresh supply of food in a further four to five. But would she be able to last out the eight or nine days that he was away and, in this wilderness of rock and snow, which seemed to have so few distinguishing marks, if once he left her would he ever find her again?

During the past few days he had thought a great deal of the Canon, and he had practically persuaded himself that he must really have been sleep-walking and dreamt the whole vision. After all, the idea that he should play a leading part in defeating the Germans was pretty farcical on the whole, but it was the height of absurdity now that he was marooned in the Antarctic and almost certain to die there. Yet, when his chattering teeth at last allowed him to sleep that night he dreamed again of Beal-Brookman, and the little Canon was saying:

" The gods help those who help themselves, Philip. Have courage, my boy, and delay no longer. Your only hope of saving Gloria is to leave her."

When he awoke in the morning he told Gloria, and she agreed that it was the only thing to do. He took enough food to keep him going for three days, trusting to reach the raft by the fourth, or, at the latest, the fifth, and left the rest with her. He also left the primus stove and all their coverings except one layer of their triple sleeping-bag in which to wrap himself at nights.

They tried to make light of their parting, but it was a pathetic effort, and they were both very near to tears. He spent a few moments consciously memorizing every detail of the landscape, and it was agreed that from the eighth day of his departure she should yodel as loudly as she could every hour in order to help guide him back to her. Then, raising a feeble smile, he said he would eat his hat if he were not back in under a week, and left her.

To have had an accident himself while crossing the broken ground would have been the end of everything, so he set off at a steady, unhurried pace and picked his way carefully. After covering three miles, he was clear of the most broken ground and able to proceed considerably faster, but there were still patches of snow and ice on the downward slopes which forced him to keep his eyes fixed on the ground ahead. In consequence, he did not see that the Antarctic landscape now held a most unusual feature which he was rapidly approaching.

The crack of a rifle startled him out of his wits. Almost simultaneously the tattered hat, which he had threatened only an hour before to eat, was whisked off his head.

As he jerked to a halt, he saw that, thirty yards further down the slope, a tall black-bearded man was standing. In his hands he held the still smoking rifle from which he had just sent a bullet within an inch or two of Philip's brain.

CHAPTER XII

THE DARK PRINCE

PHILIP was quite convinced that he was suffering from an hallucination. Somehow, when the Canon's ghost had actually been talking to him there had not seemed anything so terribly abnormal about that; but this was too fantastic to be real. For several days past he had been undergoing severe strain, cold and lowered vitality, owing to lack of hot or really adequate meals, so there could be no doubt about it—his brain had become temporarily affected.

Yet the black-bearded man looked very solid. He was clad entirely in furs, a conical fur hat like Robinson Crusoe's set at a rakish angle on his head, while behind him there was a small sledge that he had evidently been dragging. Suddenly he called out in English:

"What's the matter with you? Can't you speak?"

"You *are* real!" gasped Philip, taking a few steps forward. "My God, I'm glad to see you! But why . . . why on earth did you shoot at me just now?"

Tucking his rifle casually under his arm, the other suddenly broke into peals of boisterous laughter, and it flashed into Philip's mind that perhaps he had to do with a madman; but after a moment the man stopped and began to walk forward, as he replied: "You looked so funny, striding along staring at the ground. I thought it would be amusing to pull you up short with a shot."

"But, damn it all, you might have killed me!" Philip exclaimed angrily.

"No, no!" said the man. "There was no risk at all of my doing that because I'm a very fine shot. A very fine shot indeed."

There was something in the way he made the boast, added to the fact that, although he spoke English with great fluency, he had quite an unusual accent, which convinced Philip that the stranger was neither British nor American.

"Besides," the man went on, a grin spreading over his dark face, "would it have mattered very much if I had killed you? Who are you, anyway?"

After giving his name Philip asked that of the stranger with as much asperity as he could get into his tone.

"I," replied the man magnificently, "was born Prince Fedor Solgorukin, and I am now a King."

Philip did not believe the first statement any more than the second, and it was now clear to him that he was dealing with a dangerous lunatic; but the fact remained that the self-styled King was well clad and well fed and therefore presumably had a base much nearer than the raft. With Gloria in mind, Philip realized the imperative necessity of humouring the madman, but to address him as " Your Majesty " seemed to be overdoing it, so he said:

"Well, Prince, I'm more delighted to see you than I can possibly say. I'm the best part of five days' march from my base and, owing to an accident, I've practically run out of stores. I'm sure I can count on your help, and no doubt you'll be able to put me on the way to the whaling station."

"Whether I should be prepared to help you I don't yet know," replied the other guardedly. "How long is it since you left the whaling station, and how many people are there in your party?"

That one human being should hesitate even for an instant to give help to another in such circumstances shocked Philip and struck him as being unbelievably callous, and he stared in astonishment at the tall, dark, middle-aged man in front of him. The Prince's mouth was hidden by the curling blue-black hair of his carefully trimmed beard and moustache. His nose was thin and aquiline, his high cheekbones indicated that he was of Mongolian blood, and his eyes had all the dark inscrutability of the Tartar. It was a proud, strong face, and its striking individuality proclaimed aloud that its owner was a law unto himself. Prince or not, he certainly appeared to be a Russian and an unusual personality. Philip only hesitated a second, then he said:

"I didn't come from the whaling station. We were washed up about a hundred miles east along the coast from here, on a raft."

"Who is we? How many are you?"

"Only myself and a girl," Philip jerked a thumb over his shoulder. "She's back there about three miles away with a sprained ankle. We've been hung up for nearly five days, and I wouldn't have left her unless we'd been absolutely desperate. She can't walk yet and our only hope was for me to go off and get more food."

"A woman, eh?" The Russian whistled softly, and his eyes narrowed. "In that case I can hardly refuse you the hospitality of my kingdom. Lead me to her. As we go, you can tell me about yourself. Since you arrived on a raft I take it you were torpedoed by these filthy Germans? "

"No, not exactly; although it was owing to a German agent that the raft left the United States without a proper crew in the first place. You see, it wasn't an ordinary raft. I was carrying out a semi-scientific experiment."

" How interesting!"

" It was rather, because it proved very nearly a hundred per cent. successful, but it went wrong at the last moment, and that's the reason we got washed up here. I'll tell you about it later, but first can you give me any news of the war? Our radio faded out on us over a year ago, and we've heard nothing of the outer world since."

" I know only what had happened up to last February. It was still going on then. London had been bombed to hell, but the R.A.F. was still on top of the Luftwaffe, and the Nazis hadn't the guts to invade Britain without air superiority."

" Had the United States come in?" asked Philip.

" No, not up to the spring of Nineteen Forty-One. Roosevelt and many of their top men in both parties would bring America in if they could, because they know what she'll be up against if Britain is defeated. But the great big American public has been doped for so long by Isolationist propaganda that they haven't really got round to understanding how a Hitler victory might affect them. When I last heard they were ninety per cent. pro-Ally and stripping their own cupboards to send bundles to bombed-out Britons, but all the same they were still ninety-five per cent. against getting mixed up in this crazy war—and who can blame them?"

" If they can send bundles they can send other things as well," remarked Philip. " Thank God our Atlantic Life-Line is still open. I'm the son of a British Naval officer, and I'm particularly interested in everything to do with the war at sea."

" Really! I was an officer in the Royal Navy myself for several years."

Philip shot a sidelong glance at his companion. There could be no doubt about it: the fellow had a screw loose; yet, apart from his *folie de grandeur,* he talked seriously enough. He was continuing smoothly:

" The U-boats were taking a pretty heavy toll, of course, and it remains to be seen if British and United States tonnage will prove sufficient to see the party through. If Hitler had started the war with another hundred submarines Britain would have been starved out by now. Still, one must hand it to the British that they're a remarkable people. Nobody would have given a fig for their chances last autumn and at the very moment the world was waiting to count them out they staged a victorious offensive in North Africa."

" By Jove! Did they really?"

" Yes. General Wavell defeated an army six times the size of his own and drove the Italians helter-skelter across half of Libya. It's true that the Eyeties are not in the same class as the Germans, but, even so, they were fighting behind their own well prepared defences, they had thousands of guns, quite a lot of armour and the whole Italian Air Force pitted against about three squadrons of British fighters—so it was a pretty good show."

" Gosh yes! Absolutely marvellous! " Philip murmured. " That's real generalship. My God! What wouldn't I give to get home, though, so that I could join up! "

The Russian regarded him curiously. "What? You would like to go into the war? "

" Yes, naturally. Not for the fun of the thing, but because we've got to get these blasted Germans down somehow, and every man counts."

" I am different. I do not mind fighting man to man. In fact, I rather enjoy it. But never again will I put on a uniform and allow people to order me about."

To Philip it seemed so obvious that no country could survive if its young men refused to serve it when it was in danger that it was pointless to pursue the theme, and a few minutes later they came in sight of the tent.

Gloria was as astonished as Philip had been at the appearance of the well-fed, prosperous-looking stranger in such a desolate land; but once she had got over her first delight at being spared the long and lonely ordeal, which that morning she had made up her mind to face, she began to ply him with a dozen questions.

Where was his camp? How far away was it? How long had he been there? Why had he left it? And so on.

" Patience, Madame! " he laughed. " You shall know in good time. I came down to the coast because I had a mind to shoot a seal if I could find one, but I live three good days' march away from here in the mountains of the interior. That is quite a good distance, and will take two or three days longer if we have to carry you. However, the dried food that I have in that bundle on my sledge will last me a week, and I understand you still have rations for six or seven days, so we ought to be able to make it."

" Couldn't you help me to get her to the whaling station instead?" suggested Philip. " We're both terribly anxious to get home, and that's the only place we're likely to find a ship."

" What whaling station? " asked the Russian.

" Why, the one you spoke of yourself only an hour ago. When we first met you jumped to the conclusion that I had come from it."

" You are mistaken. I asked you only if you had come from a whaling station, because I thought that the most natural explanation of your presence." As he spoke Fedor Solgorukin's face remained quite expressionless, yet Philip felt certain that he was lying. He went on briskly : " Now, as we have far to go we should lose no time. We will make the tent into a hammock and use its support pole as a carrying rod."

" But what would this place be to which you're going to take us? " Gloria asked. "Surely you don't live all on your own up in those mountains?"

His teeth showed white against the blackness of his beard as he smiled. " There are stranger things in heaven and earth than most men wot of! Those mountains hold a secret that many a scientist would give his eyes to unravel. I shall say no more at the moment than that there is a place there where I can offer you food and warmth for as long as you wish. It is my kingdom, and you, Madame, are the guest that I shall delight to honour in it."

Never in his life had Philip had more difficulty in making a decision. On the face of it the Russian seemed to be talking the most arrant nonsense, yet, if they did not go with him, what were they to do? They could only revert to their plan of fetching fresh supplies from the raft, and that was fraught with eight or ten days of appalling anxiety for them both and the awful hazard that they might lose each other in this wilderness of rocks and rifts. The thing that finally decided him was a half-humorous taunt from the Russian, who, seeing his hesitation, suddenly said:

"Come along! What are you afraid of? I won't eat you—yet!"

"I'm not afraid of anything," retorted Philip. "I was only wondering how you've managed to come so far without any tent or even enough camp equipment to cook yourself a hot meal?"

The other shrugged. "I was born in a cold country. One of my father's estates was in the far north of Russia, and I spent several winters there as a boy. I learnt then not to mind the cold. I am very fit and on an expedition of a week or so, such as this, I require little to eat, and hot food or drink is a luxury; so why should I burden myself with a lot of unnecessary paraphernalia? I bring the sledge only so that I can drag the seal meat back on it, but a hammock will be much more comfortable for Madame. As for the nights, at this season of the year my furs are all that I require to keep me from freezing. I'm afraid you'll find it pretty cold, though, as you have neither furs nor leather clothing."

"If it's only for five or six nights I'll manage somehow," said Philip, and together they began the business of converting the tent into a hammock.

Half an hour later, after a simple meal, they set off. The Russian naturally led the way, with the fore-end of the hammock pole on one shoulder and his rifle on the other. He proved extremely sure-footed and had a quick eye for spotting the best way across a piece of broken country. Gloria lay rather awkwardly in the improvised hammock, and Philip brought up the rear with the rest of the equipment piled on the sledge, which he dragged behind him.

Soon after twilight began to fall their leader selected a camping site under the lee of a big overhanging rock. Gloria still could not rest her weight on her foot without pain, but sitting down she cooked them quite a passable dinner from their slender resources, in which the Russian did not hesitate to participate.

Philip was tired and sore from the long hours of unaccustomed exertion that he had been through that afternoon, but he was still mentally excited by the new turn which their fortunes had taken through this meeting with Fedor Solgorukin. After the meal, he began to ask their new companion all sorts of questions.

With many of them, particularly those concerning the place to which they were going, the Russian fenced and was casually evasive; but when Philip said: " You were saying this morning that you were once an officer in the Royal Navy. How long ago was that? " he replied at once.

" I entered Dartmouth in Nineteen Nineteen, after I escaped from Russia."

" You will have been in the Revolution then," said Gloria. " So was me mother. She was the daughter of an Irish merchant trading in Saint Petersburg. The Bolsheviks killed him and looted his store; but by that time me mother was married to an English war correspondent and he got her safely away to Canada."

" What a small world it is! " exclaimed Solgorukin. " I was living with my family in Saint Petersburg during those awful days, and perhaps the very same gang of murderers who killed your grandfather killed my parents. They would have killed me too, although I was scarcely more than a child, if they had had the chance. My tutor turned out to be one of the Communist students so many of whom, as we learned later, had turned our universities into secret revolutionary clubs. The little rat loathed me and planned to hand me over to the mob, but he was fool enough to tell me his intentions. I was only twelve, but the use of weapons is one of the first things taught to the boys of all noble Russian families, and things were already so unsettled that I was carrying a revolver. I pulled it out and shot him. I shall never forgot the look of astonishment on his mean, stupid face. He was the first man I had ever killed, and I rather enjoyed it."

Solgorukin paused for a moment, evidently savouring anew this jolly memory, before he went on: " That same evening the mob broke into our palace and murdered not only my father, mother, sister, an old aunt and two cousins, but nearly all our faithful servants. I was saved by our chief huntsman, little Sergi, who happened to be in Saint Petersburg on a visit. Actually, he was a huge man, and he was very fond of me. We had many adventures together and killed quite a number of Reds before we eventually succeeded in reaching the Crimea, where he handed me over to my godmother, Her Imperial Majesty the Dowager Empress.

" It was she who brought me to England when she was forced to leave Russia herself, and was taken off in a British destroyer. I was so thrilled with the guns and the sailors that she thought it would be a good thing for me to go into the Navy. As you may remember, she was 'Queen Alexandra's sister, and she used her influence to get me taken into Dartmouth, although I was by then above the usual age. Then later, when it was clear that there would be no going back to Russia for us exiles, I took out British naturalization papers and was granted a commission.

" By then I was quite disillusioned of any idea that it would be fun to spend most of my life at sea, but nothing remained of the great fortune I should have inherited, so it seemed that going into the Navy was the only way in which I could support myself until I was old enough to marry. With many of my brother officers I got on famously. For good humour, courage, sound common sense and general kindliness of nature I have never met any body of men to equal the officers of the Royal Navy; but there was one little man whom I loathed.

"He was a Socialist, and he would insist on talking about Russia without knowing anything about it. The result was, perhaps, unfortunate, although it only accelerated my leaving the Navy a year or so before I would otherwise have done. The thing that everyone seemed to take such great exception to was the fact that I used a knife, although the injury I inflicted was by no means serious. Having no source of income but my pay, I had rather a difficult time for a few months, but I contracted a suitable marriage and settled down to enjoy the sort of life that a person of my birth is entitled to expect. I have been married four times, altogether, but, unfortunately, all four of my wives were bores."

The Russian ceased his flow of reminiscences as though bored himself with the tale he was telling; but the recital had forced Philip considerably to modify his opinion. The whole sequence of events, even the details of which most people would have been far from proud, had such a ring of truth that he could no longer doubt that Fedor was a prince, or that he had been an officer in the Royal Navy. Yet, if these things were true and he were not mad, this made his references to his "kingdom" even more mysterious.

"Where's your last wife, Prince?" asked Gloria. "I mean your present one. Will we be meeting her up there?" She nodded in the direction of the chain of mountains towards which they had been heading all the afternoon.

Solgorukin threw back his head in one of his gargantuan bursts of laughter. "Good God no!" he chuckled, as soon as he had recovered a little. "I wouldn't have brought Cornelia here even if I'd had the chance. She was the worst bore of them all. It was her insistence that we should go on a trip to the Grand Canyon while I was having a very pleasant love affair in New York that finished things between us. I went—I had to, because my bankers were making an intolerable nuisance of themselves, and the woman I was in love with had no money. But Cornelia and I had our final quarrel while we were supposed to be admiring the beauties of the Yosemite Valley, and I left her there to—er—find her own way home."

"From what you say I gather you managed to lead a pretty luxurious life between the two wars," remarked Philip. "Why on earth did you chuck all that up to come to this god-forsaken part of the world?"

"I have told you that I was bored," the Prince replied sharply. "When Cornelia's will was proved it was found that she had not left me one cent of her great fortune, and by that time I was already in South America, so . . ."

F

" She's dead then? " Gloria broke in.

" Yes, did I forget to mention that? She was a very stupid woman, and when I drove off in the car—just to make her realize that money was not everything, you know, and that even a millionairess gets tired if she has to walk ten miles to the nearest road-house—she walked over a cliff in the dark; and there wasn't much left of her when they found her some days later, as she had fallen a sheer thousand feet before she hit the rocks. Anyhow, as I was saying, finding myself in the Argentine with very little money I thought I'd put my old navigational knowledge to some use.   I signed on as a second officer to do a season's whaling in the winter of 'Forty to 'Forty-One, largely for the fun of the thing, and a week or so after we landed I—er—well, I made a discovery which decided me to stay on."

Both Philip and Gloria had already learned that it was no good pressing the Prince for information about his mysterious secret, and as they were both now very tired they decided to turn in; but before he dropped off to sleep Philip could not help wondering what had really happened to Cornelia. He had an uneasy suspicion that it was Fedor who planned that trip to the Grand Canyon, and that he had pushed the wretched woman over the cliff in the hope that he would inherit her fortune. Probably as a precaution against suspicion falling on him he had got out at once to South America; then learning perhaps that it had, he had shipped out in the whaler to the Antarctic to get beyond the reach of the United States police. All that fitted in nicely, but Philip had to admit to himself that he had no foundation whatever for his highly libellous theory and that he was considerably influenced by the fact that he had taken a very strong dislike to Prince Fedor Solgorukin.

Philip's dislike of their new companion was not shared by Gloria, who found the Prince attractive and amusing. He, too, obviously liked her, and as the party trudged along during the days that followed they were always laughing and joking together.   More than once Fedor inferred that there was a special bond between them owing to the fact that relatives of both of them had been murdered by the Bolsheviks, and it seemed that he treated her as an equal on this account, quite apart from the consideration he showed her as a woman; whereas to Philip he was often barely civil.

Hour after hour, while daylight lasted, they tramped doggedly forward across barren, windswept icefields towards the great range of snow-topped mountains, which seemed to get ever higher the nearer they approached. During the daytime the movement kept Philip fairly warm, but at night he was bitterly cold, owing to his refusal to deprive Gloria of more than the single sleeping bag which he had been going to take with him on his journey to the raft. She, too, felt the cold keenly, on account of her forced inactivity, although she lay smothered in coverings both night and day.

On the fourth night they reached the base of the mountain range, and Fedor led them to a cave where they were able to make camp in considerably more comfort than they had known for some time. After the meal, an open row at last broke out between the two men over, of all things, the question of Big Ships.

The Prince had by this time heard most of their adventures, but Philip had rather skated over his original object in inventing his Raft Convoy; but when the subject cropped up again he saw no reason why he should preserve any particular secrecy about it, and went into full details of the project.

"Well, as an ex-Naval man myself, I think you're completely off the mark!" shrugged Solgorukin. "It stands to reason that the country that builds the biggest, most heavily armed battleships will secure control of the seas the moment it has enough of them."

"You're taking no account whatever of air power," protested Philip, and produced all his usual arguments.

"That's all very well," said the Prince, as soon as he could get a word in. "We know that in these days it's suicide for a big ship to go in anywhere within reach of land-based planes; but it is no longer the functions of the Big Ship. It is to carry the war to the enemy's territory in places where he has few, if any, aircraft to defend himself. No Battle Fleet now ever operates without its aircraft carriers, and they are not only its eyes but a shield against all but the heaviest scale of enemy air attack. They are also capable of striking most telling blows at enemy bases."

Philip nodded. "Yes, I agree with all that. But why not have your fleet entirely composed of aircraft carriers, with destroyers to protect them from U-boats?"

"But, my dear fellow, that wouldn't be any good if some of the enemy's big ships came on the scene. You'd lose all your carriers. You must have big ships to protect them."

"I don't see why."

"Then you must be very dense," said the Prince acidly. "From the time Naval warfare started with bows and arrows and stone shot, all other things being equal, victory has always gone to the Fleet that could fire the biggest broadside."

"Well, an aircraft carrier can fire a bigger broadside than a battleship."

"Now you're talking through your hat. Aircraft carriers mount only six-inch guns or something like that. Anyhow, the weight of their broadside wouldn't amount to that of a single sixteen-inch shell."

"I'm not talking about weight," Philip countered, "but explosive power. You know as well as I do that, to stand the pressure of being fired out of a gun barrel, nine-tenths of the weight of every shell has to be solid steel, and that there is only room for a comparatively small explosive charge inside. Bombs, on the other hand, are very different. They need only a thin metal casing to hold together the solid mass of explosive which forms their bulk. In consequence, the aircraft of one carrier can drop in a single sortie a far greater tonnage of high explosive than could be fired off by the big guns of a whole fleet of battleships. That's why it is now so hopelessly uneconomical to send a battle fleet to bombard a port. A few squadrons of heavy bombers can create more havoc in ten minutes than a battle fleet could by bombarding the place for a couple of days. It's such a waste of good steel too. Anyhow, you can take it from me that the sixteen-inch gun is now as outmoded as a Roman catapult."

The Russian's voice held the trace of a sneer, as he said: "You think yourself a monstrous clever fellow, don't you? But the fact remains that all Service opinion is against you. If you had ever been in the Navy, as I have, you would know that the men who reach Admiral's rank are not fools. What is more, it may interest you to learn that the American Navy Chiefs think the same way. When I left the States they were still building big ships as fast as they could go."

Philip shrugged. "Because the Americans and the British do the same thing it does not prove that they are right. Naturally, all these chaps can't bear the thought of the main reason for their existence becoming the responsibility of another Service which is now better equipped to tackle it than themselves. They'll continue to maintain until they are blue in the face that a battle fleet is still necessary, and anyone like yourself, who is predisposed in their favour, will continue to be fool enough to believe them."

"Do you suggest that I'm a fool?" asked the Prince angrily.

"No. But I do suggest that you're taking for granted all sorts of things that you have heard other people say, and repeating them like a parrot instead of facing the problem squarely on its merits and thinking it out logically for yourself."

"How dare you call me a parrot!"

"You shouldn't behave like one!"

"You insolent young fool! I'll teach you . . . !"

"Just a moment, just a moment," Gloria intervened as Fedor rose to his feet with the evident intention of advancing on Philip. "I think you boys have both been mighty rude to each other; but there's no sense in coming to blows about a thing that can't affect any of us here one little bit. I'm awful tired, and I'd like to get to sleep. Won't both of you say you're sorry so that we can settle down for the night?"

Philip obligingly muttered that he had not meant anything personal, and the Prince mumbled something to the effect that he had taken no offence.

Even so, Philip was greatly surprised when the Russian said to him next morning: "You know, I was thinking over what you were saying last night, and I believe you are right. Logically, all future fleets should consist of aircraft carriers with destroyer escorts. Two such fleets would not have to wait to engage until they were in sight of each other; they could fight to the death without ever being less than a hundred miles apart. And since no battleship which was with either fleet could use its big guns in such an action it really does seem that battleships are quite redundant."

"That's very handsome of you," Philip smiled and this *rapprochement* made a happy start to what proved to be a long and tiring day.

Having reached the mountain barrier, they now had to climb over two thousand feet up a steep and slippery track, then make their way through a three-mile pass. On each of the two previous days Gloria had said that she was sure her ankle was now quite strong enough for her to walk, at least a part of the way; but Solgorukin would not let her. He wanted her ankle to be given the maximum rest until they reached the mountain. Now, when she tried it out, she found she could walk quite well, but the Prince took one of her arms to help her while Philip was left to bring up the rear with the luggage.

They reached the entrance of the pass without accident and halted there for their midday meal. After it, before they set out on the next stage of their journey, during which Gloria was once more to be carried, Solgorukin addressed the other two with unusual solemnity.

"Within a few hours' time you will see things which I have little doubt will astonish you. I have offered you food and warmth, and they shall be yours, but you will then understand why, had you two been a party of men, I should have left you to fend for yourselves. I intend that this place to which we are going beyond the mountains shall be my home for the rest of my life. Therefore, I would not jeopardize it or my position there by sheltering a party of roughnecks who might turn upon me. You two are different."

He smiled and went on: "Even if you wished, I somehow don't think that you two could prove very dangerous enemies. All the same, I should like to give you a warning. As my guests, I don't think you will have any reason to complain of your treatment. But I wish you both to realize that, while you are in my kingdom, as well as being my guests you will also be my subjects. Anything that you may see there—such, for example, as my treatment of my other subjects—is no concern of yours. You will neither inquire into it nor comment on it; and you will remember that my word is law."

Rising, he added more lightly: "Come, let us go." When Gloria had settled herself in the hammock he led the way into a narrow defile between two sheer walls of rock which formed the pass. It was a long walk, steadily uphill all the time and often through an inch or more of water, which in places turned the gorge into a shallow river.

Philip could not understand this at all, as at such an altitude he would have expected the whole pass to be completely blocked with great depths of snow. Yet it was far warmer here than it had been much lower down on the mountain-side or even on the plain; and he noticed that, although the peaks of the mountains that they passed remained snow-covered, the rock was now bare to within a thousand feet of their tops, and the rock faces seemed to be glistening with moisture.

At last they came out on a plateau from which they could see a long double line of mountain tops separated by a great chasm at least ten miles wide; while, far to the south, beyond the double line of peaks, there rose another chain of mountains far vaster than the one into the centre of which they had climbed.

Setting Gloria down, they advanced across the plateau. Their view down into the great chasm between the mountains steadily increased, and the first hint of what was coming was given by a touch of green breaking the brown colouring of the rock at the far end of the valley. After covering another few hundred yards, Philip and Gloria could see that there were trees and fields down there in the valley and—yes, little, round houses with smoke curling up from their chimney pots.

Forgetting her ankle, Gloria ran the rest of the way to the edge of the plateau, and Philip ran with her. For a moment they stood there side by side, gazing down enraptured by the distant scene, then he exclaimed:

"It can't be! It isn't true! And yet it must be—this is Shangri La!"

The Prince had joined them, and he shook his head. "No, this is not Shangri La. There are no temples here, no wise men seeking to preserve all the accumulated beauties of our civilization from destruction, and you will find the people here very poor and primitive. Yet, in some ways this is much more remarkable. That was a man-made Paradise where Nature had been coaxed to give of her best in a sheltered valley. This is not. It is against all nature that anything but the very lowest forms of vegetation should live so near the Pole; and the cultivation here is only of the most primitive kind. For two-thirds of the year this valley should be deep in snow; yet no snow has ever fallen during all the months I have been here, and while perpetual clouds should hang about those mountain tops, shutting out the sun, there is hardly a day on which it does not shine."

"How absolutely extraordinary!" murmured Philip. "Yet there must be some explanation."

"There is," the Prince replied, "and it lies in that great chain of mountains to the south. Something goes on there that I do not understand. Strange things can be done with human blood, and I know just enough to have reached the decision that it is wiser not to pursue my investigations any further. I mention this now in order that we need not refer to it again. The subject is taboo."

They stood silently looking out over the valley. It was infinitely still and peaceful in the evening light, yet the Russian's strange words had now imbued the place with a slightly frightening and sinister atmosphere.

"Come," he said at last. "You have not yet seen any of my people, and they will prove another surprise for you. Let us go down. I bid you welcome to my kingdom."

CHAPTER XIII

THE STRANGEST KINGDOM

THE Prince led the way along the cliff top until they reached a break in it from which a narrow track led downward. Gloria was tired now and limping a little, but she was so excited that she hardly noticed the pain which began to throb through her ankle again during their two-mile descent into the valley. As they advanced the terrain on either side of the track gradually altered in appearance. The bare, wet rock became sparsely covered in lichens and mosses, and as the way grew less steep they passed narrow terraces which had been banked up to hold shallow patches of soil. These broadened by degrees until they became sloping fields.

Neither Philip nor Gloria knew anything about agriculture, but it was apparent to them that the cultivation was haphazard and the crops of poor quality. The countryside had all the untidiness of a huge allotment garden at the wrong end of the year, and it was clear that no common policy or organized direction for getting the best out of the soil existed here. Night was fast approaching, so none of the inhabitants were now in the fields, but Philip noticed that no ploughs, harrows or other agricultural implements had been left out; nor were any wagons or horses to be seen.

The only signs of life were a few of the cottages that they had seen from the plateau, which, on a nearer view, seemed very old, crooked and tumbledown, and some animals grazing in the fields that looked like a cross between a sheep and a dwarf camel.

Gloria asked what they were, and the Prince replied: "They are llamas, and, as far as I know, much the same species as the animal which is quite common in the Andean States of South America. What my poor subjects would do without them, heaven knows! They give us our only meat, milk, butter and cheese, and in addition, their fat, made into dips and thick candles with special markings on them, provides our only light at night and our only way of telling the time during the long winters when we cannot see the sun. And, of course, their wool, which as you can see, is long and fleecy, and their hides supply the population with ninety per cent. of its clothes. In Peru, so I have heard, the people also use them as beasts of burden, and soon after I arrived here I tried that too, but there was no end of a rumpus. Probably owing to their dependence on them, the people regard their llamas as practically sacred. Anyhow, I had to quell a mutiny, so the experiment was not worth the bother of repeating—particularly as the people themselves provide me with all the beasts of burden I am ever likely to require."

For some quarter of an hour past dim little lights had been appearing in the narrow windows of the scattered cottages, and now they were approaching the first group of buildings they had seen. It was not large enough to be called a village or even a hamlet, but was just half a dozen houses, the sloping roofs of which formed all sorts of crazy angles, set in a small clearing which was surrounded by a high spiked stockade.

"This collection of rabbit hutches," said the Prince, "is the Palace. I fear it must prove a little disappointing to you at first sight, but it is more comfortable inside than you might suppose. The reasons for its 'bittiness' and the eccentricity of its architecture are to be found in the limitations of my people as builders. They understand only how to make one type of house. They have probably been making the same thing for thousands of years longer than the African negroes have their beehive huts, and the type of house they make is perfectly adequate for their simple needs; but they are utterly incapable of making anything larger or different."

While the Prince was talking they reached a narrow gate in the stockade, and pushing it open he went on: "This is the tradesmen's entrance, but coming down from the mountain it is quicker to go in this way. As I was saying, my people have many shortcomings, but they have one virtue, which makes up for much. It is a most unusual feature to find in such an otherwise unprogressive race. They are extraordinarily clean both in their houses and their persons. You could really eat your breakfast off the floors of their cottages and see your faces in the bottoms of their cooking pots. It was that, I'm pretty certain, which saved them from becoming the victims of some frightful epidemic when I first arrived among them."

"Yes," remarked Philip; "more than one native race has been entirely wiped out through a trader or explorer giving them some childish disease like measles. It's probably thousands of years since the people here have mixed with any other race, so I doubt whether they have any immunity at all from our usual ailments. Even our common cold might prove to them as deadly a scourge as the plague."

"Exactly; and for that reason I want to impress on you how important it is to give yourselves a real scrubbing and wash your heads as well when you have your baths in a few minutes' time. Afterwards I'll give you some robes to put on for dinner, so that all your clothes can be sterilized by baking in the oven as soon as possible."

It seemed so sensible a precaution that they agreed at once. Next moment, as they entered the open space round which the cluster of buildings stood, Gloria exclaimed:

"Now aren't these little houses cute! They come straight out of Hans Andersen, an' I wouldn't be a bit surprised to see a witch in a steeple hat open the door of one any minute!"

Each of the houses had a low front door with two steps leading down to it, a small square window at either side and one above which peeped out of the overhanging thatch. The windows had no glass in them but appeared to be made from many small panes of thin horn, through which the lights in several of them glinted dully.

"The only witch in these parts is yourself, dear guest," declared the Prince gallantly, as he stooped down to throw open the door of one of the little houses for Gloria. Following her in, he added:

"Normally, each of the cottages has two rooms on its ground floor and two above, but, as you will see, I eliminated both the partitions and the upper floors, so each piece of the Palace now makes one quite good room. This is my sitting-room. Next door on the right is my bedroom, beyond it lies the bathroom, and other rooms serve as a dining-room, kitchens, store rooms and so on."

The room they entered had a large open fireplace at one end, on which a bright wood fire was burning. Its furniture was of the simplest, consisting of two long low wooden chests, the fronts of which were carved with crude symmetrical designs, and a great pile of woollen pelts which formed a divan in the centre of the floor.

As the only light was the flickering of the fire, neither Gloria nor Philip at first noticed the two small figures who were sitting on low stools in one corner of the room But, as they jumped up and came running forward, the girl exclaimed:

"You didn't tell us you had children here!"

The Prince's mouth twisted cynically as he turned to look at her, but he made no reply and just stood there, fingering his beard. Meanwhile, the two small figures had thrown themselves at his feet and were banging their foreheads repeatedly on the earthen floor, in token of abject submission.

Philip had never seen such a thing happen before, yet the scene seemed vaguely familiar to him. Then he remembered that he had read somewhere that, up to quite recent times, all people who were not of noble birth had to grovel in this manner when admitted to the presence of the Czars of Russia. He recalled, too, with a grim satisfaction that an English merchant of Elizabeth's day, on being told what was expected of him on his presentation at the Court of St. Petersburg, had stoutly refused to make such a fool of himself, and told the scandalized Chamberlain that, as he did not crawl about on his knees in front of his own Sovereign, he certainly would not do so before any foreigner.

For a moment the Prince let the two little figures grovel, then he tapped each of them gently on the back of the head with the sole of his boot and they scrambled to their feet.

When Gloria saw them face to face it was only with the greatest difficulty that she controlled her expression to avoid hurting their feelings. Although they were only just over three foot six in height, and were dressed in woollen rompers, they were not children at all; they were little old men with straggly beards and brown wizened faces like dried-up walnuts.

"Ugly little devils, aren't they?" laughed the King. "These two are my personal servants, and I've christened them Gog and Magog. They

F*

happen to be twins, but in looks they are no exception. In fact, all these queer subjects of mine look so much alike that it's difficult to tell one from another. The fact that they all dress the same way adds to the confusion. They all wear those suits of brown llama's wool and during cold spells a jerkin of dressed llama's hide on top of it." As Solgorukin had been speaking he had pulled off his furs and dropped them casually on the floor, then he spoke to Gog and Magog for a moment in a strange language, and, snatching up the furs, the two little men scuttled away.

The Prince made a gesture towards the divan of fleecy llama skins, and Philip and Gloria, tired after their long day's march, sank gratefully upon it. Within a few moments Gog and Magog reappeared, the one carrying a tray with some pottery cups and a jug on it, the other a dish covered with small, round, flat cakes.

"Sorry that we don't run to Dry Martinis here," their host apologized. "I've tried a dozen times to make alcohol by fermenting various things, but the job absolutely defeats me. Still, you won't find that drink bad. It is made from a kind of blaeberry and is very refreshing. The cakes are rather fun if you like sweet things. They're a bit sticky but that's because they're full of honey. No sugar cane or beet grows in the valley, but the people keep bees, and honey is our universal substitute for sugar."

Soon after they had eaten Gog came in and spoke to his master in the tongue they used together. Standing up, the Prince said to Gloria : " He's come to report that your bath is ready. You'd better have it at once and Philip and I will have ours immediately after. That way you won't delay dinner too much. You see, when I had the Palace built I never expected to receive any guests here, so you'll both have to share my private bathroom until I can get another made. Come along, I'll show you the way."

He led Gloria outside and along to the next house but one, where she found that the bath consisted of a large sink-like trough cut out of solid stone, but it was full of steaming water, and wooden buckets holding additional supplies of hot and cold were ranged along one side of it. Not having had a proper wash since she left the raft a fortnight before, Gloria was looking forward to her dip with as much eagerness as a hungry man does to a square meal; and the Prince kept her only long enough from it to remark that she might find the towels a bit strange at first, as they were made of wool, cotton and linen being unknown in the valley.

When he rejoined his other guest Solgorukin was at once plied with questions about this strange, rather woebegone, little country. "It's just like a Fairy Tale," said Philip. "Those two little men of yours remind me of elves or hobgoblins. Are they really normal human beings or is there something queer about them, just as there is about the climate here? "

"Oh, they're normal enough," the Prince replied, with a shrug. "You just kick one and hear him squeal. After all, they are no smaller than the pigmies that live in the forests of Central Africa, and there is nothing abnormal about them except for their size."

"Did you have much difficulty in getting them to accept your authority?"

"I did at first, but I caught a couple and demonstrated on them what I would do to the rest if they didn't toe the line; but I'd rather not talk about it now as I don't want to have to repeat the whole story again for Gloria's benefit. I'll tell you as much as I can about them during dinner."

In spite of this promise, when, greatly refreshed from their baths, they sat down to dinner in the next house an hour later, the Prince had disappointingly little to say about his people. He had no idea how long they had been settled in the valley or where they had come from, and it was quite clear that he regarded them as little better than intelligent animals which a beneficent Providence had provided to fulfil for him the role that thousands of Russian serfs had played in ministering to the needs of his forefathers. He said of his arrival there nine months before:

"I was already fed up with whaling. The smell of those big fish when they are dead is positively revolting; so I asked the captain to put me ashore for a bit with as much food as I could carry. This range of mountains seemed to be the only feature of interest hereabouts and within the limits of a twelve-day trip. I reached the range in four days, so I thought I could well risk another couple in climbing the nearest pass, and on the sixth day I came on the valley. The people were hostile to begin with, but they had no idea of organizing themselves for any purpose, so their opposition was sporadic and quite easily overcome. One could no longer go to Europe because of this stupid war, and New York society was beginning to pall on me a little, so I decided to settle here."

"Will you be telling me how you learnt the language?" Gloria asked. "That you can speak it in so short a time seems a great cleverness to me."

"Like all undeveloped peoples, their language is simple, because it is required to convey only the simplest ideas. I found it difficult to make myself understood for the first few weeks, but I had little else to think about and constant practice, so after a bit it became quite easy."

"I take it that you're an autocratic monarch," Philip grinned, "and there's no Parliament or anything of that kind."

"No. There is no capital here, no towns, not even a village. On the other hand, there are no rates and no taxes."

"That means no police, no drains and no education."

Solgorukin shrugged. "So far as I know, they have no fixed code of laws, so a law court would be superfluous. I suppose they must have personal disputes at times, but I've very rarely seen any of them quarrelling. As there are no towns, drainage can be dealt with in the manner common to peasants all over the world; and, as for education, well, perhaps they are happier without it."

"Do they have any art, at all?" asked Gloria.

"They carve crude designs such as you may have noticed on the chests and pottery, but they haven't got up to the point of making furniture with drawers, or chairs. The stools we're sitting on are the type they use, and, in order to make this table, I got them to cut a length of the largest tree I could find in half and fit legs into the rounded part. They have not discovered dyes or paints yet. That's why everything is left its natural colour, including the woodwork of the houses and the woollen clothes they wear."

" Do they practise any kind of religion? " Philip inquired.

" No. They have no gods or temples, and they don't worship anything, unless you can call it moon worship to come out each month and dance at the full of the moon."

Gloria looked up quickly. " What sort of dances? "

" It's a kind of ring-a-ring-of-roses in which groups of six or eight of them join hands and jump round in circles. At least, that's the only dance I've ever seen them do. I discovered this practice of theirs by chance one night, and, on the two or three occasions I've endeavoured to watch them, directly they've realized I'm looking on they've broken up and gone home. As I didn't want to spoil their fun I gave up my attempts to find out more about their monthly gatherings."

" Anyhow, they cook jolly well," remarked Philip. " The meat is simply delicious."

" I'm afraid a large part of its charm for you is due to the fact that it is many months since you last ate fresh meat," smiled the Prince. " It's llama, of course, and I've no doubt that in time you'll get as sick of it as you would of mutton if nothing but mutton were available."

" But the vegetables and the gravy and the little oatcakes," Gloria protested; " Philip's right, Prince—they're all just marvellous."

" Well, yes. Actually their cooking is much better than might be expected, and particularly their treatment of vegetables. They grow the most excellent salads, and they make many kinds of cheeses, but unfortunately we have very few fruits and no domestic birds—so no eggs. However, while the season lasts I occasionally make an expedition to the seashore and come back with as many gulls' and penguins' eggs as I can carry."

When they had finished dinner they moved back to the sitting-room, but all of them were tired after their long day. As the conversation languished Solgorukin stood up and said :

" As I never expected to entertain there are no proper guest-rooms. For the time being I suggest that you should make yourself comfortable on the divan here, Gloria, and I'll have some more skins put down for Philip in the dining-room."

Philip and Gloria looked at each other. For many months past they had shared the same sleeping accommodation, and somehow it had never occurred to either of them that they would now be separated.

The Prince caught the uncertainty in their glance and, stroking his curly black beard, said smoothly: " Of course, in view of your quite exceptional circumstances during the past two years, it would not be the least surprising if you had come to regard each other as husband and wife, but I had formed the impression that that was not so. If I am wrong you must forgive me, and we will make more suitable arrangements."

"Oh, no!" exclaimed Philip and Gloria together. One added: "Thanks awfully!" and the other: "I'll be fine right here!" and both of them wished their cynically smiling host a rather awkward good-night, Philip following him out into the darkness.

Next morning, after breakfast, the Prince took them for a walk further down the slope into the valley. It was much too big for them to explore the whole of it in one day, but their host told them that during the tour on which he proposed to take them they would see things typical of all that was in the whole country; and they would discover little that was fresh even if they covered the country acre by acre for a couple of years.

There were, as he had told them the night before, no villages, and the population seemed very evenly dispersed with one cottage to every six or eight small fields. Here and there the people were now working in the fields, but they had only the most rudimentary agricultural tools, such as rough spades and hoes with which they laboriously furrowed the earth instead of ploughing it.

Only the little gnome-like men were to be seen working. The women were all busy in their kitchens or in the dairies which leant crookedly against the side of each small house. Now and again, Solgorukin turned off the dirt track which served as a road, to take his guests into one of the houses. Wherever he appeared, men, women and children immediately threw themselves on the ground and banged their foreheads on the earth until he called to them to stop.

Gloria noticed that all laughter ceased among these white pigmies directly they became aware that the Prince was in the vicinity, and it was clear that he was very much feared. She was intensely interested in the women, but found to her disappointment that they were almost as ugly as the men. They all seemed very fat, but that was largely due to the great amount of clothing they wore. They all had the same type of knitted bodice and skirt of brown wool with alternate dark and light stripes, which billowed out owing to the thick garments beneath it and almost touched the ground.

Through the centre of the valley ran a stream, and at one place it broadened out into a lake, below which cascaded an eighteen-foot water-fall. On the banks of the lake two of the pigmies were fishing with primitive rods without reels.

"I suppose they catch something sometimes or they wouldn't do it," remarked Philip.

"Oh, yes," Solgorukin replied. "As a matter of fact, they are surprisingly good considering the wretched rods they have to use; and the fish here are very well worth catching. We have types of mullet, trout and salmon."

After two hours' walk they climbed the hill again towards the Palace. As they approached the front entrance of the stockade, Philip's horrified attention was caught by a thing that neither he nor Gloria had noticed that morning when they came out.   There was a fair sprinkling of trees in the valley and several quite large patches of woodland, but none of the trees were very tall.   One of the tallest they had so far seen was a medium-size oak standing a few yards to the left of the entrance of the Palace courtyard.   From one of the lower branches dangled the body of one of the little men.   As he did not wish to attract Gloria's attention to such a sinister spectacle Philip refrained from remarking on it, but next moment the limp body was swung round a fraction by a puff of wind, and catching sight of it she came to a sudden halt, exclaiming:

" Holy Saint Bridget!   What's that? "

" I regret that it should offend your bright eyes," the Prince replied lightly, " but I have found that discipline is best maintained by leaving the body of the last offender against it hanging as an example to other would-be mutineers.   You will be glad to hear, though, that it is now several months since I have been compelled to execute anyone."

" What did the poor little wretch do? " asked Philip.

" When I was out one day he got hold of my rifle and tried to shoot me. Fortunately it proved much too big and unwieldy for him, but one cannot allow a thing like that to go unpunished."

" You must have done something to provoke him," Gloria said, as she walked on again.   " Otherwise, why would he be wantin' to kill you? "

" Oh, he had a grudge, of course.   During the previous week I had killed one of his llamas for my larder.   Naturally, they hate losing their beasts, but I and my small staff at the Palace must have a reasonable amount of meat, and I spread my demands as evenly as possible over the countryside, so that no individual peasant is expected to provide more than one animal a year."

Both Philip and Gloria thought it hard that the poor little peasant should have been hanged for his futile attempt to revenge himself after being robbed of his property; yet it was difficult to argue against the Prince's contention.   He and his staff must somehow be fed.   It was pointless to say that as an interloper he was not entitled to any food at all and that by his creation of the Palace he had placed a burden on the people that they had not had to bear before.   The fact was that he had established himself as the supreme ruler of the place, and like all other rulers, whether kings, priests or presidents, he expected his people to provide for himself and his retainers.

During the next few days they made similar excursions to other parts of the valley, but they saw little, except certain vegetables and a few modest flowers, that they had not already seen.   At first, Philip enjoyed the change and relaxation.   It is true that the life on board the raft had, in the main, been a lazy one, but there always had been something to do— the vagaries of the weather needed watching, and from time to time unexpected emergencies had to be coped with. Here, on the other hand, he had no work of any kind, no responsibilities, and, even if the moderately warm spring-like weather gave place overnight to a storm, it could no longer materially affect him. Yet, after a week of eating more than was good for him and going for aimless walks, he became bored and irritable.

Gloria's behaviour was to a large extent responsible for his short temper. She quite obviously preferred the Prince's company to his own, and he felt that, after all this time, it was most unkind of her to show her preference so openly. He admitted to himself that the Prince was a handsome and amusing person, but he felt that anyone with the least discernment should also be able to see that he was an unscrupulous rogue with the most unpleasant streak of cruelty in his nature. Yet, to Philip's intense annoyance, he found that Gloria bore out all he had ever read about the queerness of women in such matters, and their frequent disregard of man-made moral standards. Whenever they were alone she would not hear a word against the Russian, and she even seemed to approve of his brutally selfish behaviour in many of the episodes which he recounted with such gusto from his unsavoury past.

Another thing that worried Philip was the future. It was owing to his dream in which the Canon had urged him to attempt to return to the raft that he had met the Prince. This had most probably saved Gloria from freezing to death in the snow and resulted in their having reached a safe and comfortable refuge. In consequence, the outcome of the dream had aroused all his old memories of his vision and revived his faith in it. When the Canon appeared during the storm he had definitely said that if Philip proved equal to the burden that had been laid upon him, no man of his generation would have done more to help bring about the defeat of Germany; and it was transparently clear to Philip that he would come no nearer even to learning what form his mission would take so long as he remained in the valley of the pigmies. By the time he had been there ten days he was beginning to wonder how by hook or by crook he could reach the nearest outpost of civilization and to make his way home.

When he spoke to Gloria about it she proved far from enthusiastic. They had, she pointed out, been faced with dangers and difficulties for an almost interminable time, yet with the help of the Virgin Mary and all the Saints they had been spared to come to a land of peace and plenty; so why should they not enjoy their blessings?

Faced with the question as to whether she would be content to remain there all her life, she replied:

"I'll not say I wouldn't. There are worse places by far, though I'm thinking I'd be heartsick for a change after a year or two. But where would you be going, Boy, should himself raise no objection—which I've a feeling he would? "

" To hell with that! " exclaimed Philip, knowing that by " himself " she meant the Prince. " If I want to leave this valley, it will take more than

him to stop me. The place to head for, of course, is the MacKenzie Sea,
a bit further west than we should have struck it. I'm dead certain there's
a whaling station there. He as good as admitted it to start with. Then he
went back on what he said, because he's anxious to preserve the secret of
his ' kingdom,' as he calls it. The night we arrived he spun that yarn
about his captain having put him ashore for a twelve days' holiday. As
though any captain would be such a fool as to let his second mate go joy-
riding ashore while he was still manœuvring his ship in an ice-infested
sea! "

"Oh, he's a lovely liar! " smiled Gloria. "But he's an ill man to cross,
Boy; so best watch your step."

On the following day Philip tackled the Russian as tactfully as he could.
"Please don't think I'm ungrateful," he began, "but I can't possibly
settle down here indefinitely. So far as we know, the war is still going on
at home, and I shall feel ashamed of myself for the rest of my days if I
don't manage to get back and take some sort of a hand in it before it's all
over."

"While no such mad desire to immolate myself on the altar of my
country is ever likely to cloud my own judgment," replied the Prince, "I
can understand it doing so in others. But how, pray, do you propose to
set about getting back to civilization? "

"We shall head for . . . "

"*We?* " interrupted Solgorukin sharply. "Surely you don't propose
that Gloria should share your crazy attempt to break out of the
Antarctic? "

"Well," Philip hesitated, "I shall certainly take her with me if she
wishes to come; but at the moment I'm not quite certain what she means
to do."

"Let us not concern ourselves with her for the time being then. You
were saying that you meant to head for . . .? "

"The whaling station on the MacKenzie Sea."

"I have already told you there is no whaling station there." The
Prince's voice was icy.

"All right then. What whaling station did the ship that you sailed in
put into? "

"We were hunting in these waters, but our base was in the South
Shetlands, which are thousands of miles from here."

"In that case I shall go to the MacKenzie Sea, then march west along
the coast until I find one."

"You are mad! " said the Prince angrily. "And in no circumstances
will I permit you to take Gloria with you. She remains here with me! "

"That is for her to say. Anyhow, I take it you won't put any obstacles
in my way and will not object to my taking all the food I can carry? "

The Russian remained silent for a moment with his dark eyes half-
closed, then he said slowly: "A week or two can make little difference

to you, and there was something I had in mind for which I should like your help before you go."

" What is it? " inquired Peter non-committally.

" As you may be aware, neither threats nor promises will induce my miserable little subjects to put one foot outside their valley. In consequence, any expeditions that I make to the coast have to be made alone. That greatly limits the number of penguins' eggs or seal meat that I can bring back. Now, I understand that you had by no means exhausted all the provisions on your raft; and many of them would be great luxuries to me. The place where the raft is beached cannot be very much further in a straight line from here than the place where I found you, so one should be able to get there and back easily in ten days. Would you be willing to accompany me on a trip to the raft before making your attempt to reach a whaling station? "

Philip hesitated only for a second. The request was not an unreasonable one. Ten days counted for little in the months it would take him to get back to England, but another ten days of rest coupled with monotony might make Gloria much more willing to join him in his bid to get home; and he was most loath to leave her behind. In fact, he had already made up his mind that, somehow or other, he simply must persuade her to come with him. So he replied: " Yes—by all means I'll make the trip to the raft with you first."

" Good! " laughed the Prince, his boisterous good humour restored. " That's settled then."

During the next two days he made no further reference to the projected trip, but he paid more attention than ever to Gloria with, so Philip supposed, the intention of dissuading her from accompanying him in any attempt to reach a whaling station.

In the evenings it had become more or less a habit for Gloria to announce when she was feeling like bed, upon which the two men would bid her good-night and leave her in possession of the sitting-room; but sometimes the Russian made a move of his own accord and sometimes, if Philip felt bored by their exclusion of him from their conversation, he would get up and go off first. Two nights after his talk with the Prince he was both tired and bored. That day he had been for a long aimless walk, and at dinner the others had hardly addressed a word to him, so, having accompanied them across to the sitting-room, he allowed just enough time for the dining-room table to be cleared before he said: " If you don't mind, I think I'll turn in."

They both wished him a perfunctory good-night, and he went back to the dining-room, where he found Gog and Magog preparing his bed of llama skins. By this time he had managed to pick up a few words of the little people's language, so he was able to thank them when they left, but he did not start to undress. Instead, he sat down to think over again the problem which had been worrying him all day. How could he ensure that

Gloria left the valley with him? The last thing he wished to do was to expose her to serious danger again, but, on the other hand, he had grown much too fond of her to leave her with anyone whom he distrusted as profoundly as he did their host.

Over an hour later he was still cogitating the same question when he thought he heard a muffled shout. Stiffening where he sat, he strained his ears to listen, and the shout came again from the direction of the sitting-room.

He had no doubt whatever that it was Gloria getting what she had asked for by setting her cap at the Prince—and not liking it. He had seen this coming for days and known that when it came it would mean a show-down between the Russian and himself, which would probably cost one of them their lives.

The cry came for a third time as he was hastily getting Eiderman's pistol out of his haversack. Thrusting it into his pocket, he dashed from the room.

CHAPTER XIV

THE SHOWDOWN

In a second Philip was across the enclosure. Flinging wide the door, he sprang into the sitting-room. Gloria was struggling on the great pile of skins, half-buried beneath the bulk of the Prince, who was holding her down. At the noise of the door being flung open, he let go of her, and they both sat up.

"What the hell d'you think you're up to?" Philip angrily demanded of the Russian.

"Get out!" snarled the Prince in reply.

"No!" Gloria panted, as she hurriedly smoothed down her clothes. "Please stay—but there's nothing to get excited about. 'Twas tickling me he was—and you know I can't stand being tickled. That's what made me shout."

Solgorukin stood up. His dark eyes were glinting dangerously and his mouth twisted into an ugly sneer. For a moment it looked as if he meant to throw himself on Philip, but apparently he thought better of it, for he suddenly relaxed and said, with a shrug:

"All right. Come in, if you wish. Gloria and I were having a romp, that's all. But we shall find plenty of other opportunities when you've left us."

"Perhaps!" said Philip dryly. "Anyhow, I haven't left you yet. Incidentally, one of the reasons for that is your own request that I should not go until I had accompanied you on a trip to collect some stuff from the raft; but you haven't shown much keenness on the idea since I promised that I'd give you my help."

Solgorukin toyed with his black beard for a moment, then he said: "All right, we will set out for the raft to-morrow, if you like."

"That's O.K. by me," agreed Philip.

"Good!" The Prince turned to smile at Gloria. "Well, if there are to be no more romps to-night I'll leave you now. Philip can retire to his couch with a quiet mind, or, if you prefer, remain here to amuse you in my stead." With a graceful bow to her and a casual nod to Philip, he marched out of the room swinging the door to behind him.

Philip was about to follow when Gloria said in a rather small voice: "Don't go. Sit down for a few minutes and have a drink." Walking over to one of the chests on which a jug of fruit juice was always kept, she poured some into a mug and brought it to him.

"Thanks," he said, taking the mug; but he did not drink from it and went on seriously: "You know, Gloria, you'll be letting yourself in for a packet of trouble if you go on leading Solgorukin up the garden path like this."

"I know," she answered, turning away from him towards the fire and beginning to prod nervously at the logs with her foot.

"Well," he went on, as he put down the unwanted drink. "Of course, it's not my affair, but . . ."

"Isn't it?" she burst out passionately. "Isn't it your affair? Whose fault is it that I'm here at all? It's two years and three months since we left New York. That's a long time at my age. And will we ever get back? If we do I'll probably be an old woman by then, and I don't want to live like a nun all the days of me life!"

Suddenly she swung round and faced him. "Oh, Boy, I know I was beastly to you about what happened before. And maybe I've been wasting my time trying to make you jealous. But if you don't want me I'm going to him! I'm going to him now, this very moment!"

As she stamped her foot Philip seized her by the arms and pulled her violently towards him. Next second she was sobbing her heart out on his shoulder, while his cheek pressed tight against her burnished curls.

It was moments later before they could even stammer at each other between kisses, and at first Philip could only say:

"Oh, Gloria, my darling Gloria! Gloria, my love, my love!"

"I—I won't expect you to . . . to marry me, if—if we do get back," she said, between her sobs.

"But, of course, I shall marry you," he declared. "You're the only girl I've ever really cared for, and I couldn't possibly live with anybody else. It's having been separated from you that has made me so desperately unhappy these past two weeks."

"Yes, me too. We'd kind of grown together, hadn't we? But really I've been loving you in me heart from the very day I first set eyes on you!"

Philip laughed then and held her away from him to smile down into her face. "You adorable little liar! You hated my very guts."

She shook her head. "Not really. I thought you were an awful old stodge. But I admired your courage and I liked your looks. They say, too, that imitation is the sincerest form of flattery. Just think of the trouble I've taken to get out of using Bowery slang and the way I've soft-pedalled my Irish accent—simply because I wanted to talk more like you."

"Oh, darling, please! You make me feel the most awful snob, and I was an absolute brute to you in lots of ways."

"'Tis meself is the snob and you weren't a brute at all. The way I plagued you it's a miracle you didn't throw me overboard, and I've no wonder at all that you took a great hate to me."

"No, no, my sweet, I never hated you. I swear I didn't," Philip protested vehemently. "It's true enough that I used to worry myself quite a bit about what you'd be up to next, but I thought you had tremendous guts and you never once let me down when we were in trouble. Then you are such a marvellous companion, and from the very first I used to love to watch your face light up when you became excited about something, and just to look at you as you moved about the launch or sat around on deck."

"Oh, Boy, stop now, or I'll hardly believe it all. In a moment you'll be going back on what you've always said and telling me I'm pretty."

"But you are; and I've never said otherwise except just once when I wanted to get my own back over that libellous portrait you did of me. You're beautiful, darling. You're beautiful with the real beauty that grows on one until one comes to realize that there is nothing to equal it in the whole world."

With shining eyes she lifted her lips to his again, and their mouths met in a long sweet kiss.

"Why . . . why didn't you tell me all this before?" she gasped when at last she could speak again.

"Because I've been a coward and a fool," he admitted. "While we were alone together there were scores of times when I ached to take you in my arms, but I simply didn't dare. Then, these past three weeks since the Prince came on the scene, I've come to realize how desperately I love you; but I thought it was too late. I've been going through positive hell in the belief that you'd fallen for him."

"Fallen for that mountebank!" Gloria exclaimed.

"Well, you admitted just now that you'd been doing your best to make me jealous and you certainly succeeded. Still, that makes it all the pleasanter to hear you call him a mountebank."

"He's something much worse than that," said Gloria, lowering her voice. "Of course, he's amusing and makes one laugh, but he's the king of all the liars that ever were, and I wouldn't trust him with a ten cent piece. He's treacherous, Boy, and as cruel as a snake, so that it's really frightened of him I am at times. Frightened for you, I mean, if you should cross him. You'll be careful, won't you? I beg you to for my sake."

"Let's not talk of anything unpleasant to-night," smiled Philip, and picking her up he laid her gently down on the soft bed of skins, and kissing her took her once more into his arms.

Yet, eight hours later, when the first glimmer of dawn began to show through the little horn panes of the windows, they perforce reverted to the subject of the Prince, as it was essential that they should decide the line of policy they meant to adopt towards him.

Philip favoured an announcement and proposed saying straight out at the earliest opportunity: "You may remember, Prince, that on the night of our arrival here you remarked to Gloria and myself that, in view of our quite exceptional circumstances during the past two years, it would not be the least surprising if we had come to regard each other as husband and wife. Well, I am delighted to tell you that we intend to regard each other in that way for the future." But Gloria would not hear of it.

"Please, Boy, do no such thing," she pleaded. "He has the very devil of a temper and it hangs only by a hair. If he lost it the Saints alone know what he'd do to both of us. I'm sure you're right about his murderin' that last wife of his, poor woman, and if he thought that I was in love with you I believe he'd shoot you without a second thought."

"But hang it all!" demurred Philip. "I *must* say something. You know jolly well that having no idea of what was going to happen later on last night I let myself in for setting out with him this morning to go and fetch stores from the raft. What other excuse can I possibly make for not going? And I'm hanged if I'll start off on a ten days' trip just when we've—er—found each other."

Gloria bubbled with laughter and pulled his head down to hers so that she could kiss him, before she murmured: "Found each other! What a lovely way to put it, Boy, when it's almost cheek to cheek we've been living all these months."

"Well, you know what I mean. After all, even if we're stuck out here almost at the South Pole, that's no reason why we shouldn't have a honeymoon—and I don't see why we should allow the convenience of that blasted Russian to interfere with our taking it when we want to, either."

"No, no, we'll not let him do that," Gloria said soothingly. "All the same, I'm not saying that the most convenient time for us is right now. For one thing we must go carefully, Boy, we really must. He might spoil everything for us if we sprung it on him. I'll be looking forward to our honeymoon every bit as much as you, but I'm sure it would be best if you went off with him, as you have arranged to do, this morning."

"What! And leave you? Within a few hours of all this? I simply couldn't. And why on earth should I?"

"So that while you're away I'll have the chance to do a wee bit of thinking. By the time you get back I'll have made a sweet little plot for getting him to accept the situation."

" But I'll be away for ten days—more perhaps."

Gloria gave him a steady look. " Wasn't I just saying that the best time for us might be thereabouts? I'm sure I caught a chill yesterday. I can feel it coming on, and I may not be feeling up to much for the best part of a week."

" Oh, well, in that case, darling—still, I just hate to leave you, and I'd far rather have it out with Solgorukin here and now."

" But you're not going to, darling. Instead, you'll be giving me the biggest kiss ever yet, then be getting back to your own room before Gog or Magog is about. And no kissing me good-bye in front of himself, either. I'd be scared into a fit if I thought you were going off with him and him suspecting something; so be good now, and I'll have thought of a way to fix things by the time you get back."

" I don't much like the idea of leaving you alone with these queer little men, though," Philip protested.

" Oh, I'll be all right. They'll never dare to harm me."

Philip produced his gun and handed it to her.

" Anyhow, I'd be happier if you'd take this, just in case they cut up rough. I shan't need it till I get back, and I hope not then."

They lingered together for another half-hour, then she positively drove him from her; and he had not been back on his own couch in the dining-room for more than ten minutes before Magog came to call him.

When they assembled for breakfast an hour later Philip was in hopes that the Prince might have forgotten all about the expedition, or for some reason of his own produce an excuse for putting it off; but this did not prove to be the case. They had hardly exchanged good-mornings before he announced that he had given Gog orders to get out the sledge and pack up a good supply of dried llama's meat and other things to go on it. He added that the meat was very sustaining and that a handful of it with a little honey would keep one going for a whole day. He also announced that he needed no coverings other than his furs, but he suggested that Philip should carry the bivouac which had served as a hammock for Gloria, so that he could sleep under it at nights.

These preparations were so simple that they were very soon completed. To his fury Philip had time only to squeeze Gloria's hand while the Prince turned his back for a moment to take his furs from Gog; then, with as little fuss as if they were going for an ordinary walk, except that the Prince was carrying his repeating rifle and Philip was pulling the sledge, the two of them said good-bye to her and set off towards the plateau.

Both of them looked back and waved from time to time as they climbed the slope, but by eleven o'clock they had reached its edge, and, after a last wave, the two now tiny figures disappeared from her view.

They did not stop for a long break at midday and halted, with military

precision, for only ten minutes in every hour; so they were down through
the pass and out on to the still crisp snow of the plain by late afternoon. Here they set a course several degrees more to the eastward than
that which they had followed on coming to the valley, and pressed on for
a further three hours before picking out a spot sheltered from the wind
by a fold in a glacier, in which to camp for the night.

It was nearly a month since Philip and Gloria had left the raft, and now
mid-November; so the weather was very much better and the days
lengthening with the advance of the Antarctic summer. Apart from having
to make a few detours round patches of soft snow in which they sank
nearly up to their knees, and one really bad day when it took them eight
hours to cross a mile of broken ice, they met with no setbacks; and on the
fifth day they reached the coast.

For a little they were uncertain which way to turn, but Philip felt sure
that he recognised a cone of black basalt that crowned a nearby headland,
which meant that he must have passed it when trekking west towards the
MacKenzie Sea, so they turned right, and after a further five-mile trudge
entered the small bay in which the raft lay.

Philip found everything much as he had left it. The raft was still
frozen in, but beyond the bay the ice had now broken up, and some of
the floes showed signs of disintegration.

The Prince was intensely interested in the whole contraption and
expressed such open admiration for the thought that had gone to planning
it all that Philip found it difficult to continue feeling hostile towards him.
They dug out all sorts of good things to eat and spent quite a merry
evening.

First thing next morning they made a careful selection of the items they
meant to take back, and among them Philip insisted on including a
number of his most useful carpenter's tools. During his stay in the valley
he had thought of several things for which they might come in handy, and
now that he meant to honeymoon with Gloria it looked as if there would
be time to carry some of them out before undertaking the attempt to reach
a whaling station. The Prince at first protested about the extra weight,
but agreed to humour him, and they set out on their return journey, both
now pulling the fully loaded sledge.

Naturally, the going was slower, owing to the weight they were dragging,
but the big, muscular Russian seemed almost tireless, and Philip felt the
strain far less than he would otherwise have done because of the exciting
thought that every step he took was bringing him nearer to Gloria.

The weather remained good, except for one heavy fall of snow that
compelled them to camp early on their fourth afternoon, and, as they were
not near any sheltered spot, drove the hardy Russian into sharing Philip's
bivvy, but by the fifth morning they reached the foothills, and by sunset
they were almost through the rock-strewn gorge that led up to the plateau.
It was no more than half a mile away, so only the crossing of it and the

descent to the valley remained to be accomplished, and after a last halt they expected to reach the Palace in time for late dinner.

They had their ten minutes' rest, and it was Philip, now burning with impatience to see Gloria, who said: " Come along! Last lap—let's get it over."

To his surprise, the Russian looked at him rather sadly, and shook his head. Then he said:

" No, Philip. I'm afraid this is where we part."

" What on earth d'you mean? " Philip asked in amazement.

The Prince was sitting on a flat-topped rock some fifteen paces distant and his repeating rifle was lying across his knees. Unobtrusively he slipped off the safety catch as he replied: " For various reasons, my poor Philip, we have become allergic to each other. To start with, there is this crazy idea of yours that you must get home to fight the Germans, so you are determined to go in search of the whaling station on the MacKenzie Sea. Of course, you are right about that. There is one there, and I was stationed at it when I decided to make the little trip inland which resulted in my discovery of the valley."

" I thought as much," muttered Philip; " but what's all this leading up to? "

" First to the point that I cannot allow anyone who has been in my kingdom to leave it. You see, when I failed to return to the whaling station last February my shipmates must naturally have assumed that I had fallen down a crevasse or met my death in some other way. For reasons which I will not go into, that suits me very well. I am sorry to appear distrustful, but I cannot risk anyone who knows that I am still alive communicating with the outside world, because some day I might get bored and wish to return to it myself under another name; and I can do that in safety only so long as it is believed that I died here."

Philip had begun to feel apprehensive. He was holding a two-pound tin of toffee that he had brought from the raft, and he shifted it nervously back and forth from one hand to the other, as he said: " Look here, what are you driving at? "

Ignoring the interruption, the Russian went on smoothly: " Secondly, there is the question of the girl. You are in love with her, aren't you? "

" Yes, I am, but what about it? "

" Only that I have never allowed any man to come between me and a woman I desired. I am not in love with her myself, but she amuses me, and I am determined to have her. By disposing of you I shall spare myself the scenes you would certainly make and achieve my object more easily."

Philip took two strides forward, but the Russian raised his rifle and snapped: " Stay where you are! I have little more to say. I have given you two very good reasons why by your own attitude you have left me no option but to kill you. I could have shot you from behind a dozen times in the past few days, but I preferred to pay you the compliment of allowing you to face your death like the brave man I believe you to be."

The thoughts in Philip's brain raced like a mill-stream. The whole situation was fantastic, impossible. No one could murder another person for their own selfish ends and in cold blood like this. Yet, he knew that was precisely what the black-bearded Prince meant to do. He was mad, of course, a megalomaniac; but that did not alter the fact that he had decided to inflict death and had the means to do it. A bullet fired by him would be just as effective as one fired by a sane man—and he was a crack shot.

Philip tried frantically to think of something to say, some argument which would appeal to the Russian's vanity or sense of humour, but he could think of nothing. For a second he contemplated hurling himself forward, but the distance was too great for him to cover it in time. Before he was halfway across the space between him and his self-appointed executioner his chest would be riddled with bullets. Beside him there was a high rock screening the entrance to a side gully. If he could slip behind that he might have a slender, a very slender, chance of getting away and behind other cover before the Prince could reach the entrance of the gully. But, even for a sideways jump into the fleeting security offered by the big rock, it was necessary to distract his would-be killer's attention for ten seconds. He was still nervously juggling with the tin of toffee. As Solgorukin lifted his rifle to his shoulder to take aim, Philip suddenly threw back his arm and flung the tin at the Prince's head.

The tin was still hurtling through the air as Philip sprang for the entrance of the gully. As he landed behind the tall rock he stumbled and almost fell, but he regained his balance and dashed on. The gully proved to be a narrow defile almost blocked by one great slab of rock some twenty yards down it. Running for his life, Philip spurted towards the narrow fissure between the block and the cliff-face. He felt that he might squeeze his way through where the Prince with his greater bulk and thick furs would find it much more difficult. If that proved the case he might win sufficient lead to find a hiding-place further up the gully where he could lie concealed until full night had fallen. Then, later, under cover of it, he would make his way down into the valley, and when his murderous enemy was asleep find some way of overpowering him.

Solgorukin had fired his rifle, but the tin of toffee had come flying towards him before he had taken proper aim, so his bullet ricochetted harmlessly down the valley, but he felt confident that he could soon get his victim at his mercy again.

Lowering his rifle with a chuckle at the unexpected sport that the Englishman now looked like giving him, he started in swift pursuit.

Philip was squeezing himself through the narrow fissure when he heard the clink of stones struck sharply aside by the Russian's swift-moving boots. The noise spurred him to fresh exertions. The close, dark cleft was about twelve feet deep, and he was two-thirds of the way along it. With an effort that almost tore his coat off his back, he burst his way out at the other end and began to run again. The gully was now a mass of broken, tumbled rock, over which it was difficult to travel fast, but offering good cover further on.

Suddenly the rifle cracked. Philip felt as though someone had hit him with a hammer on the back of his right calf. He had never before been wounded, and, as he felt no pain, he did not realise for a second that it was a bullet which had struck him; but at his next step his leg collapsed under him, and he went crashing down among the rocks.

Scrambling to his knees, he tried to get up, but his injured leg was now only a dull, useless appendage which refused its service and dangled grotesquely below his still sound knee. As he fell again he came down on his back, and for the first time saw how his enemy had managed to catch him so quickly. The Prince had not attempted to force his way through the narrow cleft. Instead, he had climbed the great ten foot high lump of rock that nearly blocked the gully. He was standing there on top of it silhouetted against the evening sky, a dominating, satanically grinning figure.

" So you thought you could get away from me, eh? " he laughed down at Philip. " Did I not tell you when we first met that I am a marvellous shot? I could have winged you at half a mile had I wished. But it's getting late and I didn't want to have to follow you too far up into the mountains to administer the *coup de grâce*. By the bye, this brief post-ponement of your end enables me to rectify a slight omission which you may have noticed in my good manners. I forgot to thank you for helping me to bring all those things from the raft."

" Damn your eyes! " snarled Philip, striving to rise again. As he did so he thought he heard some stones tinkle somewhere beyond the Prince, but he knew it must have been his imagination.

The Russian went down on one knee, brought his rifle up to his shoulder and pointed it at Philip; but he did not seem to be in any hurry to fire and went on conversationally: " As a matter of fact, fetching those stores prolonged your life for ten days. If it hadn't been that I wanted your help to bring them as far as the entrance to the plateau I would have shot you the evening you had the impertinence to interrupt me when I was making love to Gloria. Anyhow, nothing is going to stop me making love to her to-night—not even Gloria herself! "

" 'Tis wrong you are there! " came a voice from the far side of the rock, and Philip's heart leapt.

" Gloria! " he shouted.

At the same second the Prince half-turned and rose to his feet. Two shots followed each other in rapid succession. The Prince staggered, dropped his rifle and fell to his knees.

For a moment he remained there breathing heavily, then he seemed to make a great effort, and picking up his rifle raised it slowly to his shoulder.

"Gloria!" yelled Philip again. "Look out! He's going to shoot! For God's sake, get under cover!"

A third shot rang out, but not from the rifle. The Prince flinched again just before he squeezed his trigger.

The rifle cracked. There was a piercing scream, followed by another sound, a weird choking cackle. The Prince was laughing.

For a moment the noise of the last shots echoed and re-echoed round the valley, then the Russian seemed to slide forward so that he was hidden from Philip's view.

In an agony of fear Philip began to shout again: "Gloria! Are you all right? Oh, Gloria, for God's sake, answer me!"

But not even a whisper came in reply. Night was now falling fast, and an utter silence enveloped the rock-strewn valley.

CHAPTER XV

THE COMING OF THE DOG

NOT a whisper of sound broke the stillness until Philip began to drag himself over the rocks. In his mind an intuitive flash had already given him the explanation of what had taken place. Gloria had known that he and the Prince might arrive back any time from the tenth day after their departure. Carrying the pistol that he had left with her, she must have walked up to the plateau and across it to the edge of the gorge that afternoon in the hope of meeting them if they returned before nightfall. She was probably sitting up there wondering how much longer to give them before abandoning her vigil for the night, when the Russian's first shot had brought her hurrying to the scene.

Philip needed no telling that her opportune arrival had saved his life, but he was in desperate fear that she had paid for it with her own. Her first shots could only have wounded the Prince. At all events they had left him the strength to turn and take careful aim at her—and he was a crack shot. The awful silence seemed to confirm Philip's worst forebodings.

Dragging his injured leg behind him he began to haul himself as quickly as he could towards the narrow passage between the cliff-face and the great slab of rock on the top of which Solgorukin lay. He wondered anxiously if the Prince was dead. Even Gloria's third shot might not have proved fatal to him. He was a big, strong, vital man of the type that takes a great deal of killing. There came into Philip's mind an account he had read of the death of another black-bearded Russian— the evil monk Rasputin; and he remembered how extraordinarily hard it had proved to kill him.

The conspirators who had determined to murder Rasputin from patriotic

motives had invited him to a musical entertainment. They put enough
strychnine in the monk's coffee to kill ten ordinary men, but it left
him completely unaffected. One of them shot him through the chest with
a revolver, but he did not fall, and as he strode towards the door his
astonished attackers made way for him, believing that the superstition
that he could not be killed by mortal hand must be correct. As he passed
through the door a servant seized a big hunting-knife from the wall and
drove it through the monk's back; only then did he stagger and collapse.
They got him into a car and drove him down to the bank of the frozen
Neva. Having broken a hole in the ice, they pushed him in; but he was
still living and tried to struggle out, so they had to hold his head under
until he drowned.

With a pistol it had been good shooting on Gloria's part to hit the
Prince at all, so it was very possible that none of her bullets had wounded
him in a vital part. Philip hoped desperately that his enemy was dead,
but knew that he might only be shamming death or have fainted from
loss of blood.

As he struggled forward, in spite of his urgency, he felt very tired and
strangely feeble; but it was not until he had begun to worm his way
through the cleft that he understood the reason. In lifting his dead leg
over a ridge of rock at the entrance of the passage his hands became
covered with something warm and sticky, and he knew then that he must
be bleeding copiously.

He was now faced with the alternative of losing more blood if he
pressed on or saving his ebbing strength by stopping at once to bind up
his wound; but his anxiety about Gloria was such that, even had he
known his life to hang upon it, he could not have brought himself to halt
for a single moment.

Tearing his nails upon the rock, he pulled himself through the cleft and,
panting from his exertions, lay still an instant while he fished in his
pocket for his torch. He had good reason to thank his gods that
on his visit to the raft he had thought of fitting it out with a new battery,
as it was now dark in the little gorge; all the tumbled rocks were chunks
of blackness, and the entrance could only be seen as a patch of grey.
Flashing the bright beam round he searched the heavy black shadows
with it till it lit upon something white. Next second he saw that it was
Gloria's face and that her huddled body was lying deathly still.

Squirming forward again across the rocks, he flopped down beside
her, then after two sharp-drawn breaths he braced himself to shine the
torch full upon her and learn the extent of her injuries. To shoot at the
Prince she had evidently climbed part of the way up the big rock and,
when he had shot her, fallen backwards down it, as one of her legs was
twisted under her. Her face was untouched, but there was blood on the
rock beside her, and it was falling drop by drop into a little pool from a
dark patch in her side.

From what he could see she had been shot through the ribs and had fainted from loss of blood. He put his hand on her heart and found that it was still beating; but he was filled with terror that her life was ebbing from her and that, unless he could do something quickly, she would die as he lay there beside her.

Propping the torch against a nearby rock so that it shone upon her, he pulled and tore at her clothes until he had bared her side and could see the wound. There were two holes separated by about five inches and just below her right lung: a neat round one to the front and an ugly jagged tear at the back where the bullet, having smashed a lower rib, had come out.

First, Philip made a pad of his handkerchief, which he placed on top of the wound; next, he struggled out of his coat and shirt, tore the shirt into strips and tied them together, then passed the long bandage he had made backwards and forwards round Gloria's body as tightly as he could. It was a rough job, but it was the best he could do for the moment.

He was feeling very groggy now and sat for a moment swaying from side to side. He wanted to be sick, but repressed the feeling with an effort to set about tending his own wound. While he had been bandaging Gloria he had kept his leg in one position, and it had gone stiff; as he moved it now it gave him pain for the first time. He felt it gingerly, but he was already certain that the Russian's bullet had smashed the bone below the knee. The saliva ran hot in his mouth as he gritted his teeth and peeled the torn trouser-leg away from the wound. It was a nasty mess and he had nothing with which to clean it. All he could do was to tear the lining out of his jacket and bandage it up with that. He just managed to finish the job before he fainted.

When he came round, as soon as he could think clearly again, he heard a sound that chilled his blood and made his heart hammer in his throat. A sound of heavy breathing and scraping boots was coming from somewhere above on the big rock beside which he lay. It could mean only one thing: that the murderous Russian was still alive and climbing down towards them.

The torch still burnt, propped between the rocks where Philip had placed it, and it exposed both Gloria and himself in its glare. He wondered why Solgorukin had not used its light to finish them off from the top of the rock. Perhaps, having just come out of a faint himself, he took her stillness for death and was coming down the rock to verify his impression. On the other hand, he might open fire at any moment.

With that thought in mind Philip was terribly tempted to make a grab at the torch and switch it out, so as to secure at least the ephemeral protection of darkness. But there was another movement which it was even more imperative that he should make. He must snatch up the pistol that lay just beyond his present reach, where Gloria had dropped it as she fell. He dared not risk making the two movements together, in case he bungled both; and he knew that he would have only time to make one successfully before the Prince could act on the knowledge that there was still life in at least one of his victims; so the torch must be left.

Philip forced himself to remain very still. The least movement might have betrayed him. He did not even dare to open his eyes, but watched the great mass of shadow about the rock under half-closed eyelids. Solgorukin seemed to take hours in his downward climb, although the gradient of the rock was easy and its surface broken. He gasped, swore and groaned as he came, so he was evidently in great pain, even if not seriously wounded. When he reached the bottom of the rock he rested there for some time, breathing stertorously. Then, having regained his strength, he came on again.

At last the shadows parted and the Russian appeared on the fringe of the area lit by the torch. Philip could guess now why he had not shot at them again. It was either because he had no ammunition left or because he had dropped his rifle and lost it in the darkness through its sliding away down the slope of the rock. In any case, he was no longer carrying it. Instead, he had a large hunting-knife, the naked blade of which gleamed dully between the lips of his bearded mouth. It was clear, too, that one or more of Gloria's shots had struck him in the leg as he, like Philip, was now compelled to drag himself along, and was carrying the knife in his teeth because he needed both his hands.

Philip let him get within ten feet then suddenly sat up, grabbed the pistol, levelled it and fired. Solgorukin's dark eyes rolled wildly in their sockets. The knife fell from his mouth and tinkled on the stony bed of the ravine. A long, low moan issued from his lips, and like a great ship sinking he slowly crumpled to the earth.

The strain and effort had temporarily exhausted Philip. Relaxing, he flopped back against a rock and remained quite still for a while. It was a movement from Gloria that next roused him. She had opened her eyes and was trying to sit up, but she slipped back with a groan.

"Steady, darling!" He found that his words came with difficulty. His mouth was dry and parched. Taking her hand he pressed it.

"Me head!" she moaned. "Oh, me head!"

Picking up the torch, he gently lifted her head and saw something that he had missed before. There was blood on her hair. Evidently, when she fell backwards she had either cut her scalp or fractured her skull; but the bleeding had stopped and her curls were so thick that he felt fairly confident that, however badly her head might be aching at the moment, the injury was not a serious one.

He began to talk to her, telling her that the Russian was dead and that everything would be all right; that they would have to stick it out there for the night, but that, somehow, they would get back to the valley in the morning. But she did not respond, and soon he realized that she was only semi-conscious. From time to time she muttered a little, but the only words that he could catch were: " 'Tis so cold, 'tis so cold! "

Now that it was some time since Philip had exerted himself he was beginning to feel seriously affected by the cold himself. The ravine was near enough to the valley to benefit to some extent from its freak climate, so, although they were far above the normal snowline, there was no snow on the ground, but every inch of rock was dripping wet with the unceasing thaw which always seemed to be in progress on the plateau and in its vicinity. This damp cold was much more penetrating than a moderate degree of frost would have been, and Philip felt that, unless ague and rheumatic fever were to be added to their sufferings, he must do something to counteract it.

With Gloria seriously wounded and his own leg broken, he knew that any attempt to get as far as the valley would prove absolutely hopeless while darkness lasted, so the only relief from the bitter searching cold lay in securing further coverings. The sledge with the supplies from the raft, among which was a quantity of bed and table linen, was well over fifty yards away—a long and exhausting crawl for a man with a broken leg— and it suddenly occurred to Philip that there was extra clothing within ten feet of him—on the Prince's body.

Getting out his torch he crawled over to the Russian, and, fixing the light to shine upon him, began to undo his fur coat preparatory to pulling it off. To his utter horror Solgorukin's eyes suddenly opened. He was not yet dead, and his black eyes were hard and unforgiving. In a harsh, rasping voice he started to speak.

" You can make the weather you want with human blood . . . if you know how. That is the secret . . . the secret of . . . of the Lords of the Mountain. I hope . . . they get you. I . . . I should like to see you taken by the . . . the Dog."

As he ceased speaking a rattle started in his throat. The horrible sound continued for nearly two minutes. When it stopped he suddenly went limp, and Philip knew that this time his enemy was really dead.

Philip was shivering now, and it was only with difficulty that he could prevent his teeth from chattering; so without the least compunction he set about stripping the still warm body of the Prince. His useless leg hampered him considerably, and such garments as he could not get off fairly easily he cut away with the Russian's knife.

When he had done he took the whole bundle in his arms and crawled over to Gloria. Some of the Prince's underclothes he used as extra bandages for her wound and his own. Then he wrapped her in the big fur coat, pulled on the dead man's fur-lined trousers and lay down beside her. She had either fainted again or was asleep, but her body was warm to the touch and her breathing fairly regular. He now felt utterly exhausted, and even the dull throbbing in his leg formed only a part of a nightmare that he seemed to have been experiencing for hours on end. In another few moments he had fallen into a fitful sleep.

As it was now getting towards the end of November the nights were becoming very short, and Philip roused himself as soon as the morning light began to filter into the ravine where they lay. His sleep had done him little good, and he was feeling ghastly, but he knew that somehow he had to make a stupendous effort and get Gloria back to the valley. Her face was now flushed with fever, and she was muttering deliriously. Directly he moved, his leg gave him such a spasm that he almost cried out, but he fought down the pain and crawled along the ravine till he was back in the gorge and had reached the sledge.

Having eaten some chocolate and biscuits, he put more in his pocket, had a long drink of water and filled his flask. Next, he broke the tentpole in half and made a rough splint with it for the lower part of his leg, and, as he knelt, lifted it a little behind him by strapping his ankle to the back of his belt, so that the leg should no longer drag behind him and send a twinge of pain through him every time his foot bumped on the ground. Then he converted two table-cloths into thick knee-pads and taking up a sheet returned with it to Gloria.

After forcing some water from the flask between her parched lips, he folded the sheet lengthwise until it was a long narrow band. Laying the centre of this across her chest, he pushed the ends under her arms and turned her over sideways. Then he lay down back to back with her, drew the ends of the sheet under his own arms and tied them as tightly as he could on his chest. When he knelt up again he had her strapped to his back with her legs dangling behind him on his left-hand side, away from his injured leg. He then began to shuffle forwards on his hands and knees. In this way he got her as far as the sledge. Having unloaded the stores he tied her, now raving with delirium again, to the sledge, and by using another folded sheet as a kind of breast harness for himself, he began to drag the sledge slowly up the gorge.

It took him an hour to reach the entrance to the plateau, and three to cross it. The strain of covering such a distance on all fours while dragging such a weight was tremendous, and all the time his smashed leg was throbbing and burning as if it were on fire. On reaching the edge of the cliff he fainted.

When he came to again he knew from the position of the sun that it was well past midday, so he must have been out for some time; but the enforced rest had had the effect of restoring some of his strength. After he had eaten some of the chocolate and biscuits and had a drink of water he felt up to attempting the descent to the valley, which, although difficult and tricky, would at least be downhill.

He was in hopes that he would not have to drag Gloria all the way to the Palace unaided, as he was almost certain to pass fields in which some of the pigmies were working, and he meant to call upon them to provide stretcher parties.

For another hour he stumbled and wormed his way grimly down the track until he came to the region of the terraced plots; then, after a short rest, he cupped his hands and began to shout.

As there was no result he struggled on for another quarter of a mile and repeated the process. This time, after about five minutes, two of the little brown-clad farmers came running up the path, but directly they saw him they stopped dead in their tracks and, in spite of his beckonings and callings, refused to come any nearer.

Grimy, sweating, red-eyed, he wearily crawled towards them, but, to his disgust and fury, they turned and ran away. Another ten minutes plodding on his aching knees brought him to the next corner. They were both lurking there behind the angle of a low wall, and one of them had secured a short pitchfork. Suddenly he darted out and made a nervous stab with it at Philip's face.

Philip dodged the thrust, and his roar of astonished anger sent the two little men scampering to safety a dozen yards away. But, in spite of his surprise and fatigue, he was quick to realize that this new development might prove exceedingly serious. Knowing that he would need every ounce of his strength to carry Gloria, he had left both his pistol and the Prince's rifle behind in the gorge, so he was completely unarmed.

Of course, the explanation for the attack was simple. He and Gloria were covered with dried blood, and it was obvious that they were both badly wounded; while the fact that she was wearing the Prince's blood-stained furs was a fair indication that the latter was either dead or lying somewhere up in the mountains too badly wounded even to crawl. The little people had no cause to love their king, and, not unnaturally, they had associated his two guests with all his doings. Now, seeing their opportunity, they were out for revenge.

Even wounded and crawling as he was, Philip felt that he could prove a match for two or three of them; but the thought which almost brought panic to his mind was that the example of the little brute who had first thought of fetching his pitchfork might be followed by others. If a dozen or more of them launched an attack with such weapons, Philip knew that he and Gloria would be stabbed to death in no time. If ever there was a case for making a swift example this was it.

With a plan already forming in his brain, he began to advance again, while the little men, warily keeping their distance, backed away before him. Gradually he slowed down his pace, then put his hand to his head as though he was about to faint, swayed for a moment and fell forward on his face.

He was careful to let his head roll sideways, so that he could watch his adversaries through his eyelashes. Within a moment of his staging his pretended collapse the man with the pitchfork ran at him. In one swift

movement Philip grabbed the fork and tore it from the pigmy's hand.
Next moment he brought its butt-end cracking down on the little devil's
head.

With a yelp of pain and fright the victim fled screaming, his small
friend close on his heels.

Now being armed, and having shown that he still had some teeth left
with which to bite, Philip felt a little more sanguine about facing further
attacks; but the effort to deal with such a situation while he still tugged
the dead weight of Gloria had proved almost too much for him.

For a long time past she had been delirious, and he, too, was now
running a high temperature. Yet he knew that he must not give up until
he reached the shelter of the Palace. After ten minutes' rest and another
drink he set off again.

The last two miles were unadulterated hell. His leg was a red-hot flame
behind him, his hands were blistered and bleeding, his knees torn even
through the pads, the sweat was pouring off him, and he could hardly
see out of eyes that were rimmed with dust and sunken right back in his
head. At last, panting, gasping, trembling, he lurched across the com-
pound of the Palace, pushed open the door of the sitting-room and flopped
down inside it, with Gloria bubbling incoherently on the sledge just behind him.

How long he lay there he had no idea. He blacked out, came to through
a haze of pain, managed to undo the cloth that bound Gloria to the
sledge and get her on to the pile of skins, then fainted again.

When he fully regained consciousness it was the middle of the night.
Gloria had ceased her raving and was sleeping. The fire had gone out,
and the room was in complete darkness. His leg now was just a dull,
throbbing ache. He knew that there were all sorts of things he ought
to do; but the darkness was an almost impossible handicap, so he lay there
until the grey light of morning percolated through the small windows.

Moving cautiously so as not to disturb Gloria, he left the room and
made his way to the servants' quarters, hoping against hope that the
cooks and scullions, or at least Gog and Magog, had remained at their
posts; but the whole place was deserted. Fortunately they had not
sacked the larder before leaving, and in it he found a good supply of
food and blaeberry juice.

Having lit the kitchen fire, he put some water on it to heat and undid
the bandages to look at his leg. It was a horrid sight, and he thought
that, had he received such a wound on the battlefield, an Army surgeon
would have had his leg off below the knee. He felt that it ought to come
off, as otherwise there was a grave risk of gangrene from it killing him
within the next few days; but, although he had heard of people ampu-
tating their own legs in such circumstances, he decided that such a job
was absolutely beyond him; the best he could hope to do was to cauterize
the wound.

He put a poker in the fire to heat, washed his leg carefully with soap and warm water, and applied the red hot iron first to the edges of the wound, then, with an effort that took all his will, to its centre. He had expected that this would make him faint, but it did not. The pain was hideous and made him sweat, but it was just bearable. After a rest to regain his breath, he put clean bandages round the wound, rested his foot in a sling he had made for it while the poker was heating, and, using a broom as a crutch, tried moving about upright for the first time since he had been shot.

It proved a bit tricky at first, but he thought that after adjusting the height of the crutch and the length of the sling he would be able to get about fairly well. Putting some soup, llama's milk and blaeberry juice in a basket, he hopped back to Gloria. She was still asleep, so he lay down near her. He felt terribly tired now, and he wondered how, seeing that this morning's effort had proved so exhausting, he had conceivably managed to drag Gloria all that way the day before.

He realized now that he had been delirious a good part of the time and remembered that people suffering from delirium are said to have super-human strength. His head felt very heavy, and a little pulse in his temple was beating in time to the throbbing of his leg. His temperature was mounting again, and the burning pains from the cauterization were now beginning to give him hell. For hours he lay there moaning and twist-ing, and only the gradual darkening of the room told him that evening had come.

Making an effort he crawled over and lit two of the rush-lights. It was only then he noticed that Gloria was no longer asleep. Her blue eyes were open and, looking abnormally large in her white face, stared up at him. As he knelt beside her couch her pale lips framed the one word: " Boy? "

"Yes," he said, and he noticed that his own voice was harsh and cracked, even as he smiled and tried to make a joke by adding: " It's all right, my sweet. He's dead. I'm the King here now, and you're the Queen."

Her eyes just moved as though she understood, but she was obviously too weak to talk. Having kissed her lightly and held her hand for a little, he took up his crutch and hobbled over to the kitchen to heat some water with which to wash her wound. Unlike his own, it had been fully pro-tected from the dust and dirt of the hard journey from the pass, and when he examined it there were none of the blue edges to the ragged flesh which had so frightened him about his leg. The bullet had gone through her side and out of it, so there seemed no reason why in healthy flesh like hers the wound should not heal up, and his impression was that her weakness and delirium were mainly caused by shock and loss of blood.

After attending to her, he tried to settle down for the short night, but his leg pained him so that he would have given much to be able to cut it

off, and he did not get to sleep until the long dawn twilight of this
season had begun.

The week that followed was a nightmare time of hopes and fears. After
that first recovery of consciousness Gloria lapsed into a coma, broken by
periodical bouts of delirium; and for several days she could keep nothing
down. Philip's fever subsided after forty-eight hours, but he was alarmed
to see the lower part of the larger of his two wounds, where the bullet
had emerged from his leg after smashing the bone, was going a bluish-
purple colour, so he had to cauterize it again.   This time, having been
even more drastic with himself, he did faint, and the shock of the burning
set him back by making him feverish once more.   But, eight days after
their desperate encounter in the gorge, neither of them was any longer
running a temperature. Gloria was not strong enough to move, but she
could talk a little, and Philip knew that, although he would limp for the
rest of his life, the danger of his wound going gangrenous and killing him
was past.

In the latter part of the week there occurred an unexpected and startling
phenomenon in the shape of a violent electric storm.   There was no rain,
but deafening peals of thunder rolled round and round the mountains that
enclosed the valley, and the most terrifying forked lightning zigzagged up
and down without ceasing for the best part of two hours.   At the time
Philip and Gloria were in no state to give their full attention to this mighty
spectacle, but, on thinking about it afterwards, Philip came to the conclusion that this great electric disturbance had something to do with the
amazing fact that the valley enjoyed a temperate climate, although it was
situated well within the Antarctic circle.

His reason for this assumption was that, whereas it had been pleasantly
warm when he first arrived in the valley, the weather had gradually
declined up to the time of his departure for the raft, and ten days later,
when he had carried Gloria in, it had actually been quite chilly, with
clouds obscuring the sun and a cold mist rising at night from the lake in
the valley bottom; yet, after the electric storm, the late Prince Solgorukin's
kingdom was within an hour restored to the enjoyment of the equitable
and balmy climate which had been its most staggering feature when its
monarchs-to-be arrived there just on a month before.

During his long hours of compulsory inaction Philip had thought a
good deal about the Prince's cryptic utterances.   He had said quite
distinctly that you could make the weather you wanted with human blood,
that the secret of doing so belonged to the Lords of the Mountain—who-
ever they might be—and finally that he would like to see Philip taken by
"The Dog."   But where to?   And what Dog?   There were no dogs in
the valley or any animal even remotely resembling them.   Perhaps he
had been speaking of metaphysical things and referring to the passage in
the Book of Revelations which speaks of " the power of the Dog " as a
synonym for the Evil One, and had simply meant: " I'd like to see the
Devil fly away with you! "   Or perhaps these seemingly mysterious

pronouncements were no more than the nonsensical ravings of a dying man.

Philip would have liked to think that, but was prevented from doing so by his memory of the Prince's references to the great chain of mountains to the south and the strange things that could be done with human blood on the first evening, when they had gazed together from the barren plateau down into the fertile valley.

Yet once he was able to hop about on his crutch without enduring a spasm of agony every time he jarred his injured leg, he had little time for such speculations. The desertion by the Palace staff had left its occupants with only limited stocks of food and other necessities such as rushlights and wood for the fires. A very limited diet was all they could have managed in any case for some days after their return, and, although Philip would have liked more milk for Gloria, they existed fairly well on the things that had been left; but now the time had come when fresh supplies positively had to be obtained.

If he could have spoken the little people's language he would have gone out and explained to some of them that all men from the outer world were not as selfish and brutal as their late King, and that, if only they would give him their trust and help, he would find many ways of repaying them; but, as this was out of the question, he intended to try to make his actions speak for him. The only items of any quantity in the Palace which were suitable for barter were the llama skin rugs, and of these there were at least a hundred.

Rolling one of them up Philip put it in a basket and hobbled off to the nearest farm. The little wrinkled-faced good-wife saw him coming through the open door of the kitchen, and fled with a squeak of alarm. Philip went in, helped himself to some chopped meat that was on the kitchen table, vegetables, milk and butter, and left the llama skin lying there in exchange.

As he came out of the house a stone whizzed passed his ear, and as he went down the lane he was pelted for some little distance from behind the hedge; but only one stone hit him and that not hard enough to inflict more than a momentary hurt.

The following day he tried another cottage, but this time in exchange for a skin he took a baby llama from the yard and carried it back with him under his free arm to the Palace enclosure. He wanted to start breeding llamas in due course, so that in time he would have his own supplies of all their products and no longer have to extract them from the poor little peasants by threats, as the Russian had done.

It was now December. Gloria, although still too weak to get up, was improving daily and, with Philip's help, was able each morning to get out into the enclosure and spend the day in the bright sunshine. She was also able to dress his leg for him and, although the wound was now healing, it remained a nasty sight, as the lower leg where the bone had splintered remained as thick as his knee. Whether he would ever be able to walk on it again still remained doubtful, and it looked as if several months must elapse before it would even be fit to hobble on. This alone put out of court for that winter any prospect of getting to the whaling station they now knew to be on the MacKenzie Sea. In consequence they determined to make themselves as comfortable in the Palace as they could.

By Christmas Day Gloria was able to get up and take on the light work of the house, including feeding the young llamas, of which they now had four. Philip meanwhile was able to get a little further afield and so to spread his requisitioning in exchange for llama skins over a greater area. He had hoped that after a bit the pigmies would come to realize that he was paying for the things he took in the only way he could, and begin to bring their surplus produce to the Palace in exchange for skins, or at least show some signs of friendliness. But they did neither, possibly because they never traded among themselves and were still too undeveloped to comprehend the intention of barter. They still fled at his approach, and occasionally the more truculent among them threw stones at him.

By Christmas, although it should have been the hottest season of the year, the temperature had perceptibly declined again, owing to increases in the cloud formations which shrouded the mountain tops and, at times, swelled to such dimensions that they met over the valley and shut out the sun. Then, on Boxing Day they had another electric storm which was followed by cloudless skies and the warmest sunshine they had so far experienced there; the good spell lasting well into the New Year of 1942.

There was a third electric storm on January the 23rd, and on their working it out it seemed that these storms occurred quite regularly once every twenty-eight days; so Philip formed the theory that they had something to do with the new moon.

Gloria was now quite recovered, and Philip's leg was as good as it was likely to be for some months to come. He still could not bear to put his foot to the ground for more than two or three steps at a time, but it no longer pained him if he put no strain upon it, except for a dull rheumatic ache which bothered him during periods of damp weather or just before an electric storm was due.

A thing that now began to worry him was that his barter system looked like breaking down, and he wanted to keep it up even if the pigmies did not appreciate it. He was down to fifty skins; he did not wish to part with more, and his own llamas were still far too young to give him the supplies he needed.

It was now the harvest season, and he would have done a day's work on each of the nearest farms had his leg permitted, but he was still almost helpless without his crutch. This wish to do something in return for the goods he commandeered decided him to put into operation a plan that he had conceived before going to the raft, when it had looked as if he would spend some weeks at least honeymooning with Gloria in the valley before they made any attempt to reach the whaling station. But for this scheme he needed the tools that he had abandoned with all the other supplies up in the gorge.

In consequence, he and Gloria determined to make an expedition to the gorge for the purpose of recovering all the gear that had been left behind. They took supplies for five days, as with Philip's bad leg they reckoned it would take them two days to get up there with the sledge. The other two days were spent in getting all the things first across the plateau to the cliff-top, and then down to the Palace. Even in four days it proved hard work, but they were delighted when it was done as the stores gave them many luxuries for special occasions, and the tools and utensils would, they knew, prove invaluable.

The day following their return Philip started on his great idea, which was nothing less than the making of a watermill to grind the valley's corn. With Gloria's help he built a large wheel down below the lake, and with his expert engineering knowledge it was simple, once the wheel was placed and turning, to harness it to the small crude mill which he had also made. It took five weeks to complete, and the next business of the King and Queen of this strange land was to convey to their subjects the use of the contraption they had made.

This was accomplished during the following days by the simple process of taking the farmers' corn from their bins, grinding it for them and putting it back. Where the attempt to barter had proved a complete failure the mill produced results within a week. Six days after the first corn-grinding had taken place Gloria opened her door in the morning to find that one of her subjects had placed a bucket of llama's milk and a big pat of butter there during the night.

They were naturally delighted with this, and if Philip could have danced at all he would have danced for joy. Even during the time that they were laid low they had not been altogether miserable because they were together, and each day of their recovery had brought a new delight from their well-tried companionship which was now crowned with love. For a time, at all events, thoughts of the outer world had receded into the background because they were so busily occupied in finding new joys in each other. It only needed this resumption of friendly relations with the little people to complete their happiness.

During the last weeks of March numerous other gifts arrived at their front door, and it seemed that they had entered upon a halcyon period of honeymoon contentment. It was, therefore, all the more of a shock when one night, at the end of the month, just as they were going to sleep, Philip heard an unfamiliar sound   Sitting up, he exclaimed:

" What's that? "

Gloria gripped him quickly by the arm, and her voice was a frightened whisper. " 'Tis a sort of . . . of baying sound."

"You're right!" he cried. "Oh, God, you're right! It's the barking of a dog!"

CHAPTER XVI

THE WHITE MAN'S BURDEN

FOR a moment they sat quite still, then the sound came again. Gloria was right; it was not the yapping of a small dog but the deep baying of a hound.

Even in daytime the valley was far quieter than any ordinary countryside. There was no traffic on the roads, no rattle of farm machines, no crowing of cocks or lowing of cattle, and at night, when even the occasional clink of a bucket or the clatter of a churn had ceased, it was deathly still. There could therefore be no mistake about the noise they heard, yet, although they could hear it so clearly, it was difficult to judge the distance of the beast making it, owing to that very stillness that gripped the night-enshrouded valley.

"What the devil can it be?" muttered Philip, reaching for his crutches. "Anyhow, I think I'll go out and have a look; just to see if I can see anything."

"Must you, Boy?" Gloria asked a trifle hesitantly.

"Yes, I'd better, if only to see that the gates of the stockade are shut."

"All right then. I'll come with you."

While they pulled on their clothes the loud barking continued and seemed to be coming nearer. Then came the sound of a beast galloping along the track. It halted outside the Palace enclosure, and there was a scuffling noise as if a mastiff or something even bigger was worrying its way round the edge of the stockade trying to find a way in.

Gloria put her arms round Philip and clung to him. His heart was pounding in his chest. It seemed sheer madness to go out, unarmed as they were, and risk being attacked, solely to satisfy their curiosity about this probably savage brute; so they stayed where they were, within the protection of the little house.

The beast snuffled, whined, then began to bay again and cantered off up the hill. Philip undid the door and they went outside. A sickle moon bathed the valley in a faint, sinister light. Both gates to the enclosure were shut, and, as Philip made certain of the fastening on the big main gate, he said :

"I've often wondered why the Prince went to the trouble of having such a stout palisade put up. He had too much contempt for the pigmies even to contemplate their ever rising in force against him, but now we know. It must have been to keep out this mysterious beast."

Gloria shivered. "Where can it possibly come from, Boy? And how would even a big dog be able to cross the miles of frozen lands outside the valley all on its own?"

"Goodness knows! From the little Solgorukin said the inference is that it comes from that great chain of mountains to the south. There may be other valleys like these for all we know but with quite different types of people and animals living in them. But that's ten days' march away at least. No ordinary dog could go that length of time without food and be fit enough to canter about afterwards."

"Maybe it's not an ordinary dog."

"Yes, perhaps it's some beast that lives in a cave up in the mountains above the valley here and comes down into it only occasionally. It might be an Abominable Snowman."

"What in the world would that be?"

"That's the native name for an animal that lives high above the snow-line in the Himalayas. It's thought to be a kind of bear. No European has ever seen it, but parties climbing Mount Everest have come across its tracks in the snow. They say it has a footprint like that of a huge man, and from the length of its stride they calculate that it must be at least seven feet in height."

"There's lots of queer things in the world that the wiseacres don't know about yet," said Gloria, not wanting the conversation to lapse.

They were standing together hand in hand near the stockade. Both of them were feeling extremely nervous, and they were talking only to keep up their courage while they still listened intently to the baleful baying that continued to make the night hideous further up the valley.

For a moment the baying ceased. Suddenly there was a shrill scream, then dead silence.

"It . . . it's got one of the Little People," faltered Gloria.

"I know," muttered Philip miserably, wondering if there was anything that he could possibly do about it.

A moment later they heard the swift padding of feet again. The brute was approaching at a gallop. Instinctively they drew back, but they could still see the track through the openings between the big spiked stakes of which the stockade was formed.

Holding their breaths and tightly gripping each other's hands, they watched. The distant padding became a heavy drumming on the earth, and the great brute raced by, but they both saw it quite distinctly. It was a dog, but one of the biggest that they had ever seen, and it looked like a very large bloodhound or a prize Great Dane. There was nothing strange or supernatural about it, although it looked a most formidable brute, but the thing that kept them rooted to the spot with horror was that the body of one of the pigmies was dangling from the great slobbering mouth.

G*

"I must get the rifle," muttered Philip, releasing Gloria's hand.

"'Tis no good," she said swiftly. "You've never found the time to clean it yet, so 'tis still all rusted up."

"Then I must take my pistol—I cleaned that."

She grabbed him by the arm. "You'll do no such thing. I won't let you go out there."

"God knows I don't want to!" he declared quite honestly. "But we simply can't stand by and see these poor little wretches hunted to death."

"It's happened before. It must have, otherwise the Prince wouldn't have known about the beast. And why should you give your life trying to stop something that's probably been going on for centuries?"

"With a little luck I might shoot the brute if I could get near enough to have a pot at it."

"And what chance would you have if you wounded it and yourself with only one good leg? No, Boy. I'll not be left here on my own. What'll I do if you're killed, and me about to have a baby?"

"You're what!" exclaimed Philip. "Good God—when?"

She buried her face against his shoulder. "I wasn't meaning to say anything yet, though I've known for quite a while. It'll be some time in November."

For Philip this stupendous news seemed to put a new complexion on the situation, and now that he was crippled was glad enough to have an excuse not to go out to fight a dangerous beast in the middle of the night.

They returned to the house and made up the fire instead of attempting to get to sleep. That was quite out of the question so long as the hideous barking of the great dog echoed through the valley. It continued far into the night, sometimes within a stone's throw and sometimes so distant as to be very faint, but with few intervals; and, on several occasions, these were preceded by a thin cry which suggested that others among the Little People were falling victims to the beast.

In order to try to keep their minds off the horrors that the bestial visitant might be perpetrating outside, they talked of their coming child; suggesting names for it, planning how it would be dressed and educated and where it should sleep and play, just as young people all over the world do when they are expecting their first baby. But even this enthralling subject could not hold their full attention, and when, at last, at about half past four in the morning, the howling of the dog ceased they went wearily to bed and fell into a heavy sleep.

They woke late, had a quick breakfast and, arming themselves with the automatic and a pitchfork, sallied forth to try to ascertain the extent of the damage done by their midnight visitor.

The brute's tracks were clear enough in the dirt of the road, and as Philip and Gloria progressed along the valley they saw that it must have raced backwards and forwards through the twisting lanes and up to the doors of nearly every cottage. None of the pigmies were working in the fields that day, but a variety of sounds coming from their houses showed that most of those who lived in the vicinity of the Palace were still alive; and it might well be that they were mourning others who had been taken by the dog, so it seemed kinder not to disturb them in their grief.

In spite of the most careful scrutiny, Philip could see no traces of blood upon the ground, and they came across no torn or mangled corpses. It seemed more as if the mastiff acted as a huge retriever and carried its victims off to its lair. By comparison to the pigmies' average height of three foot six it stood as high as a medium sized horse to a normal man, and it had a far more powerful head and neck than a pony of the same size; so it was perfectly possible for the brute to carry humans the size of the Little People in its mouth for a considerable distance.

After a few days the normal life of the countryside was restored, and the inhabitants of the Palace renewed their efforts to achieve a better relationship with their subjects. The pigmies had no carts or barrows of any kind, but always carried their produce in panniers very nearly as big as themselves, on their backs; so Philip made a child's wheelbarrow.

As he could not secure an audience before which to demonstrate its use he just dumped a light load of his nearest neighbour's vegetables in it, then Gloria wheeled it down to the lake where numbers of the population often gathered in the evenings to stare in wonder at the watermill. Leaving it there, she and Philip retired to a distance, hid behind a hedge and watched to see what would happen. The farmer whose vegetables had been taken soon arrived, and, transferring them to his pannier, carried them home again; but a little later several other small people began to play with the barrow, and one of them being pushed over by accident into it got a ride. This resulted in rides in the wheelbarrow becoming a favourite evening sport, but it was months before they could be induced to save themselves labour by using the barrow, and others like it which Philip made for them, for any other purpose.

The Antarctic winter was now setting in, and, although the climate did not seriously deteriorate, it gradually became colder as the days shortened. Philip made himself a rough but serviceable fishing rod with a reel, which enabled him to play and land much bigger fish in the lake than the pigmies could possibly catch with their primitive tackle. By fishing two or three days a week he was able to leave presents of fish at most of the houses round about fairly frequently, and in return his neighbours now kept the Palace regularly supplied with llama's meat, butter, milk, vegetables and other products from their farms. They no longer ran away when Philip or Gloria entered their houses, but they remained shy and could not be persuaded to come within reach.

It was Gloria who was responsible for finally overcoming their fears. One day early in June she was walking past the lake where two of the little men were fishing, just above the waterfall. It was early afternoon but darkness was already falling, as at this season of the year the Antarctic world was lit by only a few hours of twilight each day. Suddenly there was a shout, and Gloria saw that one of the fishermen had over-balanced while trying to land a fish, and had fallen head first into the lake. She could not help laughing and stopped to see his friend pull him out. But, instead of helping, the friend only danced up and down in excited distress. Meanwhile, the unfortunate little man was being drawn further out by the current and seemed in danger of being swept over the waterfall. It was not until he went under that it flashed on Gloria that neither of them could swim.

Running to the bank she pulled off her skirt and went in after him. It was no small risk as she had to dive again and again before she succeeded in finding him, and she herself might easily have been swept over the waterfall, but her many months of daily bathing from the raft had made her a strong swimmer, and she managed to fish him out.

When she got him to the bank she found to her distress that he was no longer breathing, so, as soon as she had got her own breath back, she tried artificial respiration. It was now almost dark, and, seeing no signs of revival in her patient after ten minutes' hard work, she decided to carry him up to the Palace where with Philip's help and warm blankets it was possible that his life might yet be saved. The small body was much heavier than it looked, and the Palace over a mile away, but half an hour later she staggered in with it. As she put the body down she discovered to her surprise that the drowned man's companion had followed her home and was standing just behind her. He was the first of the Little People to have entered the Palace enclosure since Gog and Magog and the rest of the staff had left it nearly seven months before.

For over an hour Philip and Gloria worked on the body until their efforts were crowned with success. When he came to their patient showed considerable fright at the situation in which he found himself, but, on being reassured by his small friend, he allowed himself to be fed with hot milk and tucked up in a llama's skin to sleep near the fire.

When Gloria woke next morning he had vanished, but soon after midday he returned, accompanied by Gog, Magog and a number of friends, several of whom proved to be ex-members of the old staff. They all prostrated themselves and banged their foreheads on the ground as they had been accustomed to do before the Prince, but Philip and Gloria raised some of them up and made signs to them to tell the others to stop. There was then a great presenting of gifts, as it transpired that all of them had brought something for the Palace larder or store-room, and the little man whose life Gloria had saved produced as a thankoffering to her a live, fully grown llama. The all too brief wintry day ended in a great feast cooked in the Palace kitchen, and when most of the revellers left for their homes late in the afternoon Gog and Magog and the rest of the original Palace staff made it quite clear that they intended to take up their old posts again permanently.

Now that Philip and Gloria were in regular communication with the pigmies they began to try to learn their language. They found it far harder than they had expected, and for a time felt that the Prince must have been a quite exceptional linguist to have mastered it so well in a matter of some nine months; but later they realized that he had not really mastered it in the sense of being able to converse on abstract matters. His only interest had been to get anything he wanted brought quickly, and for that purpose the learning off parrot-fashion of the names of the principal physical objects had no doubt been quite sufficient. Philip and Gloria, too, soon acquired a useful vocabulary of nouns, but they were still a long way from being able to ask many of the things they badly wanted to know—such as the origins of the Little People and how often the Dog paid one of its terrifying visits to the valley—by the time that Gloria was due to have her baby.

At this anxious time Philip would have cheerfully given all his engineering knowledge for even a week's course in midwifery, but when the time actually came all his fears proved groundless. Four of the fat, brown-faced little farmers' wives drove him from the house and took charge of the situation. Next morning Gloria presented him with a fine, healthy son.

Later in the day, however, there occurred a disquieting episode. Philip thought Gloria was sleeping when he heard her call to him: " Boy, quickly! Quickly! Two of them have taken my baby! "

Hobbling swiftly from the little house in which he had set up a workshop, he was just in time to see the two pigmy women hurrying down the road. With a shout of reassurance to Gloria he set off after them as swiftly as he could while calling loudly on them to stop. They obeyed him, but they were obviously surprised at his anger and only handed over the child with marked reluctance.

Gloria had often remarked upon the curious fact that she had never seen one of the Little People's babies, or, for that matter, any young child of their race. Yet, there could be no doubt that they reproduced themselves just like other human beings, and quite a number of older children, who gave the impression of being from about twelve years upwards, lived quite normal lives with their parents. Philip had advanced the theory that they took their infants to some secret place and brought them up there, either in conformity with some ancient tribal custom or in order to protect them from such dangers as a visit from the Dog. This attempt by two of the midwives to remove his own son, coupled with the fact that quite clearly no trace of malice had inspired the act, confirmed him in his view.

He had lived in the valley for less than a fortnight before the injury to his leg had crippled him to an extent which made long walks impossible, so there were large sections of the eastern end of the valley that he had never explored. Yet the pigmies possessed iron implements and

utensils, such as cauldrons and cooking pots, and they also worked in
stone; so it seemed certain that they had primitive mines and quarries
in the bases of the mountains somewhere beyond the woods. It was also
possible that they had a kind of creche there where all their young were
reared together, but Philip's knowledge of their language was still too
limited for him to make satisfactory enquiries about it.

The baby had been born on November the 21st, and Gloria was doing
well, so they were soon able to enjoy the long sunny days out in the open.
They called the baby John Alphonse, the first after Canon Beal-Brookman, the second after Gloria's father. Philip did not like the Alphonse
part at all, but he was far too fond of Gloria seriously to oppose her
wish, and it seemed that the chances of his one day being able to send his
son to an English Public School, where he might be ragged about his
middle name, were for the moment decidedly remote.

The wound in his leg had long since healed, but had left it malformed
and nearly three inches shorter than the other. He could hobble awkwardly about the house on it but could not run, and to cover any
distance he still had to use crutches. This meant that any attempt to
reach the MacKenzie Sea would prove a far longer and more hazardous
project than it would have before he was wounded. Yet he had by no
means abandoned his intention of getting to the whaling station if he
could.

He would have made the attempt in mid-December, when the weather
was at its warmest and they had the benefit of the midnight sun, had it
not been for the great event in the latter part of November. Obviously,
it was quite out of the question to make the attempt until Gloria was
fully recovered and her child at least three months old. However, Philip
had an idea that the whaling season did not close till mid-March, so he
was still in hopes that they might yet accomplish the first stage of their
journey home that spring.

Christmas, and the New Year of 1943 came and went. The Antarctic
summer proved a pleasant, happy season now that they were on such
good terms with the Little People, and very different from the summer
before when they had been both desperately ill and outlawed by their
neighbours. John Alphonse was rapidly becoming a sturdy little man
who smiled, crowed and kicked to the delight of his parents, and, indeed,
of the whole household.

Gloria had feared that the child would prove a great tie to her and that
for a long time to come she would never be able to leave the house unless
she took him with her. But this proved far from being the case. Gog
and Magog were absolutely devoted to him, and these strange, ugly, little
men seemed to understand his needs far better than his mother. They
handled him with the greatest gentleness, seemed able to send him to
sleep, and he never cried when they were present; so the fortunate Gloria
had all the fun of motherhood and little of its drudgery.

It was on February 21st, when John A. was just three months old, that Philip said to Gloria, apropos of nothing:

"Well, what about it?"

She knew at once what he meant, but sat silent for a moment before she replied: "Is the urge to get back as strong in you as ever? The war may be over by now, you know."

"Even if it is we must try to get home. We've the boy to think of now as well as ourselves."

"Oh, I wouldn't be worrying yourself about him." She shrugged. "He'd be happy here all his life because he's never known anything different. It's what we're wanting ourselves and how much, is the question."

"Do you think you'd be happy to remain here always?" He took her hand and went on: "I want you to be absolutely honest with me, darling. For a long time I clung to that vision I had and the promise that I should play a bigger part than any other man of my generation in helping to defeat Hitler, but it doesn't seem remotely possible any more. The war has been on for three and a half years, so even if it's not all over the British Empire, with American supplies and the good old Navy maintaining the blockade of Europe, must be getting Hitler pretty worn down by now. And here am I, thousands of miles away in the Antarctic with only one good leg and another that it's too late for even the most brilliant surgeon to do much about; so I think we can cut out all ideas of V.C.s. Still, there are other things. We could have a real home, friends of our own kind and lots of pretty clothes for you. But I won't go into all that. I'll simply tell you for the umpteenth time that I love you, and that more than anything in the world I want you to be happy; so I'll be quite content for us either to go or stay, just as you prefer."

"Oh, Boy, I love you so much!" She leaned forward and kissed him. "I could be happy anywhere with you. We could be happy here—I haven't a doubt of it, but maybe the sameness would pall a bit later on. We're both young yet, and in the great world there's still so much to see and do. I'm as fit now as ever I've been and John A. is only waiting to get to Europe to push down the houses. Let's start our preparations and try to reach the coast by early March."

So the great decision was taken, and next day Philip set about the preparations for their journey. He had made a new bivvy of llama skins with the warm fleece inside, and began drying a considerable quantity of llama's meat as the most economical article they could take to form their staple diet. The collection of other things could be undertaken at a few hours' notice, and he planned to leave on the 26th, but John A. delayed their departure for several days by developing a slight chill.

They said as little as possible of their intentions to the Palace staff, partly because they feared that the Little People might create some sort of scene and partly because they had a vaguely guilty feeling that by leaving the valley they were in some way letting them down.

By March the 3rd John A. was completely recovered, and on the morning of the 4th, having loaded up the sledge, they said good-bye to their retainers just as though they were going off on one of those hunting expeditions on which the Prince used to absent himself when he was master of the Palace. John A. rode on a flat wooden basket which was securely tied on top of the sledge. One of the ropes which pulled it was attached to a leather belt round Philip's waist. Gloria walked beside him with the other rope over her shoulder. They set off at an easy pace and by midday were standing on the edge of the plateau taking a last look down into the valley, where they had suffered so much distress but known such great happiness.

Gloria was feeding John A., and they had taken rations for themselves for thirty days. Apart from his permanent disability, Philip was extremely fit, and by this time the use of crutches had become a second nature to him, so, even making the journey in easy stages, they hoped to reach the MacKenzie Sea in eight days. If they allowed three for the march along it before they found the whaling station, and another eleven for the return journey—should there after all be no ship or people at the station—they would still have eight days' rations in hand as a precaution against being held up by any unexpected mishap.

On the further side of the mountains they once more entered the region of eternal snows, and there were times during the first six days when they heartily wished that they had never left the valley. The strange fantastic beauties of the Antarctic still filled them with awe and wonder, but the cold was a terrible enemy, and they had constantly to be on the watch against frostbite. This was the season of unbelievably lovely sunsets which lasted up to five hours, but it was also autumn and the sun was above the horizon for a lesser time each day. Nevertheless, the weather continued good, and on the seventh evening they made camp on a low ridge from which they could see the sea. Two days later, after crossing a small headland about fifteen miles further up the coast, they suddenly saw a group of long, low huts clustered about a small inlet from the bay.

To their great disappointment no ship was lying there, but there was still a possibility that part of the crew might be at the station while the whaler was out hunting.

" Go on, darling," Philip cried; " you run on ahead. I can manage to pull the sledge myself if I take it slowly."

After a momentary hesitation, Gloria did as he suggested but he had barely covered another ten yards before he noticed that there was no smoke curling up from any of the tin chimneys of the huts, and so was prepared for the bad news that she brought when she came running back to meet him twenty minutes later. The whaling station was deserted.

Later they made a tour of the place, and it was obvious that people had been there quite recently The whole camp stank with the awful stench of decaying fish, and great lumps of waste product from a dead whale were still rotting by the wooden wharf. Apart from machinery connected with the whaling industry, the huts held only wire-netting bunks and wooden messing tables, except for one, on the door of which there was stuck a notice: " Stores for distressed Mariners," and another that was furnished as a cookhouse.

Their only important find was some dirty sheets of newspaper spread out as a makeshift tablecloth in one of the mess-rooms. These proved to be editions, or bits of editions, of various Australian papers all published during the latter part of the previous October. Although they were four and a half months old, the news they carried was twenty months ahead of the last broadcasts that the Prince had heard before leaving this same whaling station in February 1941, so Philip and Gloria, their eyes darting from one sheet to another, began to read scraps here and there with frantic eagerness.

At the first glance they both saw from the headlines that the war was not only still on but had become worldwide.

" America's in! " cried Philip; " but so are the Japs. Look! ' Americans Repulse Japanese in Solomons! ' And here again, ' U.S. Air-Sea Victory off Stewart Islands. Two Jap Aircraft Carriers and a. Battle-ship severely damaged.' "

" The Russians are in too," said Gloria.

" Good God! On whose side? " Philip exclaimed, abandoning his own sheet to look over Gloria's shoulder. A second later he sighed with relief as he read: " Germans mount fresh Attacks against Stalingrad," and added: " Thank goodness! I always said they had no use for the Nazis; but after the Russo-German pact of Nineteen Thirty-nine who could tell what they meant to do?   Where the devil is Stalingrad, though? "

Gloria pointed to a map down at the bottom of the page, and he exclaimed in surprise again: " I say, the Germans *have* made a penetration. They must be nearly a thousand miles into Russia. I wonder how long it is since Hitler quarrelled with Uncle Joe? "

" The British are attacking in Egypt," Gloria remarked, pointing at a headline with another map below it.

Philip followed her finger. " But heaven help us, what on earth are they doing there, almost in the Delta? They must have been driven back over six hundred miles since General Wavell made his magnificent advance to Benghazi."

" I wish we knew how long America's been at war, and just what brought us in," said Gloria.

Some two hours later she had the answer. They were looking through one of the dormitory huts when they noticed the front page of an American paper pasted up on the wall. It was an issue of December the 15th, 1941, and above it the sailor who had stuck it up—perhaps an American member of the whaler's crew—had written in blue pencil: "LET'S NOT FORGET."

The big splash in heavy type was Colonel Knox's official statement on his return from Hawaii, where he had been to investigate personally the dastardly attack by the Japanese on Pearl Harbour eight days earlier.

"Two battleships sunk—destroyers—minelayer—aircraft burnt in hangars—over two thousand four hundred killed," murmured Philip, aghast. "By jove, your boys must have been properly caught with their trousers down."

"Yours don't seem to have been all that slick either," Gloria cracked back, pointing at a smaller paragraph near the left-hand bottom corner of the sheet. It was a statement that the loss of life when H.M.S. Prince of Wales and H.M.S. Repulse had been sunk by Japanese aircraft on December the 10th was less than had at first been feared, but that Admiral Sir Tom Phillips was among the missing.

Philip groaned. The fact that in less than a week his own predictions had been so amply justified by two actions thousands of miles apart, in both of which a few well aimed bombs had sent great capital ships costing many million pounds to the bottom of the sea in a matter of minutes, was no consolation. For the time being he could only realize with dismay that the United States Navy had been seriously crippled before it had even had a chance to get into the war, and he thought with horror of the engine-rooms and lower decks of our own big ships as they heeled over.

On making a thorough search of the whole camp they managed to find a number of other bits of old newspapers which had been used for lining shelves, or left in dustbins.

After reading themselves almost silly during the next twenty-four hours they had succeeded in getting a good general picture of the progress of the war. There were many gaps and seemingly contradictory statements, but the main facts were clear.

Hitler had, after all, never been able to invade Britain, and, despite the Prince's stories about London having been bombed flat, large sections of it must still be standing, because the King and Queen continued to receive official guests at Buckingham Palace, and a certain amount of news was given in the Australian papers about dances and theatrical shows given in London for war charities. The U-boat blockade of Britain continued and was costing the Allies hundreds of thousands of tons of shipping, but somehow or other the Royal Navy and the Merchant Navy were still getting the bulk of the convoys through.

That was the bright side of the picture. On the other, in Africa the British had been driven back almost to the Nile. For sixteen months Russia appeared to have suffered defeat after defeat, losing millions of square miles of her territory and millions of her troops in dead and prisoners. In the Far East things were, if possible, even worse. Hong Kong, Singapore, the whole of the Netherlands East Indies, Burma and the Philippines had all been conquered by the Japanese, and the Australians and Americans were now having their work cut out to hold them in New Guinea and the Solomons.

It was evident that, far from being nearing an end, the war would go on for a long time yet and that its issue still trembled in the balance. If Britain were so hard put to it to defend Egypt she could have little to spare for other theatres. How long could Russia carry on in the face of such terrible losses? If she were forced out of the war what would there be to stop the Germans switching their huge eastern army against Turkey and driving through Persia to India for a link-up with the Japanese? If that happened would even the vast war potential of the United States and the British Empire be sufficient ever to dislodge the Axis Powers from their hold on nine-tenths of Europe and the whole of Asia?

The very grimness of these possibilities re-aroused in Philip all his old urge to get home, to join in the fight, to do something, no matter what, provided that it would help to defeat the enemy. With his game leg it was virtually certain that they would not accept him for any of the fighting services now; but he could take up his old job in the aircraft works, or, even if he was too out-of-date for that, there would be scores of jobs open to him, a skilled worker, in munitions.

But he was still a prisoner in the Antarctic, and it looked as if he must continue so for another eight months at least. The way in which the whaling station had been dismantled showed that the season was over and the last ship likely to call there gone. John A.'s arrival had caused them to leave their journey too late. The only course now was to return to the valley for the Antarctic winter and make arrangements for a second journey to the MacKenzie Sea much earlier in next year's whaling season.

Feeling that they were fully entitled to some of the "stores for distressed mariners," they took a few tins of bully beef, condensed milk, sardines, tinned salmon and chocolate and packed them with their other goods on the sledge. Then, during the second evening of their stay, Philip wrote a long letter to his father, enclosing in it the log of the Raft Convoy. Gloria also enclosed a note to her mother, but it was only a brief one to say that she was alive and happy. The whole packet was addressed to Engineer Captain R. J. Vaudell, R.N., c/o The Admiralty, Whitehall, London, and left in the main mess-room with the request that the finder would forward it.

Philip felt a certain sense of relief when he had done this. He knew now that, even if some accident prevented him from returning to the whaling station several months hence, all the data concerning his experiment with the rafts would reach the Admiralty and be examined by the experts for what it was worth. Even if it were too late to be of any use in this war, it might prove of value for commercial purposes afterwards, or, if we were unlucky enough to become involved again, in some future conflict. He was glad, too, to think that, whether he got home or not, his father would now learn that he had not been drowned off the Cornish coast in October, 1939, but had survived to enjoy much happiness with the girl he loved and to beget a son.

On the third morning after their arrival at the whaling station they left it again for what they now thought of as " home." It was a relief to get away from the fishy smell of the place, but that was not the only thing that accounted for Gloria's high spirits. She had voted for leaving the valley because she knew that Philip would not be really happy if he were prevented from doing his best to get back to England. For her the Valley held happiness and security, while Europe offered only a vague and uncertain future, so in her secret heart she was glad that they found no ship to carry them back to the haunts of men.

The journey back went well the first four days, but from then on they were a prey to constant anxiety. Fresh snow began to fall in considerable quantities. Where they struck soft patches of it their feet sank in up to the ankles with every step they took, and the going proved extraordinarily fatiguing. Then for two days and nights they were confined to their tent by a blizzard. The tent became so heavily snowed up that its sides were forced right in, so that its ground space was reduced by half, and they were compelled to lie for many hours on end jammed together almost as if they were in a double coffin, with scarcely enough room to turn over. They would, in any case, have cuddled up for mutual warmth, but the lack of power to move their limbs freely resulted in numbness and the most appalling bouts of cramp. John A. alone remained comparatively cheerful, but to achieve that Gloria had to keep him bound closely against her breasts, which was no small inconvenience.

At last the snow stopped falling. They were able to dig themselves out and proceed on their way, but they had been badly frightened, so they pushed on to the limit of their endurance, hoping to reach the valley before being caught again. On the evening of the tenth day, to their great relief, they camped in the pass halfway up through the mountains, but on the following morning when they came down into the valley they had a sharp reminder that there were times when it, too, was far from secure.

No one was working on the farms, and, although it was broad daylight, all the Palace servants were cowering in the safest hiding-places they could find. Now that Gloria and Philip could both speak the Little People's language fairly fluently, it did not take them long to discover the cause. On the previous night the valley had been ravaged by another visit from the Dog.

It was, Philip remembered, just a year since that night of horror when they had actually seen the great mastiff gallop by carrying one of the pigmies. Then he had been in no position to cross-question the Little People about it, but now he determined to find out everything he could concerning the sinister beast.

This proved no easy undertaking, as, for one thing, the pigmies seemed to have a superstitious fear of discussing the subject at all, and, for another, because he and they still found great difficulty in finding words to convey abstract ideas. The sum of many hours spent on talking to members of his household and farmers living nearby amounted to the following.

The visits of the Dog were of two kinds. First, it appeared once a year, always on the same night towards the end of March. On these annual visits it took thirteen people—never more and never less. This number was in some way connected with the thirteen electrical storms, one every lunar month, which took place above the valley during each year. Secondly, there were much worse visitations in which anything from fifty to a hundred people were carried off, but these took place quite irregularly. Sometimes, as in the year that had just gone, no such raid took place at all; other years two or even three raids occurred, so no one could ever tell on what night the dreaded Dog might appear.

It was so strong and resourceful that when it had once selected a house from which it intended to secure a victim it was virtually impossible to keep it out. The flimsy doors and window-shutters of the cottages were little protection, and to erect stout stockades, such as the Prince had made around the Palace enclosure, was beyond the capabilities of the pigmies. The Dog never killed its victims but carried them away alive. Strangest of all, it was not considered to have any will or baleful intelligence of its own, but was regarded as a servant sent by a great and maleficent power that Philip could only translate as "The Lords of the Mountain."

He wished with all his heart that he could devise some way in which to protect the Little People from this terrible menace which hung over them, and from which they were never free for a single night; but with such scanty information there seemed little he *could* do. He did not doubt that the evil came from the great chain of mountains to the south, but, crippled as he was and with Gloria and his little son to look after, he did not feel called upon to attempt the role of Jack the Giant-Killer. For one thing, he doubted if he would be able to accomplish such a journey on his own, and, for another, if he could, he had no intention of undertaking it until he had a much clearer picture of what he would have to face when he got to the other end.

All he could do was to urge the pigmies to live inside a number of stockaded cantonments which he offered to help them make; but that would have meant most of them abandoning their houses. It seemed that they were a race of fatalists and, rather than do this, they preferred to continue to accept the risk that had formed part of the lives of their forefathers for many generations.

For some time past Gloria had been interesting herself in such bits of their history and folklore as she could pick up, and she had formed her own theory about them. On one point she was quite definite; certain words in their language had a distant resemblance to the Erse which she had learnt in old Irish songs that her mother had taught her. From this she argued that the Little People, or a branch of their race, had once lived in Ireland and that the Irish legends concerning the leprechauns were based upon a memory of these real human beings.

This idea was to some extent supported by the only tradition the pigmies seemed to have concerning themselves, which was that their ancestors had at one time lived in a big island which had many lakes, rivers and mountains, and was known as the Green Land. White men and Red men of the larger races had both dwelt there, and at a time of great storms, earthquakes and upheavals some of the Red men had taken the forebears of the Little People away from their original home in ships, later to settle them in their present country of the valley.

" That sounds much more like a distant memory of Atlantis to me," Philip declared when Gloria produced her theory, and ne told her all about the Canon's account of the great Island Continent that had been engulfed by the Flood.

After discussing the matter, they agreed that, in any case, the primitive Irish would have been the Atlanteans' nearest neighbours in the west, so it was perfectly possible that the races in the two countries had been related. Philip produced the Canon's belief, and one now shared by many leading anthropologists, that all myths and legends are race memories of actual historical happenings in the distant past, and, as it seemed in some ways fantastic, Philip and Gloria came to the conclusion that they were actually living among a race of European pigmies whose ancestors, when they lived in the old lands, had provided the foundation for such stories as " Snow White and the Seven Dwarfs."

Now that they had to remain in the valley for another Antarctic winter they once more gave their thoughts to various measures for improving the lot of their people. Gloria made some crude musical instruments for them; a drum, a harp and a kind of banjo, which proved a great success; and she showed a number of the little women how to cook all sorts of new dishes that they had never thought of before. Philip enlarged the mill, made a number of small carts and introduced the rake as a new innovation in hay-making. That autumn he also showed them how to store potatoes and root crops against the winter in a barrow; but by far his greatest achievement that year was the manufacture of glass.

On one of his longer expeditions he had come across a sand-pit and, quite near it, the place where the Little People smelted the crude iron to make their forks and spades. After several failures he succeeded in producing a rough glass, which, although it was not clear enough to be seen through, gave much more light than the little pieces of dark horn which up to then had been the only material from which to make windows.

As the Antarctic spring approached they began their preparations for a second journey to the MacKenzie Sea, since Philip was determined not to leave it too late in the season to catch a ship for home. Gloria was going to have another baby, but it was not due until early January, and he planned that they should leave the valley by mid-October. By the 14th everything was ready, but to their surprise and dismay, when they woke up on the morning of the 15th, they found that John A. was no longer in his cot. During the night the now lusty fellow of eleven months had disappeared without a sound.

He was already capable of staggering about, but, quite apart from the fact that he habitually uttered loud cries while doing so, he certainly could not have wandered off on his own; so one of the pigmies with whom he was such friends must have taken him.

In an anxious flurry Gloria summoned Gog and Magog and asked them if they had any idea what had happened to the child. They had. With disconcerting frankness they admitted that John A. had been stolen away by some friends of theirs whose names they were not prepared to disclose, and without the least sign of contrition they went on to reveal the reason for this kidnapping.

It seemed that Philip and Gloria had so won the hearts of the Little People that the idea of their departure was now regarded as a national calamity. The fact that during the two years they had lived in the valley there had been no raids by the great Dog, other than the apparently inevitable annual ones, had also caused special protective powers to be attributed to them. It was admitted that when they left the valley in the previous March they had duly returned to it safe and well, but, when they had departed many months earlier with the Prince, he had not come back at all, and both of them had come back grievously wounded: so, the little men argued, it would be tempting providence to leave it again. To ensure that they should not do so it had been decided to steal the baby, without which it was felt they would certainly not leave the valley.

Flattering as was the motive behind the crime, Philip could not help being greatly annoyed at this frustration of his plans; but, although he argued, pleaded and threatened during most of the day, all the pigmies with whom he spoke displayed an unusual degree of determination in their opposition to him.

At first Gloria was not particularly worried about John A., as she felt certain that the Little People were much too fond of him to do him any harm and knew even better how to look after him than she herself did; but after a week, with Philip still vowing vengeance against the kidnappers when he found them and no hint of when John A. was likely to be re-

turned to his home, she became distinctly anxious as to how he was getting on. In consequence, one afternoon when Philip had gone down to
the mill, she tackled Gog and Magog.

To begin with they tried to reassure her as well as they could while
showing reluctance to go any further, but at length she persuaded them
to relieve her anxiety in a more practical manner. First they took her
up to the meadow in which the Little People of that neighbourhood were
in the habit of dancing at the full of the moon, and, putting her in the
centre of one of the big rings made by their dancing feet, they made her
promise that, if they took her to the place where John A. was hidden, she
would neither attempt to take him away nor tell Philip where it was. Then
they led her to the far end of the valley and into a wood. Here they insisted on blindfolding her, then after a further quarter of an hour's walk
she heard a babble of children's voices, and they told her that she might
take off the bandage.

Looking about her she saw that she was in a high cave lit by a funnel-
like opening in the roof. As she and Philip had suspected, the Little
People reared their children in a secret crèche, and this was it. In front
of her there were scores of infants, toddlers and playing children of all
ages up to about ten, with here and there among them one of the pigmy
women acting as nurse. John A. came staggering towards her with squeals
of joy, and next second she had him in her arms.

On the way home that evening she asked Gog and Magog why it
was that, if, as she supposed, the children were all brought up in the
secret retreat in the mountainous side of the valley from fear of the Dog,
all the grown-ups did not take refuge there every time the beast
appeared.

They said that the children had always been brought up there as long
as anyone could remember, but no doubt the custom had originated on
account of the Dog and its visits, which also went back into the mists
of antiquity. But the idea of any grown-up other than the nurses taking
refuge there shocked them profoundly. To attempt to do so would only
have resulted in leading the Dog to the secret place which, apparently,
was not invulnerable; and they thought it better that half their race should
be taken than that their children should be imperilled. This reply
showed a new side to the pigmies' natures and a capacity for courage and
self-sacrifice that Gloria had not till then suspected that they possessed.

While observing her promise to Gog and Magog, she told Philip that
night about her afternoon's adventure, and they agreed that, although
the Little People had succeeded in foiling their plans to get to the whaling
station early in the season, they had no cause to be concerned about their
child. The best line now seemed to play a waiting game until they could
persuade their subjects to give John A. back to them, and then, having
made fresh preparations in secret, slip away from the valley one night
when their departure was least expected.

The following week the horror of the Dog descended on the valley again in one of the surprise visits during which so many more people were lost than at the annual March raids. Gloria clung to Philip and refused to let him go out, but nearly all night they stood—he with the rifle now well cleaned and oiled and she with the pistol—behind their stockade waiting for the brute to pass in the hope of being able to shoot it. Three times they caught glimpses of it in the distance, but it was the dark period of the moon, so they had only starlight by which to see, and to their disgust it whisked away into the darkness each time before they had a chance to aim their weapons at it. During the day of mourning that followed it was found that some sixty-five people had been dragged from their homes and spirited away—no one knew where.

Philip, angry, bewildered, sick with rage about this horrible thing which went on beneath his eyes and which he seemed powerless to stop, spent the day trying to find out more about the monster and from where it came. Its tracks about the main paths crossed and re-crossed each other so frequently that it was difficult to ascertain where it had entered the valley and where it had taken its victims once it had secured them. Yet, after Philip had followed innumerable false trails that led to cottages with broken doors, or great holes torn in their wattle and daub walls, it emerged that after each outrage the Dog entered at some point or other a small wood which lay to the south-east corner of the valley. After half an hour in the wood Philip discovered the focal point where all these tracks emerged. It was at the base of the cliff, and near it a steep track led upward.

For the first time he realized that there must be a second way out of the valley and through the mountain peaks that hedged it in. Hampered by his lame leg and crutches, it took him over an hour to climb the track and reach a small plateau which lay at about the same level as the great plateau several miles further along the ridge.

There was nothing to be seen on the little plateau, save that the earth was freshly disturbed and trampled as though a number of men or beasts had been milling round on it quite recently. At the far side from the cliff up which Philip had come there was a gap between two walls of rock, which he now felt sure must be the entrance to another pass through the mountains. There could be no doubt that this was the way that the sinister beast came, but the day was now far advanced, and he was unarmed, so he decided that discretion was the better part of valour, and that he would not explore the pass that evening.

He had turned back and was just about to begin his descent of the cliff track up which he had come when his eye caught something glittering about ten feet away on the ground. At first he thought it was just a bright piece of quartz, but its colour was so unusual that he went over to have a closer look. A moment later, with a hand that trembled so much that it could hardly hold his find, he picked the thing up. It was a beautifully coloured piece of semi-precious stone. It was also the twin of that wonderfully carved ten thousand year old Atlantean musical instrument that the Canon had shown him long long ago on the first evening they had spent together at the Rectory.

Very slowly Philip made his way home, examining his find afresh every hundred yards or so to make certain that his eyes had not deceived him, and trying to figure out exactly what this extraordinary coincidence portended.

The stone pan-pipes might, of course, have been washed up on that ledge by some great natural cataclysm thousands of years ago, but that seemed most unlikely. It was far more probable that it had been dropped there by someone who had been on the plateau the night before.

If that were so, then the Masters of the Dog—the Lords of the Mountain—were the descendants of some of the Atlanteans who had escaped destruction at the time of the Flood. There was no more reason why some of their ships should not have been washed up on the shores of the Antarctic than on any other continent. The miracle was that they had survived. But then the Atlantean priests were said to have been great magicians, and there were these strange hints both from the Prince and from the Little People of the powers of the Lords of the Mountain to control climate and weather.

When Philip got back to the Palace he and Gloria talked over the matter far into the night, and, as she pointed out, his discovery fitted in with the tradition of the Little People—that they had lived in a great island and at a time of storm and earthquakes been brought to the land of snow by Red men in a ship.

Another thing that they discussed at length, but on which they could reach no conclusion, was whether the supernatural appearances of the Canon had any connection with Philip's find. Was it just a coincidence that it had been a flute such as the Canon had possessed that Philip had found, and not a necklace, a sword, a buckle or a ring? Was this one more reminder that he yet had a part to play in the distant war which would bring grievous harm to Hitler and his Nazis? No ghost could possibly have placed the thing there; that was quite certain. But the Canon's ghost might have scared its owner into dropping it up on the little plateau the previous night. Had it done so because, for some reason, it no longer had the power to appear to Philip direct? Had these circuitous means been used in one last effort designed to remind him of the Canon, of the prophecy of the Canon's ghost, and so urge him to exert himself to get home?

On the following day, taking their arms with them, they went up the cliff together and explored the pass. It was much shorter than the one they knew, but it brought them out on the landward side of the chain of mountains in which the valley was set, and from two thousand feet up they gazed for a long time across the seemingly endless plain below to the great southern range, which they now felt sure was the home of some strange and sinister mystery.

They found no other traces of recent visitors and could do no more for the time being; neither, until they got John A. back, could they get away to the whaling station, as Philip was now more than ever anxious to do.

It was not until mid-December that John A. was restored to them, and, by then, as the Little People knew perfectly well, Gloria was too near the time for her second child to risk a journey. The child, a girl, was born on January the 4th with the help of four small midwives as before; and the arrival of the new infant put out of court any question of their leaving for the MacKenzie Sea so as to reach it during the whaling season of 1943-44.

Philip endeavoured to conceal his disappointment, and playing with his children was a big consolation. The new baby, whom they christened Aurora after the Aurora Australis, was a pet, with her mother's blue eyes and Philip's fair hair, and John A. was growing apace. He could now talk a little, although, to the annoyance of his parents he seemed to pick up the Little People's language more quickly than theirs.

By early March Gloria was as fit again as she had ever been, but as the month wore on both she and Philip became increasingly silent and worried. Neither spoke of it to the other, but both could hardly get it out of their minds for a moment that at the end of the month the annual visit of the Dog was due, and that on that night thirteen more of the ugly Little People whom they had now come to love would be taken.

On the afternoon of the day Philip got out his rifle and began to give it a good clean. Gloria came over to him, laid a hand on his shoulder and said: "Must you, Boy?"

"How can I help it, my sweet?" He took her hand and kissed it, then, in an attempt to make light of the matter, he added with a little laugh: "To protect the natives from tigers and things is part of 'The White Man's Burden'!"

"You'll go up to the plateau and wait there?"

"Yes."

"I felt sure you would. Well, I'll be coming, too."

He began to protest, but she laid a finger on his lips. "Be quiet now, my own one. What would I do by meself here? If you have to die I'd much rather die too. I just hate to leave my babies, but I'm not really worried for them, because I know that they will be cared for by all our little friends and never really miss me. But I couldn't go on without you.

No more was said, but two hours before sunset they left the Palace and set out together to defy the Power of the Dog and its mysterious masters.

CHAPTER XVII

THE TEMPLE OF THE FALSE SUN

As they walked along the track between the small fields and vegetable plots that they knew so well, the countryside looked very peaceful, and it was difficult to believe that, within a few hours, it would be ravaged by an animal which had the qualities of an almost mythological beast. Yet the inhabitants had not forgotten that this was their age-long anniversary of dread, and they were already hurrying home to barricade themselves in and hide as cunningly as they could in the hope that they might once again be among the many who survived and not among the unfortunate few who were taken.

Every one of the little brown men whom they passed gave them greeting and either warned them not to stay out late that night or urged them to go back to the Palace there and then; and they all asked after the children. In every case Philip and Gloria promised to take care of themselves, and, although neither of them spoke of it, both of them had the thought that never until this evening had they realized how greatly they had come to be loved and honoured by the Little People. As they walked on past the lake where the waterwheel now lay silent, they began to talk of more plans they had in mind for increasing the wellbeing of their subjects; yet, somehow, deep down inside them, they both had the feeling that they would never pass that way again.

In spite of that and the unknown qualities of the terror that they were about to face, they felt little sense of fear. Instead, they were filled with a highly nervous excitement. It was as though the valley and all their interests in it were a chapter of their lives which was ending with the setting of the sun, and they had no more power to postpone its end than they had to slow down the solar system. Ahead of them they sensed a danger far worse than they had ever known before, yet they had the strange conviction that, if only they could surmount it, they would at long last really find their way home.

By the time they reached the little plateau the long March twilight was deepening. Sitting down they unpacked the cold supper they had brought with them and ate it; then they took up their positions for their watch. To sit with their backs to the cliff track up which they had climbed seemed to invite being driven over it backwards should the Dog charge them, so they chose a spot at the extreme right of the plateau where they could crouch with their backs to the cliff yet enfilade anything coming out of the entrance to the pass. Prince Fedor had left behind him some sixty rounds of ammunition for the rifle but they were now reduced to four rounds in the automatic, so it was agreed that Philip should do the shooting and Gloria should come to the rescue with the pistol only if his rifle shots proved ineffective and he was hard pressed.

For an hour the darkness was very black, then the moon came up. They knew that they would not now have very long to wait, as both their own experience and the tradition of the valley agreed that the Dog always began its man-hunt shortly after the moon rose.

It was very still there and suddenly Philip caught a sound. " Listen! " he breathed, touching Gloria on the elbow.

She nodded, having heard it too. Very faintly at first, but gradually growing clearer, the notes of a weird music were wafted to them, and Philip felt sure that it came from the type of pan-pipes of which he had seen two specimens.

The music continued to be soft but was now quite close at hand. They crouched at the far corner of the plateau, straining their eyes into the semi-darkness. The moon was only a sickle and, while the great patch of black shadow that marked the entrance to the pass stood out clearly, the first movements within it were difficult to see.

Suddenly a number of figures seemed to detach themselves from the blackness and stand forth quite clearly in the moon's silvery light. Four flute players headed the procession, then came a great palanquin, or covered litter, carried shoulder-high by eight stalwart bearers. After this came a second and a third litter, similarly borne, and the rear of the procession was brought up, not by a Dog, but by thirteen great dogs, all whimpering and straining at leads that were held by thirteen tall and powerful men.

The flute players halted and ceasing their music turned about. The palanquin was set down, its curtains parted, and a tall dignified figure stepped out. The other two litters were set down in the background, but no one emerged from them. The dogs were brought forward, and the man who had come out of the palanquin made a sign to one of the dog's keepers, who leant a little towards the great beast and was evidently just about to undo the leash from its collar.

Philip saw that he dared wait no longer. His bad leg was good for a few steps if he took them slowly. Carrying his rifle at the ready, he gave a loud shout and advanced a few paces, followed by Gloria.

The heads of every one of the strangers instantly turned towards them, and as Philip limped forward the man from the palanquin came to meet him. When they had approached to within a few yards of each other they both halted. Philip was six feet in height, but the man facing him was considerably taller. He was dressed in a white robe with a black pattern on it, and it was not until Gloria was within a few feet of him that she realized that it was made of penguins' feathers. The robe, which hung slightly open, disclosed some brightly coloured woven garments beneath it; a hood of the same material covered the stranger's head, and the moonlight glinted on the jewelled earrings that dangled from his ears.

His skin was a reddish-brown, his nose hooked, his chin firm, his lips thin. It was the proudest and most cruel face that Philip had ever seen.

Suddenly the man spoke, but in a tongue which they could not understand and which had not even a resemblance to that of the Little People.

Philip replied in English, and Gloria tried the language they had learnt down in the valley; but he evidently did not understand a word of either. With an impatient shake of the head he beckoned them forward and, as he turned to lead them towards his palanquin, gave a sharp order to the man who had been about to unleash the dog.

As the man again put his hand on the mastiff's collar Philip shouted: "Hi! You there! Stop that!" and by waving his own hand from side to side he tried to indicate that the man should ignore the order he had evidently been given.

Their leader turned and stared. The man with the dog just glanced at Philip, then took no further notice. Philip raised his rifle and aimed it at the dog, at the same time calling: "If you let that dog go I'll shoot it!"

Obviously none of them understood either Philip's words or his gestures, or, apparently, the purpose of his rifle. The man released the dog, and it bounded towards the path that ran down the cliff. Philip squeezed the rifle's trigger. There was a sharp report that echoed round and round among the stone crags. The dog leapt into the air with a howl, crashed to the ground just on the edge of the slope, whimpered for a second and lay still.

Lowering his rifle, Philip turned back to the leader of the strangers, trying to express by a lifting of his shoulders that he was sorry he had had to shoot the dog but had seen no alternative.

The man did not speak and he made no threatening gesture. He simply looked at Philip. His eyes were jet-black, and beneath brows drawn together in imperious anger they sparkled with sudden malevolence. As Philip met the glance he found that his own eyes were fixed and held. He could no longer look away from the stranger's eyes, which now appeared to him like balls of red fire. The eyes grew larger and larger. Philip felt as though he were being drawn towards them and must plunge headlong into those two great blazing pits which were rapidly merging into one. He felt his knees go weak, his rifle slipped from his hand, and he fell fainting to the ground.

When he recovered it was still dark. He could feel a gentle jogging motion, but for the moment he had not the least idea where he was; then, as memory returned, he realized that he was in one of the big litters that had been brought to the plateau by the strangers. As he struggled into a sitting position he felt a movement beside him and heard Gloria whisper:

"Boy darling! Are you all right?"

THE TEMPLE OF THE FALSE SUN

"Yes, I think so." He found her hand and gave it a reassuring squeeze. "But what happened . . . after that devil looked at me?"

"He looked at me, too; but only for a second. Just long enough for me to know that I'd have no chance at all if I tried to shoot him."

"What happened then?"

"He jabbered at his servants, and they put you in this carrying wagon thing. They signed to me to be joining you, so I hopped in quick before they could say different, because I was scared to death of what that witch-doctor man might have done to you. When I found your heart and breathing were all right I thought I'd be taking a peep at what was going on. The moon coming through the chink in the curtains showed me that this thing is full of camp gear: tents, cooking utensils and all that. It's some tents we're lying on now."

"Did they do the filthy job they came to do?"

"Yes. They let another of the dogs go as soon as you were knocked out, and back he came a quarter of an hour later with one of our poor little men. Then they let a third dog go, and so it went on till they'd gotten twelve victims. They've put all the captives in the other waggon. I mean, the one that the big panjandrum isn't using. I'd guess that it was about four by the time they got through, and it must be around five now. We're somewhere in the pass still. Oh Boy, darling, what'll we do? What'll we do?"

"Hush, my sweet." He squeezed her hand again. "While there's life there's hope. That sounds a silly and trite thing to say, but all the same it's awfully true."

"These Red men are evil folk, Boy, and I'm scared of what they may do to us."

"Yes, they're evil all right; but it's no good meeting trouble halfway. I suppose they took the automatic off you?"

"No. What sense was there in showing the pistol when I knew I'd never be able to use it? They don't know I've got it because it was hidden under my coat before, but as soon as I got in here I hid it in the knapsack we used for carrying the supper things."

"We'd better keep it there, then. It's quite a comfort to think that anyhow we've got one weapon. D'you know what happened to the rifle?"

"No. I think they left it where it fell. I picked up your crutches. You'll find them there beside you." Gloria yawned. "Oh, I'm so tired! It's come on me all of a sudden. It must be that I was tired before, but too worried to notice it while I was wondering if you were ever going to open your lips again."

"My poor darling!" Slipping an arm round her he drew her head down on to his shoulder. "You've had the hell of a night; a much worse one than I have. Try to get some sleep now."

The gentle rocking of the well-sprung palanquin was **very conducive** to sleep, and within a few minutes she had dropped off. Philip lay staring over her head into the darkness wondering what the future held for them. Escape, for the moment at all events, seemed out of the question. His leg would prove an almost insurmountable handicap in any attempt to get away, and, in any case, where could they go, as it hardly seemed likely that the valley would prove a safe refuge for them now that they had made enemies of these " Lords of the Mountain "?

A faint grey light began to filter between the curtains of the litter. Soon after this its pace became erratic, and it was frequently tilted forward for brief intervals at a sharp angle, from which Philip knew that they must be through the pass and descending the two thousand feet track to the plain.

They were not far down it when Gloria began to talk in her sleep. This was not a thing she often did, so Philip put it down to over-excitement, and, although he did not at first pay much attention to her mutterings, his interest was suddenly caught because she seemed to be carrying on a conversation of exceptional gravity. He heard her say perfectly clearly:

" I'm one hundred per cent. American." Then she went on, often with quite long intervals between her sentences:

" Yes. He said, ' In order that Government of the People by the People for the People shall not perish from the earth.' "

" Sure, it means a fair chance for all. It means that people are just people, and having money, or birth, or brains doesn't necessarily make them any finer or greater. So everyone has an equal right to the things that really matter; like bringing up their children the way they think best, going to what church they fancy and telling even the President he's wrong, if they honestly think he is."

" Forget all that! But I don't want to. Why should I ? "

" Oh, I see. Well that certainly makes a difference."

" That's a pretty fast one. You see, there's Boy and the children. Naturally, I wouldn't want to die."

" The vote and all that has never meant much to me; but all the same I've always thought that women and men should look on one another as equals. They're just made different, but they're not really different inside."

" Is that so? Thousands of American boys giving their lives every day now? That's just terrible. Of course, we've been out of it all from the beginning, and we've hardly heard anything of what's going on "

" If you put it that way, I suppose I would."

" Boy says I could pass for an Irish girl anywhere."

" He'll just hate doing that, same as I will."

After this her disconcerted sentences trailed off into a mutter, and Philip fell into a doze himself. They both woke at the same time when the litter was set down with a jolt.

Their first sensation on waking was one of icy cold, and on looking out between the curtains they saw the reason. The procession had reached the bottom of the mountains and had halted in the middle of a field of snow across which a bitter wind was blowing. The position of the sun indicated that it was now about midday, and seen from the snow-field it had a great double halo round it, caused by a refraction of light, which is one of the strangest features of the Antarctic world.

They had hardly taken in their surroundings when the bearers of the litter pulled the curtains aside and began to get out the equipment for making camp. All of them were dressed in the same fashion as their chief if not with the same grandeur. The patterned featherwork of their cloaks was extremely fine, and thousands of hours of labour must have gone into their making. They were also very practical for such a climate, as layer upon layer of the feathers sewn on some foundation material made the cloaks both wind- and water-proof.

Some of them gave Philip and Gloria curious looks, but no one spoke to them, and they sat in the litter shivering for half an hour, until a circle of eight round tents looking like large beehives had been erected. A lean-faced man, who was slightly taller than the rest and appeared to be the foreman of the gang, then motioned them towards one of the tents.

On entering it, they found to their surprise that, although sparsely furnished, it not only appeared quite comfortable but was most agreeably warm. The snow had been covered with thick matting over which coloured rugs were spread, and on these a number of cushions had been scattered. In the centre of the floor stood a small brazier which radiated both light and heat, but it was not burning coal or any other substance.

Philip stopped to examine it, then gave a low whistle.

" By jove, these boys have got something here! This gadget is made to function by electricity. Nothing else could possibly give this effect. Yet there is no wiring attaching it to any generator or battery. It must be animated by some sort of electrical wireless wave; that's the only explanation. It's the sort of thing our own scientists have only got as far as dreaming about yet."

Gloria had seated herself on some of the cushions and was not really listening, but the word " dreaming " caught her ear, and she said quickly:

" Boy, I had a dream while I was sleeping just now."

" I know you did," he smiled. " You were talking in your sleep like billy-oh. At least, I think you were; but I dropped off myself, and you were saying such extraordinary things that perhaps I only dreamed that you said them."

" What sort of things was I saying? "

" Oh, you were quoting Abraham Lincoln, and it sounded as if somebody had asked you to say what you understood by Democracy yourself, and then if you really thought it worth dying for."

H

"That's it," Gloria nodded. "All that came into my dream; but you'd never guess who I was talking to."

"Who?"

"'Twas the Canon."

"Really! But, hang it all, you never met him when he was alive, so how could you possibly know?"

"'Twas himself all right. I haven't a doubt of that," and Gloria began to describe the figure that she had seen in her dream. When she had done Philip said at once:

"Yes. That was John Beal-Brookman. How very extraordinary! Do tell me what he had to say."

"Well, first he was asking me if I really understood what the war was all about. Then he wanted to know if I'd be willing to face danger and death for what I believe to be right. We had a bit of an argument about that; but I cooked me own goose by saying what I've always thought, that women are every bit as good as men. After that 'twas not so bad because he said that I wouldn't be expected to do anything that you wouldn't do, and that when we had to face the music we'd be together."

Gloria paused for a moment, then went on: "The rest of it was mostly himself giving me instructions that I was to pass on to you. These people are the enemy, he said; just as much as the Germans or the Japs, because they're on the wrong side in the eternal World struggle that has been going on for thousands of years between Blacks and Whites. He said that, although our scientists don't even know of their existence, theirs know quite a bit about the outer world. They know about the war and they want our enemies to win. 'Tis for that reason we must make them believe that we're pro-Nazi ourselves."

"What!" exclaimed Philip. "No damn' fear! I'd rather tell the truth and shame the devil."

"Ah!" she nodded. "I told him you'd hate doing that; but he said to tell you that we must think of ourselves as if we were spies in an enemy country and that the further we can worm our way into their confidence the better we'll be doing our job."

"I see. Of course, that makes a difference. I doubt if it will work, though. We've never gone in for Quislings in England, so the idea isn't really plausible."

"'Twas that very thing I said to the Canon, and he replied that we'd both better think of ourselves as Irish from now on. The big shots at the place we're going to are clever, but the knowledge they have is not so hot in many ways. They'll know that lots of the Irish hate the English, but they wouldn't be able to tell people of one European race from another just on looks, or way of speaking, and they'll have no means of checking up on whatever we tell them. 'Twas the Canon's idea that we should both take me mother's name and you could say that your father was murdered by the Black and Tans during the Troubles. But he was warning me that once we've made up our story we must stick to it and act every moment of the time as if we really thought the Nazis were the tops."

Philip remained silent for a moment, then he said : " If they are capable of questioning us at all they will probably question us separately, so we must have a watertight story that we'll both be able to remember and expand in detail, if necessary, without contradicting each other. We'll never be able to do that if we try to invent and memorize an entirely false story of our doings over the past five years. I think we'll have to stick to the truth with just a few cardinal differences."

" 'Twould be much the simplest," Gloria agreed. " Otherwise, we'll be tying ourselves in knots about how we got here; it's just on the cards, too, that they may have come across our raft, although the Canon said nothing about that."

" Exactly. We'll tell the truth wherever possible then. Listen, how would this be? I am Irish, and my name is Philip O'Neil. The raft was a secret device that I was testing out because I hoped to be able to help the Germans with it. My idea was that single rafts—we must say nothing about a string of them or the launch—could be camouflaged like bits of wreckage so that the British would allow them to drift through their blockade, and that the Gulf Stream would wash them up on the coast of Norway. The scheme was to use them for running high priority war supplies from the U.S. to the Germans after the war had started. I decided to make the first crossing in one myself and went to New York in the early summer of 1939 to have it built there. I met you. We fell in love, got married and decided to make the trip across on the raft our honeymoon. After that it's pretty plain sailing."

" If your name's O'Neil what'll mine have been before I married you? " Gloria asked.

" It would prevent any chance of confusion if we say that it was O'Neil also, and that we're distantly related. That would account for our meeting in New York. I could have had an introduction to your family."

" Okay. The family came from Limerick in the west of Ireland, and if the subject of religion crops up it would look more natural if you said you were a Catholic."

For an hour or more they talked on, discussing the details of this new rôle they were to play. They had already forgotten that their plotting was inspired by only a dream.

They were interrupted by the entrance of two of the litter bearers, one of whom fixed up a low wooden folding-table, upon which the other set down a tray carrying numerous glazed bottles and bowls containing foods and liquids. This porcelain was so exquisite in design and colour and looked so frail that at first Gloria and Philip hardly dared to handle

H 2

it, but it was now sixteen hours since they had eaten, and they both suddenly realized that they were very hungry.

There were no knives, forks or spoons, but napkins had been spread for them, and the foods before them, although strange, proved delicious. There was a thin soup with a flavour faintly reminiscent of mint, a stew which they thought was based on llama's meat but spiced with many herbs that did not grow in the pigmies' valley, and, as a pudding, yellow fruits which Gloria felt sure were some form of mangoes. To wash it down there was a pot of some infusion which was not China tea but something like it, with a faintly orange aroma.

When they had eaten the men appeared, bringing a basin of warm, scented water for them to cleanse their fingers, and then cleared away.

" Well, we certainly can't complain of our treatment so far," Philip murmured. " It's very different from what I expected after the look the leader of this crowd gave me last night."

" I was meaning to ask you, Boy—did it hurt much? What really happened to you? "

" Heaven only knows! He used a form of hypnotism, I suppose. Anyhow, the look he gave me seemed to strike me between the eyes like a physical blow, and it laid me out. In a way it was as though I was being drawn forward and downwards into a fiery pit; but it didn't hurt and I felt no ill effects when I woke up."

He had barely finished speaking when the subject of their conversation entered the tent. Now that they could see him in a better light he seemed a more imposing figure than ever. He and his people appeared to be of American-Indian stock, but certain ornaments on their clothes and camp equipment all suggested a connection with either the Aztecs of Mexico or the Incas of Peru, although the art of these people seemed much more highly developed and bore some resemblance to the classic Ming period of China.

The visitor's face was as inscrutable as ever, and, although he looked in turn directly at them, his eyes did not hold even the hint of a smile. Pointing at himself he said : " Coxitl," twice, which they took to be his name, so they gave theirs as Philip and Gloria O'Neil in reply; but, as soon as he uttered a sentence, they could only shake their heads.

He spoke again, several times, each time quite slowly and in a way that seemed to differ slightly from his previous utterances, so that they gathered that he was trying them out with a variety of languages. But they could not understand one word he said and, giving a slight shrug, he left them.

Another meal was served in the evening, after which they were not disturbed till the following morning. At dawn camp was struck, and they were led back to the palanquin. There they were given plenty of rugs, foot warmers, and a thing that was the equivalent of a hot-bottle.

which kept warm all day until camp was made at dusk. From that point on the same routine continued unbroken.

Apart from the bitter cold of the daytime whenever they put their noses outside the heavy leather curtains of the litter, they had nothing of which to complain. Coxitl did not attempt to speak to them again, and the litter bearers preserved an entirely impersonal attitude towards them. They saw practically nothing of their fellow-prisoners—the twelve little men who had been retrieved from the valley by the big dogs. The brown pigmies were carried in the third litter by day and hustled into one of the beehive tents each night. They now seemed completely apathetic to their fate, and Philip doubted if they had the will to attempt to save themselves, even had he been in a position to organize a mutiny. In any case, with the litter bearers, dog-leaders, musicians and a number of cooks, etc., who completed the party, the men from the mountain numbered nearly fifty, so Philip and Gloria would have stood no chance whatever had they attempted anything against their captors.

The rate of progress varied according to the ground, as, although the great snow plain looked flat and even from a distance, it was far from being so in fact. The wind had packed the snow in a ridge so that its surface was like the waves of a frozen sea. Moreover, at times they came to places where the irresistible pressure of some slowly moving glacier had forced the ice and snow up into great rugged blocks. With the sunlight glinting on them so that they sparkled with every colour in the prism, they looked like the ruins of a fairy city; but they formed barriers that it was no easy matter to cross. Blizzards also twice delayed them, but day by day they gradually drew nearer to the great chain of mountains, the towering heights of which were lit each evening with a golden glory and fantastic colourings ranging from pale pink to deep purple on their lower slopes.

On the twelfth day the mountains bulked over them with truly Himalayan splendour, their lofty peaks hidden in cloud. By afternoon they had reached the base of the range and began the ascent of the foothills. Dusk found them at the bottom of a steeper gradient, and Philip thought that they would camp there for the night, expecting that the following day they would enter a winding pass which would lead them to another valley, greater perhaps but similar to the one they had left. But the caravan pressed on, continuing even after complete darkness had fallen, so that nothing could be seen of the surrounding scene by peeping between the curtains of the litter except the faint shimmer of snow in the surrounding rocks.

By half past eight they were missing their evening meal, but an hour later they had forgotten their temporary hunger. The gentle sway of the litter made them feel sleepy, and by ten o'clock Gloria had dropped off. Philip thought it unlikely that they would reach the valley until the following morning, so he made no special effort to keep awake and succumbed soon afterwards. Both of them woke with a start on the litter being set down, and, although chinks of light showed between the curtains, they both had the feeling that they had not been asleep very long, and that it was probably not yet midnight. Stretching out a hand Philip pulled back one of the curtains. An extraordinary scene then met their eyes.

To start with the light was neither daylight nor any form of artificial light that they knew. It came from what looked like a miniature sun high up and some distance away from them. This sun was red in colour and pulsed constantly as though it were a lump of molten lava. No sky of clouds surrounded it. Instead, it seemed to hang in a dense black void that the human eye could not penetrate, while its baleful throbbing rays bathed everything below it in a blood-red glow.

The glow lit a vast stone staircase that ascended two-thirds of the way towards the ball of fire, then ended abruptly on what Philip at first took to be a terrace; but after a moment he realized that it was the flattened top of a huge pyramid, the base and lower sides of which were so big and stretched so far into the surrounding gloom that he had not immediately taken them in. As his glance fell from the glowering sun he saw that all the men with whom they had spent the past twelve days had gone to the head of the column and thrown themselves face down on the ground at the foot of the great flight of steps.

" May the Saints defend us! " Gloria whispered. " Where are we, Boy? What sort of place is this? "

" It's a temple, and we must be inside a great cave," he whispered back. " The party must have entered a tunnel that leads here while we were asleep. Look, there's one of their priests! "

A solitary figure appeared on the top of the truncated pyramid, and advancing to the top of the steps raised its arms above its head. A single deep boom sounded from a hidden gong. Suddenly, there was a scurrying of feet and a dozen figures emerged out of the darkness. With fierce cries they came hurrying towards the litters. They were half-naked and bare-footed. Their faces and bodies were hideous from the scars of self-inflicted wounds; their eyes rolled in their heads, and they appeared to be animated with the madness of dervishes. Flinging themselves on the last litter of the three, they dragged out one of the little men and hurried with him towards the steps.

" Oh, Holy Mother, look to us now! " sobbed Gloria, and buried her face on Philip's chest. He held her tightly to him, but he could not tear his horrified gaze from the awful spectacle that followed, and, although she was not actually watching, she could tell from the noises more or less what was going on.

The wretched pigmy was half-carried and half-thrown up the great flight of stone stairs, as, one after another, the mad priests raced ahead of their companions for a few steps and snatched the little body, till finally it was lain, still writhing, at the feet of the High Priest.

All the moving figures were now distant but stood out clearly in the awful red glare that streamed down upon them from the molten sun. Stooping, the priest seized the body and lifting it raised it for a moment high above his head. Coxitl and his men had now risen. From them at the bottom of the steps and from the priests at the top there went up a fierce shout.

The High Priest laid the body down on a square slab. His right hand was raised, and the red light glinted on the shiny surface of a dagger. It flashed down into the body. There was a faint distant scream. Then the High Priest was tearing with both hands at the pigmy's chest. Next instant he had torn out the living heart and was holding it on high, offering it up to the red sun. Another fierce shout went up from the congregation and the priests. There followed the final abominable act. Lowering the heart, the High Priest bit a piece out of it, then flung it to his subordinates. Two of them struggled for it, the others tore the remains of the body to pieces and began to smear themselves with the blood of their victim.

Having completed their horrible rites, they came streaming down the great staircase again. In fascinated horror Philip was still staring out between the curtains of the litter. Gloria's curiosity overcoming her fear, she pulled the curtain further back so that she could look too.

Suddenly, one of the blood-smeared priests saw them. His eyes glaring with the lust of murder he pointed at them and screamed out something to his companions in a high falsetto. Instantly the whole mob came streaming forward. Next moment, with wild cries and clutching claw-like hands, they had surrounded the litter in which Philip and Gloria were crouching, with the clear intent of dragging them from it to be the victims of another sacrifice.

CHAPTER XVIII

THE SECRET OF THE MOUNTAIN

THE instant Philip saw the eyes of the fiendish mob fix upon Gloria and himself he heaved upon the heavy curtains to get them back into place; but the stiff leather was difficult to handle, so even that took a few seconds, and the action of the foul human herd followed so swiftly on its thought that half a dozen of the blood-smeared priests were leaping forward before he could get the curtains properly closed.

Gloria had seen them too. Her face white as a sheet, she pressed back against him. But only for a moment. Remembering the pistol she flung herself upon the haversack, and with trembling fingers strove to disentangle the weapon from the things in which she had wrapped it.

Philip meanwhile was thrusting and banging on the leather sheeting on the other side of the litter, in the hope of forcing an opening by which they might slip out. Having seen the evil hysterical rabble in front he had realized at once that four shots from an automatic would not save Gloria and himself for as many minutes once they were face to face with the priests of this grim underworld into which they had been brought.

From beyond the curtains came the shrill screaming of the priests and the scrabbling of horny nails as they clutched at the leather; but there was now also the sound of deeper voices and of trampling feet that suggested a fight was going on outside.

As Gloria thrust the automatic into Philip's hand he turned to face the curtained entrance of the litter again. For a few moments they crouched there together with their hearts beating in their throats. The sounds of the struggle outside continued. Leaning forward Philip put his eye to a small crack in one of the leather folds of the curtain, a crack which they had often cursed during their journey because of the icy draught it let in. Coxitl and his bearers were standing with their backs to the litter. They had stout staves in their hands and were laying about them lustily in an endeavour to drive off the priests.

Suddenly, the fighting ceased, and a moment later the High Priest came into Philip's field of vision. He was taller even than Coxitl and an eagle-visaged being of barbaric splendour. Great gems flashed and scintillated from his chest, ears and headdress in the weird red light. His face was hideously scarred by deliberate mutilation with lines and circles; spots of fresh blood were spattered on his robe from the recent sacrifice. The other priests had drawn back but only to form a snarling restless crowd behind him.

The High Priest spoke to Coxitl, who replied briefly but firmly; then the two of them began to argue. Although Philip could not understand a word of what they were saying, he could guess as easily as if they had been talking English. The priest was demanding that the strangers should be handed over to his people for immediate sacrifice, and Coxitl, who evidently had other views as to the future of his captives, was refusing to give them up.

"What's happening, Boy?" whispered Gloria. "What's happening?"

He told her his guess about what was going on, and she began to pray aloud to the Holy Virgin to save them.

In an agony of suspense Philip continued to peer through the crack. The High Priest was threatening now, and Coxitl seemed to be weakening. Then a new figure appeared on the scene. He was the shortest of these mountain dwellers that Philip had so far seen; an old man who walked with a slight stoop. His face was wrinkled, lined and cunning; his sharp nose and shiny bald head gave him a strong resemblance to Gandhi.

The High Priest stood his ground while Coxitl bowed low before the newcomer. The argument was renewed but only for a minute. The bald-headed old man gave an order in a surprising virile voice. Next moment, to the intense relief of its occupants, the litter was lifted and borne onwards till the shouts and curses of the disappointed priests gradually died away in the distance.

For a little time they did not dare to look out again, but when they did they found that they had left the red glow of the Temple behind and were now being carried down a long smooth-walled tunnel reminiscent of a subway in an underground station, except that, instead of being brightened by coloured tiles and gay advertisements, the walls were of a dull uniform greyness.

The party proceeded down a ramp and through another long gloomy tunnel that had doors slightly wider at the bottom than at the top, similar to the Egyptian style, set in the walls at intervals of every twenty feet or so. At last the litter was set down in front of one of these, and the bearers pulled aside the curtains. As Philip and Gloria got out Coxitl appeared, drew back a heavy hanging that filled the doorway and motioned them to pass through it.

On doing so they found themselves in a room of medium size, sparsely furnished with floor-coverings, rugs and a single cushioned divan of the same type to which they had become accustomed in the tent.

Coxitl had followed them in and, in spite of his haughty, unfriendly demeanour, they would have thanked him, if they could, for having protected them from the priests; but after a swift glance round to see that the place was in order he made a sign that they should stay there, and left them.

They were still considerably shaken by the revolting murder of the pigmy in the Temple and their own narrow escape, so they looked round their new quarters with some apprehension. The room was low-ceilinged, and in the centre stood one of the portable radiators that provided light and heat. The walls were of grey stone, and carved in panels on them were obviously conventionalized representations of strange, barbaric gods. One had an almost cubist eagle's head, which was strangely similar to that used by the Nazis. Another had a human face with huge, staring eyes; his hands gripped the ankles of a small man or doll, who dangled upside down, and he was in the act of tearing this puppet in half. There were others less respectable but no less grim, as the only decorations of a living-room.

It was Gloria who noticed that there was another curtained entrance to the room at its far end, and beyond it they found what could be better described as a wash-place than a bathroom. To the right-hand side of the doorway about a quarter of the floor space was sunken a few inches and formed a shallow trough. It was half-full of water and had a drain at one end; from a runnel set about three feet up in the wall a steady stream of warm water splashed into the trough so that it was never empty and constantly refreshed. On the other side of the doorway lay a large stone slab evidently used for massage.

As they had not enjoyed a bath for thirteen days, they quickly slipped off their clothes, and getting into the trough began to splash about in the warm water in an effort to clean themselves up. They were still at it when, to their considerable embarrassment, two people, a man and a woman appeared in the doorway.

In the dim light it was at the first glance difficult to make out much about the newcomers, but, as they came forward, it became clear that they were servants. Both of them carried towels and what transpired to be jars of oil for making lather. The couple looked about thirty years of age, and they behaved like grave, unsmiling robots; but they were evidently well used to their work. After bowing the man and maid took complete charge of Philip and Gloria; they bathed them, massaged them afterwards and then, taking away their much patched remnants of garments brought from the raft and others made since of llama skins, clothed them in kilts, tunics and outer robes of clean, plain linen.

After they were dressed the servants left them, to return with two of the low folding tables on which they served a supper so good that it seemed to Gloria and Philip well worth their long wait for it. When the meal was finished the servants cleared away, brought more pillows and rugs to increase the size of the divan, then bowed and retired. For a little while Philip and Gloria talked of this sinister underworld to which they had been brought, but it was now many hours since they had slept and they were very tired, so, while they were still speculating on what the next day would bring, they fell asleep.

The following morning the same man and woman attended them, then, after they had had breakfast, Coxitl appeared, and there seemed no alternative but to follow him when he beckoned them out into the tube-like corridor. He led them some way along this gloomy tunnel, down a long ramp to a lower floor and through a curtained doorway into a room where twelve of the litter bearers, whom they had come to know quite well by sight on their journey, were now drawn up in two rows, like a guard of honour, in front of a larger doorway to an inner room.

Coxitl left them to go inside and, returning a moment later, beckoned them forward. The room they now entered was the largest they had so far seen and was decorated with sombre magnificence. The walls were black stone, and in them were set panels depicting the same horrific gods as those in the room where Philip and Gloria had slept; but whereas those were simple carvings cut in the bare rock these were rich mosaics made of many thousands of inlaid semi-precious stones. These panels were a riot of scintillating colour against the dead-black walls, in which they sparkled like huge jewels.

Cross-legged on cushions in the centre of the polished wood floor sat a semi-circle of seven old men. All of them were of the same hook-nosed, reddish-brown-skinned American-Indian type as Coxitl. They were dressed in loose robes and smoking long pipes. Having bowed low before this group of elders, Coxitl stood aside, and the central member of the council addressed Philip:

" *Sprechen Sie Deutsch?* " he asked in a croaking voice.

" *Mein Deutsch ist nicht gut,*" replied Philip. " *Ich bin ein Irelander.*"

The old man nodded and said something in his own tongue to another elder sitting on his right, whom Philip then recognized as the bald-headed, sharp-faced man like Gandhi who had intervened in the Temple the previous night.

The bald man looked at Philip out of sharp, piggy little eyes and said in excellent English: " My name is Zadok. The Lord Toxil, who is the chief among us, has never completely mastered the English tongue, so he has directed me to question you."

He then interrogated Philip and Gloria for over two hours, translating all their replies to his companions, and occasionally being assisted in his questioning by a gaunt, bony, old creature—apparently named Rakil— who spoke good English with a strong American intonation. During this examination little was said about the war, but Philip and Gloria had ample opportunity to put over their story that they were both diehard Fenians who detested the murdering English and everything for which Britain stood.

Philip was asked why he had shot the dog just before his capture, and his explanation was accepted, Zadok commenting that he could hardly be expected to know that the annual levy of pigmies was necessary to the continuance of their own race as well as for other purposes; and Gloria was thrilled to hear him refer to the pigmies as Leprechauns, thus confirming her own theory about their origin.

There followed some discussion among the seven, at the end of which the old man in the centre, looking straight at Philip and Gloria in turn with piercing eyes, spoke a few sentences, which were then translated by Zadok as:

" The Lord Toxil has said that Rakil and I shall speak with you separately again after the midday meal. If we find no treachery in your hearts they will remain yours, but if treachery is found they will be offered to the Remorseless One."

They were then taken back to their room, and shortly afterwards their servants served them with a meal, the excellence of which was lost upon them, owing to their very natural concern as to how they would come through the further examination to which they were to be subjected in the afternoon. Philip knew from the human sacrifice that he had witnessed in the Temple of the False Sun only the night before that the threat to offer their hearts to " the Remorseless One " was meant absolutely literally and, although Gloria was not aware of that, she was quick enough to assume that the threat was synonymous with death.

The only thing they could do now was to use every moment they had left going over their individual stories again and reminding each other of various points in connection with questions that they might be asked. Having secreted the pistol under his robe, Philip made up his mind to shoot Gloria in the event of the verdict being given against them; then, endeavouring to put as good a face on the matter as possible, they wished each other luck and allowed themselves to be led away by the guides who came to fetch them.

The ordeal did not prove so severe as they had feared. The fact that it was now so long since either of them had been in Europe or the United States made it impossible for them to give much of the information which their questioners were desirous of having, and it was soon quite obvious that they had no means of checking the veracity of any private history they were given.

After half an hour, Rakil, who was questioning Gloria, left her to go into a nearby room in which Zadok was examining Philip. The two men consulted for a few minutes in the strange tongue-clicking language they used among themselves, then Zadok said to Philip:

" Rakil finds nothing against your wife, and I find nothing against you."

" Thank you," sighed Philip in relief. " May I go and tell her? "

" You may. Then bring her back with you that she may listen to my words at the same time as yourself."

When Philip returned with Gloria they all four sat down and Zadok went on: " You will find much that is strange to you here. We have no married couples in this city beneath the mountain; but as you are young and of a foreign race I will permit you to continue to share the room you occupied last night. You will on no account attempt to escape. If you succeeded you would soon die of the great cold outside. But you would not succeed, and when you were caught I should order your hearts to be offered to Shaitan. For a little time it would be best if you do not leave your room. Later the Lord Toxil will decide what use we can make of you. Then you will be free to move as you wish in this series of galleries. But beware of entering the Temple or loitering near it. The priests think of one thing only—the number of sacrifices they can make to Shaitan. To that end their whole life is devoted, and the Remorseless One is for ever crying out for more victims. I saved you last night because I thought it would be foolish to allow them to sacrifice you until we had at least found out if you could be of use to us. But the priests are always lying in wait for the unwary; so heed my warning."

The memory of the half-naked, self-mutilated bodies and the glowing eyes of the blood-maddened priests was too recent in the minds of both Philip and Gloria for either of them to make light of Zadok's words. After a moment Gloria said:

" Would you be telling us something about yourselves, now? "

"Yes," he agreed. "I will satisfy your curiosity as far as I can. My race originated in the great semi-tropical island of Atzlan."

"Is that the same as Atlantis?" inquired Philip.

"Yes. In your language it is called so. You know our history then?"

"We know only the legend that a great civilization once flourished in a large island situated in the centre of the Atlantic; and that about eleven thousand years ago it was destroyed by earthquakes, and nearly all the people were drowned in a terrible Flood."

"That is so. We are descendants of some of those who escaped. They were in a ship and managed to survive even after being wrecked on this fearful coast. It was fortunately summer. Before winter came they had found the great cavern which is now the Temple. These rooms and hundreds of others have been made by the many generations that have lived here since. But do you know why Atzlan was destroyed?"

"No. Not really. There is a vague idea that it was because the people had become evil and the gods decided to wipe them out."

Zadok shook his skinny, bald head. "There is only one god who has any power in the planet which you call Earth. We know him as Shaitan —or the Remorseless One. Atzlan was destroyed by Flood and Fire because its people forgot him and did not offer him enough hearts. He became angry. He warned us, but we heeded him not, so he tore apart the paradise in which we lived and sent the remnant of us into exile. Here we must remain until we have placated him by offering the full sum of the sacrifice that he requires. When that has been done he will free us from our imprisonment in this icy world and give us back all the rich, warm lands of the earth."

"I see," said Philip hesitantly. "That's why your priests are so eager to make as many sacrifices as they can, I suppose?"

"Yes. But here the numbers that we can afford to sacrifice are small; and we dare not take more than a few score of Leprechauns from their valley each year. They would die out. So our greatest offerings to Shaitan are made in other ways. In the meantime, we watch with interest all that happens in the outer world from which you come."

"You're talking in riddles, now," said Gloria. "D'you really mean that you're in touch with what goes on in places like the United States?"

"Certainly we are," Zadok gave her a mirthless grin. "The Lords of the Mountain—that is the seven of us who rule here—are very powerful magicians. In America you would call us scientists, but it is the same thing. In your countries television is only in its infancy. Here we have perfected it to such a degree that we can make our screens show us any part of the world we wish. We can not only focus on a room in Berlin, Washington or Tokyo; we can also listen to all that the people in it say."

"In that case you must know how the war is going," put in Philip quickly. "Do please tell us all about it. We've had no news of the out-side world since the end of October, 1942."

"That was just before the Anglo-American expeditions landed in North Africa," remarked Rakil, entering the conversation for the first time. "Unfortunately, the Germans were taken by surprise, so the Allies secured French Morocco and Algeria quite quickly; but we managed to hold them up in Tunisia all winter."

"The African landings marked the turning of the tide against the Axis," said Zadok, taking up the tale. "It was about that time that the Germans were held by the Russians at Stalingrad. Later they suffered a major defeat there. Since then the Russians have reconquered a great part of their lost territories."

"By jove!" exclaimed Philip, and he was just about to add: "What splendid news!" when he caught himself in time and substituted: "That's pretty bad. But what about the Western Allies? Don't tell me that those filthy British are going to come out top-dogs after all?"

Zadok shook his head. "This war is a long way from being over yet. It is true that with the help of the new American armies the British now control all North Africa. General Alexander's armies from Egypt joined up with the American General Eisenhower's armies in Tunisia last May. Then on July the 10th they invaded Sicily. After conquering the island they went on to Italy, and the Anglo-Americans are now fighting about fifty miles south of Rome."

"All this must be pretty worrying for Mussolini," Philip murmured.

"He has gone. His own Fascist Council turned on him soon after the landings in Sicily. They made him a prisoner but Hitler helped him to escape. He is now with the Germans who took over as much of Italy as they could after Mussolini's downfall; but he has no more power."

"The hearts of the Italian people never were in the war, anyway," Philip remarked.

"Perhaps not," Zadok replied. "But there are forty-five millions of them. Their armed forces were greater than those of Britain at the time they entered the war and within a few days of that Britain was left to face the might of Germany alone. The additional burden of having to fight a second power with a larger population than her own would have meant the end for any people less pigheaded than the accursed British. How they managed to defend their island and at the same time defeat great Italian armies thousands of miles away in Abyssinia, Eritrea and Libya still remains a miracle."

"I suppose the explanation lies in the fact that the quality of the Italian troops and generalship was nothing like up to the standard of those produced by the Empire."

"True, yet the Italians outnumbered the Empire forces by at least six to one and individually many of the Italians fought with great gallantry. For instance in 1942 two Italian sailors sank two of Britain's biggest battleships."

" *Two* men sank *two* battleships! " gasped Philip. " How on earth did they do that? "

" They entered Alexandria harbour in a midget submarine, got out and attached two limpet bombs to the bilge keels of *Queen Elizabeth* and *Valiant*. The explosion of the bombs tore holes in the hulls of the two great ships and caused them to founder on the mud of the harbour. Both of them were out of action for many months."

Gloria glanced at Philip expecting one of his usual outbursts on the lines of big ships now being as great a waste of effort in a modern war as equipping an Armoured Division with elephants, but he did not rise.

Instead he was thinking. " Well, anyway, that released their destroyer escorts to do useful work and British superiority in the Eastern Mediterranean was obviously not affected. Let's hope someone has taken the lesson to heart. Those Italian sailors were probably paid about 8 lira a day and each of them rendered £8,000,000 of British war capital useless for many months. What a commentary on our pre-war naval building programme! " After a moment he said:

" Tell us about the war at sea."

" Last April it was announced by Washington that in the year 1942 the Allies lost twelve million tons of shipping. The losses for 1943 have not been given yet, but we believe them to be heavier. The British Navy Minister—the First Lord, they call him—said in a speech last June that the losses for the previous month—May 1943—were so far the heaviest for any month since the war began."

" Twelve million tons a year," said Philip. " That's terrific. The whole British Empire only owned twenty-one million tons in 1939, and the United States less than nine million. But, of course, their navies weren't planned to fight an anti-U-boat war, and they spent nearly all their money on types of ships that were no good for that sort of thing. It's a marvel they've been able to find enough shipping to prevent Britain from being starved out."

" Once the United States started in you can bet they built plenty," remarked Gloria.

" You are American yourself, yes? " Rakil shot at her swiftly.

" No, Sir! " she lied promptly, a look of surprised innocence in her bright blue eyes. " Why would you think that? I'm Irish, and I'd only been living for a year in New York before my husband came over. I hated the place. Roosevelt and his New Deal and all that sort of thing have no appeal for me. It's just Socialism and Communism under another name. I'm all for the old countries like Spain and Italy where the Church still exercises an influence on the lives of the people. Quite apart from my family's just hatred of the dirty British, I've a great admiration for Mussolini and General Franco. That's why I'd like to see Hitler win."

" Of course," Rakil nodded " I had forgotten that you are an Irish Catholic. It is just that having lived in the States you have some idea of what American production can do. You are right about their ship-building. Without it Britain would have been starved out long ago. It is almost as much of a miracle as some of the things we do here. For many months past they have been making ships in merely a matter of days. And the way in which they turn out aeroplanes . . . " He left the sentence unfinished and held up his long, bony hands with an expression of amazed despair.

" How is the air war going? " Philip inquired.

" Not well for Germany," Zadok replied. " The R.A.F. bomber crews have proved as efficient as their fighter pilots did earlier in the war. For years now, with a force that gets bigger and bigger, they have been smash-ing at German cities. Hardly a night passes without an attack by them. And for the past year the Americans have been bombing Germany in daylight. That required great courage. They lost heavily at first, but their air fleets are now so large that the Germans can no longer effectively oppose them. By these great night and day attacks Hamburg, Cologne and Bremen have been almost wiped out. The industrial area of the Ruhr has been half-destroyed and the centre of Berlin reduced to little but a vast pile of rubble.

Philip had positively to fight to keep his delighted feelings from appear-ing in his face and to say with suitable gravity: " Then things don't look too good for Hitler? "

Zadok gave him a crafty smile. " On the surface, no. His defeats in Russia have cost him many of his best divisions. The collapse of Italy is for him a serious blow. The destruction of the German cities and industries might even intimidate a lesser man into contemplating sur-render. Fortunately, that is only one side of the picture. Much of his vital war industry is now transferred safely underground. The Russians are a long way yet from the gates of Berlin and there has been great de-vastation in their country. They also have suffered great losses in dead and prisoners. Stalin can still feed his armies, but his people are paying dearly for that. I do not believe that the Russians alone can defeat Hitler."

" There is the Anglo-American Army in Italy," murmured Philip.

" It may conquer Italy, but what of the barrier of the Alps? No, Hitler's only real danger is that the Anglo-Americans should succeed in landing an army in France. He would then be forced to fight on two open fronts."

" Is there any likelihood of that? "

" Yes. The British have been planning what they call ' The Return to the Continent ' for a long time. Even when it looked as if their own island would soon be conquered, Churchill created a special staff in his own office to plan for that. But Hitler may prevent them from ever launching their invasion. His plans are far advanced for waging a new type of warfare. His scientists have mastered the problem of the aerial-torpedo. These robot-aircraft packed with explosive will be sent from great distances against London and the other British cities. The Germans are also making rockets—huge rockets that will fly two hundred miles carrying ten tons of explosive. Then there are smaller rockets which will fly just as far and are filled with some sort of fire-making chemical. When the time comes all these will be sent in great numbers. They will destroy much of the Anglo-American shipping and all the British ports from which the invasion could be launched."

" I see," said Philip thoughtfully. " Then a sort of stalemate may result; except that, as the Allies have the lead in the air war and the German cities are already in such a bad state, the German people may rat on the Nazis and force them to ask for an armistice."

Zadok cackled with laughter. " There is no fear of that. All the German people who matter *are* Nazis. As for the rest they have no power. They could no more force their will on Hitler than the Leprechauns could force their will upon us Lords of the Mountain. Hitler's only real danger is that the Anglo-Americans might launch their invasion before his new weapons are sufficiently advanced for him to bring them fully into operation."

" Speaking of the Leprechauns," Gloria cut in quickly, " when we were before your Council this morning you said that the fetching of them was necessary to the preservation of their own race. What did you mean by that? "

" You will remember that when you lived in their valley there occurred each month what you would call an electric storm. Here we are on exactly the same latitude as the Magnetic Pole. As I have told you, my race is old in Magic—or Natural Science, if you prefer that name. We can so direct electric force as to disperse all cloud above the valley of the Leprechauns and create climatic conditions suitable for them to live there. But blood is necessary to the operation. Human blood must be spilt on the stone of the Remorseless One at the same instant as the current is sent out. The annual levy of Leprechauns provides one for each of the thirteen months. It is these sacrifices alone which prevent the rest of the race being frozen to death."

" How did they come here in the first place? " asked Philip.

" Their ancestors were brought by ours in the ship from Atzlan. To perform a major magic it was always necessary to offer up a human sacrifice to Shaitan. The Leprechauns were used for that purpose. In the first years after my ancestors' arrival the Leprechauns nearly died out, because life in the caves here did not suit them. It was to preserve their race that the valley was made habitable, and they were transferred there."

" What made you so anxious to keep them alive, then, when you've been killing the poor little things off ever since? " Gloria demanded.

" We need them as a pool on which to draw for mass sacrifices to the Remorseless One. There are certain special ceremonies. The installation of a new high Priest. The funeral of one of the Seven Lords—that is one of the elders whom you met in Council this morning. And for other exceptional occasions."

For a moment there was silence; then, to take her mind off the terrible picture that the old man's words had conjured up, Gloria said: "You haven't told us anything about the Jap war yet."

Zadok glanced towards Rakil, but the gaunt man had just stood up, and he said: "Zadok is responsible for watching London and myself for watching Washington. One of my sessions is due to start shortly, so I must leave you now. But we shall meet to-morrow. The Pacific war is very complicated, so it would be easier to explain with maps. I will take you both to see mine."

When they had thanked him a servant was summoned, and the two newcomers were led back to their own quarters. It was a great relief to be able to sink down on their piles of cushions with the knowledge that they had passed their tests satisfactorily and that it seemed unlikely that they would be called on to lie and pretend any more at least for that evening.

At first they were a little silent as their minds were still busy getting into perspective the extraordinary things they had learnt that afternoon. Then Philip said:

"Of course, the whole thing's fantastic; yet everything they said about the war makes sense. And, if they haven't got some scientific means of finding out what's going on, how could they know anything about it at all?"

"I think they're horrible," said Gloria. "And those old men are worse even than Coxitl. Zadok said just as casual as you please that they used to sacrifice the Little People to do their magics long before that was necessary to keep the valley from being frozen over like the rest of this awful country."

"The tragedy is that, although they've been doing it for all these years, it isn't really necessary at all."

"How d'you mean, Boy?"

"Well, these people are a queer mixture. Shut off like this for thousands of years from all other races, they've developed in some ways and not in others. They don't seem to have any aeroplanes or motor snowploughs, and they may know very little about chemistry and biology, but they appear to be far ahead of us where electricity is concerned. On the other hand, they evidently still believe that the fact of killing somebody in a special kind of way will result in certain physical repercussions like thunderclaps or a shower of rain; and that is pure nonsense."

"D'you mean that, if they did whatever they do do with their electrical paraphernalia and didn't bother about making a human sacrifice at all, that they'd be getting their results just the same?"

"That's it, darling. I'm dead-sure the two things haven't the remotest connection. They only go on making the sacrifices because they've made them from time immemorial and still believe them to be an essential part of the procedure.

Soon after this the servants came in to bath them and serve their dinner. Afterwards, as they had been forbidden to leave their apartment, there seemed no alternative but to settle down for the night. As it had been a day of great strain, they were by no means reluctant to do so, but before going to sleep Gloria said:

"Come to think of it, Boy, 'tis the strangest position we're in now about the war. D'you realize that, after having known nothing at all for all these months, by being here we'll know more than anyone on either side. I'll bet that Hitler doesn't know that as far back as the Battle of Britain Churchill started planning to invade him. And I don't suppose that Churchill knows about all those horrible new weapons Hitler's preparing to use."

"That's just what I've been thinking," Philip replied. "I haven't a doubt now that we've been sent here for some purpose; and I believe it is to find out all we possibly can about these new weapons."

"What would be the good of that when we've no way of getting the information back to London?"

"Yes—that's the snag, isn't it? Still, you never know. We've been saved by what almost amounts to miracles before, so another might turn up which would put us on the road for home." On this vague but comforting speculation they let the matter rest.

After their first meal on the following morning, the tall gaunt Rakil called for them, as he had promised, and took them down to the lower level, to a large room in which a number of middle-aged Atzlanteans were working.

Here there were no beautiful mosaics panelling the walls; instead, a number of large maps had been fixed up on them, but Philip was amazed at their crudity. They looked like the work of a child that had been set to draw maps of the continents and sections of them with red, blue and yellow chalks. Some, such as that of Europe, were much better than others, and showed a certain amount of detail, but most of them consisted only of the roughest outline and had few place-names marked on them.

"Before we start on the Pacific war," said Philip, "may I ask you one or two questions arising out of our talk yesterday? You were saying that the Anglo-Americans are preparing to land an army on the Continent. Do you know when the attempt will take place?"

"In about two months' time," replied Rakil. "During the first week in June."

"And how long will it be before Hitler is ready to bring his new weapons into play?"

"That is a little difficult to answer. Most of the experiments were being carried out at a place called Peenemunde on the Baltic. One night the R.A.F. sent seven hundred of their largest bombers there and smashed it. That put everything back for many months. In fact, if it had not been for the R.A.F. raid, Hitler's new weapons would be in operation now; by June all the ports in Southern England would be smashed up and there could be no invasion. As it is, the new weapons cannot now be ready much before June, and even then it will be some months before enough of them will be available to obliterate London and the other British cities."

"Then for both sides time has now become the vital factor? With the Russians still pushing in the East, if the Allies succeed in landing in the West before Hitler can really get his new weapons going, he is bound to be defeated; but, if the Allies fail to do that, the war may go on indefinitely and all Britain become devastated. It looks, though, as if the Allies will get on the Continent before Hitler is able to stop them."

Philip could scarcely conceal his excitement.

"Perhaps." Rakil's thin lips pursed themselves into a cynical smile. "But the Allied attempt to land might be defeated; and there are certain ways in which Hitler might be given time."

"What do you mean by that?"

"The European war is Zadok's affair, and no doubt he will tell you in due course."

Turning away, Rakil led them over to a large chart of the Pacific which, even if it had many apparent inaccuracies, was good enough to show the broad picture of the Japanese war, and he expounded to them on it for half an hour. During the first year the Japs had overrun millions of square miles of territory and achieved an almost unchallengeable supremacy over a vast segment of the ocean stretching from the Aleutians in the north to Java in the south; but from the winter of 1943 they had been held and pressed back on no less than four separate fronts. The Anglo-Indian armies had stabilized a front in Northern Burma, while Australians, New Zealanders and Americans under General MacArthur were gradually driving the Japanese back through the ghastly tropical swamps of New Guinea. But the most spectacular Allied progress so far had been made by the United States naval commands, which in the north had driven the Japanese from the Aleutians and in the south were systematically clearing island after island of their enemies.

Gloria and Philip were clever enough to infer that they had no time for the Japs and that in the Far Eastern war their sympathies lay with the Americans. To have done otherwise would have perhaps aroused suspicions about their proclaimed neutrality, and they had ample opportunity for maintaining their anti-British line by expressing their pleasure that the blood-sucking British had been driven from Hong-Kong, Borneo and Malaya.

When he had brought them up to date Rakil went on to discuss possible future moves in the Pacific. Apparently, the Planning Staffs in

Washington and London had for many months been discussing two lines of policy for defeating the Japanese. One line was to launch offensives from east and west which would drive the Japs from Burma, Malaya, New Guinea and all the Dutch East Indies until the two forces met and advanced northward against Japan; the other was to make it mainly a sea-air war and strike direct at the Philippines or Formosa and thence against Japan, leaving all the Japanese forces to the south still in possession of Malaya and the Indies, but cut off from their bases.

As Philip listened, his hair almost rose on his scalp at the awful thought of the Allied military secrets which were in the possession of these Lords of the Mountain, and the incalculable damage they might do if they had any means of communicating them to Berlin and Tokyo. When Rakil had finished speaking he said:

"It must be absolutely fascinating for you to be able to obtain particulars of the plans of all the warring nations in advance. That really is my idea of magic."

Rakil smiled. "Magic yes, but not a very big magic. No sacrifice is required, and the process differs little from what you would call going to the movies in your world. We hold sessions every day. Later to-day those who work under me will be holding one. If you would like to see it, I will fetch you before it starts. For the time being perhaps you would like to remain here and look at the other maps."

When he had left them they spent nearly two hours studying the crude maps and bringing themselves up to date with the progress of the war. After they had finished they went up to the Atzlantean who appeared to be in charge of the place and, although he spoke no English, he seemed to know what they wanted, as he detailed one of his juniors to lead them back to their room.

As soon as they were alone Philip remarked to Gloria: "You heard what Rakil said about the R.A.F. blotting out the German experimental station. That shows clearly enough that our people are wise to what Hitler's game is already."

She nodded. "Sure, and I spotted that myself. So it won't be to warn our own folk about those aerial-torpedoes and rocket things that we've been sent here."

Their midday meal was served by their own servants. Soon after it Zadok came in and, sitting down, asked if they had found their morning with Rakil interesting.

"Very," Philip replied. "It is utterly amazing that you should know so much of what is going on in all the different war headquarters."

Zadok nodded his bald head. "These results are achieved by hard work. The Lord Toxil is a fine German scholar. He makes himself responsible for knowing everything of importance that is decided in Berlin or Berchtesgaden. Rakil, as you know, overlooks Washington. My province is to follow the way that the big minds in London are working. Others of the Lords keep a constant watch on Moscow, Tokyo and Rome. It means many hours of hard concentration every day for all of us and the several hundred men and women whose duty it is to help us. In this way we miss very little."

"Why do you burden yourselves with such a fatiguing task?" Philip asked with a puzzled frown. "It's natural enough to wish to know how the war is going, but it's quite another thing to go to the immense labour that all this entails in order to find out the plans of every General Staff in advance."

Raising his eyebrows in surprise Zadok exclaimed: "But if we did not inform ourselves of each country's intentions how could we help those we wish to help or bring our influence to bear on the situation?"

"Influence!" repeated Philip. "Do you really mean that you can influence events in the outer world? How can you possibly do that?"

"By informing ourselves in advance of the plans of all countries participating in a war we can create conditions favourable to those who will best serve our own interests."

"Will you be telling us what your interests are?" said Gloria.

Zadok shrugged his skinny shoulders. "Why, the propitiation of Shaitan, of course. As I told you yesterday, we are in no position to make large sacrifices here. Our greatest offerings to him are made in the outer world. Every man, woman and child who dies an unnatural death is a sacrifice acceptable to Shaitan; and all such sacrifices that are brought about, even in part, by our efforts are counted to our credit by the Remorseless One. Therefore our life's work is to foster conditions favourable to the Four Horsemen of the Apocalypse—War, Famine, Pestilence and Death. Every earthly ruler whose ambition opens the gate to those is our ally and, although he remains unaware of it, receives all the help that it is in our power to give."

While they were still revolving this terrible doctrine in their minds Zadok went on:

"The weapon which through many generations of scientific experiment we have forged and brought to perfection here is the control of those natural forces that create heat and cold, drought and tempest. Our provision of a climate suitable to the Leprechauns to maintain life in their valley is no more than a small local example of what we can do in this way."

"Do you mean that you could cause a great storm in the Atlantic or weeks of drought in China?" exclaimed Philip.

"Certainly. In times of peace China has always proved a very profitable field for our endeavours, but it is wars which pay us the highest dividends. Armies are extremely vulnerable to long spells of unexpected heat or rain, and in the past thousand years we have many times so ravaged great hosts that they have afterwards fallen an easy prey in battle to those unconscious champions of Shaitan whom we have wished to help."

Philip was utterly aghast. "And in this war your greatest champion is Hitler?" he said, almost in a whisper.

Zadok's parchment-like face broke into a self-satisfied smile. "Through our magno-electric installations we have been able to give him most valuable aid in almost every critical stage of the war. It was we who in May and June of 1940 gave the Germans six weeks of unbroken sunshine in which to overrun Holland, Belgium and France. We caused the falling of the great rains in Tunisia during the winter of 1942 which gave the Axis time to rally and held up the junction of the two Allied Armies in North Africa for six months. This year, to give Hitler time to reorganize his Eastern front, we have given Russia the mildest winter she has had in a hundred years, and so greatly helped to spoil Stalin's winter offensive."

"You—you'll do your best to prevent the Allies landing on the Continent?" Philip murmured, fascinated in spite of his repulsion for the vulture-like old Atzlantean.

"Of course. Hitler is the finest instrument we have ever had to work through, so we shall continue to aid him to the utmost limit of our powers. We did great work in the years of the Mongol Empire and during the Spanish Conquest of South America. The religious wars after your Reformation were the best time we ever had in Europe until Napoleon arose to play our game. Then there were the First World War and the Russian Revolution. Yet never before have the number of killed been quite enough. As the population of the world increases Shaitan sets his price higher. But now we have Hitler we shall obtain our freedom.

"It is not only the thousands that die fighting in his war every day. His concentration camps are even more profitable. The Jews whom he has starved and tortured to death run into several million—and he is now endeavouring to exterminate the whole Polish nation. He has built ovens in which he can burn great numbers of them every day—more than would be killed in several hours of battle. Yes. It will not be long now. If we can prevent Hitler from being defeated for another year or two, he will have paid the price that Shaitan demands to set us free."

CHAPTER XIX

AMONG THOSE OLD IN SIN

PHILIP and Gloria sat there appalled at this monstrous thing that they had just been told. Credible or not, the thought behind the whole idea was the very essence of Evil. Strive as they would to conceal their revulsion, it was impossible for them altogether to keep out of their faces some of the horror they felt.

Zadok saw it, and his dark eyes narrowed, as he said: " You appear distressed. Does not the thought of the wholesale destruction of your enemies please you? "

" Yes." Philip forced the syllable from his lips, and, realizing that now of all times he must not be found wanting in his part, went on: " It would be a great day for the world if every one of the murdering English and Scots were blotted out to-morrow. I was only thinking of all the other people who must get killed or hurt in such a huge war—particularly if you exert all your powers to keep it going indefinitely."

" Everyone must die some time," Zadok shrugged; " and a swift death by violence is in most cases less painful than a slow one caused by illness or old age. Why, in any case, should you concern yourself for a host of people who are unknown to you? However, you do not appear to be burdened with these absurd scruples in the case of the British. That is good, as actually I came here to ask if you would be willing to give us your help in ensuring their liquidation."

" Certainly." Philip was on his toes now and did not pause a second before replying. If some great power for good had directed his steps to this domain of evil, so that he might learn what was being done there, he must reject no opportunity to find out more about the powers wielded by these Satanists.

Rakil came in at that moment. As he did so, Zadok stood up and said: " That is well. I will ask the Lord Toxil for his consent to my project. If he agrees to my using you, I will speak with you again to-morrow morning."

After Zadok had gone Rakil told them that his screening was about to begin and took them to a room on the lower level, which was very long and almost bare. Fixed to the centre of the wall at one end was a sheet, about eight feet long by four feet high, of silvery, shimmering substance that looked like frosted glass. In front of it was a low stand, on top of which some form of gyroscope was spinning at a terrific speed; before it was a frame like the back of a telephone switchboard with hundreds of fine wires and a seat facing the screen. Halfway down the room stood a narrow table with three stools at each side of it and one at the far end. The wall at the other end of the room was filled with a strange array of cylinders and retorts, reminiscent of the laboratory of a mediaeval alchemist.

There were three men and three women in the room, all of whom were middle-aged except for one of the women, who was very old and stared before her with sightless eyes. Rakil introduced them as his assistants and, as they took their places, described their functions.

As the old woman walked slowly and unhesitatingly to the seat in front of the screen and sitting down began to run her fingers lightly over the wires, he said: " Sonsig is what you would call our operator. I tell her what we wish to see and long practice enables her to tune in to the required scene almost immediately. If I wish to change the scene in the middle of a screening, I have only to tell her." Then he added casually: " We always blind our operators—it increases the delicacy of their sense of touch."

Philip made no comment on this brutal custom, but it confirmed his view that, whatever the scientific achievements of the Lords of the Mountain, they were still savages at heart.

One of the men had seated himself in front of the complicated array of retorts at the other end of the room, and pointing towards him Rakil said: " He controls our supply of magno-electric power. It is generated in a far part of the mountain, but it cannot be sent out unless the blood vapour has been passed through one of these retorts. Whenever power is required he causes one or more of the retorts to fill, and at my order it is discharged, much as you would send out a directional wireless beam, to any part of the world that we wish to affect."

The other four assistants were grouped around the table in the centre of the room, and as Rakil introduced them he went on to say that they all understood English, and that it was their business to interpret and record all that took place during the screenings. The assistants all bowed to Gloria and Philip, eyeing them with great curiosity, but, apart from a few words of greeting, they made no attempts at conversation, possibly owing to Rakil's presence.

Rakil then sat down at the top of the table facing the screen, and motioned to his two guests to sit on either side of him. The two men observers sat each side of the other end of the table, and the two women sat between them and the visitors. Raising his voice, Rakil spoke to the old blind operator for some minutes, giving her instructions about what he wished to see. As her back was towards them, Philip and Gloria could not observe her hands, but from the rapid movement of her elbows it was clear that she was flicking her sensitive fingertips over the complicated web of wires in front of her. With a quick glance over his shoulder Rakil gave an order to the man at the other end of the room, the lights dimmed, and the screening then began.

The silvery screen began to vibrate, but its movement gradually lessened until it had changed to a continuous series of smooth undulations like a swell upon an oily sea running lengthwise along its surface; then its opaqueness commenced to clear, and Philip and Gloria suddenly realized that they were looking at a moving picture.

They seemed to be on a wide road in a great stream of traffic which was approaching a huge, many-storied, modern building standing by itself. The traffic stream entered the building by a big arch. The cars, runabouts, box-wagons and single decker buses disgorged their passengers, ninety-five per cent. of whom wore American uniforms. There were hundreds of men, mostly officers, but also scores of women; as the traffic line moved off down the great ramps the constant stream of arriving people was whisked away in elevators and distributed itself through the vast building.

Staring at the picture on the undulating screen, Philip and Gloria felt as though they were behind a travelling movie camera with a muted sound track attached. They were carried smoothly down seemingly endless corridors, pausing only to look in at a number of doorways inside which the scene was almost identical—innumerable officers seated behind innumerable desks, either talking together or dictating to stenographers, and all the multitudinous noises of this enormous hive of war organization came faintly but fairly clearly to the watchers.

Eventually the field of view passed through a closed door into a larger room. A number of middle-aged officers, some of them in naval uniform, was seated at a long table. From the number of medal ribbons that most of them wore, the gold bands on the sleeves of the sailors and the general air of brisk authority that emanated from them, it was clear that they were all of high rank. Round the walls sat an even greater number of younger men, evidently there to take notes or supply information to their seniors at a conference that was just about to begin. During the next five minutes several more officers arrived, some sitting down at the table with breezy greetings to their neighbours, and others slipping quietly into places by the wall; then the buzz of conversation ceased, and they settled down to business.

At first Philip and Gloria found great difficulty in grasping anything at all of what was going on, because there were so many allusions to things that meant nothing to them. Gradually, however, it became clear that the conference was discussing the plans for an assault on another Japanese-held island in the Pacific.

From time to time one or other of Rakil's male assistants spoke a few words in his own tongue, and one of the women took them down in strange hieroglyphics on a sheet of papyrus spread before her on the table.

Gloria soon became bored with the whole proceedings. The novelty of the thing had been great fun at first and, she felt, might have continued so if the magic mirror had gone on showing all sorts of different scenes, but to sit and watch a number of old men arguing the pros and cons of things she did not understand was proving inexpressibly dreary.

Philip, too, gradually became bored. When some of the officers spoke, who either had naturally soft voices or had never been taught to speak up, it was a great strain trying to catch what they said. He also found that the undulations of the screen had the effect of slightly distorting the whole picture, as though it were seen through a layer of very gently moving water. It was this, he suddenly realized, which accounted for the crudity of Rakil's maps. If the screen always had this slight wobble, it was obviously impossible for an observer to copy the detail of an intricate coastline with any accuracy; and, of course, for the same reason it was impossible to read any of the documents which lay on the table, or any type of a size much less than a newspaper headline. The movement, too, was very tiring to the eyes, so the visitors were both glad when the conference broke up, and Rakil terminated the screening.

Afterwards, he explained to them that normally he would have carried his observers direct to the room in which he knew that these important conferences were held almost daily, but he had thought that his visitors might like to see something of the great Pentagon Building, which had been specially erected at Washington in an incredibly short time to house the War Staffs of the United States Armies. He then took them into the room where the maps were hung and pointed out the position of the tiny coral atoll off the northern coast of New Guinea that General MacArthur was shortly proposing to take, and placed a hieroglyph, representing the date on which it was to be attacked, against it.

While Rakil was still talking one of his women assistants had come up behind him, and when he had finished spoke to him in their own tongue. After listening to her for a moment, he said: " Marlig asks if you would care to take your evening meal with her and her companions. You have my permission to do so if you wish."

Gloria and Philip accepted with alacrity. Marlig and the other assistants were mostly middle-aged people, but there seemed at least a chance that they might prove more human than Zadok, Rakil and the other ghoulish old men.

Marlig, like all the other Atzlanteans, had black hair, a reddish skin and an aquiline nose. She was not a particularly attractive-looking woman, and they soon discovered that her English was extremely limited. As she explained to them in halting phrases, many of which had a distinctly American twist, it was one thing to learn enough of a language to listen to conversations and catch the gist of what was being said, but quite another to make one's own rebellious tongue master the strange noises that composed the languages of the outer world. She went on to say that the Seven Lords were exceptional in this respect; but that it was part of their training for their high office that, during the ten years of preparation which they underwent, they should completely master at least two of the world's most important languages.

While they were talking she led them down a ramp to a still lower floor and along a broad corridor which ended in a pair of wide and heavy curtains. On passing through them the eyes of the newcomers were at first quite dazzled by the contents of the extraordinary apartment into which they had been taken.

It was far bigger and loftier than any of the rooms they had so far seen, although not so large as the Temple, and it was laid out as an indoor garden. But the amazing and rather awful thing about it was that all the flowers were made of gold.

Marlig seemed very proud of it and struggled to find words to convey that she had seen nothing to compare with it in any television picture of the outer world. Philip was reminded of Prescott's account of the garden of solid gold flowers which the Spanish Conquistadores had discovered, and promptly looted, at the back of the Incas' Temple of the Sun in Peru. He did not doubt that the idea of creating both that and this ornate colourless and perfumeless pleasance had had a common origin in the long since sunken island of Atlantis.

His speculations were cut short on their being surrounded by several of Rakil's assistants whom they had met that afternoon, and a number of other Atzlanteans. All of them had questions to ask in poor to moderate English, and for the next hour the two strangers were kept hard at work giving the same account of themselves as they had given the day before to the Council, and an additional mass of miscellaneous information on life in Europe and America.

From the garden of gold flowers they were led to other recreational apartments. There was a fine swimming-pool with a variety of steam and other medicinal baths beyond it, a number of large and lofty squash courts in which some of the Atzlanteans with basket-like racquets bound on to their right hands were playing a game which was no doubt the ancestor of Basque Pelota, a fine concert hall where the strange, unfamiliar music was being played, and other rooms in which several couples were playing games that looked like chess and draughts, or just sitting in small groups talking All of the rooms were well equipped, yet not one of them had even a suggestion of homely comfort about it; they all had the bleak impersonal atmosphere of a well-endowed but rigidly ruled institution.

There was no general dining-room for the considerable concourse of people, and it transpired that they fed in messes. Marlig's mess consisted of some twenty people, all working under Rakil and all speaking a limited amount of English with an American intonation acquired from listening to practically nothing but American voices during their work.

However, when the time came to dine a heated discussion broke out among the Atzlanteans, and it appeared that Zadok's English-speaking observers, headed by a thick-lipped man named Quetzl, insisted that Philip, being Irish, should feed with them. After much argument he won his point, so Philip and Gloria had to put as pleasant a face as possible on their separation, and they did not see each other again until they were escorted back to their own room some hours later.

As soon as they were alone they sank down among their cushions almost exhausted from the ceaseless questioning to which they had been subjected, but they had picked up a good deal themselves and were not too tired to exchange information while they undressed and settled down for the night.

Philip had discovered that the valley of the pigmies was not the only one in which a scientifically controlled climate made it possible for human beings to live in the open all through the year. There were two or more valleys nearby in this larger range, and it was from these that the Atzlanteans obtained all their food. This also explained why there were no young people to be seen in the underworld; they farmed the valleys. It seemed that the Seven and their hundred-odd assistants were the privileged minority of the race, and that only by years of hard application to study and an unshakable devotion to the way of Shaitan was it possible to secure a place among this hierarchy. On the other hand, all those unfortunate Atzlanteans who failed to be appointed to one of these comparatively rare vacancies were, at the age of forty, given over to the priests and sacrificed to the Remorseless One.

Gloria sighed. " My bunch were throwing a special party, but you'd never guess why. 'Twas because a fat-faced dame called Agnil was giving her eyes to Shaitan to-morrow. They're going to blind her with redhot needles, Boy, and they haven't yet got to anæsthetics down here. And, would you believe it she was just itching to play. To be a tip-top screen operator is the highest a woman can get among these nuthouse-hoodlums. But what gets me down is that they never laugh. They're so terribly earnest all the time, and they seem to think of nothing but ways in which they can serve what they call Atzl—by which I suppose they mean the State "

" That's it," agreed Philip. " And what a State! Their dreary earnestness about it reminds me of the accounts one used to read of the young Russian Communists in the old days; but the ideals of these people are nearer to those of the Hitler Youth. They want *lebensraum,* and for generations they've been told that Shaitan can give it to them if they'll pay up enough in blood and death."

" 'Tis strange, though, that they seem to give no thought at all to souls."

" Yes, I noticed that too. Apparently they're interested only in destroying bodies. It looks to me as if the Powers of Good have made them slip up somewhere during their long history and caused them to go off their original track. Races that are shut away from all outside contacts for many centuries do tend to lose sight of the origins of their religion and get set in a rigid pattern. Look at the Egyptians. Not only their religion, but their art, clothes and way of living from the cradle to the grave all became static and formalized through their being boxed up for the best part of three thousand years in the Valley of the Nile. Still, whether these people are following the original Satanic cult or not, it would be difficult to conceive a more hideous doctrine. This remorseless fanaticism of theirs and its consequences now they've got a naturally brutal people like the Germans to work for them just don't bear thinking about."

In spite of the terrible things they had learned that day, they both slept soundly. The magno-electric science developed by the Atzlanteans had enabled them to provide their underground domain with perfectly balanced air-conditioning as well as heat and a pale, diffused though rather dull light. Another factor that no doubt contributed to their all being in excellent health was the food. As Philip and Gloria had learned from their visits to the messes, everyone had exactly the same food, and, as they had already noticed, while the quality was excellent there was always just barely enough of it, so that no one ever actually left hungry, but there was no chance of anyone suffering from over-eating.

Soon after they had breakfasted Zadok came to them. Sitting down on some cushions he proceeded to rub his hands together. The skin looked like old parchment and rustled slightly as he said:

"I have spoken with the Lord Toxil, and he agrees to my plan. Yesterday with Rakil you saw how we obtain our information. The present is a very busy time, particularly in London where all the planning is now going on for D-Day."

"What's D-Day?" asked Philip.

"The date for the Anglo-American invasion of the Continent. My idea is that you should help us by becoming one of those who gaze and listen for me."

Philip thought it well to make it appear that he was by no means eager to accept, so he said doubtfully: "I don't know that I should be very much good. I hardly understood anything I heard at Rakil's screening yesterday."

"It's only a matter of practice," Zadok assured him quickly. "These Planning Staffs have a language of their own. That is why it is difficult to understand them unless, to use a phrase they use themselves, one is 'in the picture.' Their work is so secret that secrecy has become second nature to them. Even when they talk to one another they use code-words to express many of these things they are discussing."

"I know," Philip nodded. "I noticed that yesterday. It doesn't convey very much to hear a General say, as one of the Americans did, 'If we do BULLET, why would we want to do BABYKILLER?'"

"That is true. But we get to know the meaning of all these code words in time, through the context in which they are used. I should provide you with explanations for the most important ones that are being used in London at the moment, and you would soon become familiar with them. No, it is not the code-words alone that are the difficulty; it is the extraordinary inability of the British to talk plain English or to give anything its proper name."

"Whatever do you mean?"

Zadok scowled. "They are constantly using the words 'Radar, Bolero, Bottleneck, Window,' to mention only a few. These do not appear to be ordinary code-words, and they are used in such a great variety of connections that it is difficult to decide their real meaning. The one word 'Whale' may mean the great fish-like mammal which frequents our southern waters, a concrete construction of which the British are making large numbers just now, or the Chief of their Naval Staff. They refer to Sir Henry Wilson, their Supreme Commander in the Mediterranean, as 'Jumbo,' and to the Prime Minister's principal Staff Officer, General Sir Hastings Ismay, as Sir 'Pug'! But they are not even consistent in their nicknames. These important people are not always called after animals or fish. The Chief of the Imperial General Staff, Sir Alan Brooke, is just known as 'Brookie,' and the Chief of the Air Staff is called 'Peter' Portal, although his name is really Charles."

"Of course, that does make things a bit awkward," Philip commented sympathetically.

"Then there is this puzzle about the fruits," Zadok went on angrily. "These high level people are always talking about Raspberries, Strawberries and Mulberries. We know what a Mulberry is. I will explain that to you this afternoon. But the other two remain a mystery. Seniors speak of giving Raspberries and Strawberries to their juniors. Strawberries are popular, but raspberries are not. Yet it cannot be the real fruit of which they speak, because we never see a General or an Admiral present his planning staff with a basket of either kind. However, we sometimes hear a junior officer say that he has had one of these 'baskets' that we have never yet seen. Sometimes, too, they speak of having been giving a 'bottle' which, curiously enough, they appear to dislike. But perhaps it has some connection with the mysterious and ubiquitous 'bottleneck' which also causes them so much annoyance."

"I expect there are a lot of initials, too, used in referring to different people and departments in the Service Ministries, aren't there?" Philip remarked, with memories of his father discussing Admiralty matters when brother officers were present.

"Yes. But we solved those straightforward minor riddles quite early in the war. It is these infuriating colloquialisms which trouble us much more. One would think that to 'have a crack at a thing' would mean the same as an attempt to 'shoot a thing down.' Yet it seems the exact opposite. I cannot always be giving my thoughts to such problems, and my assistants have little aptitude for these things. It is in this way that you could be of invaluable service to us."

"Well, I'll have a shot at it if you wish. There's only one thing, though. From what I saw yesterday each man who is watching has a woman opposite number who takes down the running commentary that he makes. I suppose you'd have no objection to my wife taking down for me?"

"Certainly not. For a long time past I have had two teams of assistants watching London. So much is happening there now that in a few days' time I propose to start a third team. You and your wife shall become regular members of it." Zadok stood up, adding as he did so: "You know where my room is? The room that we talked in the first afternoon you were here. Come to it after the midday meal, and I will give you a broad picture of the way in which the Anglo-Americans are planning their invasion."

When Philip and Gloria had had their lunch they went to Zadok's room. Instead of inviting them to sit down, he took them at once to a room exactly similar to the long chamber in which they had witnessed Rakil's screening the day before.

"This is my Number One Team," he said, introducing them to the Atzlanteans who were present, most of whom they had already met the previous evening. "I have arranged that for this afternoon they shall abandon their routine work for a general probe round London. That will make you acquainted with the spots you will most frequently have to watch. If we are lucky I shall be able to point out many of the leading personalities. Whether they are individually for or against certain policies is often of the first importance. That is why you must not only get to know them by sight but also learn their nicknames. By so doing you will often be able to ascertain their views from hearing members of their staffs quote their opinions to one another. Now, let us proceed."

Exactly the same routine was followed as that at Rakil's screening except that, in this case, the blind operator was an elderly man. Within a few moments of their having seated themselves on the stools on either side of the narrow table, the screen in front of them began to undulate.

As the first picture formed within it, Philip felt an awful twinge of homesickness; it was Trafalgar Square. The magic camera entered it from the north and advanced through it towards Whitehall. Pausing a little way down the famous street it turned through a stone archway on the right, and Zadok said:

"This is the Admiralty. On the left of the courtyard are the private apartments of the Navy Minister. He is always styled First Lord." The field of vision slewed towards the main building and went upstairs to the first floor. There it entered several rooms where a number of Admirals seated in them were duly named, and their jobs briefly outlined.

Zadok then took them across the street to the War Office, down Whitehall to Combined Operations Headquarters, back again past the Cenotaph to Downing Street, through the Foreign Office and across the inner courtyard to the Air Ministry; at each of which a similar procedure was followed.

The picture then descended Clive Steps, showed a swift panorama of St. James's Park with its lovely lake, now made yet more lovely by the tender spring green of the budding trees that surrounded it, and came to rest on the back of a huge block at the end of Whitehall.

"This building," said Zadok, "is for our purpose much the most important that we have yet visited. It is the offices of the War Cabinet. In its upper floors many gifted people connected with the Government do highly specialized work. On its main floors all the most important meetings governing the strategy of the Armed Forces of the British Empire are held. In its basement live the little band of officers, Captains and Commanders, R.N., Colonels, Lieutenant-Colonels and Majors, Group-Captains and Wing-Commanders, less than thirty in all, who work under the direct instructions of the Chiefs of Staff. From this small body germinate the broad plans which eventually animate the nine million six hundred thousand men the Empire now has in arms. The Prime Minister first disclosed their existence to us. He was heckled in the House about lack of co-operation between the Services, and he retorted that these officers of the three services ate, slept and lived together as part of his own Ministry of Defence."

Passing Special Police, Home Guards with revolvers strapped to their waists, soldiers armed with tommy-guns and finally a special guard of Royal Marines, the picture entered the building and visited the offices of a number of key personalities. As it swept through the basement, Zadok remarked:

"It was these people and their predecessors who did all the foundation work on the operation which most concerns us—the Return to the Continent. In certain ways some of them still play a part which will have an enormous bearing on its success or failure. So they need careful watching But the broad plan passed out of their keeping last autumn. A British General named Morgan—his friends call him Freddy—was charged with examining the whole plan and working it out in detail. He was given a large special staff of British and American Navy, Army and Air Force officers to assist him. Then, early this year, the American General Eisenhower—he is always referred to as Ike—was recalled from North Africa, appointed Supreme Allied Commander in Western Europe and made responsible for the invasion. We will now go to his headquarters."

The picture on the screen dissolved to form again a moment later as the outside of a big block in a London square. It passed between the white-helmeted American sentries and upstairs to a long series of rooms. The Supreme Commander was not in, but they found his Chief of Staff, General Bedell-Smith, talking to General Morgan and the Deputy Supreme Commander, Air Chief Marshal Sir Arthur Tedder. The conversation did not mean much to Philip, but Zadok later remarked that having come in on it had well repaid his otherwise fruitless afternoon.

By this time the screening had lasted for very nearly three hours, so when General Bedell-Smith's visitors left him Zadok brought it to a close. Owing to the variety of scene, both Philip and Gloria were far more impressed than they had been on the previous afternoon, and they were much more inclined to look forward to their new work now that they knew a little about some of the important people they would be watching.

During the next few days they sat in with Zadok's Number One Team, gradually accustoming themselves to the colloquialisms used by the high-level planners, the nicknames of the war leaders, the meanings of the principal code-words and the rooms in certain buildings where special information was most likely to be picked up.

The Number One team was mainly concerned with the War Cabinet, the Chiefs of Staff and General Eisenhower. The Number Two team overlooked the Service Ministries, the Foreign Office, the American and Russian Embassies and attended all Secret Sessions that were held by Parliament. But recently a new factor had entered the picture. General Eisenhower had charged General Sir Bernard Montgomery, the C.-in-C. 21st Army

I

Group, with the responsibility for the actual assault on the coast of France. In consequence, the final plans would now be made at his Headquarters in Western London, and it was in order to keep himself informed of any new development which might arise that Zadok had decided on the creation of a Number Three team.

Philip had asked that Gloria should take down for him deliberately with the idea that between them they might be able to fake or distort all the most important evidence that they secured before turning in their reports; but at their first sitting they had to abandon all hope of this.

To their annoyance they found that Zadok had appointed the thick-lipped Quetzl, and a woman called Velig, to act as their collaborators, and both were old hands at the game. The result was that, as soon as Philip tried misinterpreting a policy which was being enunciated by one of General Montgomery's Staff Officers, the Atzlanteans promptly came to his assistance with corrections. They might not be able to speak very good English, but it was clear that, apart from the colloquialisms which some-times foxed them, they understood it very well. After three futile at-tempts, in all of which he was caught, but which were fortunately put down to his lack of experience at the work, he decided that he had better give up.

To have persisted would have inevitably aroused suspicion, and Philip knew that if he once did that it was almost as good as signing death war-rants for Gloria and himself. It was already clear that they could be useful to Zadok, but they were certainly not indispensable; and the fana-tical Atzlanteans appeared ever ready to seize any excuse which gave them an opportunity to make a sacrifice to their terrible god.

Philip and Gloria at first found it difficult to become accustomed to the ubiquity, depth and fierceness of this sadistic craving, but after a time they came to realize that their companions were animated by the same type of fanaticism as had caused the priests of the Spanish Inquisition to com-mit such terrible atrocities in the name of their religion.

When Zadok's Number Three team started work in earnest it was de-cided that the newcomers should henceforth be given the freedom of the recreational apartments and take their meals with their fellow-workers. They were allowed to keep their own room for sleeping or resting in, which was a great relief to them, but the new arrangement enabled them to learn much more about the strange and sinister community of which they had perforce become members.

Most of their companions had been married but were so no longer, as their marriage partners had failed to make the grade and had been sacri-ficed to Shaitan at the age of forty. Such studious and gifted couples as had qualified for the hierarchy were no longer regarded as husbands and wives and saw little of one another if their duties, as was most frequently the case, caused them to be assigned to different messes.

Every individual had his or her own apartments, similar to those

assigned to the newcomers, but they were the only couple allowed to share
a room, this concession being made solely on account of their youth and
the fact that, since they were of another race, they could be treated
differently without the risk that the exception made in their case would
have an ill effect on the discipline of the community. All manifestations
of sex were forbidden on pain of death to these middle-aged Atzlanteans
of the underworld, as it was considered that love affairs would have the
effect of weakening their powers of concentration. On receiving their
appointments to the hierarchy they had left their youth behind, just as
they had left any children they might have had, since the chances were
all against their ever seeing any of their offspring again.

There were two ways only in which they might possibly do so. Ranking
immediately below the Seven, there existed a Council of Eleven, the members of which were responsible for the administration and supply of the
underworld. The Eleven, of which Coxitl, who had brought Philip and
Gloria from the valley of the Leprechauns, was one, were the only people
who were allowed to leave the underworld after having been given a
permanent place in it. They might, therefore, see their children when visit-
ing the valleys. The other possibility was that a child of one of the hierarchy might be brought into the underworld as a servant. But such an
occurrence was a matter for dread rather than rejoicing, since for the least
offence the servants were dismissed—and dismissed meant being dragged
by Coxitl's troops of litter-bearers to the Temple and there handed over
to the ferocious priests for sacrifice.

The more that Philip and Gloria saw of their companions the more fully
they realized the utter impossibility of making any real friends or allies
among them. Generations of iron discipline in this Totalitarian State had
moulded them into a cold, cruel race from which the milk of human kindness seemed to have drained entirely away. They were human now only
in appearance. Their hearts were the steel organs of robots and their
perverted minds functioned only to plan and gloat upon the destruction of
mankind.

The Atzlantean week consisted of five days instead of seven, and
theoretically the teams of operators, gazers and recorders were supposed
to have every fifth day off, but whether they actually got it or not depended on the amount of activity going on in the spheres they covered.
Zadok's Number One team had not had a day off for many months since,
even when the War Cabinet and Chiefs of Staff Committee were not sitting, they had to follow the indefatigable Prime Minister to Chequers and
often listen there to his brilliant discourse far into the night.

Number Three team was more fortunate since General Montgomery and
his two colleagues who held equally responsible posts in the other services,
Admiral Sir Bertram Ramsey, and Air Marshal Sir Trafford Leigh-
Mallory, and General Omar Bradley, the Commander-in-Chief of the
United States Army of Liberation were all away from their headquarters

a great deal, making personal inspections of the formations which were to take part in the invasion and witnessing demonstrations of secret equipment which was to be used for the first time in connection with it; and to follow them, except for some special purpose, was considered unnecessary. In consequence, Philip and Gloria got their days off fairly regularly and utilized a good part of them in finding out as much as they could about what was going on in the other spheres.

By putting all sorts of bits of information together, they formed a picture which Philip put into words one night when discussing the situation with Gloria.

" It's clear that the Russians have been pressing the Anglo-Americans to form a second front for a long time past. We know that Roosevelt and Churchill, accompanied by their Chiefs of Staff and other high-ups, had a big conference with Stalin and his boys at Teheran last January. As far as I can make out, Uncle Joe put the screw on. He probably said: ' Apart from your occupying a dozen German divisions in North Africa and a few more in Italy, I've done all the fighting so far. It's quite time you chaps did a bit—and this time I really mean it. I've already lost ten times the number of men in killed and prisoners that you have, and my food situation behind the lines is deteriorating pretty badly. Hitler would be only too pleased to call off his war with Russia at practically any price now. I don't like Hitler and I don't want to let you boys down; but if you're not prepared to give me a definite promise that you'll open a second front this summer I really will have to reconsider the situation.' "

Gloria nodded. " That's about it, Boy. Although the President seems to have been mighty keen on opening a second front for ages past."

" So has Churchill for that matter. We know now that he had put his people on to plan the taking of Cherbourg in an operation called ' Sledgehammer ' before the United States had even entered the war; and if it hadn't been for the mess-up in North Africa he would have done ' Round-up ' as a full scale invasion in 1943. The only reason that the big shot sailors, soldiers and airmen have hesitated is because they realize better than anyone else the appalling risk of such an operation. After all, the Germans couldn't do it. They funked it even when they were at the height of their power, and Britain was almost unarmed, and alone. The trouble with an invasion is that once it's started there can be no pulling back; no breaking off the battle and cracking in again a fortnight later a bit further along the line. If this thing does go wrong it will have the most appalling repercussions. To start with, a great part of the best manhood of Britain, the States and Canada will certainly be killed. And, if it looked as if the Allies would never be able to land an army in France at all, that's the one thing that really might make U.J. throw in his hand. That brings us back to what I started to say. I don't believe for a moment that Uncle Joe ever had the least intention of ratting on us, but one can hardly doubt that the Anglo-Americans came back from Teheran definitely committed to opening a second front this summer."

" To my mind 'tis just as well they did," Gloria remarked. " What hope would they have of defeating Hitler if they left it even to the autumn? By then poor old London will be a heap of rubble from his V-bombs, and all these fine landing-craft we see on the screen when we take a trip down to the South Coast will be smashed to smithereens or sunk in the mud of the harbours."

" I know. It's the very devil, isn't it? Even if we could escape and get home and, more fantastic still, persuade them to call off the invasion, it wouldn't do any good in the long run. Yet, the alternative is to sit here and see the whole thing sabotaged by a most frightful storm."

" But do you really think, Boy, these devils here will be able to create such bad weather as to sink all these fine modern ships? "

" God alone knows! " Philip muttered. " We've never had a chance to see what they can do yet, because they've been husbanding every ounce of power they can put by for D-Day. But it's not a matter of sinking the ships; if they can raise even a moderately heavy sea that will be quite enough to prevent our landing-craft getting their freights safely on to the beaches."

As it so happened they were to witness a demonstration of the Atzlan-teans' powers to control weather conditions many thousands of miles away on the following afternoon.

Zadok did not always conduct the screenings personally. He spent most of his time with Number One team, and one of his deputies named Kishdil usually directed Number Three's operator. On this occasion the two senior teams both happened to be observing scenes of which Zadok was particu-larly anxious to have a record, so he came hurrying in to Number Three.

He gave quick instructions in Atzlantean, which neither Philip nor Gloria understood, but they saw the picture at which they were gazing suddenly dissolve and, a moment later, its place was taken by a wide expanse of sea.

As the picture came into focus they could see two groups of warships several miles distant from each other. From what Philip remembered of his father's books showing the silhouettes of the principal ships in the navies of the world, the first group consisted of the German battle-cruiser *Hipper* and a light cruiser of the *Köln* type. The second included a British battleship mounting a four gun barbette forward, which made him be-lieve her to be of the *King George V* class.

Visibility was fair, and the sea moderate. They could see two British aircraft darting high above the flak the Germans were sending up and evidently keeping their own ships informed of the enemy's position. Zadok meanwhile had given some orders to the assistant who was sitting up at the far end of the room near the retorts. A lever was pulled over, electric flashes came and went in a number of tubes and bulbs, then a large retort gradually filled with what appeared to be red vapour. At another order from Zadok the lever was pulled back and the red vapour disappeared.

Philip stared at the sea-scape, expecting every moment to see rain come sheeting down, but nothing happened. Zadok noticed his anxious expression and said in English:

" Number Two team was observing a conference at the Admiralty when a signal was brought in for the First Sea Lord. Fortunately, he read it out to his companions. It was a report that the spotting aircraft of a British Squadron had picked up the *Hipper* off the Norwegian coast and that the Squadron was closing in. I've done my best to save the Germans, but it needs half an hour for any action taken here to affect the weather in Europe."

It was difficult for Philip and Gloria to restrain themselves from cheering the British Squadron on during the half-hour that followed, but the ships seemed well matched for speed, and the British gained only very slowly on the Germans as they raced through the water towards the shelter of the Norwegian fjords. With only a few minutes to go the British battleship fired two shells at maximum range. They sent up great fountains of water only a few hundred yards from the *Hipper's* stern. Then the outline of the ships became very faintly blurred. It had begun to rain. The battleship fired again—a four gun salvo this time. The *Hipper* heeled right over under the impact of the explosion close on her port side, and tons of water cascaded down on to her deck; but the scene had now gone misty. It was raining hard. Rocking back on to an even keel, the German changed her course. The next salvo from the battleship missed her by a quarter of a mile. It was evident that the range-finders could no longer see the target, and the German was now shrouded even from the aircraft overhead by the pouring rain. Zadok heaved a sigh of relief, while Philip cursed silently as the *Hipper* altered course again and slipped away unseen to the security of her hideout in the Norwegian coast.

It was only a few days after this that Zadok spoke one morning quite openly to Philip of the Atzlantean plans to sabotage operation OVERLORD, as the Anglo-Americans had named their plan for the return to the Continent.

" OVERLORD," he said, " is by far the greatest and most complicated operation of war that has ever been undertaken. Its complexity far exceeds the much weightier Russian offensives because, to be effective, an entire army must be landed on the coast of France within the space of a few days. That means not only getting ashore several hundred thousands of men but also many thousands of lorries, hundreds of tanks, each weighing several tons, hundreds of guns, millions of boxes of ammunition, motor cycles, staff cars, petrol, food, balloons, ground equipment for airfields, and the innumerable other items all of which are absolutely essential to the waging of modern war. And it does not end there. It is not enough to get these huge swarms of men ashore with their initial requirements. They will be eating, firing and consuming petrol every hour of the day and night from the second they land. If their supplies run out even for an hour they will be in great danger; if their supplies are cut off for a day they will be lost. Yet everything for their maintenance must be sent in day after day over the open beaches."

"Yes," Philip agreed with apparent cheerfulness. "If you can get a really good storm going they won't stand a hope in hell."

Somewhat to his surprise, Zadok replied: "We must prevent their ever starting if we can. It is a pity that we cannot let them land in good weather, then stop their supplies of food and munitions reaching them a few days later. I feel that, if we could keep them cut off for even three days, that would be quite sufficient to enable the Germans to drive the whole Anglo-American army back into the sea. But the Lord Toxil does not agree with me. He says that the risk is too great. He fears the tremendous tenacity which both the British and the Americans display once they have committed themselves to a course of action. He thinks, too, that the opposition we shall be up against will make our own task no light one."

"What sort of opposition?" asked Philip, striving to keep out of his voice the excitement he felt at the thought of the secret machinations of the Atzlanteans being met with any opposition at all.

Zadok shrugged his skinny shoulders. "OVERLORD is the crucial operation of the Second World War. If the Anglo-Americans succeed in establishing an army in France during June, Hitler will be caught between two fires. We may be able to help him to keep going for a year or so, but in the end he will be inevitably crushed. On the other hand if the Anglo-Americans fail in June they will never be able to land an army based on Britain in France at all. Years must elapse before any other method of doing so could become a practical proposition. Long before that Russia will become exhausted and Hitler will have rockets with a great enough range and power to destroy the big city ports of the American eastern seaboard. It will then only be a matter of time before Hitler is able to soften Britain sufficiently to invade and conquer the island. Once that is accomplished the shipbuilding yards and aircraft plants of all Europe will be at his disposal. Then it will be the turn of America. That is what hangs on the success or failure of OVERLORD. Others are just as well aware of that as ourselves. I speak now not of the living but of the dead. On D-Day every spiritual force, even to the most distant past, which has contributed to the Anglo-Saxon civilization and the making of the Free Democracies in both hemispheres will be thrown in against us."

"You mean," said Philip slowly, "that, as well as a down-here battle on the physical plane, there will also be a titanic conflict in the unseen spiritual world above?"

"Exactly. That is why the Lord Toxil is not prepared to take the risk of allowing the Anglo-American spearheads to get ashore. But not doing so we miss a chance of offering a fine sacrifice to Shaitan in the thousands of Anglo-Americans who would be killed and drowned if their Army was driven off again; but as against that, if we succeed in preventing the invasion altogether, in due course Hitler will be able to offer up the whole Anglo-Saxon race, in the same way as he is now eliminating the Poles and countless thousands of other people in his concentration camps."

Philip nodded. " Yes, I see the idea. But how long will you be able to ensure really bad weather in the Channel in midsummer? Even if the Allies can't go in on June the Fifth, as they have planned, they might still be in time to overrun Hitler's V-weapon sites if they go in at the end of the month."

" They would never be able to get ashore then, and they will know it; so the attempt will not be made," Zadok replied with a crafty smile flickering over his thin lips. " This enterprise is so vast that one human brain can hardly grasp it. You have already seen some of the hundreds of ships and landing craft that are assembling along the south coast of England, but there are many hundreds more on the west coast and in the great ports up in the north; then there are the naval task forces which are still up in Scotland. All these must be brought down to the assembly point off the Isle of Wight. That cannot be done in a day. The movements southward will start at least a week before D-Day. By D-minus Two there will be such an armada massed within a hundred miles of Southampton that any German reconnaissance plane seeing it will know that the invasion is due to start immediately."

" Then the Anglo-Americans will not be able to achieve surprise in any case? "

" They might still do so if the R.A.F. can keep all German aircraft off from D-minus-Two. But even if the concentration is reported on D-minus-One that will not allow sufficient time for the Germans to bring their strategic reserves into a suitable position to resist the blow."

" You hope then to hold the concentration there by bad weather long enough for the Germans not only to spot it but to move up their reserves? "

" That is our plan. On June the Third, D-minus-Two, we shall start our storm. The cloudy weather should ensure a German aircraft being able to slip in and out without being shot down by the R.A.F. On June the Fifth, or at the latest the Sixth, the Germans will know that the invasion is imminent. If we can give them till June the Tenth they should have completed their redispositions. The R.A.F. will see and report these German troop movements. From that point the Anglo-Americans will know that it would be suicidal to attempt the operation, so the invasion forces will be dismantled and the project of landing an army on the Continent will be indefinitely postponed."

It was on the same day as this discussion that Zadok first pointed out General Gale to Philip. For some little time now the block in the West End square and the headquarters in Western London had both been semi-

deserted. General Eisenhower and General Montgomery had moved to
their Invasion Headquarters. Such changes were easy for the gazers to
trace as, if some prominent personality disappeared for a few days, he
could almost certainly be picked up by one of the teams on his next visit
to the Offices of the War Cabinet, and his car with its flying pennant
followed back when he left for his new location. So the principal places
of interest for Number Three team were now a great area of hutments
covered with camouflage netting in Bushey Park, a little way outside London, and a lovely old country house set in fine private grounds down in
Hampshire.

That afternoon the Number Three team had been overlooking a conference about marshalling areas, at which General Montgomery was present, and when it broke up he took aside another General, a big, power-
fully built man who stood half a head taller than most of the other people
in the room, to have a word with him alone.

Zadok was standing behind Philip at the time, and he said: " I want
you to take careful note of the big man to whom General Montgomery
is now talking, so that you will recognize him again. His name is Richard
Gale, and he is the Major-General Commanding the Sixth British Airborne Division."

Philip found himself looking for a moment straight into a broad, tanned
face with a short brown moustache. It was a face that radiated humour,
kindliness and great personality. When the General spoke his voice was
slow, deep and full of quiet confidence. Then, at something that the little
pointed-nosed Commander-in-Chief said he gave a grand, infectious laugh.

" That man is dangerous," said Zadok in his reedy voice from behind
Philip's head. " He is not only very brave and very clever, but he knows
how to win the confidence of his men. I have kept my eye on him for a
long time. He was one of the original members of the Joint Planning
Staff that now work in the Offices of the War Cabinet. Very early in the
war, when Britain had no airborne forces, he was among the first to realize
the enormous possibilities of this new arm. He managed to get away
from the War Office and has played a leading part in the training and development of the parachutists and glider-borne troops. It was his division,
the Sixth Airborne, that went into Sicily. He has now been chosen to play
a key rôle in the invasion. Whenever you pick him up listen carefully to
all he says and see that it is included in your report."

When Philip told Gloria the Atzlantean plans to counter the invasion,
in the privacy of their room that night, he also told her of the other,
greater battle which was preparing between the powers of Darkness and
the powers of Light.

" 'Tis no surprise to me at all," she said, when he had done. " If the
Good God has thought fit to rob us of our babies and send us to this hell-
ish place for some purpose of his own, 'twould be giving ourselves airs to
think that we're the only ones receiving the great guidance."

" Yes, that must be so," Philip agreed with a smile. " Although I must confess the idea had never occurred to me before. D'you really think, though, that at this time lots of people are seeing visions and dreaming of dead friends who set them on a certain course as the Canon did with us? "

" I wouldn't know." Her blue eyes were very serious. " But if any proof that some such thing were going on were needed just look at the Mulberries."

They had literally been looking at the Mulberries at the same time as Admiral Tennant, who was responsible for them, had been doing two days before. This code-word covered the greatest secret of the war. It had first been laid down that a prime essential to a successful invasion was the speedy seizure of a port in order that heavy equipment could still be got ashore, even if the weather suddenly deteriorated. Then various people had expressed the opinion that the Germans, knowing this, would concentrate all their toughest units round the ports, and thus the Allies might find it impossible to capture one during those all-important early days of the operation. The only alternative seemed to be to face the risk of going in over the beaches. But suddenly the idea had been advanced that the Allies should build two great ports in Britain, tow them over to France in pieces, and plant them on chosen strips of coast. The scores of huge floating piers—many of which were over two hundred feet in length and forty feet broad and deep—now lying along the south coast of England, were the result. If the Mulberries proved successful the unloading of the ships supplying the invading forces would be able to continue, whatever the weather.

" Of course," said Philip, " I see what you mean. Bad weather in the English Channel in June is almost unheard of, so some outside entity, such as the Canon was to us, must have put it into some living person's head that the chance that the weather might be rough was much greater than most people thought, and therefore every possible precaution *must* be taken."

" Yes, and more than that, Boy. The Blessed Saints must have had a high old time persuading the old diehards that these new-fangled things, with the mountain of work they entailed, were both necessary and practical. Just think now what Zadok told us of the labour that went into the making of those Mulberries."

Philip did think. He remembered Zadok saying weeks before that every engineering firm of any size in the whole of Britain had been called in to help. Millions of tons of steel and concrete had been required, thousands of labourers; and so many tugs would be needed to tow these huge piers across the Channel that there were not enough in all the ports of the United Kingdom, so that further fleets of sea-going tugs were now being brought from North Africa and the United States. To do the job at all production had had to be stopped on scores of other items of urgently needed war equipment, many of them of the highest priority. And all this for what? To attempt the seemingly impossible. To try out something that never even had been contemplated in the history of the world before. No less than the prefabrication of two huge harbours in which many thousands of tons of supplies could be unloaded in a single day; and their towage over nearly a hundred miles of open sea to a hostile shore where they were to be fitted together and made serviceable in a matter of days in the very face of the enemy. And this mad scheme with all the gargantuan labour it entailed had been undertaken solely because the English Channel *might* become rough in midsummer.

As Philip drew Gloria's head of flaming curls down on to his shoulder, he murmured: " Yes, darling. Such a scheme could never have got past all the conscientious but unimaginative people who would normally have opposed it, if there weren't hundreds more like ourselves who are being inspired by those Great Powers who do not mean to see the Light perish from the world."

The thought was a great comfort to them, yet, as they fell asleep, but for each other they still felt very much alone.

The weeks had slipped by, and May was now well advanced. Each day brought new evidence that the preparations for the Allies' return to the Continent were nearing completion. Every harbour and every rivermouth from Harwich right round the South Coast to Avonmouth were packed with shipping in endless variety, great and small according to the anchorages. Huge areas of England had been closed to visitors. In Sussex, Hampshire and Dorset, great tracts of country had been cordoned off for the reception of the invasion forces who were to be sealed into them and no longer allowed to communicate with the outside world once they had been briefed in the parts they were to play.

Thousands upon thousands of British and American soldiers were moving to their battle stations. Night after night endless columns of tanks, guns, lorries and jeeps moved steadily southwards; hundreds of trains with millions of tons of munitions steamed slowly but methodically from every part of the United Kingdom towards the southern ports. Every airfield in the southern counties was packed to capacity with aircraft. Day by day the fighter screens that were put up became more numerous and more vigilant in their task of protecting all vital ground preparations from being observed by the enemy. Night and day Bomber Command and the United States Eighth Air Force sent out ever greater numbers of their heavies to destroy such important targets as the bridges over the Seine and innumerable communications centres, often far in the interior of France, while the Tactical Air Forces made great offensive sweeps and the aircraft of the Coastal Command hurled their explosives at the enemy lairs, from which submarines and E-boats might be sent to play havoc among the great armada, once it sailed.

To Philip and Gloria these days were a time of ever increasing anxiety.

Having reached this sinister underworld in such a strange succession of circumstances, they had not the least shadow of doubt that they had been sent there for a definite purpose; yet they could form no idea of what that purpose was. Each night they prayed with all their strength that the Canon would again appear to one of them in a dream and give them some new direction. But he did not do so, and at length they came to the conclusion that, the gods having given them free will, they were not to be ordered to do anything. This was to be the test of their courage and integrity; it was to be left to them what action, if any, they should take.

Yet what action *could* they take which would have any material effect against the natural forces controlled by this powerful and well-organized body that lived for the sole purpose of abetting Evil?

For weeks past they had endeavoured to learn something of the secrets of the magno-electric forces which the Atzlanteans could wield with such terrible effect; but there they had come up against a blank wall. The only thing they had found out was that the operative power was generated in great caverns in another part of the mountain, and by an entirely separate group of Atzlanteans with whom those they knew never came into contact. The only actual manifestation they had ever seen was the red vapour that filled a large retort on the far wall of the medium chamber whenever an operation was actually in progress. They did not even know how to start to get to the caverns where the power was generated, so there was not the faintest possibility of their being able to sabotage the main source.

Philip still had his automatic with four bullets in it. He thought of endeavouring to assassinate as many as possible of the Seven, but he had never seen more than two of them together since the day of his arrival. He could shoot Zadok or Rakil, or perhaps both, but their colleagues would carry on for them, and there seemed no reason at all to suppose that the killing of these two evil old men would have the least effect on events in distant Europe.

Again and again Philip and Gloria discussed the matter, but they could see no way in which by giving their own lives they could strike a blow that would aid their countries or harm one single German. When they woke on the morning of June the Third, which was D-minus-Two, they had still made no plan and were near despair from their fruitless efforts to think of one.

That afternoon Zadok assembled all his assistants, and with the aid of a map gave them details of the final invasion plan. The operation was to be launched against selected beaches along approximately fifty miles of the Normandy coast between the base of the Cotentin Peninsula and the mouth of the River Orne. The Americans were to go in on the right and the British on the left. The two flanks were to be covered by the Airborne forces of the respective armies, which would be put down just after midnight on D-minus-One. The landings on the beaches were to take place some six hours later, early in the morning of D-Day. The first main objectives after establishing a firm bridgehead were—for the Americans, to cut the Cotentin Peninsula, then to capture Cherbourg at its tip—for the British, to secure the line of the River Orne and seize the town of Caen as a pivot in order to be able to resist the counter-attack of the major German forces which were known to be in the area of the Seine and, it was appreciated, would endeavour to roll up the whole Allied invasion force by attacking its left flank in great strength.

Zadok went on to say that from now onwards all the teams available would be kept in practically perpetual session by using a certain number of trainees as reliefs in addition to all trained operators and observers. Those who could not understand either English or German were to be used for subsidiary tasks connected with the invasion, in which over-looking was more important than overhearing. His Number One and Number Two teams were to concentrate on the Prime Minister and In-vasion Headquarters in order to get early news of the weather if the Allied military leaders advised a postponement and of any communications about it which might pass between the Prime Minister and the President of the United States. His Number Three team was to keep the Headquarters of the Sixth British Airborne Division under observation, as these troops would be the first to be irrevocably committed if the operation were on.

Philip and Gloria slept for the rest of the afternoon as their first tour of duty was not until the evening. At the evening meal they found that a tense excitement had now gripped all the Atzlanteans, and a whisper was running round that the largest number of victims for more than a hundred years had been turned over to the priests for sacrifice that night.

When they reached the screening room everything was proceeding smoothly. They were told that all the troops were now assembled in their marshalling areas and in process of being briefed; and that the great flotillas of shipping were beginning to close in on Southampton.

Zadok came in himself to start off the session with a new operator. The picture that came on to the screen was a permanent R.A.F. Station in Southern England with well designed brick buildings and comfortable quarters. They had seen this aerodrome on numerous occasions recently and knew it to be the Headquarters of the Sixth British Airborne Division. It was still light and a pleasant summer evening.

Parked round the great airfield were the scores of aircraft which were to take the paratroops to France or tow in the gliders. Both aircraft and gliders looked strange because they had all just had broad bands of colour painted round their wings. The picture carried the gazers across the grass to the Officers' Mess. On the large stone-pillared porch, where there were a number of basket chairs, a group of officers stood chatting. The domin-ant figure of the group was General Gale. He was standing in what the observers had come to know as a characteristic attitude; his feet were set wide apart and his hands were stuffed into the pockets of the beautifully cut light grey jodhpurs that he always wore instead of the conventional battledress.

Philip began to say a few sentences from time to time, either giving a brief summary of a conversation or any special item of information for Gloria to take down. They learned that the camp had been sealed the day before. No one in it or entering it from that moment could leave it or telephone or send a letter until the invasion had begun. They learned, too, that the new bands of colour on the aircraft were special recognition signs which, for reasons of secrecy, could not be put on until the camp had been sealed.

From recent observations Philip already knew the names of most of the senior officers present, and he said: "Wing-Commander Macnamara has just introduced another Wing-Commander to the General, but I didn't catch his name. He's not a real airman, as he has no pilot's wings on his chest, but he says he's come down from London this afternoon.'"

Zadok peered into the globe. "Ah!" he exclaimed softly. "I know that little man well by sight. He is one of the Joint Planning Staff, but never before have I seen him outside the Cabinet Offices."

Philip proceeded with a routine description for the record. "The man from London is short and dark. He is plump, wears several medal ribbons and is rather red in the face. He and the General have just found that they have several friends in common and that they were both born in Eighteen Ninety-Seven. The General said, 'And a damn' good vintage too!' I doubt if they'll say anything of interest about the war in the middle of a crowd like that though, so we might as well see what's going on elsewhere."

The picture moved through the hall of the mess to a big lounge. The whole place was packed with about half and half officers and glider pilots of the Sixth Airborne Division, in khaki, and the R.A.F. officers who were to fly them over, in Air Force blue. They were all mixed up together and in tremendous spirits. None of them yet knew the date that had been fixed for D-Day, but they did know that, the camp having been sealed the day before, it could not be far off. Philip recorded that they were betting that immediately the invasion was started the Germans would retire to the Rhine because they would not dare to face the Anglo-Americans on so long a front as the Atlantic Wall. Clearly their morale and confidence in their own fighting powers were terrific.

The picture next toured the station offices. These were now semi-deserted but the Station Commander, Group-Captain Surplice—a tall, well-built fellow with very blue eyes and white even teeth—was just receiving some weather reports which made him frown. This, together with Zadok's self-satisfied smile, gave Philip cause to assume that the Atzlanteans' counter-invasion measures had already started.

Back in the mess an airman was asking the General what weapon he personally was going to take for the battle. He roared with laughter and replied: "Weapon! What the hell do I want with a weapon? If I have the good luck to get anywhere near those so-and-so's my boots are good enough for me!"

As there was nothing going on that was worth recording it was suggested that the screening should be broken off for a while. Zadok agreed and left them. Philip walked over to the instrument board and stood for a little beside Arkitl, the member of Number Three team who always attended it when they were on duty. The red vapour was swirling into the big retort. Arkitl watched it carefully and each time it filled turned over the lever that released it into the tubes that carried it away.

For some time they sat about, then Zadok's deputy Kishdil came in, and the screening was resumed. The aerodrome was now dark and almost deserted. In the mess everyone had gone to bed except the General and the man from London. They were discussing the qualities that made a good leader.

The General insisted that only one thing mattered—efficiency. If the men knew that you really knew jour job they would follow you blindly anywhere.

His companion asked him why he wore his grey jodhpurs instead of the conventional battledress.

"What's that got to do with it?" he wanted to know. "Anyhow, it's not because of the look of the thing. I wear them because they're comfortable and I hate the feel of that beastly khaki serge."

"Just as I thought," replied the other. "That's simply another way of saying that you're independent-minded and the jodhpurs are an expression of your strong personality. Good leadership may be nine-tenths efficiency, but the odd tenth of personality must be there as well."

Deciding that the argument was of no particular interest, Kishdil did not wait to hear the end of it, but took the picture outside. In the open a strong wind was now blowing, and storm clouds were piling up to hide the stars. There seemed no point in continuing the screening, so it was closed down for the night.

When Philip and Gloria got to their room she said: "What d'you think will happen, Boy? D'you think they'll go to-morrow night, storm or no storm, or not?"

Philip smiled at her. "Can you imagine men like Richard Gale being put off by a capful of wind? And your people are just as tough as mine. Of course, it will make things much more difficult. If the weather's very bad a lot of the gliders will break away from the towing planes and a lot of the landing-craft will be swamped, so our casualties are bound to be much heavier. But they'll go in just the same. They can't afford not to now that all that shipping is on the move."

He was, therefore, all the more shocked and distressed when he learned in the middle of the following morning, that, owing to the extraordinarily adverse weather conditions which had developed in the past twenty hours, the Allied High Command had decided to postpone the operation. Against all his expectations the Atzlanteans had won the first round hands down.

A screening revealed the personnel of the aerodrome going about their respective businesses as usual. Very few people there had ever known the date of D-Day, so they were equally unaware of the postponement. The only two who could have any idea of its full implications were the General and the Wing-Commander from London. As they talked of it quietly together, the latter was saying gloomily that during the night over four thousand ships and many thousands of smaller craft had moved up and were now massed round the Isle of Wight. The cloudy weather was ideal for the Boche aircraft to sneak through, and it only needed one to nip in and out again for the whole works to be blown. If that happened the Germans might decide to throw in every available Luftwaffe plane that could cover the distance; in which case there would be the most appalling massacre among our close-berthed stationary shipping.

Everyone else, completely unaware of the terrible menace that now overhung this great operation for which they had spent so many months in training, remained in excellent spirits; and that night there was a spontaneous sing-song in the mess in which senior and junior alike joined in all the old choruses at the tops of their voices.

By midnight the sing-song was practically over, only a few roisterers remained, and Kishdil was just about to close down the screening for the night when Quetzl caught sight of the General's A.D.C.—a good-looking young lieutenant, whom they knew by his Christian name of Tom—hurrying down the corridor towards his Chief's room.

The picture followed him into the General's bedroom. The General had left the sing-song only three-quarters of an hour before, but he was already in bed and asleep. Tom woke him and handed him a flimsy with a single code-word written on it.

The General glanced at it, then looked at him and said: " The job's on, Tom! This time to-morrow night we'll be on our way."

Zadok was sent for immediately. When he came in his parchment-like face had gone a yellowish colour under the natural red tint of his skin. His dark eyes were bilious, and he could not control his skinny hands which were trembling with rage. But he was not at a loss for long.

Having spoken to the others in Atzlantean, he turned to Philip and said: " It is typical of the pig-headed British and their crazy American allies to launch a forlorn hope instead of having the sense to admit defeat. But they will be made to pay for their folly. We shall put Plan Two into operation at once.

" The Lord Toxil has approved that, in the event of the Anglo-Ameri-

cans deciding to go in, we should conserve the energies that we have at
our command for the next five days. The energy already released is
sufficient to cause sea-sickness among the troops and difficulty for the
landing-craft. On D-plus-Four we shall create the biggest storm that there
has been for a hundred years in June in the English Channel. In this way
we shall cut the invasion force off from its base before it has had time to
gain a secure foothold, and break up the Mulberries before they can be
got into working order. Stunned and disorganized as the Germans are by
the ceaseless bombing, they should at least be able to do the rest."

Zadok paused for a moment, then went on: " In addition, there is
a local operation which I shall direct personally from this room. The
most vulnerable spot in the Anglo-American Invasion Army will be its
left flank. There are neither the troops nor the room at the base of the
Cotentin Peninsula for the Germans to attempt a major counter-attack
against the Americans on the right; but the Twenty-First Panzer Division
will be within easy striking distance of the British on the left, and it could
be supported by many other good formations. If the British flank is left
open, their destruction is inevitable. By smashing it we can make a German victory certain. To-morrow night it will be for us here to ensure
that the British Airborne Forces never get in! "

When Philip and Gloria got to their room he was smiling. " I knew
it," he said. " I knew they'd have a cut at it whatever the weather. And
we've got the finest seamen in the world. By hook or by crook the
Navy will get the Army ashore. But it's going to be a sticky wicket after
that."

Gloria took his crutches from him and helped him to lower himself on
to his cushions, as she replied: " I'm so glad it's come at last. 'Tis the
waiting that's been the worst part. Tell me, Boy, what's the best we can
hope to do? "

He drew her down beside him and lowered his voice to a whisper.
" You heard what Zadok said. The success or failure of the whole opera-
tion depends on the Sixth British Airborne Division securing the left flank.
The counter-measures to wreck it are to be conducted from our room.
That gives us a real chance. If we play our cards properly I believe we
can win for our Airborne Forces just one hour."

CHAPTER XX

THE VITAL HOUR

As they walked down the gloomy tunnel to the first screening of the following morning, there were two things that filled them with acute anxiety. One was the possibility that some unforeseen factor might arise to disturb the normal routine of the coming night's procedure. The other was the latent power that lay in Zadok's eyes.

They had sat up far into the night planning their *coup* and settling the details of the action they proposed to attempt; but, if anything happened to throw the routine out of gear, their whole plan might be ruined.

That Zadok would take the screening himself they felt reasonably certain. Thousands of tons of paper had been consumed by the Allied Staffs in planning the innumerable aspects of the Invasion, thousands of telegrams had been exchanged between London and Washington, and thousands of hours had been spent in conferences. But that was all over now, and at this eleventh hour not even one more sheet of paper would be used to amend the rôle of a single man. Again the likelihood of a second postponement, now that the word to set going the million wheels of the vast machine had actually been given, was practically out of the question. In consequence, Zadok's Number One and Number Two teams had become overnight little more than interested spectators, and his Number Three team was bound to receive the lion's share of his attention.

In any case, they had made their plan on the assumption that he would be present, but the thing that perturbed them most was their lack of knowledge about his hypnotic powers. Coxitl had paralysed Philip with a single glance, and it seemed certain that, as one of the Seven, Zadok would be possessed of even more remarkable powers. But could he, for example, paralyse a person's brain and strike them down by looking through the back of their head? There was no possible way in which Philip or Gloria could answer this, and they knew that they must now leave the success or failure of their plan on the knees of the gods.

When the first screening opened the activities on the aerodrome and in its vicinity appeared little different from those on the previous day. Very few people yet knew that this was D-1, and it was not until lunch-time that the whisper went round: " Final briefing at three o'clock."

In due course the picture followed the General and most of the senior officers from the Mess some distance across the camp to a long hut with blacked-out windows. At one end, beyond a raised platform, the Intelligence officers had arranged a large map of the Channel and the invasion area, with the routes to be taken by the aircraft, and dropping zones for the paratroops, marked clearly upon it.

The rest of the hut was filled with wooden tables and benches crowded with R.A.F. Pilots and glider Pilots of the Airborne Division all mixed up together. General Gale now had another General with him, and the two of them were shortly afterwards joined by an Air Vice-Marshal. As the two newcomers were introduced Philip caught their names and the particulars that emerged about them.

They were General Crawford, D. Air of the War Office, and Air Vice-Marshal Hollinghurst, the A.O.C. of the Group which was to fly the Airborne Division in. Both had played a great part in the organization and training of the Airborne Forces, and both of them were going to fly over to France that night as passengers, to see what further lessons they could learn from the actual operation.

The proceedings were opened by the Station Commander, who read Orders of the Day from General Eisenhower and Air Marshal Sir Trafford Leigh-Mallory; after which he explained the general lay-out of the sea-borne assault.

General Gale then stepped up on to the platform and said that his task was to protect the left flank of the Allied Armies. To do this three separate landings would be made to the east of the River Orne. A château that contained a local Headquarters had to be taken, and a powerful battery that enfiladed the assault beaches had to be destroyed. Then two adjacent bridges crossing the River Orne and the Dives canal about five miles from the coast had to be seized intact, and further inland other bridges had to be blown up. The General meant to establish his battle H.Q. between the two seized bridges; to infest with his men all the territory to the east in order to delay a German attack against the British flank, and, when the attack came, as come it must, to fight with his back to the double waterline.

When the General had finished, the Station Commander briefed his pilots, and the Signals Officer, the Meteorological Officer and the Secret Devices Officer in turn gave their technical information to the air crews. The first briefing, which had taken just an hour, was then over, but two further briefings of a similar nature for other parties were to follow. For these Zadok relieved his Number Three team with trainees, so Philip and Gloria were free to leave the screening room.

They had already decided that to fail to take a meal might arouse suspicion, so, loath as they were to spend any of their remaining time with the Atzlanteans, they went to the Mess, fed as quickly as they could, then retired to their room. Their next tour of duty did not start till nine o'clock, so they had over four hours in which to be together undisturbed.

Both of them had been a little worried about this interval, fearing that they might be overcome by thoughts of the results to themselves if the thing they contemplated should break down; but they began to talk of the way they had played each other up during their first weeks on the launch, then of the great happiness that had been theirs during the two and a quarter years they had lived as husband and wife in the valley of the Little People, and almost before they realized it the final hours had sped.

Philip had already greased his pistol and seen that it was in proper working order. He now took it from the old knapsack in which they had brought it from the valley, and hid it securely under the folds of the loose tunic he was wearing. Gloria slid into his arms, and for a few moments they embraced closely. As she relaxed, she murmured:

" You'll not let those fiends get me, Boy, will you? "

" No," he replied, a trifle hoarsely. " I'll keep a bullet for you as I promised, whatever happens. It will be very quick."

" Sure it will. I'm not frightened of that. 'Tis no more than thousands of our boys will be getting in these next few hours, so we'll be in good company. May the Blessed Saints give us our courage to the last. That's all I'm asking."

" I think they'll do that for us." He smiled, and added to rally her: " But will they forgive you for living in sin for two and a half years with a Protestant? That's far more important."

" Oh, Boy! " She smiled back. " What a dear fool you are! They'd never be holding out on me over a thing like that when there was no priest to marry us. And if they did I'd boycott them, so I would. They can keep their heaven if they won't let me bring you into it! "

Again they had a quick snack in the mess for the sake of appearances, then went to the screening room. Old, bent and evil Zadok came in to take control himself; black-browed Arkitl was at the instrument board. As Philip and Gloria sat down side by side on two of the stools, thick-lipped Quetzl and the woman Velig sat down opposite them. The old blind operator took his place before the mesh of wires and spinning gyroscope, Zadok gave his instructions, and the screening began.

As the lights dimmed the silvery, frosted screen began to vibrate, and the first humming of the soundtrack impinged upon the silence; then the vibrating lessened and the ripples took its place until on the gently undulating surface a picture began to appear.

It was the crowded ante-room of the R.A.F. Mess. Every one of the scores of leather armchairs in it was occupied now that dinner was over, and the room was hazy with tobacco smoke; but its occupants were not settling down to read books or papers to-night. The soldiers were exchanging addresses with the airmen and cracking jokes as they made plans for great reunions after the job was over. Some were seated at the desks writing letters to their loved ones, others were smoking a last pipe or knocking back a last pint before going out to the battle.

No roomful of men could have been more representative of the British

Empire; the Dominions were well to the fore, and there were a number of Colonials. In the great babel of sound Philip could catch snatches of speech in accents ranging from Oxford to Glasgow, Dublin to Devon, and Cardiff to Cockney London.

The picture shifted to the big entrance hall. This, too, was crowded. Gathered round a table were the two Generals, the Air Vice-Marshal, Wing-Commander Macnamara, the Planner from London, a Major and young " Tom," General Gale's A.D.C. On the table was a hock bottle, the long neck of which was wrapped in gold foil as though it were champagne.

Quetzl, who for some time past had acted only as checker to Philip, remained silent while the latter began to make his report.

" They are about to drink success to the enterprise in a bottle of wine produced by the man from London. The Major's name is Griffiths. He is the pilot of General Gale's glider. Macnamara will pilot the aircraft that tows the glider. General Crawford is to fly in and back with him. ' Holly,' as they call the little Air Vice Marshal, is going in another aircraft. He reminds me rather of a Roman Emperor as he sits there sipping his wine.

" Apparently he is a connoisseur of hock. They are all remarking that it is something quite exceptional. They say it is very heavy—like a liqueur—like Imperial Tokay. It's called Ruppertsberg Hoheburg Gewurztraminer Feinste Edelbeer-Auslese 1920. I think that's what General Crawford said when he picked up the bottle and read out the label just now. The red-faced chap who produced it is laughing. He says he always calls it Pharaoh's Wine, because he doesn't believe that anything like it has been vintaged since the Golden Age.

" Another Major has joined the party. He is the Divisional Intelligence Officer. He, Gale and the man from London are now talking about the forthcoming operation. The Planner says he thinks the real crisis will come in about a week, when the Germans have had sufficient time to mass for a counter-attack in force, and the Allies are still building up over the beaches.

" The General disagrees. He puts his faith in the immense air superiority of the Allies and the fact that the R.A.F. have already destroyed all the bridges over the Seine. He says that the bulk of Rommel's forces will now have to come right round Paris. That wherever they mass the Tactical Air Forces will find them and break them up. He says that, if the Allies can secure their first objectives, he does not think there will be any need to worry.

" Group-Captain Surplice has just come in. He is about to make a tour of the aerodrome in his car. The party is breaking up. A stream of officers is now leaving the ante-room. They are going to put on their flying-clothes and collect their equipment."

As Philip stopped talking the picture began to move about carrying them from place to place, only pausing for a moment or two here and there. Outside the weather was still not good, but it had improved a little; there were breaks between the clouds, and the twilight faded almost imperceptibly into moonlight. The paratroops in their camp were getting into their harness and blacking their faces so that they looked like demons. The Control Room was full of officers and W.A.A.F.s taking constant telephone calls, typing records and checking signals. On the aerodrome scores of ground crews were now getting the aircraft for the first wave into position. The Station Commander's car had put him down at the Watch Tower, where he was now standing with three Wing-Commanders. The picture came to rest, and after listening for a few seconds Philip said:

" The first wave is to consist of fourteen paratroop-carrying aircraft, followed by four aircraft towing gliders containing special material needed as soon as possible after the paratroops have landed—explosives for blowing up the bridges, and so on. The wave is to be led by Wing-Commander Bangay, and the Air Vice-Marshal is going with him. They are to take off at three minutes past eleven."

At this point Zadok stopped the picture and walked down the room to speak to Arkitl. They examined some of the instruments together. Then Zadok came back and said to Philip:

" The skies over the Normandy beaches are clear under two thousand feet, with broken cloud above which would let the moonlight through, so that the pilots should be able to pick up their dropping zones without difficulty. But we shall alter that. We can force the cloud down to five hundred feet. If they have to work by instruments some of the paratroop-carrying aircraft may lose themselves, and in any case the gliders will break away and fall in the sea."

Philip nodded and dug his nails into the palms of his hands under his tunic, as he strove to control his anger at this foul and murderous design. He knew enough about aeronautics to realize that the accurate dropping of parachutists on a given spot was a difficult enough business even under good conditions in daylight, and that, unless a glider pilot could see the tail of the plane that was towing him, his glider would get out of control, begin to swing and after a few minutes snap her towing-rope. Thick, low cloud was the one thing absolutely guaranteed to render this airborne operation abortive and make at least fifty per cent. of the men engaged in it casualties before they had even landed in France. Yet it was just the sort of thing that he had expected Zadok to lay on.

When the screening was resumed they returned to the Watch Tower. The aircraft of the first wave were all lined up, and they now began to take off. With a great roar of engines each of the fourteen paratroop-carrying aircraft raced past at thirty-second intervals and lifted into the air; they were followed at one-minute intervals by the four tugs each towing a glider containing the special material that the paratroops would need so urgently on their arrival. In eleven minutes the first wave, the spearhead of the mighty invasion, had taken off without the slightest hitch.

Zadok stopped the screening again and gave an order. Arkitl pulled over a lever, the red vapour swirled into the retort. When it was full he threw the lever back again. The effect would be operative over the Normandy coast in half an hour's time. The aircraft would take approximately seventy minutes to get there from the time of their take-off, so the cloud would be down over the coast long before they reached it.

When the screening was resumed once more the picture travelled about the aerodrome again. In the Control Room Philip picked up the news that the Air Commander-in-Chief was making a midnight tour of his principal airfields and was expected in at any moment. The aerodrome was swiftly cleared, and shortly afterwards Sir Trafford Leigh-Mallory arrived in his private plane. The Station Commander received him and took him over to the Mess where they had a short talk with the two Generals. Then the Air Marshal returned to his aircraft and was whisked away into the darkness of the night sky.

The picture now moved into the dark empty spaces above the Channel. Nothing was to be seen below, but through the sound track there came the noise of a sharp rhythmical drumming.

" Someone is beating a drum, somewhere," said Philip, " but I can't imagine where it can be."

Zadok looked across at him, and the old Atzlantean's face was creased into a sneering snarl, as he replied: " That is Drake's Drum you can hear, Drake sailed with his ships again last night from Plymouth Hoe. He and Nelson, Beatty, Rodney and the rest mean to throw the dark shadow of the fleets they once commanded between the invading forces and the German patrol boats that might yet give warning where the Anglo-Americans mean to strike."

There was nothing that Philip or Gloria could say, but they were immeasurably heartened by this great gleam of brightness in this dark night's work. Yet a few moments later they were plunged in gloom again.

The operator had located the first wave of the Airborne Division. It was about ten miles off the French coast. Grimly Philip began to record.

" The aircraft of the first wave are keeping station well at about fifteen hundred feet, but there is a bank of heavy cloud ahead of them. The leading aircraft is diving now in an attempt to get beneath it. The rest follow suit. They can't make it. The cloud is too low for them to dare go under it. The pilots are cursing, but they are going through. The glider tugs are entering the clouds now. We are still about five miles from the coast of France. They've gone down to about eight hundred feet, but are still in thick cloud. It's like a fog. The glider pilots can no longer see the tails of their tugs. They can no longer make their gliders follow the action of the tugs. They are beginning to sway. Did you hear that report? One of the towing-ropes has snapped. There goes another! The aircraft are flying on, but the two gliders are adrift. A third tow-rope has snapped. The three gliders are planing down towards the sea. The first one has hit it with a splash. There goes the second. We're almost over the coast now. The fourth rope has snapped, and the last glider is now adrift too. The third one has crashed in shallow water. I'm following the fourth one down. He'll never be able to reach his proper landing-place. There! He's smashed up in the middle of an orchard. We're three or four miles inland now—perhaps more. But there's no flak. What are the Germans up to? Are they all asleep? They must be able to hear the roar of the aircraft engines."

"It's those accursed women and the poets!" Zadok broke in.

"What?" exclaimed Philip, startled by the interruption.

"Why, all the non-combatants, of course," Zadok snarled. "Don't you understand? All of what we term 'The Mighty Dead' are out to-night. Those who did not fight physically in life rarely wield the flaming sword when they return. But they have other weapons. All the artists, statesmen and writers of a score of nations, who were rebels in their time, have wooed the Germans into sleep with fair, deceptive dreams. The musicians of ten centuries are stopping their ears with dream music, and the thousand million women, who have always longed for peace, are pressing in one vast pall upon their eyes. But this is only the beginning. There is a limit to what the dead can do, and the final decision must be reached by those who are living now. If we can hamstring the invasion, Hitler and Shaitan will triumph yet. Go on now! Keep on recording."

"The paratroops are going down," said Philip. "A lot of them are off the mark. They're pretty widely spread. Ah! There's a flak gun—and another. Some of the Germans have got into action at last. There is a tremendous roaring behind us now. Can we turn back a little? Yes, it's a great force of heavy bombers coming in over the coast. They're putting down their bombs. God! What a flash! That must have been an eight thousand pounder. And another—and another! Right dead on the battery that could have enfiladed the assault beaches. There they go again! Huge white flashes! There can't be much living down there now. That's one job the Airborne Forces won't have to bother about! The paratroop-dropping aircraft are turning back now. There's quite a lot of flak. Three, six, eight, ten, eleven. Where are the others? Yes, there they are. All fourteen are safely out and heading for the coast of England."

Zadok broke the picture. "Not too bad," he commented, after a moment. "We compelled the paratroops to scatter so that they'll have great difficulty now in finding their rallying-points in the dark, and we prevented all four gliders from getting in, so the paratroops have been rendered almost ineffective through the loss of their special materials. If only we can do as well with the main body and send the General's glider crashing into the sea, we shall have achieved a ninety per cent. success. The Germans will only have to mop up the stragglers in the morning. Let us see what is happening at the aerodrome."

A series of pictures showed them the Mess, the Control Room, the Watch Tower and various other parts of the faintly moonlit R.A.F. Station. At last they located General Gale with his A.D.C. and a number of other officers in the men's camp, drinking beer with them. They were all laughing and in the best of spirits, little knowing that many of their comrades were already drowned or hopelessly lost in the Normandy cider-apple orchards. After a time they began to make their way towards their respective gliders, and, as the General left them to walk over to his, there was a great burst of cheering, and scores of the tough, black-faced paratroops spontaneously broke into the chorus of " For, He's a Jolly Good Fellow."

Another little party had already rendezvoused at the General's glider to wish him good luck, among them the Station Commander and the man from London. Philip then began to record.

" General Gale is still wearing his jodhpurs, and he now looks a more massive figure than ever. The innumerable pockets of his special kit are bulging with maps and all the other things he will need when he lands in France. Over everything else he is putting on a light coloured mackintosh. Wing-Commander Macnamara and General Crawford are just saying good-bye to him. He is joking with Macnamara. The second wave is to consist of twenty-five Albemarle aircraft, all towing gliders. Macnamara is to lead them in, and the General is saying that he'll break his neck next time they meet if he lets anyone get ahead of him so that his glider does not fetch down first.

" Macnamara and General Crawford are now walking across the grass to the other limb of a V in which two runways meet, on which their aircraft is parked. General Gale's officers are saying that he ought to put on his Mae-West—that's what they call the life-saving jacket that one blows up. He says he can put it on later if necessary. They say it would be a bit tricky if he leaves it to the last moment, when the glider might be diving head foremost into the sea.

" He turns to the man from London and gives that deep laugh of his, as he says : " I'm supposed to be commanding this damn' D'vision, yet just look how these fellows bully me ! ' Then he says to the others : ' All right. I'll put it on if you like.'

" Several people are now helping him into it. Tom is saying to him : ' The tapes should go up as high under your shoulders as possible, sir.'

" He is burbling with laughter again. He has just said : " I know what you're up to! If we fall in the water you want my head to go under and my bottom to be left sticking up in the air!' Now he's slapping his enormous inflated chest and exclaiming: 'Good God! Look at me! I must look like Henry the Eighth!'

"The man from London is pointing to the huge chalked letters on the nose of the glider, just under its number—Seventy. He says: 'I know you christened your glider Richard the First because you, Richard Gale, will be the first British General to land in France for many hours; but it ought to have been Richard Cœur-de-Lion, because he was just such another big man, and you are leading another Crusade.'

"They are ready to emplane now, and all saying good-bye. Group-Captain Surplice has come forward with a tin of Golden Syrup. Apparently the General saw some on the breakfast table a few mornings ago and exclaimed: 'By jove, I love Golden Syrup, and I haven't seen any for years!' They are all laughing now as he accepts the tin and thanks the Station Commander for his hospitality. The man from London is pressing a sealed tin of chocolates into the A.D.C.'s hand to eat on the flight. They are clambering in. The doors of the glider have been closed.

"The Station Commander and his party are walking across the grass to the Watch Tower. One-fifty is zero hour for the departure of the second wave. The minutes are being counted out. The engines of Macnamara's aircraft are already roaring. The signal's been given! They're off! The aircraft is speeding smoothly down the runway. As it doubles its distance from its starting-place to the point of the V, the tow-rope suddenly becomes taut, and the glider slides forward. The aircraft has lifted. Now the glider is airborne too. Richard Cœur-de-Lion is on his way to France!

"The next aircraft has already run out. It picks up its glider with equal smoothness. At the Watch Tower they are checking the timing. The aircraft are leaving to the split second at one-minute intervals. Several of the officers who were with the Station Commander have got into a car and are driving over to the Control Room. They are going upstairs and out on to the balcony. They are watching the procession of aircraft and gliders as they mount into the air. From the moment of General Gale's departure to the last glider becoming airborne will take twenty-five minutes. The officers on the balcony are now looking at a great cluster of moving lights in the sky to the west. One of them just said: 'That's part of the American Airborne Division making for the base of the Cherbourg Peninsula. Good luck to them!' The sky is now alive with aircraft. The rest of the Sixth Airborne Division is being flown in from a dozen different airfields that all lie in Air Vice-Marshal Hollinghurst's Command.''

Once again Zadok cut out the picture and spoke to Arkitl. The lever was thrown over, and the big retort on the instrument panel began to fill with red vapour again. Philip needed no telling that an additional voltage of the magno-electric current was about to be sent out to counteract the natural thinning of the cloud-bank which would otherwise have taken place before General Gale reached it. He turned and looked at Gloria.

At that second Coxitl walked into the room. It was the one thing that Philip had been so much afraid of—the unforeseen factor which might ruin everything. But it was too late to do anything about it. Without a word Gloria stood up, picked up her stool and began to walk with it towards the instrument panel.

Zadok's glance left his team and followed her. " What is the matter? Where are you going? " he called out in a surprised voice.

While his gaze was averted Philip had drawn his pistol. From the corner of his eye he saw Gloria falter and halt. He knew then that she was being held against her will by some swift hypnotic command sent out by Zadok. He squeezed the trigger of his automatic twice. There were two spurts of flame, and the two bullets hit Zadok in the middle of his emaciated body. The old Atzlantean coughed, his eyes bulged hideously, and he crumpled to the floor.

Gloria, as though released by a spring, bounded forward and began to run.

At the sound of the shots the old blind operator staggered up from his seat, and the screen instantly went black. Quetzl and Velig had leapt to their feet. The former dashed round the end of the table and flung himself upon Philip. They crashed to the floor together, but Philip was still clutching his gun.

While they were rolling over and over together he caught two sounds. One he had feared; it was the musical note of Coxitl's silver whistle summoning his company of bearers. The other he was praying for; it was the crash of broken glass, and he knew that Gloria had succeeded in her share of their plan. With her heavy stool she had smashed the big retort that held the red vapour.

The thick-lipped Quetzl was on top of Philip and glaring down into his face. But knowing nothing of firearms the Atzlantean made a cardinal mistake. Instead of trying to get the gun away from Philip, he grasped him with both hands by the throat. For a moment Philip felt the awful pains of strangulation, but he lifted his gun, jammed it into Quetzl's ribs and fired. The Atzlantean's whole body jerked as though animated by an electric shock, then he suddenly went limp and slumped sideways.

Philip wriggled out from beneath him. He could see Gloria struggling gamely with Arkitl at the far end of the room. Normally he could not cover a dozen paces without the aid of his crutches, but the imperative necessity of reaching Gloria lent him both abnormal strength and re- sistance against pain. He had promised her the last bullet, and he was determined to spare her the horror of being taken alive. Scrambling to his feet he set off at a run towards her.

He had hardly covered half the distance before he felt himself checked. He faltered and could not force one foot in front of the other; his bad leg gave way under him, and he crashed to the floor. His brain seemed to be going numb, and he knew that Coxitl had stabbed him in the back with that terrible hypnotic force that the chief men among the Atzlanteans wielded with such devastating effect. And, even as he fell, he could hear Gloria calling to him:

" Help, Boy! Oh, help, help ! "

She was facing him and still struggling with Arkitl, but the Atzlantean's body was now between them and covered most of hers so Philip did not dare to risk his last remaining bullet. He knew, too, that his thoughts were swiftly becoming slow, vague and indeterminate. It was as though the room were growing larger and dimmer, the noises in it becoming more distant and himself beginning to float in space.

With a great effort he turned over on his back. The proud, cruel face of Coxitl was now right above him. The dark eyes in it pinned him to the floor. They were turning into the fiery pits he had seen before. For what seemed an age he forced his own eyelids slowly down and strove to lift his right hand, which still clutched the gun. It seemed to be twenty times its normal weight.

Then, for some unaccountable reason, there flashed into his bemused mind the last lines of the letter that the Canon had written to him just before he died. " From to-day I shall fly the flag of Saint George from the spire of the church, with the prayer that he may give you his special protection." Within a second his lips were framing an appeal they had never uttered before.

" Saint George! " he gasped. " Saint George! "

There was a blinding flash, a shattering report; his pistol, lifted now to within a few inches of his own head had exploded. The bullet struck Coxitl under the chin. His face was smashed upwards as though struck from beneath with a great hammer, and he fell backwards, spurting blood.

Instantly, all Philip's faculties were fully restored to him; but with sinking heart he realised that his last bullet was now spent. Rolling over, he staggered to his feet and lurched towards Gloria. Even as he did so, he was aware that behind him the room was full of Coxitl's bearers.

In one glance he saw that Gloria had clawed open Arkitl's face, but was now gripped firmly by him and being forced back, so that her hands could no longer reach his head. Hurling himself on them, Philip struck out with his left fist across Gloria's shoulder. He caught the Atzlantean full between the eyes. Arkitl gasped and let go. As Gloria fell backwards Philip threw his left arm round her neck so that her chin was in the crook of his elbow. Lifting his right hand he brought the butt of the gun down with all his might on the crown of her head. He heard her skull crack, yet he hit her again and again, and he was still hitting her as a dozen strong hands grabbed at and seized him.

As they dragged him away, she fell to the floor, and he caught one glimpse of her face. The bright blue eyes were wide and staring. He laughed then, because he knew that she was dead, and that he had saved her from the final torment.

All that followed seemed like a nightmare. He was pulled, pushed, hustled out of the room, up the ramp and along the gloomy tunnels. Before he even had time to collect his thoughts he was hauled into the Temple of the False Sun. Once more he caught a fleeting glimpse of the great truncated pyramid in the vast cavern. The baleful red glow of the fiery ball that seemed to hang suspended in mid-air coloured every-thing about him. The hidden gong gave out one deep boom. The horrible crowd of stinking, self-mutilated priests came surging up out of the red twilight. They tore him from the bearers and thrust him up the great flight of steps. Sharp-nailed hands grabbed and clawed at him from all directions. He was barely conscious when he reached the summit, and they flung him face upward on the great altar stone of basalt. He glimpsed the High Priest towering above him, the obsidian knife clutched in his right hand. It descended with a thud between Philip's breast-bones, and ripped its way down to his stomach. His body was one frightful searing pain. He screamed aloud. Then he seemed no longer to be spreadeagled on the altar.

He was above it and looking down on his own body. He saw the High Priest tear out his heart and bite at it, yet he felt no more pain. A moment later the priests were tearing the carcass that had once been Philip Vaudell limb from limb, and smearing themselves with its still warm blood.

But Philip's eyes were no longer dazzled by the red glare of the False Sun. They were bathed in the refreshing darkness of the night sky beyond the Mountain. He knew that he was travelling swiftly, faster than the fastest plane, over land and over sea towards Europe.

In earthly time barely twenty minutes had elapsed between the moment that he had shot Zadok and the moment that the High Priest of Shaitan had torn out his heart. By half past two he was above the Bay of Biscay; but here he seemed to come up against a great wall of blackness that as he advanced dissolved into a mass of screaming, evil figures that drove him back.

Swerving like an aircraft that is attacked by flak he sped out into the Atlantic, and came in again across the Cornish coast. Instinctively, he made for Southampton and from there struck out across the Channel.

He could see now with the eyes of the spirit as well as with those of the flesh. More than halfway across the Channel he sighted the Allied Armada There were countless ships in line upon line, with all lights out, heading for the Normandy coast. But there were other ships that he could see as well: frigates and men-o'-war, dreadnoughts, galleons and caravels. Squadron upon squadron of them were sailing in front of and to either side of the physical Armada. The shade of *Victory* had left Portsmouth hard. Sir Richard Grenville's *Revenge,* the *Golden Hind,* the first *Royal Sovereign*, the *White Ship,* the little, high-decked floating castle that had carried Henry V to Agincourt, all were there.   And there were others that flew the Stars and Stripes of the United States and the Fleur-de-Lys of France.

A moment later Philip caught the roar of aircraft engines. To right and left and before him they were streaming in, and they, too, had their shadow escorts; strange, old-fashioned biplanes that had fought in France and Flanders during the First World War, Gladiators that had taken their toll of the Luftwaffe in the azure skies of Greece and Africa, early Hurricanes, Spitfires and Blenheims that had held Britain for the British when Britain stood alone.

Moving faster than the fastest plane, he caught up with a string of glider-towing aircraft ahead. He knew at once that it was the spearhead of the 6th Airborne Division's second wave. Streaking forward by a single impulse of his will, he reached the head of the line. Macnamara was still leading, but right in front was a dense bank of cloud.

For a moment Philip's heart sank. Had he failed after all? Then, as he watched, the cloud lifted as though some giant hand had brushed it aside, and he heard the voice that he had held dearest in all the world say:

" 'Tis a marvellous part we were given to play, Boy; and it's proud I am to have earned the right to see the finish."

Gloria was there beside him, laughing and smiling into his face But he had hardly cast an arm about her when the coast of France rose up below them, and battle was joined.

With a howl beyond that of any tempest a vast concourse of black and evil figures descended upon them from the upper air. All unconscious of the spectral battle now raging, the crews of the gliders were still cracking jokes as they made their last preparations before going down. Yet, in the dark night outside their flimsy structures, countless horrible, bat-winged things strove to foul their engines, snap their stays, fray the tow-ropes and bring the gliders down.

But Philip and Gloria were alone no longer. A great host of known and unknown figures flew beside them, each armed, as they now found themselves to be, with a flaming sword.

For what seemed endless time they battled with the dark, satanic legions, driving them back and back as the planes flew on. Then at last they heard the order given: " Cast off! " Macnamara's aircraft drew away.

There came a sudden eerie silence as General Gale's glider hovered above the River Orne. Slowly it went down and down while the battle overhead continued in all its fury.

With aching arms they slashed and slashed at the evil faces which still beset them, till it seemed that they could wield their weapons no more. Yet they kept on.

Dawn came, and with it a slight lull; just enough time for them to survey the scene below. The three big, widely separated fields that had been chosen weeks before as the dropping zones of the 6th British Airborne Division were now like three flypapers upon which clouds of white flying-ants had settled; barely half a dozen had come down outside their concentration points. But for the tragic loss of the four that had snapped their towing-ropes in the first flight, it was now clear that this brilliant operation had proved a hundred per cent. success. In the neighbourhood of each dropping zone scores of little figures were carrying boxes of ammunition and supplies into the nearby woods, and busily digging in the anti-tank guns. Both the vital bridges were intact and now under guard. On one there was a busy group running out telephone wires and establishing the Divisional Headquarters. In its midst a splendid figure wearing light grey jodhpurs now bestrode a newly requisitioned milk-white horse. General Gale had captured his first objectives, and the vital flank of the Allied Armies was secure.

Turning, they looked back along the beaches. A choppy sea was creaming angrily upon them, but for mile upon mile hundreds of landing-craft were nosing in towards the shore, while further out scores of warships flashed and flickered under palls of drifting smoke as their guns pounded the redoubts in Hitler's vaunted Atlantic Wall.

There came a roar like the approach of the vortex of a cyclone, and the unseen battle in mid-air was on again. The Powers of Darkness had thrown in their last reserves. For a few moments everything was one hell-torn screaming confusion, then the attack of the satanic legions began to slacken. Suddenly, they gave and broke. A great shout of triumph went up from the Shining Host above, and at that moment down below, amidst the spatter of machine-gun fire and the crashing of mortars, thousands upon thousands of British and American soldiers threw themselves into the surf. Cheering and shouting as they plunged through the shallow water, the Armies of Liberation came up out of the sea on to the shores of France.

It was only then that Gloria and Philip were at last able to withdraw their gaze and smile into each other's eyes.

They were still doing so when they heard a well-remembered voice behind them and, turning, saw the Canon.

" It isn't finished yet," he said; " but now that our flank is protected they'll never be able to drive us off the beaches. Hitler is caught between the Soviet Sickle and the Sword of the Western Allies, so this day's work is the beginning of the end for the Germans. Come with me now, and I will lead you to the Garden of Eternal Peace, warmed by the sun of Fulfilment and watered by the river of Contentment, where all things are understood, and Love sings litanies down the wind of Time."

THE END